Passage to Mutiny

Richard Bolitho novels by Alexander Kent

in chronological order

ALEXANDER KENT

PASSAGE TO MUTINY

G.P. PUTNAM'S SONS
New York

First American edition 1976
Copyright © 1976 by BOLITHO
MARITIME PRODUCTIONS LTD.

SBN: 399-11772-5

Library of Congress Cataloging in Publication Data

Kent, Alexander.
  Passage to mutiny.

  I. Title.
PZ4.K369Pas3 [PR6061.E63] 823'.9'14 76-14819

PRINTED IN THE UNITED STATES OF AMERICA

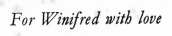

For Winifred with love

Contents

Where lies the land to which the ship would go?
Far, far ahead, is all her seamen know.
And where lies the land she travels from? Away
Far, far behind, is all that they can say.

ARTHUR HUGH CLOUGH

I

All Things Remembered

It was almost noon, and the sun which blazed across Sydney harbour was pitiless in its intensity. The sky above the capital of the infant colony should have been bright blue, but it was blurred as if seen through a crudely made glass, and the air around the waterfront buildings and anchorage alike felt gritty and humid.

Isolated and apart from the varied collection of local shipping and heavier merchantmen, a man-of-war stood above her reflection as if she had been there forever, as if she would never move again. Her ensign flapped only occasionally above her high poop, and the commodore's broad pendant which flew from her mainmast truck was only a little more enthusiastic.

But despite the heat and discomfort her decks were alive with watching figures, as they had been for some while, since another British man-of-war had been reported entering the anchorage.

The commodore leaned his palms on the sill of his cabin windows and withdrew them hurriedly. The dried wood felt like a heated cannon. But he watched nevertheless, conscious of the unusual silence throughout his command as the newcomer crawled closer and closer across the glittering water, her masts and yards and then her curved beakhead taking shape and clarity above the haze.

The commodore's flagship was the old *Hebrus*, a small two-decker of sixty-four guns which had been ready for disposal after nearly thirty years of service. Then she and her commodore had been given just one more commission. Now, on this October day in 1789, anchored as senior British naval vessel in Sydney harbour, she was still expected to act if need be with her old efficiency and relish, although many of her officers secretly believed she would be hard put to reach England if her recall was ever offered.

The other ship was a frigate, common enough in times of war and at any other place where their agility and speed might be required at short notice. But out here, thousands of miles from home and familiar faces and customs, a King's ship was rare, and all the more welcome.

Her presence accounted for the *Hebrus*'s silence. Every man watching her painstaking entrance in the merest breath of wind would be seeing her differently. A town in England perhaps. A voice. Children he could barely remember.

The commodore grunted and straightened his back, the effort bringing a prickle of sweat across his spine. It was absurd. The new arrival was the thirty-six-gun frigate *Tempest*, and she had never been to England at all.

He waited as his servant padded around him with dress coat and sword, the trappings of officialdom and ceremony, remembering what he had heard about *Tempest*. It was strange how circumstances could affect a ship's purpose as well as the lives of the many who might serve her.

Six years earlier when war with the American colonies and the Franco-Spanish alliance had come to a close, ships which had been worth their weight in gold in battle were, like most of their companies, no longer wanted. A country soon forgot those who had fought and died for it, so a ship's survival seemed of even less importance. But peace between the great powers had never been very secure, at least to those who had been involved in the price of each bloody victory.

And now there was renewed tension with Spain which could just as easily fan into something worse. It was over rival claims to various territories which each hoped to exploit for trading and colonial purposes. Once again the Admiralty had been directed to search around for more frigates, the life-line of every fleet.

The *Tempest* had been built in the Honourable East India Company's yard at Bombay just four years back. As with most of John Company's ships, she was constructed of the finest Malabar teak and to the best available design. Unlike the Navy, the Company's ships were always built with long usage in mind, and with some regard for those who had to work them.

The Admiralty's agents in Bombay had purchased her for the King's service without her ever sailing under a Company flag. She had cost them eighteen thousand pounds. The Admiralty must have been desperate to pay such a princely sum, the commodore thought privately, or else, as was equally likely, a little extra gold had changed hands in other directions.

He gestured for his silent servant to offer him his telescope. He waited for the *Hebrus* to swing very slightly to her cable and then trained the glass on the slow-moving ship. Like most sea officers he was always impressed by the sight of a frigate. This one was heavier than he was used to, but still retained the graceful proportions, the appearance of latent speed and manoeuvrability which made them every junior officer's dream.

Despite the damned haze he could see a cluster of figures around her forecastle, one anchor catted and ready to let go as she glided purposefully above her twin on the blue water, her stem barely raising a ripple. Under topsails and jib only, her canvas filling and then flapping emptily while she changed tack to take advantage of the poor breeze, he could almost feel the excitement across the water. The sight of a port, any port, always dulled the memory of hardship and sometimes brutal conditions which had got them this far.

The commodore had been expecting the *Tempest* two weeks or more earlier than this. She had come from Madras, and despatches he had already received from a courier brig had left him in no doubt *Tempest* would arrive on time.

But he was not irritated as he might have been with other ships. *Tempest* was under the command of one Captain Richard Bolitho. Not a friend exactly, but a fellow Cornishman, and that, out here in this misery of convicts and foul conditions, fever and corruption, was worth almost as much.

He levelled the glass again. He could now make out the frigate's figurehead, a wild-eyed girl with streaming hair, her breasts out-thrust as she held a horn fashioned like a great shell to her lips. Her hair and torso were painted in bright gilt. Only her eyes were blue and intense while they stared far ahead as if to follow the makings of her tempest. The gilt on her and the gingerbread around the part of the poop yet visible must have cost Bolitho a small fortune, he decided. But in these waters there was little else to spend your money on. He winced as he heard his marines stamping along to the entry port. Even their boots seemed loud and heavy enough to shake the poor old *Hebrus* apart.

A lieutenant peered respectfully through the screen door.

The commodore nodded curtly, not wishing his subordinate to see that he was so interested in the other ship.

'Yes, yes, I know. I'll come up.'

Even as he reached for his hat the first bang of the salute echoed across the harbour, making the dozing birds lift from the water, flapping and squawking to reprimand the newcomer for disturbing them.

On the quarterdeck, and despite the spread of an awning, it was like a kiln.

The flag captain touched his hat and studied his superior's mood.

'*Tempest*, thirty-six, sir. Captain Richard Bolitho.'

Gun for gun the salute continued, the dark smoke pressed down on the water as if by something solid.

The commodore thrust his hands behind him.

'Make a signal as soon as she is anchored. Captain repair on board.'

The captain hid a smile. The mood was good. He had known times when he had made a dozen signals right in the middle of another ship's last-minute manoeuvring. As if he had enjoyed the apparent confusion caused. There must be something special about this one, he thought.

With her topsails shivering to the regular crash of her eleven-gun salute to the commodore, His Britannic Majesty's frigate *Tempest* continued slowly across the harbour. The glare on the surface was so fierce that it was painful to look much beyond the rigging or gangways.

Richard Bolitho stood aft at the quarterdeck rail, his hands locked loosely behind his back, trying to appear relaxed despite all the usual tensions of entering an unfamiliar anchorage.

How still it was. He glanced along his ship, wondering how she would appear to the commodore. He had taken command of *Tempest* in Bombay when she had been commissioned for the Navy, just two years ago.

The thought of the actual date made him smile, changing his grave expression to one of youthfulness. For it had been his birthday, as it was today. On this, the 7th of October, 1789, after making one more in a countless line of forgotten landfalls, Richard Bolitho of Falmouth in the County of Cornwall was thirty-three years old.

He glanced quickly to the other side of the deck where Thomas Herrick, the first lieutenant, and his best friend, was peering beneath the shade of one hand while he studied the set of the braced yards and the shortened shapes of the bare-backed topmen. He wondered if Herrick had remembered. Bolitho hoped not. In these waters, with week following week of disagreeable climate and persistent calms, you were all too conscious of the passing of time.

' 'Bout five minutes now, sir.'

'Very well, Mr Lakey.'

Bolitho did not have to look round. In the two years of his command in *Tempest* he knew the voice and temperament of all those who had served with him for most of the period. Tobias Lakey was the lean, taciturn sailing master. Born and raised in the spartan reality of the Scilly Isles off the tip of Bolitho's own Cornwall, he had gone to sea at the age of eight. He was about forty now. In all those years, in every sort of vessel from fishing boat to a ship of the line, there was little of the sea's ways he had still to learn.

Bolitho glanced slowly along the deck, trying to recall all the other faces which had vanished in the two years. Death and injury, disease and desertion, the faces had come and gone like the tides.

Now *Tempest*'s company was much like any other in a vessel which had never touched a British port, and as mixed as the waterfronts she had seen in her voyages. Some were men who really wished to make the Navy their career. Usually they had signed on other ships in England and had transferred to any available when their own had paid off. They better than most would know that conditions in England, six years after the war, were in many circumstances far worse than life aboard a man-of-war. Here at least they had security of sorts. With a fair commander and a large portion of luck they could make their way. In their own country, for which many of them had fought long and hard, there was little work, and the seaports were too often full of the war's cripples and those rejected by the sea.

But the remainder of *Tempest*'s people were a real melting-pot. French and Danes, several Negroes, an American, and many more besides.

As he looked at the men at the braces and halliards, the boat handlers waiting to lower his gig outboard, the swaying line of sweating marines on the poop, he tried to tell himself he should be content. He knew that if he were in England he would be fretting and worrying about getting back to sea. Trying to obtain a new ship, *any* ship. That was how it had been after the war. Then he had already held two commands, a sloop and his beloved frigate *Phalarope*.

When he had been given the *Undine*, another fifth-rate, and despatched to Madras on the other side of the world, he had felt only gratitude that he had been spared the fate of the many who daily thronged the Admiralty corridors or waited in the coffee houses, hoping and praying for just such a chance as his.

That had been five years in the past. And apart from a short visit to England he had been away from home waters ever since. When he had taken command of *Tempest* he had expected to be recalled to England for new orders. To be sent to the West Indies perhaps, to the Channel Fleet, or to the territory which was in dispute with Spain.

He looked at Herrick again and wondered. Herrick said nothing of his own views now, although he had once made them plain enough. Apart from his coxswain, John Allday, Bolitho knew of no other who risked his anger by such plain speaking.

It had all come back to him when *Tempest* had anchored at Madras two months ago. Even as his boat's crew had made their desperate efforts to pull him through the angry surf without getting their captain soaked to the skin he had remembered his first visit. When he had carried Viola Raymond, wife of the British Government's adviser to the East India Company, as passenger. Herrick had spoken out then to warn him of the real dangers, of the risk to his name and advancement in the one life he loved.

Automatically he touched the shape of the watch in his breeches pocket. The watch she had given him to replace one broken in battle.

Where was she now?

During his brief return to England he had gone to London. He had told himself he would not really try to see her again. That he would just pass her house. See where she lived. At the same time he had known it was a lie. But he could as easily have stayed content with her memory. The house, apart from the servants, was empty. James Raymond and his wife were away on the government's business. Raymond's steward had been offhand to a point of rudeness. Aboard a King's ship a captain was second only to God, and many said *that* was merely due to seniority. In the streets and terraces of St James's he ranked not at all.

He heard Herrick call, 'Stand by to let go, Mr Jury!'

Jury, the barrel-chested boatswain, needed no advice about watching the anchor party, so Herrick must have sensed Bolitho's mood and was trying to jerk him from it.

Bolitho smiled wearily. He had known Herrick since taking command of *Phalarope*, and they had rarely been apart since. He had not changed much. Stockier perhaps, but the same round, open face with those bright blue eyes which had shared so much with him. If, as Bolitho now suspected, his brief affair with Viola Raymond had made its mark in high places, then Herrick was being punished too, and without cause. The thought angered and saddened him. Maybe the commodore would shed some light on things. But this time he would not hope. He did not dare.

He thought of his despatches, of the extra news he would give Commodore James Sayer. He remembered Sayer quite well, and had met him in Cornwall once or twice. They had served in the same squadron on the American station before that. Both lieutenants.

With the echoes of the final shot hanging in the air *Tempest* glided the last half cable to her prescribed anchorage.

Bolitho said curtly, 'When you are prepared, Mr Herrick.'

Herrick raised his speaking trumpet, his reply equally formal.

'Aye, aye, sir.' Then he shouted, 'Man the lee braces there! Hands wear ship!'

The motionless seamen sprang into life.

'Tops'l sheets!'

Bolitho saw Thomas Gwyther, the surgeon, hovering by the larboard gangway, trying to avoid the hurrying seamen. How unlike the last surgeon Bolitho had had. He had been a violent, towering drunkard of a man. One who had let his passion for drink and the memories he had tried to contain with it destroy him entirely. Gwyther was a stooped, dried-up little man with wispy grey hair, whose frail looks were at odds with his apparent toughness and durability. He attended to his duties readily enough, but showed far more interest in plants and vegetation in whatever place the ship touched land than he ever did in humanity.

'Tops'l clew lines!'

The master said in his flat, unemotional voice, 'Put the helm a'lee.'

Tempest, obedient to rudder and to the dying breeze, turned slowly above her own image, losing way, her decks even hotter as the last canvas was manhandled and fisted to the yards.

'Let go!'

Bolitho heard the familiar splash beneath the bows, and pictured the massive anchor shattering the stillness of that inviting water. He repressed a shudder. He recalled the two large sharks which had patiently followed the ship for several days almost into the harbour itself.

'Signal from Flag, sir. Captain repair on board.'

Bolitho looked at Midshipman Swift. He was in charge of the signals party, and at seventeen was no doubt full of hopes and impatience for a chance of promotion. He shifted his gaze to Keen, the third lieutenant, wondering briefly if he was remembering when he had been in Swift's shoes aboard the *Undine*. It all seemed so long back. Now Keen was twenty-two. As brown as a berry, with the clean good looks which would conquer any girl's heart, Bolitho thought. Keen, who had joined his first ship because his father wanted him to learn to 'find himself' before entering the family's city business, and who had stayed on because he actually liked it. Keen, who had taken a wood splinter the size of a marlin spike which had been blasted from the deck into his body within inches of his groin. Even now he grimaced whenever it was mentioned. Allday, mistrusting any ship's surgeon, and *Undine's* in particular, had taken the splinter from the boy's body himself. The burly coxswain had surprised Bolitho yet again with one more unsuspected talent.

'Away gig!' Herrick cupped his hands. 'Mr Jury, put some more hands to the tackles, and lively so!'

Allday was watching the hurried preparations, his eyes critical as the boat was swayed up and over the nettings. In his blue jacket and flapping white trousers, his hair tied to the nape of his powerful neck, he looked as solid and as dependable as ever.

He said quietly, 'Another place, Captain. Another task no doubt.' Then he yelled, 'Watch that paintwork, you clumsy bugger! This is for the captain not the bloody cook!'

Some of the old hands grinned, others, newer or with less knowledge of the language about them, cringed at the outburst.

Allday muttered, 'By God, if we don't get back to proper work, I can't picture what sort of hands we'll be using!' He shook his head. 'Seamen indeed!'

Bolitho did not know what Allday meant by 'proper work'. They performed regular patrols amongst the growing spread of trading stations which were scattered across the seas from Sumatra to New Guinea. They had made long passages many hundreds of miles to the west to search for and act as escort to some valuable merchantmen on passage from Europe. *Tempest* was always kept busy. For with the spread of trade, and with it the exploitation and expansion into settlement and colony, so too came those who preyed on it. Pirates, self-styled princes, old enemies sailing under letters of marque, it was dangerous enough without the additional hazards of hostile natives and tropical storms.

Perhaps he meant, like Herrick, getting away from heat and

thirst, the daily risk of an uncharted reef, or attack by warring savages.

The explorers and the great navigators had done much to disperse the mystery and the dangers of these waters. But those who had followed in their wake had less noble motives. For a handful of nails, some axes and a few strings of beads a captain could buy almost anything and anyone.

For the sake of their trade and possessions Britain, France and Holland carried the main share of protecting the vast sea areas so that vulnerable merchant vessels could go about their affairs. Unfortunately, the oceans were too large, the forces employed too small to be much more than a gesture. Also, the countries who had the most invested in the Indies and the islands of the Great South Sea did not trust each other, nor had they forgotten old wars and debts still left unpaid.

Bolitho heard the gig's crew clattering into the boat, and saw that the side party of marines and boatswain's mates were waiting to see him safely away.

He looked up at the drooping masthead pendant and then across the shimmering water to two large transports which were anchored well clear of the shore.

And now there was this additional responsibility. The growing colony of New South Wales. He studied the big transports for some sign of life. Convict ships. How many poor wretches had been transported out here to provide labour and the power for clearing land and founding a nation. He tried to imagine what it would be like in such a ship battling round the Cape of Good Hope or, worse, around the dreaded Horn. Men, women and children. The law was as impartial as it was tragic.

Herrick touched his hat. 'Boat's ready, sir.'

Bolitho nodded gravely and looked at the red-coated marines and their captain, Jasper Prideaux. It was rumoured that he was in the marines because he had been made to leave society for killing two men in duels. Bolitho, more than many, had cause to understand that.

For two years he had tried not to dislike Prideaux. Despite sun and salt air the marine captain remained pale and unhealthy looking. He had sharp, almost pointed features. Like a fox. A man who would enjoy duelling and winning. Bolitho had not succeeded in getting rid of his dislike.

'Attention in the boat!'

Allday stood by the tiller, one eye on Bolitho's sword as he clambered down the side to the twitter of calls and the slap and thud of muskets on the deck.

'Shove off! Give way all!'

Bolitho shaded his eyes as the boat pulled swiftly around and beneath the tapering jib boom and blue-eyed figurehead.

Tempest was a well-found ship, but as Lakey had said often enough, she was a Company vessel, no matter what flag flew above her taffrail. With thirty-six guns, which included twenty-eight twelve-pounders, she was more powerful than any ship he had yet commanded. But she was so heavily built of teak, and her timbers and spars matched accordingly, that she lacked the swift agility expected of a King's ship in close combat. She had been built to protect heavy Indiamen from pirates and to strike fear into any such island or inlet which might be harbouring them.

Herrick had remarked from the start that if challenged by a real fighting ship they would have to close the range and hold on to it. Any sort of feinting and last-moment manoeuvres were not even to be considered.

On the other hand, even the most doubtful had to agree she was a fine sailer under good conditions. With just her plain sail set, and she carried over seventeen thousand square feet of it, she had been known to log fifteen knots. But Lakey, always down to earth, had said, 'Trouble is, you don't get good conditions when you needs 'em!'

Bolitho made sure his despatches and his own report were safely stowed below the thwart and turned his attention to the *Hebrus*.

Another castaway. Perhaps events were moving so fast in Europe that they had already been forgotten. Around the world lonely, solitary ships like his and the commodore's patrolled and tacked back and forth in complete ignorance of what was happening in the very countries whose decisions shaped their destinies.

'Way 'nough!' Allday swung the tiller, his eyes slitted against

the sun until they were covered by the flagship's great shadow.
'Hook on, bowman!'

Bolitho stood up and took a deep breath. He always remembered a captain he had once served. He had caught his legs in
his sword as he had come aboard for the first time and had
sprawled headlong at the feet of his startled marines.

At the top of the steps and just inside the entry port he removed his hat and waited for the din of calls and muskets being
snapped to the present to subside.

The commodore walked to greet him, one hand outstretched.
For a split second longer Bolitho's mind told him he was
mistaken. This was not Lieutenant James Sayer of the American
Station, or even of Cornwall. He had been another sort of man
altogether.

The commodore said, 'Good to see you again, Richard. Come
aft and tell me your news.'

Bolitho returned the handclasp and swallowed hard. Sayer
had been a well-built, lively man. Now he was round-shoul-
dered, and his face was deeply lined. Worst of all, his skin was
like old, unusable parchment. Yet he was only two or three
years older than Bolitho.

In the comparative cool of the great cabin Sayer threw off his
heavy dress coat and sank into a chair.

'I've sent for some wine. My servant keeps it in a specially
cool place in the bilges. Only Rhenish, but lucky to get *that*
out here.' He shut his eyes and groaned. 'What a place. An
island of felons surrounded by corruption!'

He brightened up as the servant entered with some bottles
and glasses.

'Now your despatches, Richard.' He saw his face. 'What is it?'

Bolitho waited for the servant to pour the wine and leave the
cabin.

'I was delayed on passage here, sir. We were struck by a squall
three days out of Madras, and two of my people were badly
injured by falling from aloft. Two others were lost overboard.'

He looked away, remembering the pity he had felt at the
time. The squall which had come with the swiftness of sound
in the middle of the night had departed just as quickly. Two
dead and two permanently crippled for no reason.

'I decided to put into Timor and land the men there. I have had business with the Dutch governor at Coupang and he has always been most helpful.'

The commodore watched him above the rim of his goblet. 'Yes. You've had fine successes against pirates and privateers in that area.'

Bolitho faced him. 'But for my unplanned visit I would not have heard the news. A ship, a King's ship, had a mutiny aboard, some six months ago, according to the governor. She had been outward bound from Tahiti when it happened. I am not certain of the reasons for it, but one thing is clear, the mutineers cast their officers and loyal men adrift in a small boat. But for the commander, I am told his name is Bligh, they would have perished. As it was, he found his way to Timor, over three thousand, six hundred miles, before he could summon help. The ship was an armed transport, sir. The *Bounty*.'

Sayer stared at him, his face grave. 'I've not heard of her.' He stood up and walked to the broad stern windows. 'So the mutineers will probably use her for piracy. They have little choice, other than hanging.'

Bolitho nodded, feeling his own uncertainty. *Mutiny*.

Even the word was like the touch of some terrible disease. He had felt it aboard his first frigate, *Phalarope*. It had not been of his doing, but the memory was still sharp in his mind.

As the commodore remained silent and continued to stare through the windows Bolitho added, 'I up-anchored and headed south-west and then around the southern coast of this colony, sir. I put into Adventure Bay in Van Diemen's Land. I thought the mutineers might have gone there before the news broke about their crime.' He shrugged. 'But they have vanished. It is now my belief they have no intention of returning to a civilized country where they might be seized. They'll stay in the Great South Sea. Add to the list of renegades and murderers who are living off traders and natives alike. But a *King's ship*. It does not bear thinking about.'

Sayer turned and smiled sadly. 'You have cause to hate the word mutiny. I am glad you discovered what you did. But higher authority than ours will decide what to do next, have no doubt.' He sipped at his goblet. 'Bligh, you say?' He shook his head. 'Must be a determined man to survive such a journey.'

Bolitho felt himself relax in the chair. Ever since he had spoken with the Dutch governor he had held the story of the mutiny on his mind. Now, under Sayer's influence, he could face it in its proper proportion. He had reacted like most captains, seeing himself in the same predicament. Without knowing the ship, the men or the exact circumstances it was like baying at the moon for more light.

He watched Sayer with sudden compassion. Tired out with this unenviable appointment, broken by some past fever, he was nevertheless the senior officer. Just as Bolitho had been the only representative of the world's greatest navy as he had covered many hundreds of miles in search of pirates and the local rulers who gave them encouragement. Perhaps one day he might fly a broad pendant of his own, but he doubted if he would carry Sayer's self-assurance to go with it.

The commodore said, 'I shall see the governor without delay. I suggest you return to your ship and take on water and whatever stores you need.' He studied him calmly. 'I am afraid I'll be sending you to sea very quickly. I would have done so anyway. Your news hastens the event.' As Bolitho rose he added, 'If you need extra hands, I daresay it can be arranged. After two years of Botany Bay it is hard to discover where a transported convict leaves off and an honest man begins!' He winked. 'I'll speak with the receiving officer ashore.'

At the entry port Sayer stood with Bolitho looking across at *Tempest*. In the bright glare her rigging and shrouds shone like black glass.

'Fine ship.' He sounded wistful.

Bolitho said, 'I imagine you will soon be returning to England, sir.'

The commodore shrugged. 'I would wish to see Cornwall again.' He reached out and touched the worn gangway rail. 'But like my poor old *Hebrus*, I expect I will die out here.' He said it without rancour or bitterness.

Bolitho stood back and removed his hat to the quarterdeck.

As the side party paid its respects to him once more and he climbed down to the waiting gig he found himself thinking of the fine houses in St James's. Would anyone there care if they read Sayer was dead?

But he thought he already knew the answer, and he was frowning when he ordered Allday to cast off.

As he sat in silence and the boat left the flagship's shadow and moved into the blazing heat he glanced at the faces of the oarsmen. What did he really know of these men? It was different in war. The enemy was clear to see, the cause, though vague, was always a just one because it was your own. Holding together, cheering and hitting back were all part of that desperate world. But now, miles from real civilization, what would men like these think if pressed too far?

Allday glanced down at Bolitho's squared shoulders, at the black hair which as always was tied neatly above his gold-laced collar. The captain was going over it all, as he usually did. Fretting and bothering himself for other people's sakes. He could guess what was uppermost in his mind. Allday had been aboard Bolitho's ship in the mutiny, a pressed man at that. He'd not forget it either. He looked at the oarsmen, each picked and trained by him. They knew about the *Bounty* mutiny, and by sundown every man-jack and convict in the colony would, too.

Allday had never known his parents, and could not properly remember at what age he had first set foot aboard ship. He had been at sea all his life but for a short while in Falmouth, where he had been pressed by men from Bolitho's own ship. Over the years before that time he could recall several captains who would warrant a mutiny. Cruel, vindictive men who seemed to delight in making their people suffer. Men such as those could make even the tiniest act of kindness in the crowded world between decks seem like a kind of miracle. It was wrong that it should be so when there were others like Bolitho who cared for their responsibility.

Bolitho snapped, 'If you do not watch your helm, Allday, we'll be inboard by way of a gunport, I'm thinking!'

Allday swung the tiller and grinned at Bolitho's back.

That was more like it.

The dusk which quickly enclosed the harbour was like a seductive velvet curtain. It helped men to forget the heat of the day and the strain of re-provisioning the ship with anything which Benjamin Bynoe, the hard-eyed purser, could obtain at the lowest barter.

Bolitho leaned back on the bench beneath the open stern windows and watched the lights winking from every level of the town. It was to be their second night at anchor in Sydney, but his first on board. Commodore Sayer had kept him busily engaged, mostly ashore, meeting the assistant governor, his superior being elsewhere in the colony attending to some petition from *those damned farmers*, as he described them. The first settlers, even with the available if reluctant aid of the convict labour, were not finding their lives easy.

Bad crops, some floods and theft by natives and escaped prisoners had left them in no mood for tolerance.

Bolitho had also met the officers of the local military. He had got the distinct impression they were not eager to discuss their affairs with anyone from outside the colony. He had said as much to Sayer, who had smiled at his doubts.

'You are quite right, Bolitho,' the commodore had said. 'At first the governor was content to use marines to keep order and contain the transported convicts. But they were required in England, and most have been shipped home. These "soldiers" you spoke with are some of the New South Wales Corps. They are specially recruited at high expense, and in many cases are more dishonest than those they are supposed to be guarding! I would not wear the governor's coat for a sack of gold.'

Bolitho's impressions of Sydney had been equally mixed. The dwellings were rough, but well sited for the most part, with ready access to the waterfront. Some, like the huge windmills behind the town, standing on the slopes like gaunt onlookers, showed signs of the Dutch influence. Practical and well designed.

Bolitho was well used to the crudity and drunkenness of seaports in many countries, but Sydney's rash of grog shops and worse made some he had seen appear quite mild. Sayer had told him that many of the shanty-keepers were actually employed by the officers of the Corps, who openly encouraged immoral liaisons between their own men and the convict women who served in such places. He had scornfully described the men who enlisted in the Corps as either 'blacklegs' or 'blackguards', and none in it for anything but personal gain.

Aboard his own ship again he was able to find some satisfaction and escape from the busy life ashore. Sayer had discovered nothing more of *Tempest*'s new instructions, which would eventually come from the governor upon his return.

Opposite him, lounging contentedly in another chair, was Herrick. They had dined together on an excellent mutton pie which Noddall, the cabin servant, had obtained specially from an unknown source ashore. They had consumed all of it, and Bolitho realised it was the first meat not taken from a salt cask he had eaten for months.

He said, 'I think some claret, Thomas.'

Herrick grinned, his teeth white in the glow of a solitary lantern. They had soon found that to increase the light only encouraged a host of buzzing insects which immediately destroyed the blessing of the cool air.

He said, 'No, sir. Not this time.' He beckoned Noddall from the shadows. 'I took the liberty of getting some good French wine from the barracks' quartermaster.' He chuckled. 'They may not be much as soldiers, but they live well enough.'

Noddall busied himself at the table with his wine cooler.

Bolitho watched him, recognizing every movement. Noddall was small, like a little rodent. Even his hands, which when not in use he held in front of his body, were like paws. But he was a good and willing servant, and like some of the others had come to the ship from Bolitho's *Undine*.

Herrick stood up, his head clear of the deck beams as evidence of *Tempest*'s generous proportions, and raised his goblet.

He said, 'To you, sir, and your birthday.' He grinned. 'I know it was yesterday in fact, but it took me a day to discover the wine.'

They continued almost in silence, their long pipes lit, their glasses readily refilled by the watchful Noddall.

Overhead, through the skylight, they could see the stars, very large and close, and hear the regular footsteps of a master's mate as he paced back and forth on watch, the occasional shuffle of boots from the marine sentry beyond the bulkhead.

Bolitho said, 'It will be late autumn in Cornwall now.' He did not know why he had said it. Maybe he had been thinking of Sayer. But he could see it all the same. Gold and brown leaves, a keener edge to each dawn. But still fresh and bright. It always held off the winter in Cornwall. He tried to recall the ordinary sounds. The ring of chipping hammers as the farm workers used their time building or repairing the characteristic stone and slate walls which separated their fields and houses. Cattle and sheep, the fishermen tramping up from Falmouth to one of a dozen tiny hamlets at the end of the day.

He thought of his own house below Pendennis Castle. Square and grey, the home of the Bolithos for generations. Now, apart from Ferguson, his steward, and the servants, there was nobody. All gone, either dead or, like his two sisters, married and living their separate lives. He remembered his feelings when he had met the marine captain, Prideaux, for the first time, and his attendant rumours of duels fought and won. It had reminded him of his own brother, Hugh. He had killed a brother officer over a gambling debt and had fled to America. To desert his ship had been a bad enough shock for their father, but when he had joined the Revolutionary Navy and had risen to command a privateer against his old friends and companions it had been more than enough to speed his death. And Hugh was gone, too. Killed, it seemed, by a runaway horse in Boston. Life was difficult to fathom out.

Herrick sensed his change of mood.

'I think I should turn in, sir. I have a feeling we'll all be up and about tomorrow. Two days in harbour? Tch, tch, someone high-up will say! It'll never do for the *Tempest*, and that's the truth!' He grinned broadly. 'I truly believe that if all our people were allowed ashore in *this* place, we'd *never* get 'em back!'

Bolitho remained by the stern windows long after Herrick had gone to his cot, or more likely the wardroom for a last drink with the other officers.

Herrick always seemed to know when he needed to be alone. To think. Just as he understood that it only made the bond stronger between them.

He watched the smoke from his pipe curling slowly out and over the black water which surged around the rudder. It was bad to keep thinking of home. But he had been away so long now, and if he was to be banished he would have to do something to change his future.

He heard a violin, strangely sad, from below decks, and guessed it was Owston, the ropemaker, who played for the capstan crew, and entertained the hands during the dog watches.

Tempest would make a fine picture from the shore, if anyone was watching. Gunports open, lit from within like yellow eyes. Riding light and a lantern on the starboard gangway for the officer-of-the-guard to climb aboard without losing his footing in the darkness.

He thought of some of the convicts he had seen. Surely none could be here for serious offences? They would have been hanged if they were hardened criminals. It made him ashamed to think how he had just been brooding on his own separation from home. What would these transported people be suffering if they could see his ship, know that she would eventually weigh anchor and perhaps sail for England? Whereas they . . .

He looked up, off guard, as there was a rap at the outer door. It was Borlase, the second lieutenant. As officer-of-the-watch he was no doubt the only officer aboard in full uniform. He was twenty-six years old, tall and powerfully built, and yet his features were rounded, even gentle, and his expression was usually one of mild surprise that he should be here. Bolitho guessed it had originally been a guard to hide his feelings, but had since become permanent.

Borlase had been first lieutenant in a small frigate. The ship had run hard aground near the Philippines and had been a total loss. Fortunately, there had been an East Indiaman nearby, and all but three hands had been rescued. At the hastily convened court martial the frigate's captain had been dismissed from the Navy for negligence. Borlase had been officer-of-the-watch at the time, and his evidence had helped to send his captain into oblivion.

Bolitho asked, '*Well*, Mr Borlase?'

The lieutenant stepped into the lantern light.

'The guard boat has sent this despatch for you, sir.' He licked his lips, another childlike habit. 'From the governor.'

Bolitho saw Noddall hurrying from the dining compartment carrying another lantern, his little shadow looming giantlike against the white-painted screen.

As he slit open the canvas envelope he found time to wonder if Borlase's part at the court martial had been as much to clear himself as to bring down his captain.

He read swiftly along the neatly written paper. All at once the stresses and anxieties of the past weeks faded, and even Borlase, who was watching him with a gentle smile on his lips, seemed to have vanished.

He said sharply, 'My compliments to the first lieutenant, Mr Borlase. I'd like to see him directly.'

The lieutenant opened his mouth as if to put a question, and shut it again.

Bolitho walked to the stern windows and leaned as far out as he could, letting the sea air explore his throat and chest. He wished he had not drunk so much or dined so well on the mutton pie.

He tried to clear his mind, to concentrate on the despatch. *Tempest* was to weigh and put to sea as soon as it was prudent to work clear of the harbour limits. He felt the air cooling his hair and cheek. It felt stronger, but would it last? He checked his racing thoughts and heard Herrick coming into the cabin.

'Sir?'

'We are ordered to sea, Thomas. A transport ship is overdue, although she was reported safely on passage three weeks ago by the mail packet. The packet's master made signal contact with her south-east of Tongatapu.'

Herrick was tucking his shirt into his breeches, his face frowning.

'But that's over a couple of thousand miles from here, sir.'

Bolitho nodded. 'But the ship, she's the *Eurotas*, is a regular visitor. She supplies the colony and some other islands as required. Her master is well versed with these waters. It is no use deluding ourselves. She should have been here, at anchor, days ago.' He recalled the grog shops and the brazen-eyed girls at the windows. 'The governor knew she was expected. He kept it a secret, even from his subordinate. The *Eurotas* is filled with guns, powder and supplies. And money to pay the military and civil authorities.'

'And you think the *Bounty* mutineers may be in that area, sir?'

Bolitho did not reply immediately. He was thinking of the governor's instructions, feeling their anger and urgency. Most of all he was remembering the last paragraphs. The *Eurotas*, apart from her valuable cargo, was also carrying more convicts, and he could almost see the rest in his mind. The newly appointed adviser and acting governor for yet another colonial project, James Raymond, and his wife were passengers.

He turned from the glittering lights and reflected stars. They had gone cold.

'Rouse the master, Thomas. Find out the first possible moment we can proceed. I'll warp her clear with boats if need be. It may be a false alarm. *Eurotas* might have put into an island for water or wood. Or she could have been becalmed as we have often enough.'

Herrick was studying him, his eyes very still.

He said, 'Doubtful.'

Bolitho walked past him, touching the chairs without feeling them, and the old sword which hung on the bulkhead, where Allday watched over it like a keeper.

He continued, 'Sayer will be sending the courier brig when she returns, and the governor will despatch two small schooners to the north and east.'

'Like a needle in a haystack, sir.'

Bolitho swung on his heels. 'I *know* that, damn it! But we must do something!'

He saw the instant look of surprise and hurt on Herrick's homely features and added, 'I'm sorry. Too much wine.' Herrick would have to know sooner or later. Bolitho thrust the papers across the table. 'Read them for yourself.' He walked to the door and said to the sentry, 'Call the midshipman-of-the-watch. I want all officers in the cabin without delay.' He turned aft again and saw Herrick watching him.

Bolitho said simply, 'I *know*, Thomas. I even know what you have been thinking. But it was five years ago. A long while to remember.'

Herrick eyed him grimly. 'Aye, sir. If you say so. I'll go and assemble the officers outside and bring them in together.' He left the cabin.

Bolitho sat down on the bench seat and after a slight hesitation drew the watch from his pocket. It was a very good timepiece, made by Mudge and Dutton, and it had a neat cylinder escapement and a firm, air-tight guard.

He saw none of these things, but clicked open the guard to read the engraved inscription on the inside.

> *Conquered, on a couch alone I lie,*
> *Once in dream's deceit you came to me,*
> *All dreams outstripped, if only thou were nigh!*

He closed the guard and thrust it into his pocket. His head and mind were quite clear, and when his officers filed into the cabin they saw nothing to make them believe he was in any way different. Except for Herrick, and he could do nothing about it.

2

Isolation

Bolitho paused on the companion ladder and allowed his eyes time to adapt to the harsh glare.

It was almost eight bells, with the men of the forenoon watch listlessly assembled below the quarterdeck rail to make the changeover.

Bolitho had been on deck two hours earlier, as was his habit. Then, even with the sure knowledge of another scalding day to come, it had seemed refreshing and alive. There had been a dampness on canvas and rigging to add to the deception, but now the sun's heat had expanded and magnified, and as he stepped on to the quarterdeck he found himself wondering just how long they could continue searching for the *Eurotas*.

Since leaving Sydney they had made good two thousand five hundred miles. Nearer three thousand with all the changes of tack and the maddening perversity of the wind. Herrick had remarked that it *felt* twenty times that much.

Three weeks of searing heat and endless, empty miles.

Bolitho squinted his eyes to try and see beyond the gently pitching bowsprit, but the glare was already so fierce that the sea appeared as polished silver without division between it and the sky.

Slowly he examined the set of each sail. Drawing, but only just, with the yards braced round to hold the vessel on a starboard tack.

He heard the master's mate report to Lieutenant Borlase, 'The watch is aft, sir.'

Then Borlase's heels squeaked as he crossed the deck, his shoes clinging to the hot pitch between the seams.

Both he and Keen, who was relieving him, were well aware

that their captain was present, but were used enough to his ways to know he would not interfere with the routine of changing the watch.

Bolitho heard Keen say, 'Aye, sir. Nor'-east by east. Full and bye.'

Then Borlase, curt and impatient. 'As usual, nothing to report. I have logged Peterson for insolence. The first lieutenant can deal with him later.' He wiped his streaming face and neck. 'Relieve the wheel, if you please.' Then with a nod he vanished through the companionway.

The hands went about their allotted duties and the watch began another long four hours.

Bolitho had seen Herrick right forward with the boatswain and some working parties. The tasks were unending. The ship, like any other, was like a finely tuned instrument, with every inch of rigging and canvas designed and arrayed to play its part. Splicing and stitching, painting and blacking-down rigging, *Tempest* took a lot of sweat and backbreaking effort.

Herrick saw him and strode aft along the weather gangway, his stocky frame barely angled to the sun-dried planking. It was hardly surprising, for even with courses and topsails set to the wind the hull was hardly heeling to its thrust.

Herrick observed, 'Another hard one, sir.' He looked at each mast in turn. 'I've had the hands turned-to early. It'll save them from the worst of it. Mr Jury has some heavier tasks on the orlop for this afternoon.'

Bolitho nodded, watching Keen as he moved restlessly around the wheel and compass. Like the other officers he was dressed only in shirt and breeches, and his fair hair was plastered across his forehead with sweat.

He said, 'Good, Thomas. I know they'll curse us for the heavy work, but it will save them from other troubles.'

Herrick knew as well as any officer that too much leisure under these conditions could lead to arguments and worse. In cabin and wardroom it was bad enough. For the company crammed together in their screened quarters or messdecks it would be like part of hell.

Herrick watched him, judging the right moment.

'How much longer, sir?' He stood his ground as Bolitho

turned towards him. 'I mean, we have covered the full distance. That mail packet reported *Eurotas* in these waters, safe and on passage. She must have run into trouble. We could barely miss her at this snail's pace.'

Bolitho walked to the quarterdeck rail and gripped it with both hands. The heated woodwork helped to steady his mind, hold back his uncertainty.

He saw Jacob Twig, the cook, walking purposefully beneath the shadow of a gangway, on his way to see the purser, no doubt. The fresh food and extra stores they had obtained from Sydney had to be eked out within the usual issue of meat from the cask. Salt beef, salt pork, some so hard it was like the ship's teak. Twig was very dark and extremely tall. When he was in his evil-smelling galley he loomed over the pots and platters like some kind of sorcerer brewing potions.

Bolitho said slowly, 'I agree that we have run the full course.' He tried to picture the missing ship, guess what could or might have befallen her.

In the whole three weeks they had spoken with only two other vessels, small Dutch trading schooners. They had been a week apart, but neither of the masters had reported sighting anything except the usual clusters of native craft amongst the many islands. And it was always prudent to give them a wide berth.

He added, 'According to the chart, we are once again due south of Tongatapu. If we come about and steer to take advantage of this wind, I think we could sight land early tomorrow.'

Herrick waited. Reading his mind.

Bolitho said, 'I'll not hazard the ship amidst the reefs, but we can put boats ashore. The local chief is alleged to be friendly. Our ships are not unknown to him, according to Mr Lakey.'

Herrick grimaced. 'I'll take a loaded brace of pistols with me nevertheless, sir! There have been too many good sailors cut down without warning.'

Bolitho turned to watch a sudden flurry in the sea alongside. A shark falling upon a smaller fish, the incident over in a second. Then the surface was smooth again, with just the occasional pointer of the shark's fin to reveal their patient escort.

B

He replied, 'Some of these islands have had good reason to hate us.' He unconsciously touched the lock of hair which hung above his right eye.

Herrick saw the movement. It was as familiar as Bolitho's level grey eyes. Beneath the lock of hair was a deep, savage scar which ran right up his forehead. As a junior lieutenant Bolitho had been struck down and all but killed by a native when he had been on an island with his ship's watering party.

Herrick persisted, 'I'll shoot first, all the same, sir. I've come too far to have my brains spilled with a war club!'

Bolitho was suddenly impatient. The thought that the *Eurotas* might have been overrun by warring islanders appalled him.

'Call the master, Thomas. We'll lay off a new course and decide what we must do.'

Herrick watched him stride towards the poop, his face completely absorbed.

He said to Keen, 'Keep an eye on your watch. We will be needing all hands within the hour.'

Keen did not answer. He remembered Viola Raymond. She had nursed him when he had been put ashore after being wounded. Like some of the others he knew about the captain's involvement and what Herrick thought about it all. Keen was fond of them both, but especially so of Bolitho. If he was going to search for Viola Raymond, and more risk was to come from their reunion, then it was their business. He watched Herrick's troubled face. Or was it?

In the small chart room beneath the poop and adjoining the master's cabin Bolitho leaned over the table watching Lakey's fingers busy with brass dividers and rule.

'If the wind holds. Noon tomorrow.' Lakey looked up from the table, his lean face silhouetted against an open port.

Beyond it the sea was glittering and painful to look at. How much worse in a big transport loaded with convicts. If the *Eurotas* was aground somewhere, then the first fear would soon change to something more dangerous. The desire to escape, to be free with even the tiniest chance of survival, could make men do the impossible.

If the wind holds. It must be engraved on every sea officer's heart, Bolitho thought.

He eyed Lakey thoughtfully. 'So be it. One hundred and forty miles to Tongatapu. If we can log five knots and no more once we have changed course, I think your estimate a fair one.'

Lakey shrugged. He rarely rose to either praise or doubt. 'I'll feel happier when I've examined our noon sights, sir.'

Bolitho smiled. 'Very well.'

He turned on his heel and hurried to the quarterdeck, knowing Lakey would be there when he was needed.

'Ah, Thomas, we will bring her about on the half-hour and steer nor'-west. That will allow us sea room when we are closer to the reefs. Also, if the wind veers we will be better placed to select one of the other islands in the group.'

When a ship's boy turned the half-hour glass beside the binnacle the hands manned the braces and hauled breathlessly at the frigate's great yards.

As *Tempest* wallowed round and allowed herself to be laid on the opposite tack Bolitho was very aware of the time it took to perform the change. Even allowing for the poor wind, he had every available man employed on deck and aloft. He knew the folly of allowing slackness and taking short-cuts even on routine work. In battle, with the biggest proportion of seamen required at the guns and repairing damage, the ship would have to be handled by far fewer. And yet *Tempest* had answered helm and canvas more with the slow dignity of a ship of the line than a frigate.

It was so easy to get complacent, to put off the back-breaking and thankless work of gun and sail drill with a battle in mind. Out here, with sometimes months on end and no sight of any other man-of-war, it was hard to build up enthusiasm for such drills, especially when it was only too easy to turn your own back upon it.

Bolitho had one bitter reminder, however. In the years when he had commanded *Undine* he had been forced into open conflict with a powerful French frigate, the *Argus*, commanded by Le Chaumareys, an experienced veteran of the war and one of Admiral Suffren's most capable commanders. Although serving under a letter of marque for the self-styled prince, Muljadi, Le

Chaumareys had remained a French officer in the best sense of the word. He had even warned Bolitho of the foolishness he would display in trying to fight his *Argus*, Muljadi's pirate fleet and the dithering incompetence of governments on the other side of the world. Just two ships could decide the fate of a great area of the Indies. Bolitho's little *Undine* and Le Chaumareys' powerful forty-four.

As in *Tempest*, Bolitho had been blessed with a motley collection of seamen, some of whom had been gathered from prison hulks to make his complement adequate.

All he had had against the Frenchman's experience and his equally well-trained company had been youth and a freshness of ideas. Le Chaumareys had been away from home for years. His work under another's flag was to have been his last before returning honourably to his beloved France.

It had been Le Chaumareys' familiarity with an established routine, his reliance on the same old methods and manoeuvres, which had cost him a victory, and his life.

Bolitho wondered how long it would take him to get too complacent, or so weary with endless patrols and chases after pirates that when a real challenge offered itself he would find himself without the steel to repel it. Or if indeed he would recognize the weakness if there was no one to tell him.

'Course nor'-west, sir. Full and bye.' Herrick wiped his forehead with his wrist. 'And no fresher on this tack either!'

Bolitho took a telescope from Midshipman Swift and trained it beyond the bows. Through the taut rigging and shrouds and above the figurehead's golden shoulder, on and on, to nothing.

'Very well. Dismiss the watch below.' He stopped Herrick as he made to hurry away. 'I believe Mr Borlase wishes you to punish a seaman today?'

Herrick watched him gravely. 'Aye, sir. Peterson. For insolence. He swore at a bosun's mate.'

'I see. Then *warn* the man yourself, Thomas. A flogging for such a triviality will do nothing to help matters.' He looked at some seamen on the deck below and along the gangways. Almost naked, and tanned in a dozen hues, they appeared strong enough, able to control any sudden flare-up of temper which could end in flogging, or worse. 'Then have a word with

Mr Borlase. I'll not have him or any officer passing over responsibility in this manner. He was in charge of the watch. He
should have dispersed the trouble as soon as he saw it.'

Herrick watched him leave the deck and cursed himself for
not stepping into the matter earlier. For letting Borlase get
away with it, as he did so often, when you stopped to think
about it. When you were tired, sun-dried and dying for a cool
breeze it was often much easier to do the work yourself instead
of following through the chain of command.

Which is why I'll never rise above lieutenant.

As Herrick moved up and down the weather side of the deck
he was watched for much of the time by Keen and Midshipman
Swift.

From midshipman in the *Undine* to *Tempest*'s third lieutenant.
When Keen had been raised from acting rank and had passed
his examination for lieutenant he had imagined that no reward
could provide greater satisfaction.

While he tried to stay under the shadow of the mizzen topsail
he watched Herrick and wondered, not for the first time, where
the next move would come. Some lieutenants seemed to soar
to post rank and higher, like comets. Others remained at the
same level year after year until rejected by the Navy and thrown
on the beach.

If only he had been old enough to have served with men like
Bolitho and Herrick in the real way. Against the French, and
the American Revolution, or anyone who faced them across
the water and challenged a flag as well as a broadside.

He heard Lakey's light step beside him. 'I have been
thinking –'

The sailing master smiled grimly. 'My old father on Tresco
used to say, leave thinking to horses, Tobias. They've bigger
heads than yours.' It seemed to amuse him. 'We've a course to
run out, Mr Keen. And no brooding or pining is going to
change our captain's intentions, not by one inch.'

Keen grinned. He liked Lakey, although their worlds were
so different.

'I'll try to contain myself.'

Below in his day cabin Bolitho sat at his desk and worked slowly through the day's affairs. As in most forenoon watches he received a regular stream of visitors.

Bynoe, the purser, requesting a signature on his ledger of newly opened meat casks. Hard of eye, more so of heart, Bolitho suspected, the purser was better than many he had served with. His rations were fairly issued, and he did not dock a seaman's meagre pay for some article he had not received and would not remember when the ship eventually paid off.

The surgeon came with his daily sick report. The hands kept remarkably free of hurt and illness, Bolitho was thankful to discover. But when it struck it was without warning or mercy. As with the men lost overboard, and the two left in the care of the Dutch doctors at Coupang.

While he studied each book and ledger placed before him by Cheadle, his clerk, he was conscious too of the life above and around him. They were all extensions of the ship herself. If a man died or was removed the ship lived on, gathering replacements to sustain herself.

He heard the rumble of gun trucks as one by one each cannon, from the long twelve-pounders on the main deck to the snappy six-pounders aft, were hauled inboard and examined by Jack Brass, *Tempest*'s gunner. It was Brass's routine arrangement that every week he would check each weapon, and God help the gun captain whose charge failed to reach his standards.

Bolitho had been lucky with his warrant officers and more seasoned men, and was grateful for it. Even his four midshipmen, sent to him originally by parents who wished them to gain experience and advancement which was harder to get elsewhere in peacetime, were more like young lieutenants after two years' continuous service. Swift and Pyper were seventeen, and already thinking of the time when they would be able to sit for promotion. Fitzmaurice, a pug-faced youth of sixteen, had had much of the arrogance knocked out of him. He came of a very rich family indeed, and had imagined apparently that his commission in *Tempest* was to be something akin to a courtesy cruise. Herrick and Lakey had taught him otherwise.

The youngest, Evelyn Romney, was fifteen. They all made

a change from the usual twelve- and thirteen-year-olds you found in most ships, Bolitho thought. Romney had improved the least. He was a naturally shy youth, and lacked the firmness required when dealing with men old enough to be his father. But if Fitzmaurice cursed his family for sending him packing to sea, Romney, who was less able to face up to the demands made on the 'young gentlemen', seemed desperately determined to do well. He obviously loved the Navy, and his attempts to overcome his shyness were pathetic to watch.

Bolitho heard the measured tramp of boots as the marines trooped aft from their daily drills on the forecastle and in the tops. Prideaux would not be with them. He would leave the sweat and discomfort to his sergeant. Then later he would emerge and criticize, his foxy face peering at each of his men in turn. Bolitho had never heard him offer one word of encouragement or praise, even when a marine had been promoted.

More muffled than the sounds near the quarterdeck, he heard the thump of hammers and the occasional rasp of a saw.

Isaac Toby was the ship's carpenter. Fat, slow-moving and rather vacant-looking, he had the appearance of an untidy owl. But as a carpenter he was an artist. With his own small crew he kept the repairs up to date, although with a vessel built of teak that was the least of his worries. At this moment he would be completing his latest challenge, the building of a new, additional jolly boat. It had been something of a joke to begin with, a casual remark made by the gunner about waste of valuable wood when a seaman had been caught throwing some offcuts over the side.

Toby had taken it as a personal affront and had said he would build a boat with his own hands out of all the oddments which Brass could discover. The boat was nearly completed, and even Brass had had to admit it was far better than *Tempest*'s original one.

Bolitho leaned back and ran his fingers through his hair.

Cheadle gathered up the last document and made sure the signature was dry. The clerk was a strange, withdrawn man, as were many of his kind. He had deep, hollow eyes and large, uneven teeth, so that he appeared to be smiling, something he never did, as far as Bolitho knew. To discover anything of his past Bolitho had had to drag it from him word by word. He had been transferred from another ship which had been paid off in Bombay. His captain had assured Bolitho that Cheadle was a good clerk, if somewhat reticent. He had once worked in a grocer's shop in Canterbury, and prided himself on his service to 'the quality'. But so far, even after two years of daily contact, Bolitho had never heard him mention it.

Noddall entered as the clerk left and placed a glass of wine on the desk. With fresh water so much in demand, and the uncertainty of supply a constant worry, Bolitho usually took wine as an easy alternative. He recalled when he had been guided to the famous shop in St James's, how he had purchased the many fine bottles before his voyage to the other side of the world in *Undine*. The wine had been reduced to broken glass and spillage during his fight with the *Argus*, but the memory stayed with him. He touched the watch in his pocket. Like so many others.

Allday sauntered through from the sleeping cabin and watched him gravely.

'Reckon we'll find 'em, Captain?'

He stood with arms folded across his deep chest, his face and body relaxed. He was more like a companion than a subordinate. How much they had shared together. Bolitho often wondered if Allday missed England. He would certainly be missing the girls. Allday had always had a reputation with them, and more than once had been glad, if not eager, to set sail in haste for fear of husband or irate father.

'I hope so.'

Bolitho sipped the drink. Cheap and stale. Not like the French wine which Herrick had got for him. The Sydney garrison had probably bought a stock from a French ship, or some ambitious trader. If you were prepared to risk your fortune and your life, and pit your wits against fierce natives, pirates and the constant dangers of shipwreck you could sell anything out here.

In the wake of navigators and explorers like Cook had come the others. On some islands, where the natives had lived in simple, idyllic surroundings, the ships had introduced disease and death. The merchant adventurers had set one tribe against another by offering shoddy goods and cheap cloth in exchange for secure moorings from which to barter.

And now everyone was paying for it. Soon, some over-greedy trader would start supplying a tribe with muskets. Bolitho had seen it happen in the Americas, where the French had trained Indians to track and kill the British, and the British had done the same to them.

Afterwards, with their independence won, and with both British and French gone from their newborn country, the Americans had been left with another army in their midst. A nation of Indian warriors which, if joined together, might still drive the settlers into the sea and isolate the new ports and cities.

He added, 'I doubt very much that we could have passed the *Eurotas* without sighting her. We have had double lookouts, and at night have shown enough lights for a blind man to see. Her captain would know of the concern for his late arrival and would try to make contact with any ship of size.'

Allday's eyes were distant as he watched the sea through the stern windows. With the wind across the larboard quarter the ship was leaning slightly under the pressure, so that the sea appeared to be on the slope. Like most professional seamen, Allday seemed able to stare at the sea without a blink, and yet the horizon was shining fiercely like a tautly stretched thread of gems.

'My guess, Captain, is that she's put in somewhere for water. Her supply might have gone foul, as ours did once.' He grimaced. 'With a hull full of convicts and the like, her captain'd not want to add to his worries, and that's no error.'

'True.'

Bolitho looked away, remembering the way she had looked. Their carefree disregard for discovery and what *might* have happened. At Madras, and afterwards. In that wretched, fever-infested colony to which Bolitho's ship had been sent to lend authority to yet another governor. Often he had sweated at the thought of those possibilities. A door being flung open, her face and shoulders pale as he tried to hide her from her husband. But nobody had come to break their passions, and the ache of losing her was even harder to accept.

He felt anger, too. What could James Raymond be thinking of to drag her out here again? European women found the climate cruel and demanding, and for Raymond there was no such need. His fine house, his authority, all he had gained at others' expense would have made it easy to leave her in security and comfort amongst people and customs she understood.

There was a rap at the door and Borlase peered through the screen, his face less mild than usual.

'I was wondering if I might speak with you, sir.' He looked quickly at Allday. 'But if it is inconvenient . . .'

Bolitho gestured to Allday, and as he left the cabin said, 'Be brief, Mr Borlase. I intend to exercise the twelve-pounders before noon.'

He knew why the lieutenant was here and that too depressed him.

Borlase licked his lips. 'I had occasion to log a seaman, sir.'

'Peterson. I know.'

He saw the merest flicker of surprise before Borlase hurried on, 'I see, sir. But I intended that Mr Herrick should award punishment. Peterson was defiant and insolent to his superior, and twelve lashes, at the very least, should be his just deserts!'

The speech had brought a flush to his cheeks. Like a petulant but triumphant child who has found a weakness in authority, Bolitho thought.

He answered quietly, 'The bosun's mate who was *defied* was Schultz, is that so?' He did not wait for an answer but continued in the same level voice, 'He is an excellent seaman, and we are lucky to have him. *But*,' the word hung in the air, 'less than two years back he could speak no tongue but his native German. What language he has mastered is made up of sailors' talk and slang, the commands needed to obey and instruct others.'

Borlase stared at him blankly. 'I don't see . . .'

'Had you bothered to investigate this matter.' Bolitho could feel his anger mounting, despite his care to control it. Why were men like Borlase never able to learn from mistakes and to accept the lessons? 'You would have treated the incident with a minimum of fuss. I believe that Peterson was slow to respond to an order, and Schultz shouted that *he were better on a gallows*

than on the main yard?' He waited, seeing Borlase's fingers opening and closing like claws. 'Well?'

'Yes, sir. Something like that. Then Peterson called Schultz
a pig and a heartless devil.' Borlase nodded firmly. 'It was then
that I ordered him to be taken below.'

Bolitho locked his fingers behind his head. He felt the sweat
trickling down his chest and armpits, the shirt, newly washed
and fresh on today, clinging like a wet shroud.

Maybe this was what had occurred in the missing *Bounty*, or
aboard the *Eurotas*. Men tormented by climate and unceasing
work taken off guard by some stupid remark made without
real thought. The rest could explode like a powder cask.

He said, 'Peterson's father was hanged at Exeter for murder
and theft. But he was wrongly identified, and the real murderer
was caught and executed a year later.' His tone hardened. 'But
not before Peterson's mother and family had been driven from
their home by the dead man's friends. They received a pardon,
but it was somewhat *late*.' He saw Borlase pale and added, 'I do
not blame Schultz, because his language is limited. I cannot
blame Peterson either. The very mention of a gibbet, the suggestion, no matter how casually made, that he were better use
hanging from one, would drive *me* to rage!'

Borlase muttered haltingly, 'I am sorry, sir. I did not know.'

'Which is why I blame *you*. That man is in your division and
was of your watch. I knew, so did the first lieutenant. I trust
that you will do something, and soon, to restore his respect.
Something you have to *earn*, Mr Borlase, it does not come with
the King's coat!'

Borlase turned about and left the cabin, and for several
moments Bolitho remained quite still in his chair, letting the
sea noises intrude again to cover the fierce beats of his heart.

Allday said, 'That was a rare quilting, Captain!'

'I told you to leave the cabin!' He stood up, furious with
himself for losing his temper, and with Allday for his calm
acceptance of it.

'But I did, Captain!' Allday kept his face stiff. 'I thought you
were calling me aft again.'

Bolitho gave in. 'Was it *that* loud?'

Allday grinned. 'I've heard worse, but I guessed you had

pressing matters on your mind, and might wish to be reminded of them.'

'Thank you.' He felt his mouth giving way to a smile. 'And damn you for your insolence.'

The coxswain took down Bolitho's old sword from the bulkhead and rubbed it against his shirt.

'I think I'll give it a polish, Captain. Might bring us fortune.'

Bolitho looked up at the open skylight as bare feet pounded over the deck and he heard the sudden squeal of blocks, the boom of canvas. The watch on deck was trimming the sails and resetting the yards again. The wind getting up? A change of direction?

He left the chair and walked swiftly through the day cabin to the outer door.

Keen was still in charge of the watch, and was as competent and reliable as any young officer could be. But Bolitho knew his one weakness. That Keen would rather die than call his captain to aid him if the wind began to change. He also understood why Keen was so unwilling, and the knowledge had so far prevented him from warning the lieutenant of the danger which delayed action could bring.

He reached the quarterdeck and saw the hands at the braces and the yards trimmed to take a slight alteration in the wind's direction.

Starling, master's mate-of-the-watch, touched his forehead and reported, 'Wind's backed a mite, sir. An' 'tis risen, too.'

His voice was extra loud, and Bolitho guessed he was warning his lieutenant that the captain was about.

Bolitho consulted the compass and the set of the sails. They were hard and filling well. They might gain another knot for a few hours, with any luck.

Keen came hurrying from the quarterdeck rail, his face anxious.

Bolitho nodded impassively. 'We will call the hands to exercise the main armament in an hour's time, Mr Keen.' He saw the surprise and the relief on Keen's face. 'Something wrong?'

Keen swallowed yard. 'N-no, sir. Nothing. I just thought . . .' He broke off.

Bolitho turned aft to the poop. Keen would never make a good liar.

Keen watched him walk to the comparative seclusion of the stern and then whispered fiercely, 'Did he say anything, Mr Starling?'

The master's mate eyed him cheerfully. Like most of the others he liked Keen. Many, once raised to the rank of lieutenant, thought themselves too proud to speak with mere sailormen.

He replied, 'I think 'e just wanted you to know 'e was *there*, sir. In case you needed 'im like.' He showed his teeth. 'But o' course, we *didn't*, did we, sir?' He walked away chuckling to himself, and to supervise the flaking down of disordered halliards.

Keen thrust his hands behind him as he had seen Bolitho do so often and began to pace the deck, ignoring the heat and the thirst which was making his mouth like clay. It was difficult to fathom the captain sometimes. To know if he was sharing something with you or holding it to himself for his own amusement.

Keen had heard his voice through the cabin skylight, although he had not known what was said. But Bolitho's tone, and Borlase's face when he had appeared on deck, had told him far more.

It never stopped for a captain. Never. He saw Allday walking along the gundeck carrying the sword under his arm. He could almost envy him his confidences with the captain. More even than Herrick he seemed to be the one who really shared them.

He swung round, startled, as Bolitho called from the taffrail, 'Mr Keen, I fully realize your intention to keep your body in a healthy condition by walking back and forth under the sun, but would you please exercise your mind also and send some hands to the foretops'l brace. It too needs your urgent attention.'

Keen nodded and hurried to the rail.

No matter what other problems might be on the captain's thoughts his eyes were in no way affected.

3

A Strange Message

Bolitho raised a telescope to his eye and winced as the hot metal touched his skin.

Since first light, when the masthead lookout had reported sighting land, *Tempest* had continued her slow approach, the first excitement giving way to a feeling of tension.

He studied the islands with methodical care, noting the various hills, the one on the nearest headland which looked for all the world like a bowed monk with his cowl pulled over his head. How close it looked through the powerful lens, but he knew that the first spit of land was a good three miles away. Beyond it, and further still, other islands and tiny humps of bare rock overlapped in profusion, giving an impression of one ungainly barrier of land.

A seaman's head and shoulder loomed through the glass, and Bolitho steadied it as he focused upon *Tempest*'s cutter which had been lowered soon after dawn. Under a tiny scrap of sail, it was pushing ahead of the frigate, and he could see an occasional splash beyond the bows as a leadsman took regular soundings to mark their approach.

For if the sea looked placid and inviting, Bolitho knew danger was rarely far off. Close to the nearest headland, where the sea was green rather than blue, he had seen a darker smudge beneath the surface. Like a giant stain, or a submerged patch of devil's weed. Reefs were here in plenty. There was no room at all for taking chances.

Without lowering the glass he said, 'Let her fall off a point, Mr Lakey.'

'Aye, aye, sir.' The sailing master sounded tense.

Bolitho continued to study the nearest island. Uninhabited,

or did those lush slopes hide curious eyes? He recalled how he had landed on one such beach. Lulled by the heady scents of palms and unfamiliar vegetation, free for a while from the spartan life aboard ship, he had been totally unprepared for the sudden rush of screaming, stabbing savages. It still came back to him, especially at moments like this.

'Nor'-west by north, sir! Steady as she goes!'

'Very well.' Bolitho turned slightly towards Herrick. 'Nothing, Thomas. Not even smoke from a fire.'

Herrick replied, 'I don't like it.' He too had a glass trained on the islands. 'At this crawl any lookout would have sighted us long ago.'

As if to confirm his words six bells chimed out from the forecastle. Eleven o'clock. *A long while since dawn.*

Bolitho bit his lip. Too long. He did not know the *Eurotas*, but she was a well-found ship and no stranger to these waters. Her captain, James Lloyd, had an equally sound reputation. But even if the ship had foundered on a reef, surely some survivors would have got clear in the boats?

He lowered the glass and watched a shark rise momentarily to show the whole of its sleek back to the sunlight, barely an oar's length from the side.

Midshipman Swift said, 'Cutter's signalling, sir.' Even his voice was hushed. Like the hot breeze. Like the ship.

Bolitho raised the glass again and saw Starling, one of the master's mates, standing upright in the sternsheets, his arm outstretched.

'Take note, Mr Lakey.' Bolitho shut the glass with a snap. 'The boat has sighted shoals to the nor'-west.'

He looked up, shading his eyes with his forearm. Under topsails and jib only *Tempest* was making poor headway. But they had to stay alert. Be ready to come about, in a baby's breath if necessary, and fight clear of those hidden reefs.

He watched the sails, barely filling, and the shortened shapes of the lookouts. Just to watch them made him feel dizzy. One was not even holding on to his perch in the crosstrees, and Bolitho could see his leg jerking up and down, probably in time with a song only he could hear.

Lakey left the wheel, where two helmsmen stood crushed by the blazing sunlight, and walked to the quarterdeck rail.

Bolitho turned to face him, dragging at his shoe which had stuck to the deck seams.

Lakey said quietly, 'Been thinking, sir. There's another island. To the nor'-east. On the chart it shows no name, but sailors call it the Island of Five Hills.' He shrugged. 'For the hills are all there are of it. I went ashore there some years back when I was serving in the old *Fowey*. The hills give good shelter to an anchorage, and there's a beach, too. We put in looking for water.' He sighed, remembering. 'But apart from rock pools we were unlucky.'

Herrick said, 'Well, *Eurotas* is hardly likely to be there, is she?' He could barely hide his impatience. Like most of those around him he was feeling the strain.

Lakey was unmoved. 'It's not that, sir. If the ship *was* damaged, holed mebbe. Well, she could be beached in safety, with far less chance of attack by natives an' the like than on the larger islands.' He frowned. 'I should have thought of it earlier.'

Bolitho looked at him, thinking hard. 'No matter. It makes good sense, and as we have to pass through the islands anyway, we'll lose nothing by extending the search a little.'

'Mr Starling's signalling again, sir.' Swift's tanned face was screwed up with concentration as he watched the cutter through the big signals telescope. 'Reefs close to larboard, but still no bottom.'

Lakey breathed out slowly. 'The chart is right about that, anyway.'

Bolitho plucked the shirt away from his chest. It was wringing wet.

'Nevertheless, we will begin sounding ourselves. Pass the word forward to the leadsman.'

Soon afterwards he heard the leadsman's cry from the chains, 'No bottom, zur!'

It must be like a great spiky cavern down there, Bolitho thought. He could picture *Tempest*'s hull as it would be seen by fish or merman. Dull against the glittering surface, idling forward between the reefs, while far beneath her keel the sea fell away to blackness. To a silent world.

Somebody must have sighted the ship. Even if the lookouts could see no sign of life there would be other eyes about. The word would be passed through the islands quicker than any known signal. A ship was near. A man-of-war. Once *Tempest* had passed by the people would emerge to continue their lives in their own way. Preying on each other, hunting, fishing. Killing.

'No bottom, zur!'

Bolitho watched the cutter thoughtfully. 'Call away the quarter boat, Mr Borlase. Take her yourself, and run close inshore once we are through the reefs. No risks, but keep an eye open for wreckage washed into caves or on the beaches. Arm your people and mount a swivel in the bows.'

Borlase, who had been a spectator like most of the ship's company, forced his sun-dulled mind to react.

'Aye, sir.' He cupped his hands. 'Quarter boat's crew lay aft!'

Tempest was moving so slowly that it was not even necessary to heave to while the men tumbled into the boat and thrust off from the side.

Bolitho watched until Borlase had got his men working the boat properly and had a sail hoisted to the solitary mast. It was better to do something than merely stand still and brood.

It would also confuse any hostile eye on the shore. Boats in the water without obvious purpose could mean anything, and would delay the passing of messages until the reason became clearer.

'By th' mark twenty, zur!' A pause as the leadsman hauled in his line hand-over-hand. 'Rocky bottom!'

Bolitho looked at Herrick. If the tallow in the bottom of the lead held no sand it was likely they were right above the reef at its safest point. Twenty fathoms were as secure as a hundred.

Starling in his cutter would not even have known it was there, for with a boat's smaller lead and line of half that length he would be unaware that the worst was over. But his sounding was still essential. A sudden uplift of reef, an uncharted pinnacle, no matter how small, could tear out *Tempest*'s bilge like an axe through a hammock.

He watched the surf writhing beneath another headland. No wonder old sailormen kept their audiences enthralled with tales of sirens and mermaids luring ships to their deaths. It all looked so peaceful, so inviting.

'No bottom, zur!'

Bolitho moved restlessly to the starboard side and tried not to think of fresh, cool drinking water. Like that which you found in streams and brooks in Cornwall. So clear and refreshing it was like wine.

He saw Keen watching him, his face in a frown. Probably thinks me mad to keep on looking, searching.

He heard the rattle of canvas and blocks as another weak gust filled the sails to make the masthead pendant lick out like a long tongue. Few of the seamen and marines were speaking, or even showing much interest in the passing islands. The gurgle of water alongside, the creak of the wheel were the loudest sounds to be heard.

'Deep nineteen!' It was like a dirge as the leadsman hauled in his line yet again.

Lakey said suddenly, '*There's* the island, sir! Fine on the starboard bow. The hills overlap from this bearing, but five there are, with the anchorage beneath the second and third, as I recall.'

Bolitho took a glass from Midshipman Romney who had been hovering nearby with his sextant in readiness for the noon ritual of shooting the sun under Lakey's demanding eye. Poor Romney could not even do that properly. The other three midshipmen were now as proficient as any lieutenant. Better than some.

He saw the hills, stark and bald of vegetation nearer the top. But for Lakey's hoard of sea knowledge he would never have guessed there were five hills in a row. What a terrible place to be shipwrecked or marooned. No vessel, unless driven off course by a storm or on some unlawful mission, would pass this way. A man could die of madness as easily as of thirst.

'By the mark fifteen!'

Bolitho touched Romney's shoulder, feeling his skin jump beneath the grubby shirt.

'You keep an eye on Mr Borlase's boat. If it becomes hidden

around a point, or lost from view for any time, inform Mr
Herrick at once.'

He saw the boy looking up at him. As ever, desperately
eager, yet already fearful of making some new mistake.

Bolitho added quietly, 'You are excused noon sights, Mr
Romney. I *know* our position well enough. But I do not wish
to lose a boat's crew.'

Romney touched his forehead and hurried to the nettings,
his telescope making him all the more pathetic.

Lakey said gruffly, 'Never make a sea officer. Never in this
life.'

'By the deep twelve!'

Bolitho looked away. He doubted if it would get much
shallower just yet, but the leadsman's regular reminder calls
helped to steady his thoughts.

Without turning he knew Allday was behind him. Despite
his solid build Allday could, when he desired, tread like
a cat.

He said, 'I could fetch you a drink, Captain?'

Bolitho shook his head. 'Later. It's not time.'

Allday strode forward to the rail, his head to one side.

'Cannon fire!'

If he had voiced some terrible obscenity against King and
country his words could not have had a more startling effect.

Ross, master's mate-of-the-watch, said scornfully, 'My empty
stomach more like!'

Then they all heard it, a solid, re-echoing bang, like a drum
in a cave.

Lakey nodded firmly. 'From that anchorage. *Must* be. The
sound would be bounded seaward.'

Bolitho saw the faces along the gundeck upturned towards
him. Seeing what he would do. How he would begin.

He said, 'Signal Mr Starling to maintain his distance, and
then recall Mr Borlase.'

Romney exclaimed wretchedly, 'I c-can't see the other boat,
sir!'

They all stared at him.

Herrick said harshly, 'You *what?*'

Romney had been distracted by the distant gunfire and the

sudden excitement on the quarterdeck. Like everyone else who was not below, he had been looking ahead and not where he had been ordered to watch.

Bolitho gripped his hands behind him. The gunfire was very irregular and obviously from only one cannon at a time. Whatever the reason, it was not the action of someone trying to hide.

He looked past the midshipman and watched an out-thrust shoulder of land. Borlase must have gone right into the beach to pursue his search. It was unfortunate that Romney had looked away at that moment, but it could not be helped now. Borlase would know how to take care of himself. He had already shown he was more than capable of that.

Bolitho said sharply, 'Set the fores'l, Mr Herrick. Alter course two points to starboard.'

Herrick snatched up his speaking trumpet. 'Pipe the hands to the braces! Lively there!'

As *Tempest* swung heavily on her new course and the hurrying seamen freed and set the big foresail, Bolitho felt the slight increase in speed. With the wind now almost astern, and the additional span of canvas to contain it, she gathered way and began to overhaul the cutter.

Bolitho raised a glass again, seeing the first hill sloping down towards the weather bow, so that through the lens it appeared to be touching the figurehead's left shoulder.

'Deck thar!' All eyes were turned up towards the foremast lookout. 'Ship at anchor round th' point!'

Another crash echoed and grumbled across the blue water, and Bolitho saw hundreds of sea-birds circling above the nearest hill like tiny white feathers.

He waited until the seamen had finished belaying the weather forebrace and then turned and walked aft to the wheel. He could feel the helmsmen watching him, and knew Keen and Lakey were also following his movements.

The senior helmsman said hoarsely, 'Nor' by west, sir. Steady she be.'

Bolitho consulted the compass and examined the trim of the yards and loosely flapping sails. Then he looked at Herrick, recalling in fleeting seconds all those other times.

'Very well. You may beat to quarters now, and clear for action.'

Herrick nodded, his features impassive.

The two marine fifers came pounding aft, dragging out their sticks and adjusting their drums before starting a staccato tattoo, while the bosun's mates ran from hatchway to hatchway bellowing, 'All hands! All hands! Beat to quarters and clear for action!'

Bolitho realized that Midshipman Romney was still standing by the rigid helmsmen and asked, 'What is keeping you?'

The boy, a small, unmoving figure in a helter-skelter of outward confusion as *Tempest*'s seamen and marines ran to quarters, stammered huskily, 'I – I am sorry, sir, I thought . . .' He trailed into silence.

Herrick said sharply, 'Starboard side forrard. Report to Mr Jury. He is already shorthanded.' He raised his voice. '*Move yourself*, Mr Romney!' He watched the midshipman hurry away and murmured, 'God help that one.'

The leadsman, forgotten by almost everybody, called, 'By the mark ten, zur!'

Bolitho watched the cutter passing abeam, Starling standing in the sternsheets to wave as they ploughed past.

He took out his watch. It was all taking too long. But he dare not set any more sails. If *Tempest* had to come about to avoid grounding, the extra canvas would make it almost impossible.

Herrick called, 'Cleared for action, sir!' His eyes were on Bolitho's watch and he added, 'I regret that it took all of fifteen minutes, sir.'

Bolitho returned the watch to his pocket. For once he had not been thinking about his standard requirement of ten minutes or less for clearing for action.

'Yes. We must try to lop five minutes off it.'

It would do Herrick more good to worry about that than to know his captain was feeling new anxiety.

He looked over the rail and along the gundeck, at the bare-backed seamen by each twelve-pounder, and on to the forecastle where the long bow-chasers and stubby carronades were also ready and waiting.

Gun captains and marines, seamen and warrant officers. As mixed a company as he had ever encountered.

But whatever lay around the point, or beyond the next horizon, they were all he had.

He said slowly, 'Well then, Mr Herrick. Run up the colours.'

With her canvas filling and emptying as if drawing breath, *Tempest* steered unwaveringly towards the Island of Five Hills. Bolitho could not recall such a frustrating and slow approach, and he was conscious of the tension all around him.

He raised a glass to his eye again, trying not to count the number of times he had done so since sighting the little island. The rocks at the foot of the first headland were like broken teeth, and he could see the trapped water lifting and surging amongst them, and further still to a tiny crescent of beach. Too steep to climb from that place, he decided, even if he could get a boat through the rocks without stoving in her planks.

Bang! The sound of a solitary cannon echoed around the next headland, above which a lopsided hill seemed about to slide straight into the sea.

He steadied the glass and examined the black topgallant masts and yards of the anchored vessel, the careless flapping of her brailed-up sails. She was so close inshore that she must have been beached at some time. Possibly to repair damage, as Lakey had suggested.

He said, 'Alter course to weather those rocks, Mr Lakey. We will cross the bay and show ourselves, though I cannot imagine what they are firing at.'

Bolitho had voiced what Herrick and some of the others had been thinking since the first sound of a shot. *Eurotas*, and there seemed no doubt it was she, was well armed, as a merchantman had to be in these waters, but as there was no obvious sign of another ship she was either being harassed by natives or from the shore itself. Her cannon should be well able to drive off any such threat, and as they had heard no heavy weapons fired in reply the mystery was all the greater.

'Hands to the braces!'

Men moved slowly in the blazing glare, and then with haste as their petty officers bustled amongst them.

'Put up th' helm!'

Bolitho watched the masts' gaunt shadows swaying across the dried planking as *Tempest* responded to helm and wind. Round and further so, with the humped island swinging away to larboard, revealing the bay around the second hill, and the one beyond it.

'Steady as you go!'

'Nor'-east by north, sir!'

Tempest seemed to take it upon herself to increase speed, as with the wind following almost in her wake she threw droplets of spray over the beakhead and the men crouching at the carronades.

Herrick exclaimed, 'I can see 'em, sir! A dozen or more canoes! Big ones with outriggers!'

A gun fired from the other ship's concealed side, and a fin of spray ripped past one of the nearest canoes.

Bolitho studied the low, darting hulls, the gesticulating figures who were controlling the men at the thrusting paddles.

'Clear away a bow-chaser, Mr Herrick. I want a ball amongst those canoes. The range is too much for grape.'

Herrick looked at him, his eyes as blue as the sea. 'Will I pass the order to the gundeck to load and run out, sir?'

'No. It would be taking an axe to kill an ant.' He smiled, the effort making his parched lips crack.

He realized he must have been moving about this pitiless deck for hours. A few feet either way, oblivious to the heat and the discomfort as he had fretted over what he would discover.

'She's making a signal, sir!'

Bolitho halted in his restless pacing and waited for Midshipman Swift to add, *'What ship?'*

Bolitho shaded his eyes as some of the canoes back-paddled vigorously and turned end-on towards him. They had at last realized that *Tempest* was in the bay.

He ignored the bright hoist of flags as Swift's signal party sent them dashing up to the yards. He could leave all these things to others. He had to think. To hold his mind absolutely clear. Something was wrong. Like a picture where the artist had forgotten to include a face or a shadow.

From right forward he heard the cry, 'Larboard bow-chaser ready, sir!'

'Very well.' He raised his hand. 'Fire!'

The bang from the long nine-pounder was expected, but made most of the watchers start with alarm nonetheless. It was always like that.

Bolitho watched the ball's progress as it touched the crests of two steep breakers which were receding from the rocks and then slammed down amidst the untidy clutter of canoes. Paddles thrashed wildly, and acting on some signal of their own the slender hulls began to move away towards the headland which *Tempest* had just cleared.

'Another ball, sir?'

'No. If we hit one of the canoes it would tell us nothing. And the others will be through the rocks and away up the other coast before we had even found the wind to come about.' He shook his head. '*Eurotas* is in some sort of trouble.'

'Beg pardon, sir.' Lakey looked worried. 'But I feel the wind rising a bit. Not much as yet.' He gestured with a hand tanned so dark it looked like carved mahogany. 'Look astern. Tongatapu is all but hidden in mist. The glass won't tell us much, but I'm for caution.'

Bolitho nodded. The main island which they had sighted first was no more than a green and purple blur. Yet the eastern coastline was all of ten miles long, according to the latest chart. To be hidden in thick mist, while out here, just a few miles away, the wind was freshening, warned of something fiercer to come.

'Yes. I'd not wish to be caught amongst these reefs in a real squall. We'd drag our anchor and be aground in no time.'

He looked towards the open water. Open but for occasional feathers of spray to mark the scattered humps of reef and coral.

He made up his mind. 'Heave to, if you please, and call away the launch. I want a boarding party sent across immediately.' He saw Herrick patting his pockets and added, 'Not you, Thomas.' He sought out Keen's slim figure on the gundeck. 'Send the third lieutenant.' He held Herrick's attention by saying, 'I want it to look very normal. If I sent my first lieutenant, or,' he hesitated, 'did what my heart directs and went myself, I think it might appear unusual.' He nodded. 'Carry on.'

While the frigate laboured round into the wind, and the business of swaying out the big launch got under way, Bolitho sent for Captain Prideaux. He made the same point to him as to Herrick, and knew he was equally mystified.

'Just send your sergeant and a squad of marines.' He tried to smile at Prideaux's foxy face. 'Their uniforms, no matter how uncomfortable in this heat, will reassure *Eurotas*'s master that we are not pirates.'

Prideaux touched his hat. 'Yessir.' He hurried away, snapping for his burly sergeant.

Keen was on the quarterdeck, already staring across at the anchored ship, his face creased with responsibility.

'Pass my compliments to the *Eurotas*, Mr Keen.' He waited for the lieutenant to turn. 'Ask if we can be of assistance, although from out here the ship seems in good condition.' He knew Herrick was listening at his elbow as he continued, 'There are some passengers aboard. I would be obliged if you would enquire of them also.' He saw the sudden understanding on Keen's face. 'Now off with you.'

With Herrick he watched the launch shove off from the side, the oars rising and falling like wings as it ploughed into the first steep swell from the rocks. Even aboard *Tempest* Bolitho could feel the powerful undertow and current in the way his ship was swaying and rattling, her sails in disorder as she drifted heavily with the wind.

Bolitho braced his legs and followed the launch with his telescope. It was in calmer water already and making good speed towards the *Eurotas*. He could see activity at her entry port, a touch of blue and white to mark at least one officer awaiting *Tempest*'s boat.

No matter what reason *Eurotas* had for being here, and hull damage seemed the most likely, it must have cheered every heart aboard to see the unexpected arrival of a King's ship.

Herrick said, 'I'm not sure Mr Keen will know what to look for, sir.' He sounded anxious. Excluded from something he did not recognize.

Bolitho lowered the glass. '*Look* for, Thomas?'

Herrick grinned awkwardly. 'I know you too well, sir. You head into the bay with gunports sealed and only a chaser to speak our authority. Then you send Mr Keen instead of me, or even Mr Borlase, when he eventually reaches us.'

Bolitho smiled. 'The weather signs are not good. I want to speed things along. Also, I want to know why *Eurotas* did not fire all her guns at those canoes. One scattered broadside would have made kindling of them.' He turned to watch the boat hooking on to *Eurotas*'s chains. 'And only her captain can tell us that!'

'Quarter boat's in sight, sir!' A bosun's mate was pointing over the nettings. 'Mr Borlase is standing well out to clear the rocks.'

Bolitho nodded. 'Hoist his recall at once.'

The man knuckled his forehead. 'An' the cutter is in sight too, sir.'

Bolitho tried to keep his face impassive as he examined his actions, seeing his men in their various roles at this moment of time.

'Mr Starling had best remain where he is. We may need more soundings directly.' He looked at Swift. 'Signal the cutter to that effect.'

Prideaux's marines were on the *Eurotas*'s upper deck now, their coats like droplets of blood on the gangway. Bolitho trained the glass and tried to keep the scene steady as his ship wallowed heavily in the swell. Then he forgot Herrick and everyone else as he saw some women right aft by the poop. One in particular, with long, autumn hair, holding a broad-brimmed straw hat with her hand as it caught the wind. Viola. He almost spoke her name aloud. She was there, across the strip of restless water, her dress the colour of fresh cream, as she stood watching the captain speaking with Keen, while Midshipman Fitzmaurice, arrogant even at that distance, waited a little behind him.

He heard Herrick remark, 'I can *feel* the difference now.'

Then Lakey said, 'Aye. We're in for a blow before another dawn. Sharp and savage it'll be.'

Herrick must have turned to Allday as he said, 'Like some of the girls you've known, eh?'

Allday replied, 'They were the days, sir.'

Bolitho saw a marine returning to the launch. They were coming back.

He raised the glass again, climbing on to a quarterdeck six-pounder to get a better view as *Tempest* swung crablike away from the land. He was in time to see Keen shake hands with the ship's master, and then saw Viola Raymond move a few paces from the other passengers. It was like a silent play. The youthful lieutenant pausing with one foot on the entry port grating, the figure with the broad-brimmed straw hat and cream gown raising one hand to delay his leaving. Between them, like the jilted lover of any melodrama, *Eurotas*'s captain was looking from one to the other. Then the contact was broken, and Keen climbed down after the rest of his men and the cutter shoved off for the long pull back to their own ship.

Lakey swore as Ross, one of his mates, called, 'Wind's backed, sir! Almost due south, I'd say. If it keeps a'backing we'll be –'

Lakey snapped, 'I *know*. We'll be hard-pressed to avoid a lee shore.'

Bolitho knew that all these remarks were for his benefit if not directly put. He was as worried as Lakey about the wind and the dangerous proximity of reefs. But he was also troubled about the *Eurotas*. Viola's husband was supposed to be going to some new appointment. Their paths might never cross again. He felt something like panic. He should have gone in the boat himself and ignored his stupid caution. Everything was exactly as Lakey had suggested it would be, and had there been no search ordered by the governor in Sydney, *Eurotas* would have arrived safe and sound in the end.

It was common enough for ships to be delayed after the wearisome and often hazardous passage around the Horn, and Bolitho suspected that but for her rich cargo no such efforts would have been called for.

Borlase and his boat were tossing and pitching around the stern as Keen's launch hooked on to the chains, the oarsmen gasping and sweating from a hard pull.

Keen came inboard and hurried aft.

'Well?'

Bolitho watched him, partly wondering what Keen thought of his captain's strange whims.

Keen took a breath. 'As we thought, sir. She was damaged and holed some while back, and put into this bay to complete repairs. I spoke with Captain Lloyd, and he assured me that all is now satisfactory. He thanks you warmly for your support, especially as he was being attacked by some savage natives.' He answered Bolitho's unasked question. 'He had landed most of his artillery to lighten ship while the hull repairs were carried out.'

Herrick nodded. 'Makes good sense.'

Keen frowned, trying to miss out nothing. 'He did say that if you are returning to Sydney he would be obliged if you would reassure the governor that cargo and convicts are safely on passage.'

Convicts. Bolitho had almost forgotten about them. Again he was reminded of their plight below decks. Transported perhaps forever from their own country, and then, after weeks at sea, to be under siege in an island they did not even know.

He said slowly, 'Thank you. Have the launch hoisted inboard and prepare to get under way, if you please.' He looked at the master without seeing him. 'Lay a course to take us clear of the north'rd headland. Then which ever way the wind chooses to turn we will have the sea room to use it.'

He turned back to Keen as his ideas were translated into orders and action by the others.

'Was that all?'

Keen glanced at Herrick, but he was already calling the hands to the tackles to hoist the boat and to the braces in readiness for bringing the drifting ship under command again.

He said quietly, 'As I was about to leave, sir, the lady, the wife of –'

'Yes, Mr Keen, I do know, please continue.'

'She called out to me. The passengers had been told who was in command of *Tempest*. She wished to be remembered to you. I think she might have said more, but I was about to take my leave.' He sounded apologetic.

Bolitho smiled gravely. 'Did she look well?'

Keen nodded. 'Very, sir.' He frowned. 'But she did mention something I did not fully understand. Captain Lloyd interrupted her by asking me for information about the missing *Bounty*.'

Bolitho saw it once again in his mind's eye. The little cameo. The three figures on *Eurotas*'s deck.

'Try and remember *exactly*.'

'Yes, sir.' Keen looked across at the other ship. 'I was at the entry port when she called something like, *I hope your captain was able to have his watch repaired*.' He shrugged helplessly. 'Then Captain Lloyd saw me to the side, sir. I am sorry I can tell you nothing more.'

Bolitho looked at him for several seconds. 'You told me a great deal.'

He took the watch from his pocket and turned it over between his fingers. She had thought of the one thing which would make him suspicious. He chilled despite the sun as the reality crowded in on him. When his watch had stopped a musket ball it had saved his thigh from a bad wound, but it had been smashed to fragments in the process. She had known it, and had given him this one as a gift to replace it. It was the one thing she would remember.

He asked sharply, 'Was Mr Raymond present?'

'Aye, sir. But he remained aft with some of the others.'

'I see.'

Herrick strode from the gangway and said, 'Ready to get under way, sir. I have had word passed to Mr Starling of our intentions, and he will proceed ahead of us right away.' He sensed Bolitho's mood. 'Is something wrong?'

'Everything.' Bolitho thrust the watch into his pocket. He felt angry and sick at the same time. To think of her across the water, suffering God knew what torment, and trying to find a way of warning him through Keen.

She would never mention the watch in the presence of her husband. It was their own secret. And in any case, she would not have forgotten the truth of the story.

He said, 'Then get under way, Mr Herrick.' He looked up at the masthead pendant. 'It's backed a point more by the look of it. We will try and stand clear of the islands before it gets worse.' He looked at the lieutenant and said simply, 'The *Eurotas* is taken. We must land our people and attack before they know what we are about.'

They stared at him as if he had just gone raving mad.

'But, but . . .' Herrick floundered for words. 'I heard most of what Mr Keen described, sir. I can find no hint of trouble there, especially as we have chased the attackers away.'

'I believe the real enemy is within that ship.' He dropped all formality and stood between them. 'You both know about my watch, even though you are careful never to mention it. *You both know*, and none better than Mr Keen himself, that he was nursed by Viola Raymond after his cruel injury. She was, I believe, very good to you.' He looked at each in turn. 'Do you honestly believe she would falsify one fact and omit to mention the other altogether?'

Keen answered, 'No, sir, I do not.'

'Thomas?' Bolitho watched his friend, the emotions on his open face. 'I must know.'

Herrick bit his lip. 'Perhaps not, sir. But to assume the ship to be in wrong hands, well . . .'

Bolitho turned away. 'Do any of us know Captain Lloyd? Have we ever spoken with *Eurotas* before?' He swung round, making Keen start. 'There is no other reason for such careful deception!'

Herrick rubbed his chin. 'That being the case, sir, I think we should make haste.' He sighed. 'If you're wrong . . .'

'And if I'm not?' He watched him gravely. 'What then, Thomas?'

Lakey called, 'All ready aft, sir!'

His voice broke the spell.

Bolitho said, 'Once clear of the next headland I want you to set the t'gallants, Mr Herrick. Now send your topmen aloft and let us be about it, eh?'

Awkwardly at first, until her yards were braced round to receive the freshening wind, *Tempest* tilted to the pressure and began to turn her jib boom towards the next headland. High above the decks the seamen worked busily and expertly, untroubled by the menace which Viola Raymond's message had thrown amongst them.

By early evening the Island of Five Hills lay sprawled far astern across the larboard quarter, its shape and outline lost in haze and reflected glare.

In the cabin Bolitho sat at his table, an untouched meal pushed to one side.

The wind had backed still further, and it would take some while to beat round the northern tip of the tiny island they had just left. But equally, the wind would prevent *Eurotas* from sailing.

He thought about the attacking war canoes. An accidental encounter, or an attempted settlement of past scores? But without them it was doubtful if they would have discovered *Eurotas*'s anchorage. Her captain, whoever he was, would have had lookouts ashore, and they must have seen *Tempest*'s patient and persistent search amongst the islands. If he had not been forced to fire guns at the canoes, and remained silent, *Tempest* might have missed the little island completely.

But there were too many *ifs*. Bolitho moved restlessly to the stern windows and sought out the dorsal fin close astern. There had been a firm link between the two ships which the other captain could not have suspected in any way. He touched the watch in his pocket.

The fear was that the brave gesture might already have cost her life.

4

After the Storm

True to the sailing master's prediction the weather began to
worsen rapidly soon after midnight. The wind, although hot
and without freshness, mounted in power, and as moon and
stars vanished beyond low layers of scudding cloud *Tempest*
prepared to fight it out.

Even Bolitho found it an eerie experience. After heat and
searing glare, the slow and patient changes of tack to use what
little wind they had had at their bidding, this violent motion,
the distorted roar and hiss of waves were unnatural. Their
world had shrunk again, confined to familiar objects and hand-
holds about the decks, while beyond the bulwarks the water
seethed and boiled like a cauldron before fading into the surrounding darkness.

He found plenty of time to pity the men working aloft on
the quivering, thrumming yards and shrouds. Occasionally
during a brief lull in the wind's strange moaning he heard the
topmen and their petty officers yelling to one another, high
above the deck, voices distorted and wild, like demented
spirits.

Herrick lurched up the tilting quarterdeck and shouted, 'All
secure, sir!' He waved one arm, his blurred outline gleaming
dully with blown spray. 'She should ride it out well enough if
all holds together!' He ducked, cursing as a frothing wave
rolled along the weather side and burst over the nettings,
drenching everyone in reach. 'With all respects to the late and
lamented Captain Cook, sir, I think he was wrong to name these
the Friendly Islands! God damn them, I say!'

Bolitho groped his way aft to where Lakey and his mates
and three helmsmen who were lashed to the wheel swayed and

bobbed in a tight, breathless group. He peered at the compass bowl, unnaturally bright in the tiny lamp, and tried not to consider what this delay might mean. He was thinking like the French captain he had fought. Le Chaumareys had started to plan too much beyond the present. At sea you could not take even the next minute for granted.

He pictured his command, reeling and plunging, with spars and cordage under savage pressure. He could have run with the wind, and even now might have been well clear of the worst of it. But if the wind continued to rise, *Tempest* might have been driven many miles to the north, with little hope of getting back to the island in time to act. These violent tropical storms were frequently followed by intense calms, and if that happened Bolitho knew the chances of a quick passage were destroyed. As it was, his ship was standing into the wind as well as could be expected. Under her great maintopsail only, shortened and under constant watch, she was lying-to like a floundering, glistening hulk.

He heard the occasional clank of pumps, but knew they were being used merely to clear the water which swept over the weather side and thundered along the gundeck like surf before finding its way below. Any other frigate Bolitho had known would have been working badly in this sea, and the pumps would have been manned and busy through each backbreaking minute. But *Tempest*, with all her faults in manoeuvrability, was as tight as a powder cask, and her stout teak timbers barely leaked a drop.

Bolitho watched the water sluicing down the lee side, cascading over each tethered twelve-pounder, eager to catch a spluttering, half-blinded seaman and knock him senseless into the scuppers as it passed.

He gripped the hammock nettings and tried to think, although he felt half-numbed by sea and wind.

The *Eurotas* should be safe in her sheltered anchorage. But if her cables carried away she could go aground and break up even there.

Suppose after all this he was wrong? That Keen had been mistaken in what Viola had said to him, or had tried to invent something just to please him. Maybe she had blended her

C

message with sarcasm that only he would understand, so that should they meet again he would stand clear and keep his place.

Or perhaps she did want to see him, and thought such a message would bring him back anyway.

He pushed his hair from his eyes as the spume and ragged spray drifted through the mizzen ratlines like darts.

No. If he was right about her, he had to be equally so about *Eurotas*.

He felt Herrick lurching to the nettings beside him.

'Mr Lakey stakes his reputation that this'll last till noon, sir!' Herrick waited, squinting into the darkness. 'But at least we'll be able to see what we're about! I've trebled the lookouts, but we're drifting too much for comfort!' He sounded raw from shouting orders. 'Maybe we should've gone closer to the *Eurotas*. Grappled her, and to hell with the weather.' He was thinking aloud. But it sounded like criticism. 'I'm not sure of anything now.'

Bolitho replied, 'If I'm right, Thomas, I think both ships would have been in danger. The passengers, the convicts, who knows how many more might have been murdered, or killed in the attack.'

Herrick wiped his mouth with his sleeve. 'Aye. I suppose so. My guess is that the convicts were released out of humanity when the ship struck, and then seized control.' He turned, waiting for Bolitho's opinion.

'*If* the ship struck, Thomas. There's something too clean about all this.'

Starling, one of the master's mates by the compass, yelled, 'I heard somethin' carry away aloft, sir!'

As if to mark his warning two heavy blocks and some fifty feet of cordage clattered across the quarterdeck like a twin-headed snake.

Starling was already bellowing for extra hands to get up the treacherous shrouds and secure the damage. It was small enough, but if unchecked might spread to something worse.

Bolitho listened to the master's mate and marvelled. Starling had been hoisted inboard with his cutter at the last possible moment so that his leadsman could give the ship as much speed as possible to clear the reefs. A misjudgement, or a man losing his nerve, and the cutter might have been left astern. In this sea it would be unlikely to survive.

And yet Starling, who had begun life as a drummer boy in a foot regiment, and had run off to join a King's ship for preference, had showed little excitement when he had reported to the quarterdeck.

'Right on time, sir,' was all he had said, and now he was up and about, shouting and instructing the afterguard as if nothing had happened out of the ordinary.

Bolitho saw the legs and ragged trousers of one of the seamen hurrying up the ratlines, the bare feet moving rapidly like paddles. He recognized the man as Jenner before he vanished into the maze of rigging above the deck. Another piece of human flotsam. Jenner was an American, who had fought in the Revolutionary Navy against the British. A good seaman, although something of a dreamer, he had joined his old enemies as if he had become bored with the independence he had helped to win.

Just beneath the quarterdeck, ducking and jumping clear of the thundering crests which swept over the twelve-pounders, was another mystery. A giant Negro, he had been found half dead in a drifting longboat shortly after Bolitho had taken command. He had been naked and cruelly savaged by sun and thirst. Worse, when he was taken below to the surgeon, Gwyther had reported in his precise manner, 'The fellow has no tongue. It has been cut out.'

In the drifting longboat they had discovered a metal disc. All it had cut on it was the name Orlando. The name of a ship, a man, a piece of cargo, nobody knew.

Bolitho suspected the boat had been from a slaver and that the big Negro had either tried to escape or had been cast adrift as a warning to others.

But when *Tempest* had reached land again their survivor did not want to be put ashore, despite all that was said to him in every language which the ship's company could muster. And that was quite considerable. So, with his new name and rating entered on the muster book as Orlando, a landman, he had been accepted.

Because the American, Jenner, seemed to get on with him

better than most, Herrick had put them both in the afterguard. The mizzen mast and its attendant sails and rigging was by far the least complicated of any square-rigged ship, and Orlando's inability to speak and Jenner's dreamy attitude, which even the touch of the boatswain's rattan had failed to cure, would leave them less chance of suffering or causing an accident.

That was typical of Herrick, of course. Always watching over his men. As he had been when Bolitho had first met him in the *Phalarope* during the war. A ship beset with discontent and in-human treatment, where a junior officer could reasonably be expected to keep his silence rather than provoke a tyrannical captain. Not so Herrick. His ideals, his stubborn yardstick of right and wrong, had more than once put him into real danger.

Bolitho always hoped that Herrick would get a chance of the promotion he richly deserved. But peace, the countless numbers of sailors thrown on the beach without work or hope had blocked his chances. He was lucky to be employed at all. Unlike Bolitho, whose family and upbringing had been set in tradition, with the sea and ships the only possible career, Herrick came from a poor family. What he had he had worked for because he needed it. The fact he loved the sea was a hard-won bonus.

'Sir! The fore t'gans'l is tearin' adrift!'

Bolitho dashed the salt from his eyes and tried to see up through the rigging. Then he heard it, the irregular crack and thunder of canvas freeing itself from the yard, threatening to fill with wind and change the trim of the ship.

Herrick cupped his hands. 'Mr Borlase! Send your people aloft! Mr Jury, stand by the main stays'l!'

He turned, panting, 'If the t'gans'l carries away without ripping itself to pieces we'll need the stays'l to give us balance.' He showed his teeth. 'God, how quick the mind skips when you need it!'

Bolitho nodded. Herrick had acted well and without waiting for approval. If, as could still happen before the topmen fought their way up the foremast shrouds, the sail freed itself entirely, it would slew the bows round, and their situation in the rising gale could be suddenly critical.

He saw the boatswain mustering his men beneath the mainmast, others wading through waist-deep water to reach their stations. Familiarity, harsh, and sometimes unfair discipline had made them so. In pitch darkness, or in a raging storm, they could find their way about a ship as a blind man will know his own cottage.

Borlase was busy too, his voice matching the wind as he urged the foretopmen into action. When he shouted his voice tended to be shrill and piercing, and Bolitho knew the midshipmen often made unflattering comments about it behind his back. It was strange that few people ever thought about the cabin skylight on the poop. Voices from the watchkeeping officers reached the captain very easily. Bolitho had learned his lesson early as a midshipman when his captain had called from the skylight, 'I am sorry, I did not hear that. *Where* did you say you met the girl?'

All these things and more he had tried to describe to Viola Raymond when she had sailed with him as a passenger. He had expected her to be bored, or tolerantly patient. Perhaps from those first conversations had grown the ache he now felt for her safety with each dragging hour.

'I think they are in trouble, sir.' Herrick was leaning over the quarterdeck rail, his back and legs streaming with water. He yelled, '*What is it?*'

Borlase strode aft, his figure leaning over against the ship's steep angle.

'Mr Romney, sir! He's out on the fore t'gans'l yard!' Despite the din of wind and sea he sounded irritated. 'There's enough risk as it is without – '

Bolitho cut him short. 'Send up a bosun's mate! Or someone senior enough for him to trust!' He looked at Herrick, his voice bitter. 'Midshipman Romney may never make a lieutenant, but he tries as hard as ten men. I'll not have him fall because Mr Borlase has not the sense to see the danger.'

He swung away, trying to hold on to the picture of the island, their position and bearing from it. What he must do or avoid when the time came.

Yet all he could see was that terrified boy, clinging to a yard, some hundred and fifty feet above the deck, with a great billowing mass of wind-hardened canvas trying to smash him down and hurl him to certain death. A quick end if he hit the deck, slower by a little if he fell into the sea. He might live long enough to see his ship fade into the darkness, for no boat could be lowered now, and *Tempest*'s drift would outpace any swimmer.

Bolitho thought too of the shark which was there to greet each new day.

Midshipman Swift blurted out, 'I'll go, sir.' He faltered as both Bolitho and Herrick turned towards him. 'He'll trust me. And besides . . .' He hesitated. 'I promised I would watch out for him.'

They all looked forward as someone yelled, 'He's gone!'

Something pale fell through the rigging and struck the lee side of the forecastle near one of the carronades. It made a sickening sound, and then Bolitho saw the body bounce over into the creaming water which surged back from the stem.

Nobody said anything for several seconds, so that the roaring noises of the storm swept in on them like a fanfare of brutish triumph.

Midshipman Swift said thickly, 'I – I'm sorry, sir. I should have – ' Then he pointed along the gundeck. Swaying like a puppet, and suspended on a bowline being lowered rapidly from the foretop, was Midshipman Romney.

Several seamen ran to catch him and lay him on the deck, while Schultz, the bosun's mate who had been sent aloft to assist him on the yard, hurried aft and stood below the quarterdeck, his face upturned as he said in his thick, guttural voice, 'Mr Romney is safe, zur.' He showed his teeth as if in pain as more water surged over the nettings and doused him from head to foot. 'He vas trying to save a man from falling.' He shook his big head sadly. 'It vas too much, by God. Zey both nearly die!'

'Dawn coming up, sir!' Lakey slapped water from his watchcoat. 'Young Mr Romney is lucky to see it.'

Bolitho nodded. 'Who was the seaman?'

The bosun's mate replied, 'Tait, zur.' He shrugged. 'Good man, I tink.'

By the time the topmen had finally mastered the rebellious sail and returned to the deck the sea had opened up on either beam in a violent, rearing panorama of broken crests and dark troughs.

Herrick said, 'And you always hope you're going to get by without losing a man.' He sighed.

Bolitho saw Allday climbing through the cabin companion-way and replied, 'That is true.'

He turned with surprise as Allday said, 'I've brought you something to cheer, sir.'

It was brandy, and Bolitho felt it going through him like fire.

A seaman observed, 'That bloody shark's still arter us, th' bugger.'

Another answered, 'Reckon old Jim Tait made a good meal, eh?'

Bolitho looked at Herrick. No words were needed. Life at sea was hard. Too hard perhaps to reveal weakness, even when a friend had died.

Lakey closed his telescope with a snap.

'I think I know where we are, sir.' He sounded satisfied, separated from the drama which had just left them. 'I'll be able to fix our position very shortly.' He tugged out his watch, which if set beside Bolitho's would have looked like a chronometer. 'Aye, I'll be able to do that.'

Bolitho looked away, searching for the tiny islet which Lakey had marked as one which he would be able to identify if the wind dropped. He sighed. Not *if*. Lakey meant *when*, and that was enough.

If only he was as confident and as spared of doubts in his own ability, of what he would do when they returned to the island.

He saw Romney walking aft, pale and dazed, and seemingly unable to understand why the sodden, unshaven seamen nodded and grinned to him as he passed.

Bolitho looked down at him. 'That was well done, Mr Romney.'

The midshipman would have fallen, but Orlando's towering shape, shining in spray like wet coal, caught him and carried him beneath the quarterdeck.

When he recovered, Bolitho thought, he might be able to use that one wild gesture as a prop or a lifeline. It could make all the difference.

Herrick watched him narrowly, seeing the signs of uncertainty and searching enquiry which made Bolitho so dear to him.

Each one aboard had a job of work to do, hard or less demanding according to rank or station, carried out well or just well enough to suit a man's individuality. But it all came from aft. From the one man who now stood with a dented goblet in one hand while he gripped the nettings with the other. Bolitho's black hair was matted with salt and blown spume, and his shirt stained with tar and grease from a dozen enounters with guns and tackles during the night, yet he stood out as their captain as if he were in a dress uniform.

Bolitho said abruptly, 'That rogue of a cook will not be able to light his galley fire for hours yet, Mr Herrick.' He had to raise his voice, for the wind's noise, like the light, was strengthening. 'Pass the word to Mr Bynoe to broach some spirits for the people. They'll not care what it is, I think. Rum or gin go down as well with salt spray as brandy!' He met Herrick's glance, his grey eyes suddenly bright. 'Then we will decide what to do.'

The heat in the cabin was overwhelming, and Bolitho had to use something like physical strength to control his nausea.

All day, while *Tempest* had fought sea and gale, and they had been buffeted slowly and inexorably around the islands and the protective barriers of reef and shoal, he had examined his ideas and plans from every angle.

By noon he had known they were winning their battle with the weather, and from the faces and voices of many of his men he knew they were proud of what they had done together. It was strange how quickly men could change. Men penned together for months, sometimes years on end. Who saw and examined each others' habits and flaws like misers counting their gains and losses. An argument could flare into blood and harsh punishment. Using their common understanding could bind them just as easily into a single body.

And then, with the wind still ripping the crests from the long banks of waves, the sun had emerged again, pinning them down with its old familiar force. It had seemed as if the ship was afire, and to some of the less experienced men it must have looked as if *Tempest* was about to become their pyre. From every plank and timber, spar and piece of rigging, the sun had raised great clouds of steam, and even the seamen's bare bodies had left tendrils of it behind them as they had worked to splice and make good the damage left by the storm.

It was night now, but with a difference. Outside the great cabin windows the moon had laid a firm path on the sea, rippling in a light wind which mercifully brought them this far. Everything else shone darkly, like black liquid glass.

But it was hot, and in the crowded cabin it was hard not to think of cool, transparent water. Jugs and jugs of it. Filling yourself until you felt like bursting.

Bolitho watched the bottle of stale wine going round the table. Herrick, Keen, Lakey and Captain Prideaux of the marines were refilling their glasses, looking at the master's chart, wondering, saying little.

A storm at sea knocks the stuff out of a man, Bolitho thought. Like a physical fight, all bruises and anger. Then it was done, and all you wanted to do was creep away and be alone.

He said, 'We are now standing off the nor'-west shore of the island. I dared not beat in earlier for fear of lookouts on the hills. The island is only a mile wide at this point. Our approach would be easily recognized.' He paused, hearing Borlase's feet moving about the deck above, as near to the cabin skylight as he could prudently get.

He knew Herrick was watching him. He even knew what he was thinking, preparing to say.

Bolitho continued evenly, 'Mr Lakey is certain that we can reach a small cove without too much difficulty. The moon will assist, and once inshore the land will afford some shelter against the wind.' He looked round the table. 'I intend to land a small but well-armed party. It is already being arranged,' he saw Herrick nod, 'but the important part is *afterwards*.'

Prideaux said tersely, 'I think it would be better to land *all* the marines, sir. A show of force, no matter the reason for showing it, usually works wonders.'

Bolitho looked at him. Prideaux was very relaxed. He was

enjoying it. He obviously thought discussion unnecessary and stupid. That his captain was totally out of depth with his plan, as well as with the execution of it.

Bolitho said to the cabin at large, 'We will take thirty men, and the marines selected will be your best sharpshooters, Captain Prideaux. The sergeant will be one, and he is picking six more. I do not want a *show* of anything. If my fears are justified, we will have to act with haste, and with stealth.'

There was a tap at the door and the midshipman-of-the-watch stepped into the lanternlight.

'Mr Borlase sends his respects, sir, and wishes you to know that the boats are ready for lowering.' His eyes moved round the cabin as he spoke. Midshipman Pyper was seventeen, and probably already saw himself as a captain in some fine ship.

'Very well.' Bolitho leaned over the chart, knowing they were watching his every move. 'Once the landing party is ashore the boats will return to the ship. There are too many eyes about for my liking, and I want no evidence of our movements left in the open. Then *Tempest* will steer south and round the southern headland, much as we did originally. Mr Herrick knows what is expected once you arrive there, and will pass his instructions in his own tine. The landing party will divide into halves. One under Mr Keen, and the other will go with me. We will cross the island to the bay.' He pulled out his watch and flicked it open. The hands showed two o'clock in the morning. Dawn came up fresh and quick in these waters. There was no room for doubts now. 'After that, gentlemen, we will think again.'

They all stood up, and Bolitho added, 'And remember to tell the people exactly what we are doing. Explain that protecting lives is as much part of the Navy's work as taking them in battle!'

They moved to the door, already grappling with their own parts of the pattern he had thrust on them.

Herrick stood his ground, as Bolitho knew he would.

'I think I should take charge ashore, sir.' He sounded very calm but determined. 'It is my right, and in any case – '

'*In any case*, Thomas, you think I am foolhardy to go myself, eh?' He smiled gravely as Allday came out of the shadows and took down the old sword from the bulkhead. 'It is my decision.

Many of you probably think it is a wrong one. I have doubts too over some things.' He waited for Allday to buckle the sword round his waist. 'I'll feel more at peace amongst chaos of my own making than fretting aboard this ship and worrying that you may have fallen because of me.' He held up his hand. 'It is done, Thomas. I know you relish a good argument, but leave it until my return.' He clapped him on the shoulder. 'Now see us away and do your part.'

On deck the air was a little cooler, but not much. Bolitho walked to the starboard gangway and looked down at the jostling figures who were being sorted out and having their weapons and meagre supplies checked by Jury, the boatswain.

He tried to appear relaxed, to recognize and acknowledge each of these silent men. Once the boats had gone from the beach they would be entirely self-dependent. There was no water on the island, as Lakey had long since discovered. Just a handful of men, their small resources, and an unknown enemy.

He heard someone whisper, 'By God, the cap'n's comin' with us! Must be important!'

Another said hoarsely, 'Wants to stretch 'is legs, more like!'

'Silence on deck!' That was Jury.

Borlase touched his hat. He looked enormous against the moon. 'All mustered, sir.'

Bolitho looked at Herrick. 'Heave to, if you please. Then we will lower the boats.' He touched the sword against his hip. 'After that . . .' He shrugged.

With her canvas flapping noisily, *Tempest*'s shadow rode across the moon's path, while the three boats were swayed out and the seamen and marines scrambled into them.

Two boats would have been sufficient under normal circumstances, but with the additional hands required to pull them back to the ship, overcrowding would have added a full hour to the operation.

Bolitho made a last check in his mind. Lieutenant Keen, aged twenty-two, was his second in command. James Ross, master's mate, a thickset Scot with dark red hair, would add weight and experience to the party. Sergeant Quare and his six sharpshooters, all strangely unrecognizable without their usual scarlet coats, and hugging their long muskets like backwoodsmen. Midshipman Swift and Miller, a boatswain's mate, completed the authority.

The bulk of the men had been chosen for their skills, their ability to obey under almost any conditions, and some because they would kill without hesitation if such was the need.

He took a long breath. 'Carry on, Mr Ross.'

He saw the master's mate raise his fist and then the cutter began to move away. From the deck it looked crammed with men, oars and weapons. Next *Tempest*'s launch, and her largest longboat, idled clear of the side, oars in momentary confusion until the current swung them away from the ship's undertow. Bolitho saw Keen, very upright in the sternsheets, his shirt holding the moonlight like a banner. Allday was already in the gig, as were Midshipman Swift and the rest of the last group.

Bolitho touched Herrick's arm. 'Perhaps when this is done you may have more respect for Captain Cook's description of the islands.' He smiled grimly. 'Take care, Thomas.' Then he lowered himself down the side and jumped out into the gig.

Allday said, 'Shove off! Out oars! Give way all!'

The gig plunged and rose steeply in the swell, and now they were clear of the ship's hull Bolitho could hear the hiss and boom of breakers.

He glanced along the boat at the regular rise and fall of the oars. It was not easy to pull smoothly with the boat filled with arms and legs. He noticed too that his gig's crew had donned their chequered shirts which they always wore for taking their captain on his normal affairs of duty.

This was hardly normal, and he was moved to say, 'Thank you, lads.' But nobody spoke, and the only sound to match the sea was the steady creak of oars.

When he looked astern again *Tempest* was only a tall shadow with the moon's silver across her flapping topsails.

As soon as the boats were safely hoisted inboard again she would set every stitch of canvas she could carry to stand clear of the land as fast as possible.

A shuttered lantern blinked from the leading boat. Ross had sighted the first elbow of rocks. They must follow through one gap and then a second. After that it was no more than a cable to the beach. *If it was there.*

'Watch your helm, Allday. This is the worst part.'

He saw the quick exchanges throughout the boat. It was best for everyone to know all the risks and not just some of them, he thought.

The sea noises changed again, the great surge of water against the outer reef muffled slightly as the three boats forged steadily around the glistening crags of rock. Little waterfalls changed to surging torrents as the tide cascaded over and around the rock barrier, making pools and lakes and just as quickly draining them again.

The bowman called, 'Beach dead ahead, sir!' A pause. 'Cutter's already there!'

By the time Allday had steered the gig through the last scattering of rocks and lined up the stem with the tiny patch of beach, the cutter was already passing on the return trip.

The bowman leapt down and almost fell as he guided the boat into the shallows, and more men waded out to stop her from broaching to.

Men, weapons, discipline. Bolitho watched his gig backing water with the oars, the crew's check shirts already more distinct in the first hint of dawn.

He felt Allday's grip steadying him as he climbed up the wet sand and on to some fallen boulders. They were all cut off. And he had brought them here.

He said, 'I will lead with my party, Mr Keen. You will bear south and then east as soon as we get off the beach. Good luck.'

With Allday and Midshipman Swift at his heels he turned and looked up the steep, sun-cracked slope. If ever he had needed his confidence, it was now, he decided.

5

Now or Never

'We will rest here.' Bolitho lowered himself on one knee and unslung the telescope from his shoulder. 'Sergeant Quare's scouts will be back directly.'

The gasping, sweating file of seamen climbed over the lip of a small gully and found what shelter they could amongst thick, prickly bushes. The sun was higher, and the heat which was thrown back from the hillside and cracked boulders fiercer than ever.

Bolitho trained his telescope on the nearest of the island's five hills. It was more rounded than the others, so that it looked hunched, leaning away from him towards the sea on the other side. He saw a brief glitter of reflection, probably on a weapon, as one of the scouts paused to examine one of the many small gullies.

But nothing else moved. It was like a dead place. Harder now to believe that the *Eurotas* was anchored beyond the big hill. That she had ever been there.

Midshipman Swift scrambled over loose stones, his tanned features shining with sweat.

He liked Swift. More so since his willingness to go aloft in the storm to rescue Romney. He had pleasant, regular features, and hair so bleached by sun and salt Bolitho doubted if his mother would recognize him. Swift had been barely fifteen when she had last seen him. When she saw him next, with any kind of luck, he would be a lieutenant.

Bolitho said, 'Pass the word. Just take a sip of water. See that they don't drink the whole lot at once.'

He felt the wind ruffling his hair, and shifted his glass towards the sea. It was rarely out of sight in this island. It was hard to believe they had come through a storm. How blue the sea looked with just the cruising movement of white horses to betray the wind which had carried *Tempest* away to the south under full canvas. Now, it was empty, reaching away towards the larger islands and sluicing over the long reef barriers to show the set of the tide and yet another change of wind.

Sergeant Quare strode through the dusty bushes, his boots covered in salt and sand. He was a tall, powerful man, with intense pride in his marines and what they could do.

Bolitho nodded to him. 'Seems quiet enough.'

Quare lowered a musket to the ground and slitted his eyes in the glare.

'Two more hours and we should see something, sir.' He had a round, Devonian dialect which was like a touch of home. He hesitated, ' 'Course, the ship might have up-anchored already, sir.'

'Yes.'

Bolitho took a flask from Allday and let a little water trickle over his tongue. Brackish from the ship's casks, yet it tasted like the best wine in St James's.

Quare straightened his back, his eyes on the opposite slope. 'Here comes Blissett, sir.'

The scout in question loped down the slope towards them, seemingly without effort, his musket held high to avoid striking the ground.

Bolitho knew something of Blissett's past, and why Quare had selected him as a scout. The marine had once worked on a vast estate in Norfolk. As one of the gamekeepers, and a fine shot to boot, he had enjoyed a good and fairly comfortable life. Until, that was, he had set his cap at the niece of his lord and master. Bolitho imagined that the matter was probably more complicated than Quare knew, but the end result was that Blissett had been thrown out of work and had gone into town to drown his sorrows. A recruiting party had been at the inn also, and the rest, marked down in a haze of despair and bravado, was now history.

The Island of Five Hills must seem very different from Norfolk.

Blissett arrived beside them. 'It's pretty fair going once you get up that slope, sir.' He pointed. 'I reckon the sea is just yonder, with the bay below that shoulder of rock.' He took a flask gratefully.

Quare nodded. 'Mr Keen's party will be about an hour later than us. It's a longer route round the other side of the hill.' He cocked his head. 'Still, we should meet up mid-afternoon. What d'you say, Tom?'

Blissett shrugged. 'Reckon so, Sarnt. I found a few fire places in the gullies, but not new ones.' The last piece he added hastily as some of the seamen in earshot moved with sudden apprehension. 'No natives around here for some while.'

Bolitho reslung his telescope and gestured to Swift. 'Get the men on the move again. Same distances as before. You take two hands to the rear and make sure we're not being followed.' He looked up at the sunbaked slopes. There would be no cover here. A perfect place for an ambush.

He could sense the men as they followed at his back. Breathless and tired already, and totally unused to tramping over land, they would never respect him again if they found he had led them on a fool's errand.

He tightened his belt. But better him than Herrick. Herrick had taken enough knocks on his behalf.

Bolitho concentrated on the land ahead, keeping his pace slow but regular as he tried to picture the other side of the hill.

Tomorrow, if the wind was favourable, *Tempest* would tack around the southernmost headland once again. And if there were lookouts on the shore they should sight her immediately. More to the point, Bolitho's scouts should see *them*.

It should appear quite natural. Deception was a game any number could play.

After a fierce storm it might even be expected for a King's ship to return to the bay, if only to ascertain that *Eurotas* was still intact.

Allday broke into his thoughts. 'A scout's signalling, Captain. I think he's sighted the other party.' He grinned unfeelingly. 'God, Mr Keen's people will curse when they see the hill they've still got to climb!'

Sergeant Quare hurried across the lip of another gully and dropped out of sight. He appeared eventually on a fallen landslide of loose stones, while slightly above him another marine gestured and pointed like a deaf mute.

Quare came back, breathing fast. 'He says to stand fast, sir. A runner is coming from Mr Keen.' He mopped his face and neck. 'He'll not run for long in this lot.'

Bolitho's party sank gratefully into the bushes again and waited for the messenger to arrive. It took a full hour, and when he was finally dragged out of a gully, the man looked almost spent with exhaustion.

It was Miller, boatswain's mate, nimble enough when dashing about the deck in a full gale, or urging the hands out on the swaying yards, but no match for this island.

'Take your time.' Bolitho concealed his impatience, wondering why Keen should send him and delay the worst part of the journey.

Miller gulped noisily. 'Mr Keen's respects, sir, an' 'e – ' He gulped down air again like a landed fish. 'We found some corpses.' He pointed vaguely. 'In a little cove. Their throats was cut, sir.' He looked suddenly sick as the memory came back to him. 'I – I think they was officers.'

Bolitho watched him, not wanting to break his train of thought.

But Quare asked bluntly, 'You *think*?'

Miller looked past him. 'Aye, George. You just know them things.' He gave a violent shudder. 'Mr Ross reckons they've bin dead for days. Covered with flies, they was. Still are.'

Bolitho nodded. Despite the horror of the story he realized that either Keen or Ross had managed to keep his head and not do what every decent man would wish and bury the unknown bodies. *But they were not unknown.* The *Eurotas*'s senior officers in all probability. Murdered after being taken to the little cove. He wondered if Keen had thought the same. As he had shaken hands with the man he had thought to be the ship's captain he had been facing a murderer in his victim's coat.

The realization moved through him like sickness. Viola had tried to warn him. She might have died just as horribly because of it.

He snapped, 'Get back to Mr Keen. Fast as you can manage. Tell him we will meet as arranged, but with double the caution.' He watched his words sinking in. 'Nobody must see our approach. If we are sighted before we can act, Miller, the ship may weigh, and Mr Herrick will have no chance of catching her.' He did not add that it might as easily mean the landing party would be murdered beforehand. The expression on Miller's stubbled face told him he had already considered it.

Bolitho looked at Quare and the others. 'Come along.' He strode up the slope again, the heat and discomfort suddenly forgotten.

'You'll need to stay down, sir.' Quare spoke with a whisper as Bolitho crawled beside him between two great boulders. The stones were like heated metal, and Bolitho was conscious of the cuts and bruises he had gathered on his limbs and body in the final part of the journey.

The big hill was quite different on the other side, and different again from the way it had looked from seaward. There was a broad cleft halfway down, and then another slope which continued down to the beach and the bay.

And there, hazy in the sunlight, lay the *Eurotas*. Still at her anchor, and with several boats alongside and two drawn up on the sand clear of the surf.

There were a few figures visible on her poop and maindeck, but no sign of work being carried out on the hull, or anything else.

Bolitho wished he could use his telescope and study the ship more closely. But with the sun blazing down at an angle he dared not risk a sudden reflection warning of their arrival above the bay.

Quare had already sent Blissett and another scout to see what they could discover, but Bolitho had to guess what was happening aboard the ship if he was to be of any use.

Quare hissed, '*There*, sir!'

Several men had walked into view from the bottom of the hill. They were moving slowly. Untroubled. But all were armed to the teeth. One was drinking from a bottle, and had to be aided over the gunwale of a small boat before they pushed it into deep water and started towards the ship.

That left one boat ashore. Bolitho blinked the sweat from his eyes. But how many men?

Swift crept up behind him. 'Mr Keen's party is coming, sir.'

Bolitho looked at him. 'Keep them away from here. And no talking. You make sure the weapons are unloaded. I don't want a musket going off in error.'

He looked at the anchored ship and tried to think what to do. She lay a cable's length from the beach, and the boat which had left the island was barely halfway to her. Exposed. Helpless against even the smallest weapons.

But where were the guns which Keen had been told were unloaded to lighten the ship? They were certainly not in the empty ports along the nearest side. Nor were they on the beach. Surely they had not been jettisoned. It would take a long time, and there seemed no point in it.

Unless . . . He stared towards the southern headland, almost black against the glittering sea. Another ship perhaps. The *Eurotas*'s guns may have been off-loaded into her. He closed his eyes tightly. He could form no pattern at all.

Blissett came round the side of the great rocks without a sound.

Quare asked, 'What is it, Tom?'

The marine wiped his mouth and stared at the ship. 'We found a dead girl down the bottom there. She must have put up quite a fight, poor lass. But they done for her all the same when they'd had their way.'

Bolitho looked at him, his mind reeling. He barely recognized his own voice. 'What sort of girl?'

Blissett frowned. 'Young 'un. English, I'd say. Probably bein' deported to Botany Bay or th' like, sir.' He said nothing more, but his eyes proclaimed bitterness. His anger at those who had sent the unknown girl to this.

'Easy, Tom.' Quare turned to Bolitho. 'You were right, sir.'

'I wish to God I'd been wrong. The ship has been taken. Not by the convicts.' He saw the question on Quare's face. 'They'd not waste time and labour hoisting big guns over the side. They'd be weak and frightened after what they've been through. I believe our enemy is something far more dangerous and without mercy.'

He rolled on his back and dragged out his watch, despising himself for his relief. He had feared it was Viola lying down there.

It would not be dark for several hours. He said, 'Post a good watch, Sergeant. Then join me.'

He hurried down the slope and into a tangle of dried-up bushes. The whole place seemed scorched by the sun and covered by the droppings of countless sea-birds.

Keen and the others crowded round him.

He said, 'I believe there's a boatload of men ashore some-where. They're probably out on the headland. It's too danger-ous to run a boat through those rocks, which is why they were taken by surprise by the canoes. It's my guess they've mounted a guard there. To watch for ships and to drive off any native canoes before they can pass through the rocks.'

Keen nodded. 'And *their* boat is unguarded!'

Ross ran his thick fingers through his red hair. '*Now* it is, Mr Keen. After night it'll be another story entirely.'

Bolitho said, 'We'll take cover. As soon as it's dark we'll go to the beach.' He glanced at Keen. 'When you boarded *Eurotas*, did you see many of her company?'

Keen looked surprised. 'Well, no, sir. I suppose I assumed they were working below decks.'

With a King's ship entering the bay and a pack of yelling warriors nearby in canoes, Bolitho thought it was unlikely that any seaman would be so set on his work. It was strange he had not thought about it earlier. So there had to be a second, even a third ship.

He turned and scrambled back up the slope to the two boulders and crawled beside a watching marine. He studied the ship for several minutes. There was no doubt about it. The *Eurotas* was standing higher in the water. All those cannon, a valuable cargo and ship's stores. No wonder there were so few hands visible about her decks. Just enough to watch over the ship, the wretched convicts battened below. He tried not to think of the murdered girl.

He returned to the others. Keen watched him, his face tight with anxiety.

Bolitho said, 'It will be a gamble.' He saw Allday's hand

drop to his cutlass. 'But I intend to board that ship as soon as it's dark. Once there, we can hold her until *Tempest* arrives.'

Ross said flatly, 'The wind's no helping Mr Herrick, sir. It's veered quite a piece since we stepped ashore.' He looked at the clear sky. 'Aye, we may have a long wait, I'm thinking.'

Keen said, 'Why don't you take a rest, sir? I will stand the first watch.'

But Bolitho shook his head. 'I must go and have another look at the ship.'

Keen watched him climbing towards the twin boulders. 'He *should* rest, Mr Ross. We'll need all his edge tonight.'

Allday heard him and stared up at the boulders. Bolitho would not rest or close even one eye until it was done. Until he knew. He drew his cutlass and sliced its heavy blade through the sand.

Allday had grown to like Viola Raymond very much. She had been good for the captain when he had needed her most. But he had been secretly grateful when she had sailed for England. She represented trouble, a threat to his captain's future.

Fate, or Lady Luck, as Lieutenant Herrick would have it, had decided otherwise. No matter how it had all begun, it looked as if it might well have a bloody ending before another dawn.

Bolitho licked his lips and felt sand grate between his teeth. Waiting for darkness had been a test for everyone in his party. Scorched by the sun, stung and pestered by flies and crawling insects, it had been torture.

He saw the splash of oars in the gloom and knew a boat was heading for the beach. All through the afternoon and evening, while they had tried to find shelter amongst the scrub and eke out their rations of water and biscuit, Bolitho had watched the occasional comings and goings between ship and shore. The boat had made several trips, but never fully manned. It seemed likely there was a constant picket or lookout on the headland, and few hands could be spared for manning the boat. But the timing was haphazard, and it was impossible to gauge any sort of routine.

One thing was certain, once it had begun to grow dark the boat was always challenged.

Aboard the anchored ship there had been hardly any sign of movement. But what there had, had struck dismay and anger into the watching sailors.

A woman had been seen on deck in mid-afternoon, her dark hair hanging over bare shoulders, her screams shrill across the heaving water as she was chased and finally dragged to one of the hatchways.

Later, a body, that of a man, had been carried to the bulwark and hurled into the sea. It floated away from the hull and made no effort to swim, so it seemed there was another murder to their account.

The boat grounded violently in the surf and the men struggled with oars and then a small anchor to kedge it on to hard sand. From the din they were making, and the attendant clink of bottles, it was obvious they were all drunk, or nearly so. One slumped down on the beach, his shoulders against the dripping boat, while his companions trudged away towards the headland.

Bolitho touched Keen's arm. It was now or never. The men might be back for more drink, or to change places with their comrades aboard *Eurotas* within the hour.

He said, 'Tell Sergeant Quare to begin.'

He looked at the sky. There was cloud about, but not enough to hide the moon. The wind was fresh, and with the hiss of surf and the distant boom of waves over the reef they might be able to get near the ship unheard.

Bolitho strained his eyes into the darkness, but the shadows played tricks with his vision. He heard the seamen breathing and shifting along the cleft in the hillside, and guessed they were imagining what was happening. Blissett creeping towards the boat, smothered in sand which they had plastered on his body with the aid of their precious water.

Only the unending line of writhing surf separated land from sea, against it the grounded longboat lay like a dead whale.

Bolitho stared towards the ship. There were no anchor lights, but he could see a faint glow through some of the open ports, and knew they were where the remaining guns were stationed. Loaded with grape, they would make short work of any clumsy attack. But there were no boarding nets. Once alongside, the odds might alter.

He stiffened as he heard something like a dry cough. Then Quare said hoarsely, 'All done, sir.' He sounded pleased.

Bolitho drew his sword and rose to his feet. At two hundred yards, plus the distance down the final slope, they would be invisible. He started to walk towards the beach, his shoes scraping noisily on loose stones, while the seamen emerged in a ragged line behind him, most of them hunched forward as if expecting to meet a volley of shots.

This was the worst part so far. As he walked Bolitho tried not to think of the muskets and pistols, now all loaded and primed, the rasp of steel from axe to cutlass.

He turned with surprise as he heard a man humming quietly as he strode behind him. It was the American, Jenner, walking in his familiar loose gait, his hair flopping over his eyes. He saw Bolitho turn and nodded companionably. 'Fine night for it, sir.'

Beyond him was the Negro, Orlando, a boarding axe over his powerful shoulder like a child's toy.

What they were doing here, the cause they represented were of no value now. They were going to fight, and if possible stay alive.

All at once Bolitho was standing beside the boat while the seamen gathered into tight groups as they had been ordered.

The marine, Blissett, took his musket from Quare and looked at Bolitho.

'I left him, sir.' He touched the spreadeagled corpse with his foot. 'He's not carrying anything but his weapons. He could be anyone.'

Bolitho looked at the dead man. Around his head and shoulders the sand looked black where his blood had soaked away. He forced himself to kneel beside him, to examine him for some sort of clue. The moon swept momentarily between the clouds, so that the man's eyes came alight in the glow as if to rebuke him. His clothes were poor and ragged, but his belt, pistol and cutlass were in perfect condition.

Bolitho touched his wrist and arm. The skin was warm, but quite still. There was no wasting, no loose flesh. This man was a sailor. He stood up slowly. *Had* been a sailor.

Keen whispered, 'I've got my party around the boat.' He sounded out of breath. Excited or frightened, it was hard to tell.

'Ease her into the water.'

Bolitho stood back to look at the ship while two groups of men began to slide the boat through the lively surf. There had been five in the boat before, and never more than six. He watched as the selected seamen clambered into the hull, thrusting out the oars and muffling them in the rowlocks with food sacks and pieces of clothing. He saw Miller rip off the dead man's shirt and pass it into the boat, one foot planted on the corpse to steady himself as he did so.

Miller, probably more than any other here, was in his element. He had come through the war and had survived cutting-out expeditions, cannon fire and every other sort of risk without a scratch. As a boatswain's mate he was above average. But in a hand to hand fight he was something else again. A killer.

Allday said, 'I'll take the helm.' He looked at Bolitho. 'Ready, Captain?' He spoke so casually he might have been suggesting a stroll.

Bolitho knew him so well that he could see past the calm voice. Like himself, Allday was stretched like a halter. Only when they were finally committed would he show his true self.

The boat lifted and splashed in the shallows, the men on either side easing it into deeper water as more of the boarding party clambered into her and flattened themselves on the bottom boards like corpses.

'Enough.' Bolitho looked for Quare and Midshipman Swift. 'Keep the rest of the men out of sight if you can. If any more "pirates" come from the headland, you know what to do.'

He nodded to the sergeant. The work of the marines was over, and if things went wrong Quare and his little group would have to hide and wait for Herrick to come for them.

He climbed into the boat very carefully, his sword bared against his chest.

'Shove off!' Allday crouched forward. '*Easy*, you noisy bugger!'

The clouds had thickened even in the time taken to get this far. It might mean a tropical downpour, but not for some while. Bolitho drove the doubts aside. If he waited for rain to deaden his approach, he might wait forever. He looked at the panting oarsmen. They had pulled only a few yards and were already finding it hard work with so many inert passengers. If he stopped the attack now he doubted if he could rouse them to fight again.

Keen whispered, 'Shall I tell the swimmers to leave now, sir?'

Bolitho nodded, and saw two figures, their naked bodies shining in the filtered moonlight, rise up and then slide over the gunwale with barely a ripple.

It had all sounded so dangerous and difficult when they had discussed it on the island. Now it seemed impossible.

He tore his eyes from the two swimmers and concentrated on the ship. How large and near she looked now. Surely somebody would challenge them soon? Maybe they had already been seen for what they were, and the loaded guns were being quietly depressed towards them.

Bolitho heard one of the oarsmen curse and then gasp as something rolled between the boat and the dipping blades. It was a corpse, turning over loosely as a man will do in bed. The one they had seen cast overboard, caught and carried by the current, unable to free itself from the bay.

'Easy on the stroke, Allday.'

Bolitho felt the pistol in his belt. They must give the swimmers time to reach the anchor cable and haul themselves aboard without discovery. It was all too easy, but then, why not? The pirates, or whoever they were, had bluffed their way past a British man-of-war and had sent away a boarding officer convinced of their identity. At anchor in a safe bay, with sentries posted ashore, why should they not feel secure?

The challenge when it came was loud and startling.

'Boat ahoy?' An English voice.

Allday dragged two empty bottles from between his feet and hurled them into the bottom of the boat, throwing back his head and roaring with laughter as he did so.

Bolitho heard other voices from the ship, but no further challenge. The empty bottles were more convincing than any password.

'I saw one of the men on the beakhead, sir!' It was Miller straining his head above the gunwale. 'They're aboard, by God!'

The boat was very near the side now, and Bolitho saw the entry port, two dark figures watching their slow approach. He could even smell the ship, the familiar tang of tar and hemp. One of the men by the port swung towards the forecastle as a figure appeared in a shaft of moonlight swaying from side to side and snatching at rigging for support.

Allday hissed, 'That's Haggard, Captain! A better actor than topman by the looks of him!'

But the seaman called Haggard had the full attention of the watch on deck, as with sudden dignity he reeled and fell over the side with a violent splash.

Two things happened almost at once. The watch left the entry port and disappeared towards the bows, imagining that one of their own had fallen over the side. And then out of the darkness came a terrible thrashing sound, like something being hauled through water at a great speed.

They all heard Haggard yell, *'My leg!'* Then he screamed, the sound cut short as he was dragged bodily under the surface.

Bolitho's mind accepted all these things even as he dashed towards the bows of the boat, and a grapnel soared up and over the *Eurotas*'s bulwark. He had not thought about sharks, had never imagined they would enter the bay. The drifting corpse must have attracted one, and Haggard had been seized and crushed to bloody pulp in those great jaws.

He heard himself yell, 'Up, lads! Let's be at them!'

The spell snapped, and the horrified seamen were all at once on their feet, fighting like wild things to reach the steps to the entry port.

A pistol exploded from the gangway and a ball sang past Bolitho's face as he hauled himself on to the deck. The two men on watch were caught in the pale light, one looking at Bolitho the other still gaping towards the forecastle as if expecting to hear another scream.

Seamen surged on to the deck, knocking each other aside in their eagerness to reach the two men. Cutlasses swished in the air, and the men fell with barely a sound.

From the poop came more shouts, and it sounded as if others were clambering through the forward hatch towards the forecastle.

But Keen and his men were already dashing along the gangways, firing into the hatch and towards the starboard cathead where a man had been clinging to get a view of the shark, or to hide.

Bolitho ran wildly towards the poop, almost falling as a figure loomed from behind a companionway and barred his path. He ducked aside and cut out with his sword, feeling it jar against steel as the man met his attack. Hilts locked they lurched towards the wheel, while seamen charged past, and others paused, feverishly trying to reload their weapons.

In the far distance Bolitho heard the crackle of musket fire and knew Quare was dealing with the sentries from the headland. He could feel nothing but cold hatred for the unknown man who was pressed against him. It was like being somewhere else. An onlooker. The man's breath, strong with brandy, the heat of his body, were all part of the unreality.

Bolitho felt the heavy thrust of the man's forearm. He stepped back, catching him off balance and swinging him round against the bulwark. Something flashed past his eyes, and he heard the sickening crunch of steel in bone as Allday sent the man pitching down a ladder. Allday spun round again, reaching out with the cutlass, as a dark figure ran from the poop, saw him and hesitated just too long. Allday, his legs carrying him across the deck like a charging bull, hacked the man across one shoulder, and as he fell shrieking finished him with a heavy blow on the neck.

Another was on his knees, babbling and pleading in a language which might have been almost anything, although the meaning was clear enough.

Miller seized him by the hair and then drove one knee into his face before lifting him bodily and pitching him over the rail. The attendant thrashing and bursting spray alongside showed there were other sharks hurrying to an unexpected prize.

Light flowed from a door below the poop, and Bolitho saw a man framed in it, crouching as he peered blindly towards the din of steel and yelling seamen. Bolitho dragged out his pistol and squeezed the trigger. Nothing happened, so he hurled it at the door and ran straight for it, the speed of his charge almost dragging the sword from his grip as he plunged it into the man's body.

He half turned, hearing cries and more shots, seemingly from the water itself. Someone was getting away in a boat.

But he could leave that to Keen. He kicked the door aside, thrusting the dying man off the coaming, and then leapt into *Eurotas*'s poop. It was like a scene from bedlam. Cabin doors hung open or were smashed down. Clothing, weapons and all manner of personal belongings were strewn everywhere.

On the deck above he heard a voice, shrill with terror, and then Miller's loud and menacing, 'Stand still, you little bastard!' The sound ended with a body slithering across the poop deck and one final gasp.

Bolitho stepped slowly aft, his sword across his body, his feet stepping carefully so as not to trip in the scattered and looted confusion.

'*Easy*, Cap'n!' He recognized Jenner's drawl. 'Next cabin.'

He ducked past Bolitho, his shadow swaying across the screen doors, with two more seamen close on his heels. His face lit up as a pistol exploded from the cabin, and the man nearest him fell clutching his stomach, blood already gushing from his mouth. Jenner drew back his arm and a small dirk flew through the door like a flash of lightning.

When Bolitho reached the door Jenner was already tugging the blade from the victim's chest, wiping it carefully on the man's leg.

More feet clattered along the maindeck, and Keen burst into the poop, a curved hanger in one hand, an empty pistol like a club in the other.

'We've taken the forecastle and the rest of the upper deck, sir.' He was breathing very fast, and his eyes were shining in the lanternlight with the desperate wildness of battle. He added,

'Some got away in a boat, but I think the sharpshooters are trying to mark them down.' He looked at the corpse. 'We managed to seize two prisoners.'

Bolitho said tightly, 'Open the after hatch, but be ready for tricks. Tell Mr Ross to take over the upper deck. Someone might try to cut the cable.'

He walked past the last of the cabins to the large one in the stern. Again the disorder of clothing and sea chests. A meal half-eaten on the master's table. A woman's dress too, with blood on it.

It was suddenly very quiet, as if the whole ship was listening, stricken with terror.

'Come.' He strode out of the cabin, Allday behind him, his head turning from side to side as if to protect Bolitho from attack.

When the hatch was opened, and not without difficulty as it was wedged tight with bars and chains as if in a slave ship, Bolitho was sickened by the stench of bodies and fear which rose to meet him and his men.

Still no sound at all. Just the regular creak of spars and rigging. Perhaps they had killed everyone aboard?

Allday whispered, 'If anyone's down there, Captain, they must think hell itself has boarded the ship.'

Bolitho stared at him. Why hadn't he thought of that? The horror they must have endured, the sheer terror of the past weeks, and then the deafening onslaught of *Tempest*'s seamen. No wonder there was no sound.

He stood on the edge of the hatch, ignoring Allday's sudden anxiety and the fact he was probably framed against the moonlight.

'*Stand fast below!*' He waited, hearing his voice echo around the deck. 'You are in the hands of His Britannic Majesty's Ship *Tempest!*'

For a moment longer he imagined his worst fears were realized, and then as if out of the bowels of the ship he heard a mounting, combined chorus of cries and sobs.

'Down quickly, lads!'

Bolitho waited as more seamen dashed to the hatch with lanterns and then stumbled with them to the deck below. Here there was another hatch, beside which stood a chair from the officers' quarters, a tankard near it to mark where a guard had been sitting at the moment of attack.

They withdrew more heavy bars and lifted the hatch. It was a small hold, one which had been used for cabin stores, without light or much ventilation. It was packed from side to side and bulkhead to bulkhead with people. It was like looking down at a solid carpet of upturned, terrified faces. Men and women, dirty, dishevelled, and at the last stage of survival.

Bolitho kept his tone as level as he could. 'Have no fear. My people will take care of you.'

He thought about his small boarding party. He did not yet know how many of them had died or were wounded. If this crowd chose to attack them, they would stand little chance, weapons or no weapons. There must be close on two hundred souls down there.

Miller strode to the hatch. He seemed calm again, his voice crisp as he gestured for some hands to enter the hold. But from the side of his mouth he said quietly, 'Mr Ross 'as three swivels loaded with canister and trained inboard, sir. If they start to show their metal he'll sweep the deck afore they knows what's 'it 'em.'

So he was not fully recovered from the killing.

It was terrible to watch as the people began to emerge from the packed hold. Some held on to each other from weakness and from fear. For whatever Bolitho's voice may have implied, he knew he and his men did not look like part of the King's Navy.

One man, cut above the eyes, and his face so bruised it was almost black, was wearing the jacket of a sailor.

Bolitho asked, 'Who are you?'

The man stared at him blankly until Allday took his arm and guided him away from the slow-moving procession.

Then he said, 'Archer, sir. Ship's cooper.'

Bolitho said quietly, 'The passengers, where are they?'

'Passengers?' It was an effort even to think. 'I – I think they'm still on the orlop deck, sir.' He gestured about him. 'Most of these are being deported.' He almost fell. 'We bin down there for days.' He stared around. '*Water*. I must have water.'

Bolitho snapped, 'Broach every cask you can find, Miller. Sort them out. You know what to do. Tell Mr Ross to send a boat for Sergeant Quare's party at once.' He sheathed his sword, his mind rebelling against the necessary details. To Allday he added, 'Orlop. Lively now.'

Another hatch, another ladder, and down below the water-line. Even in a ship of *Eurotas*'s tonnage and girth there was no room to stand upright between deck beams.

Lanterns swayed to greet them as more seamen entered the orlop deck by another hatch further forward.

Tiny cabins, like hutches, lined the sides of the hull. Much like those in a man-of-war where the ship's professionals lived and slept, always cut off from natural daylight. Sailmakers and coopers, like the man Archer. Carpenters and quartermasters.

'Open the doors!'

He heard a woman weeping hysterically, and a man further down the line of cabins pleading with her to be brave.

Allday snapped, 'Here, Captain!'

Bolitho strode to the door while Allday held a lantern for him. She was sitting on an upturned chest, her arm around a girl with long black hair, probably the one they had seen chased around the upper deck.

The girl was moaning, her face hidden against Viola Raymond's shoulder, her fingers digging into the cream-coloured gown like small, frantic claws.

Bolitho could barely speak. At his back he could hear the confused cries and sobs of people being reunited, and others looking for friends and relatives without success.

But it was all part of something else.

Viola stood up slowly, taking the girl with her. She said softly, 'Go with him.' She tightened her grasp as the terror shook the girl's body. 'He is a good man and will do you no harm.'

The girl moved from her, one hand still held out. As if she was being cut adrift, Bolitho thought.

Allday had left the lantern and closed the door behind them.

Bolitho reached out and held her shoulders, feeling her reserve crumbling as she threw her arms round his neck and buried her mouth against his cheek.

'You came!' She gripped him even tighter. 'Oh, my darling Richard, *you came back for us!*'

He said, 'I'll take you aft!'

'*No*. Not there.' She looked up at him, and he could sense her disbelief. 'Take me on deck.'

They made their way through the jostling crowds of men and women, seamen and the newly arrived marines until they reached the high poop. Then she stood facing the wind, repeatedly pushing her fingers up and through her hair, and taking long breaths as if each was to be her last.

Bolitho could only watch her. Afraid for her. Wanting to help.

He made himself ask, 'Your husband? Is he safe?'

She nodded slowly and then turned towards him. 'But where is your ship?'

He replied, 'It was too great a risk. They would have killed everyone by the time *Tempest* worked into the bay.'

She walked across the deck, her gown swishing on the worn planking. She did not speak, but kept her eyes on him until their bodies touched.

Then, and only then, did she break down, sobbing into his chest, oblivious to the ship and everyone around her.

Keen paused with one foot on top of the poop ladder, his mouth set to frame a dozen questions for his captain. Seeing them together he changed his mind and returned to the maindeck, his voice suddenly firm after the madness he had seen and shared.

'Lay aft, Mr Ross. Mr Swift, tend to the wounded, and then report to me!'

Allday watched him, remembering him as the young midshipman he had once saved from an agonizing death. Now he was a man. A King's officer.

Then he turned and glanced towards the poop. Well he should be a good one, he thought. He had the best there was as his example.

6

Revenge

Bolitho put down the pen and stretched his arms. It was early evening. Too soon for a lantern, but not bright enough for any more writing. He glanced around *Eurotas's* big cabin, picturing it as it had been when he had burst through the door. Now, with the deck cleared of looted boxes and clothing, it looked almost normal.

He stood up and walked to the tall windows. Away on the starboard quarter, leaning to a fresh breeze, his own ship, *Tempest*, made a perfect sight, her topsails and topgallants pale pink in the sunlight, her stem throwing up spray as she ploughed indifferently across each rank of rollers.

Herrick was holding *Tempest* well up to windward, just in case there should be another attack. If anyone was foolhardy enough to make such an attempt, he would bring the frigate dashing down at full speed, presenting the other face Bolitho had seen just three days back.

As he had taken *Eurotas* carefully from her anchorage in the bay, *Tempest* had tacked around the headland, exactly as he and Herrick had originally planned. It was the first time Bolitho had seen his own ship cleared for action from outboard. She had looked more than hostile with her guns run out like black teeth, her big courses brailed up to the yards to reveal the crouching marines in the tops and against the hammock nettings, muskets already trained on the slow-moving merchantman.

As Herrick had explained later when he had come aboard, he was taking no chances. Even *Eurotas's* flag hastily run up to the peak, and Swift's signals from the deck, had not convinced him. His best gun captains had dropped two twelve-

D

pound balls almost alongside even as *Tempest* had made the signal to heave to and receive boarders.

While he had listened to Bolitho's story, and had seen the chaos and disorder for himself, Herrick had reacted much as Bolitho had expected. His relief at finding Bolitho alive, and the attack completed successfully, had given way to reproach.

'You should have waited for us, sir. Anything might have happened. You could have been killed or taken by those scum.'

Even when Bolitho had explained how the American, Jenner, had discovered one of the pirates hiding in a magazine with a lighted slow-match and had forced a confession from him that his orders were to blow up the ship and everyone aboard, Herrick remained stubbornly critical.

Bolitho smiled grimly, recalling Herrick's attempts to maintain his sternness. It never lasted for long.

In the three days it had taken to stand clear of the islands and head towards Sydney again he had done a great deal of thinking, also he had examined the evidence and made out a report for the governor, and for Commodore Sayer.

The attack had broken out within the ship after fire had been reported in a forward hold. In the ensuing confusion, which had been hardly surprising in a vessel filled with civilians and deported prisoners, the poop had been rushed and seized by some of the 'passengers' who had boarded *Eurotas* at Santa Cruz where she had put in for fruit and wine for the long voyage around the Horn. *Eurotas*'s comings and goings must have been watched and checked for many months.

By the time the crew had discovered the fire to be nothing more than oiled rags in a large iron pot, the ship was in new hands. Some of the prisoners had been brought on deck and had immediately gone over to the attackers. Some had tried to protect their wives and had been instantly killed. Captain Lloyd had been ordered at pistol-point to change tack and head towards the islands. That had apparently been a bad moment for the pirates as they had been sighted and had received recognition signals from a mail packet en route to Sydney.

Once within sight of the islands all hopes of retaking the

vessel or putting up any sort of resistance were dashed. A large, heavily armed schooner had escorted them to the bay, and had sent aboard two boatloads of men.

As one of the loyal seamen had exclaimed, 'The most terrible villains you ever seed, sir!'

It had been then that the real horror had begun. Looting and drunkenness had been the order of the day. While some of the pirates had directed the unloading of cargo and weapons, money and stores, using the dazed and frightened prisoners like slaves, others had gone on a wild rampage through the ship. Several people had been beaten or hacked to death, women and young girls raped time and time again in a frenzy of brutal cruelty.

Captain Lloyd, no doubt dismayed that his own lack of vigilance had allowed it all to come about, had made a final attempt to overcome his guards and rally the loyal men to his aid.

It had been in vain, and the next day there had been no sign of Lloyd or his mates, or indeed most of his senior men.

Bolitho found himself moving round the cabin, recalling Viola's eyes as she had described the nightmare. Every hour was filled with despair and terror. The pirates came and went, abusing men and women like beasts, sometimes fighting with each other in a daze of brandy and rum.

Although battened down on the orlop, she was convinced there was also another ship in the bay for part of the time. She had heard the guns being moved from the *Eurotas* and into a ship alongside. It sounded as if the vessel was lower than *Eurotas*, perhaps the same size as the schooner.

She had been imprisoned in the little cabin on the orlop for much of the time, sharing it with a young girl who had been deported for theft.

Every day the girl had been dragged screaming from the cabin, while the pirates had left Viola in no doubt that the fate reserved for her was to be the worst.

Only once had she broken down as she had described the sacking of the *Eurotas*. It had been when she had recalled her feelings as *Tempest* appeared in the bay.

Eurotas had been harried and attacked by hostile natives, and she had heard it was because the schooner had raided one of the islands and had left more carnage behind them there.

Viola had said quietly, 'I knew you had come, Richard. I have been following your career, watching for fresh appointments in the *Gazette*. When I saw young Valentine Keen appear over the side I *knew* it was your ship.'

She also described how the leader of the pirates left to guard the *Eurotas* had threatened them all with instant death by firing the magazine if one made the slightest attempt to warn the boarding party.

'I could not just stand there, Richard. That brute had paraded a handful of passengers to make it appear normal. He and some of the others had donned company uniforms. There had been so much killing. So many terrible things.' She had raised her chin, the brightness in her eyes making her sudden defiance fragile. 'Had it been any other ship but yours, Richard, I could have done nothing. But the watch. I *knew* you would remember.'

'It was a terrible risk.'

She had smiled then. 'Well worth it.'

Bolitho looked around the cabin. She had been brought here to meet the real leader of the pirates. Her description had been a good one. A giant of a man, with a beard halfway down his chest. His name was Tuke, and he was English, or so it seemed.

Viola had said, 'A man with neither mercy nor any sort of scruple. His language was as foul as himself. He goaded me. Raped me with his words. He was enjoying my helplessness, my complete dependence on him whether I lived or died. But for my husband's importance, and his usefulness as hostage, I think I would have quickly followed the fate of the others.'

Bolitho found he was pacing more urgently, his stomach muscles contracting as if he were already in close-combat with the pirate called Tuke.

Now the schooner and her consort, if there was one, were somewhere in hiding. Gloating over their loot and the women they had taken with the first load. An island, or islands, not too far from here, he thought. The chart told him nothing, and the two pirates taken alive, little more. They were typical of their calling. Brutalized by murder and hard living. Their leaders might grow rich on their spoils, but men such as these lived hand to mouth like the savages they were.

Even threats had left them untouched. They would die on a gibbet anyway. There would be no torture, and their fear of Tuke was greater, even in the hangman's shadow, than of anything their captors could offer.

Including the luckless swimmer, Haggard, who had been killed by a shark, Bolitho had lost three men. Considering the darkness, the unfamiliarity of the ship, it was a miracle. Even the wounded looked as if they would recover within a few weeks. The risk had been justified. *Vital.*

The outer door of the cabin opened and James Raymond walked aft through the screen. He was freshly changed into a clean shirt and neat green coat, and displayed little sign of his ordeal. For several seconds he stood looking at Bolitho, his features giving nothing away.

He was about the same age as Bolitho, but his face, once handsome, had become marred with a permanent frown. Petulance, disapproval, it was all there.

He acted as if he owned the ship. Had been behaving like the one dependable man aboard since Bolitho had seen him released from another tiny cabin. He had not met him for five long years. All the while he had imagined that Raymond's path to better things had been furthered by his work in the Indies, by his treachery to the governor he had been sent to advise.

Now it seemed different. While Bolitho had fretted at being kept at sea, far from the scenes of greater happenings, Raymond had been sliding towards ignominy. This appointment he had been sent to occupy sounded even lower than the one held five years ago. It was impossible to read his reactions on the matter from what he said.

Raymond remarked coolly, 'Still writing your reports, eh, Captain?'

'Aye, sir.' Bolitho regarded him evenly, trying to conceal the anger he felt for him. 'There's more to all this than I first imagined.'

'Really?'

Raymond walked to the windows and stared towards the frigate.

'This man Tuke.' Bolitho checked himself. Once before he had shared too much of his confidence with Raymond. He said, 'From this ship alone he has equipped himself royally.'

'Hmm.' Raymond turned, his face in shadow. 'It is a pity you could not have taken him and his damned hirelings!'

'It is.'

Bolitho watched him, the way his hands opened and closed at his sides. He was less calm than he pretended. He wondered what would happen when they reached port, what story Raymond would tell. From what he had already gathered, Raymond had been pleading for his life when Tuke's men had seized the *Eurotas*.

It was to be hoped Raymond had not bartered secrets for personal safety. The Great South Sea was attracting the flags of a dozen countries. Always the search for more trade, further influence and territory.

Perhaps the authorities in Sydney knew more than they said. Bolitho hoped so, for with only *Tempest* and the elderly *Hebrus* to represent the King's authority, any additional threat in these vast waters did not bear consideration.

Raymond complained, 'I have lost a great deal of money. Those damned rogues – ' He faltered, caught off guard by his own disclosure. 'I'll see then all hanged!'

The door opened and Viola Raymond stood with one hand steadying herself against the screen as the deck tilted heavily.

Bolitho watched her, the stiff way she held her shoulder. Again he felt the rage churning inside him. Tuke had pressed the heated tip of a knife against her bare skin. *His mark*. It must have been agony.

She said, 'Who will you see hanged, James?' She did not hide her contempt. 'I do not see you as a man of action.'

Raymond replied harshly, 'That is enough. Your stupidity might have cost us our lives. But for you –'

'But for her quick thinking most of the prisoners and loyal men would have been burned alive in this ship.' Bolitho faced him. 'Maybe you would have been spared. I cannot tell. But the deaths of so many set against money and personal trappings seems too great for my reasoning.'

He looked away, feeling Raymond's hatred and Viola's compassion.

'I lost some good men, too. Did you think to ask about them? To know if a young seaman called Haggard, who was seized by a shark, has a family or a widow in England?' He shrugged. 'I suppose I should be used to such indifference, but it still snares my throat.'

Raymond said hoarsely, '*One day*, Captain Bolitho, I'll make you regret your insolence. I am not blind, nor am I a fool.'

She asked, 'Are you going on deck, Captain?' She glanced at her husband. 'I have endured enough for one day.'

They walked between the other cabins, and Bolitho heard Raymond slam a door with such force it sounded as if it would tear from its hinges. He paused in the shadow, one hand on her wrist.

'Three days. I can't stand seeing you with him. Perhaps I should have returned to my ship and put a lieutenant in command. It will be three weeks before we make a landfall.'

He felt her skin in his touch. Soft and warm.

She was looking at him, her eyes very steady. 'And I have been waiting and hoping for five years. We were wrong. We should have dared. Have broken with convention.' She raised her hand to his face. 'I have *never* forgotten.' Her teeth showed white in the gloom. 'Even the special smell you have. Of ships and salt. I'd have thrown myself to the sharks which killed your poor sailor rather than submit to that monster Tuke!'

Bolitho heard the chime of a bell, the attendant slap of bare feet as the watch changed. Someone, Ross or Keen, might come aft at any moment.

He said, 'Take care, Viola. You have made a bad enemy in your husband.'

She shrugged. 'He has made himself *that*. He did not even lift a finger to protect me.'

Allday clattered down a companion ladder and shot them a brief glance.

She asked calmly, 'What do *you* see, Allday?' She smiled at him. 'More things to worry you?'

Allday scratched his head. Viola Raymond was part of a world he had never shared, and rarely trusted.

'Squalls, ma'am. I see plenty o' them. But I've no doubt we'll manage.'

Bolitho watched him go. 'You have him at a loss for words. That is rare indeed.'

They walked forward, past the big double wheel, and out on to the broad deck.

The air tasted fresh after the cabin, and from the set of the topsails Bolitho guessed they were making fair headway. He wondered if Herrick was watching them through his glass, worrying like Allday at what might happen.

She slipped her hand through his arm and said lightly, 'The deck is very unsteady, is it not?' Then she looked up at him, her eyes challenging. Pleading.

In a quieter tone she said, 'Three weeks, you say?'

He felt her fingers digging into his arm.

She continued, 'After so long, I could not bear it.'

Keen stood with Ross at the lee side and watched discreetly. The master's mate asked, 'What d'you make of it, Mr Keen? The cap'n seems to weather as many risks here as he does in battle.' He chuckled. 'Man, he's fair taken wi' th' lass, there's no doubt to it!'

Keen cleared his throat. 'Yes. Yes, I'm sure.'

The big Scot stared at him. 'Mr Keen, sir, you're blushing!' He strode away, enjoying his discovery, and leaving the lieutenant with his confusion.

Midshipman Swift hovered nearby and asked, 'Is there anything I can do, sir?'

Keen glared. 'Yes. Attend to your duties, damn you!'

The two figures by the weather rail heard none of this. The savagery of hand to hand fighting and what had gone before was momentarily lost against the darkening blue sea, and the future still lay out of reach and without form.

Perhaps it had all been quite hopeless from the beginning, and yet Bolitho felt restored.

Commodore James Sayer moved wearily to avoid the bright sunlight from the stern windows as his flagship swung heavily to her cable.

He had just returned from the governor's residence, and was still wearing his dress coat. Beneath his shirt his skin felt cold and clammy, even after the pull across the anchorage in his barge, so great was the contrast in his cabin.

Through the quarter windows he could just see the frigate *Tempest*, her outline bending through the thick glass as if she was in a haze. She had anchored at first light that morning, and Captain Bolitho had come aboard the flagship in response to Sayer's signal, and had delivered his written report, as well as a verbal account of the *Eurotas*'s plundering and murder.

The important passenger, James Raymond, had not visited the flagship, but had gone straight to Government House.

Sayer breathed out slowly as he recalled his own reception there. Usually he got on quite well with the governor, allowing for the usual span between government and the Navy. This time he was surprised to find him fuming with rage.

'If things weren't bad enough, Sayer, we've now got that animal Tuke on our hands. He stripped the *Eurotas*, and God knows what use he'll make of her artillery. I'm sending the brig *Quail* to England with my despatches immediately. I *must* have more support here. I can't be expected to take incoming prisoners, build their accommodation, tend to their security *and* keep our trade routes patrolled.'

Commodore Sayer had never met Raymond, and he had not known what to expect. He had heard that he had been promoted from being a government adviser to the East India Company to his present post out here. As far as Sayer was concerned, being posted to the Great South Sea could never be seen as promotion. Punishment more like.

But Tuke he did know. Mathias Tuke, like many of his trade, had begun life at sea in an English privateer. It had seemed the natural thing to take the next step and act merely for himself. Against any flag, and with every means at his disposal. He had missed hanging by inches many times, and all the while his influence and the stories of his horrific deeds had spread across two oceans. He had sailed these waters before, and had then set up a base near more prosperous routes in the Caribbean and the Spanish harbours of the Americas.

Cruel, ruthless, feared even by his own sort, Tuke had given many an admiral a headache wondering where he would strike next. And now he was here.

Sayer had said, 'I have a full report of the happenings in *Eurotas*, sir. But for Captain Bolitho's prompt action, with no little risk to himself and his landing party, I fear we would have lost everything, and all the people aboard the vessel slaughtered in a most callous manner.'

'Quite.' The governor had fiddled with papers on his great desk. 'I am furious with *Eurotas*'s master for acting so *stupidly!* Taking extra passengers at Santa Cruz with so many convicts and too few guards on board!' He had thrown up his hands in despair. 'Well, he has paid for it, poor devil.'

Sayer had said nothing. He had known for some while that most of the captains of merchantmen on government warrants had added to their payment by taking extra passengers. Like deck cargo, they paid handsomely, and many a sea captain retired rich. But not Captain Lloyd of the *Eurotas*.

'It puts me in the very devil of a position.' The governor had moved around the room despite the sullen heat. 'Mr Raymond has important work to do in the Levu Islands. It is all arranged. Now, with *Eurotas* virtually disarmed and in need of competent officers and replacement crew, I dare not allow him to proceed there without escort.'

Sayer had still remained silent. The Levu Group, adjacent to the Friendly Islands where Tuke had run *Eurotas* to ground, had been under discussion for many months, and almost as long as the colony in New South Wales had been founded. The local chiefs were friendly and open to barter. They hated each other, but that was safer. There was a good anchorage on the main island, with fresh water and plenty of timber. The group, or parts of it, had been claimed and reclaimed over and over again by any ship's captain who chose to anchor there in search of water and food, and hoist his country's flag.

But now, with a bad situation brewing once again between Britain and His Most Catholic Majesty of Spain, the island group represented more than a mere extension of trade and local influence. With Sydney and the rest of the great colony growing and spreading by the month, the newly opened trade and supply routes and the flanks of the colony itself had to be protected. The Levu Islands would easily act as a base for men-of-war to patrol the routes from the South Americas and Cape Horn.

He could not picture Raymond there at all in any capacity. He looked too spoiled by comfortable living. There was a hardness to him also, but it seemed to come from the heart and not the body.

Raymond had said, 'Yes. I *must* have an escort.' He had looked at Sayer. 'You command the squadron here.' It had sounded like an accusation, one which Sayer was used to, but resented. 'Surely you can manage that?'

'I have a few schooners, some armed cutters and the brig *Quail*.' He had gestured towards the window. 'Now, I have *Tempest*, thank God, and a captain with the experience and dash to make good use of her.'

Sayer had seen the quick exchange of glances. They had been discussing Bolitho. Strange there should be an atmosphere of unease. Fear perhaps that Bolitho's commodore might say something not meant for his ears.

Then the governor had said, 'You will send *Tempest*. I am drafting orders for her now. I have also instructed that *Eurotas* be restored with whatever supplies we have available. The guns and the money are another matter,' he had added bitterly.

Raymond had excused himself and had gone to another part of the residence where he and his wife were being quartered. Sayer would have expected Ramyond to show some sign of gratitude for being alive, compassion for those less fortunate. It was as if the whole incident had been shut from his mind.

But once alone with the governor, Sayer had received his second surprise.

'I can assure you, Sayer, that but for Bolitho's recovery of the ship, his obvious bravery and his successful rescue of many of the people, I would order you to arrange his, his court martial.'

Sayer had been astounded. 'I must protest, sir! I know his record, he is a fine officer in every sense, as was his father.'

'And his brother?' The governor had watched him coldly. 'Mr Raymond tells me that Bolitho's brother was a traitor during the war. A bloody renegade!' He had held up one hand.

'That was unfair of me, Sayer, but I am *feeling* unfair. I am overworked, beset with strife in the colony and the incompetence of my administrators. Now this. James Raymond, an important man from London, who has the Prime Minister's ear, the King's too in all probability, is accusing Bolitho of having a liaison with his wife.'

So that was it. Something like a bell had tinkled in Sayer's mind. Four or five years back. Bolitho had commanded the frigate *Undine* and had given support to another newly founded possession. In Borneo. That was it. The governor appointed to that godforsaken place had been a retired admiral. There had been talk of an attachment between the wife of a government official and the young frigate captain.

The governor had said crisply, 'I see from your face, Sayer, that you have already heard something of it.'

'No, sir. A long time ago. Just rumours.'

'Maybe. But some damned fate has drawn them all together out here. But it is *not* the same as before. Bolitho is still a frigate captain, but Raymond has grown in influence if not in charity. Try to see it from my point of view. I cannot afford more trouble. I will send word to London with my despatches and ask that *Tempest* be replaced. I am not such a tyrant that I would suggest the removal of her captain.'

The governor had more or less admitted that he had not liked Raymond. It was just as well, Sayer had decided.

Now, as he stood in his own cabin again, Sayer was uncertain how to face Bolitho when he came aboard. He was a fine officer, better still, he was a good man. But Sayer had his own responsibility. It was the chain of command again.

His captain peered into the cabin. '*Tempest*'s gig approaching, sir.'

'Very well. Receive Captain Bolitho and show him aft.'

He turned towards the windows again. Mrs Raymond was a very beautiful woman, or so he had heard. He supposed she had taken passage here merely to keep her husband company. She would hardly fit into the Sydney society, he thought. Officials, officers of the Corps, their wives and their women. Sayer had seen more social gatherings in Cornwall than he had out here. Not quite the thing for a lady of breeding.

He heard the stamp of feet, the trill of the boatswains' calls as the side party paid its respects to a visiting captain. He turned and faced the door, bracing himself without knowing why.

When Bolitho entered he looked as he had that morning. In his dress coat, with his gold-laced hat tucked under one arm, he was, Sayer thought, enough to win any lady's heart. He was very tanned, and his black hair with the rebellious lock above one eye gleamed in the filtered sunlight like a raven's wing. He looked at ease, and with none of the strain Sayer had seen when he had first sailed into Sydney harbour.

'Sit down, Richard.' Sayer looked at him awkwardly. 'I've just come from the governor. Been with him for hours. I'm about dead with weariness.'

'I'm sorry, sir. But I hope the visit was worthwhile.'

'Worthwhile?' The commodore looked at him grimly. 'I thought he was going to have a fit!' He wrenched open a hanging wine cooler and took out a bottle and some glasses. 'God damn it, Richard, is it true about you and Raymond's lady?' He swung round, wine slopping unnoticed over his shoes. 'Because if it is, you are pleading for trouble!'

Bolitho took the proffered glass, giving himself time. It was to be expected. After what had happened, it had to be, so why was it a surprise?

He replied, 'I do not know what you were told, sir.'

'Oh, for Christ's sake, Richard, don't play with words! We're both sailors. We know how these things happen. God, with your attack and rescue, I'd think every woman in Sydney would give herself to you tonight!'

Bolitho put down his glass. 'Viola Raymond is not a whore, sir. I met her five years back. Then, I thought it was over when in fact it had only begun. She is married to the wrong man. He is vain, arrogant and dangerous.' He could almost listen to the level tone of his voice. Again, like a bystander. 'I have no regrets other than the regret for the lost years. When she returns to England, she will leave her London residence and await my return.' He looked up, his voice quiet. 'I am deeply in love with her.'

Sayer eyed him gravely. He was shocked by the disclosure,

but touched by Bolitho's sincerity and his willingness to share his hopes with him.

He said, 'The governor is sending his despatches to England tonight in the *Quail*. In them will be a request for *Tempest*'s transfer to home waters. What you have wanted, if for other reasons. But it will take months before those despatches are delivered and replied to. By then anything may have happened.'

'I know, sir. And thank you for telling me.'

Sayer had shown his concern by disclosing the governor's plans. Bolitho could now, if he so wished, put his own report and letters aboard the same brig. If he lacked influence, he had plenty of friends. He was moved that Sayer had laid himself open for his sake.

Sayer said heavily, 'I know little of James Raymond, but what I have seen I regard as unfriendly.'

'We are both firmly set on our course, sir.'

Bolitho could see her eyes in his mind, feel her skin, the touch of her long autumn hair.

'She will wait for my return to England.'

'She is not going to England, Richard.' Sayer felt sickened by his own words. 'She is to go with Raymond to his new appointment in the Levu Group.' He stood up quickly. 'Believe me, she has no choice. The governor is bound to offer his assistance and support to Raymond, and no amount of pleading or finance on your part can put her aboard the *Quail* for England.'

Bolitho stared at him. 'Then she will remain in Sydney until . . .'

'Would you have that?' Sayer looked away. 'How they would delight in sneering at her. Scandal is news here, rumour the pathway to jealous and petty minds.'

Bolitho could not believe it, and yet he knew it was exactly what Raymond would do. If he could not break them apart, he would ensure that she was trapped.

He said, 'But the Great South Sea, sir. How long can a woman survive in the islands? It is bad enough here, but the conditions are like a palace compared with the primitive islands. She has been through all this before. No man, no *real* man would ask it of anyone, let alone her.'

'I know.' Sayer looked at him sadly. 'But Raymond is under stress to make this work successful. There will be some convict labour too, a showing of occupation, which should inspire confidence until proper arrangements have been made.'

Bolitho leaned back in the chair, his eyes seeing nothing.

That third night aboard *Eurotas* he had gone to her in the great cabin. She had shared it only with the girl she had taken under her protection. The wretched girl barely spoke, and was still shocked and terrified whenever a man went near her. For Viola she would do anything.

Raymond had been given a separate cabin, just as before when they had sailed in Bolitho's ship. But this time there had been a difference.

Desperation, desire and an overwhelming relief at finding each other again had broken down all barriers of caution.

He could hear her voice as if she were here, and not Sayer.

'We are in a ghost-ship, darling Richard. We are alone. I want you so badly that I am ashamed. Need you so much that you may be ashamed of me.'

He came out of his despair as Sayer said, 'You will be under orders to escort *Eurotas* to the Levu Group.' He watched the pain in Bolitho's eyes, imagined how he would feel under similar circumstances. Forced to watch the woman he loved and be unable to reach her. 'The governor has no other forces at his disposal, and Tuke may be intent on another attack.'

Bolitho said quietly, 'I will kill him.'

Sayer looked away. Who did he mean? Tuke or Raymond? When he spoke again Bolitho sounded calm. Too calm.

'How long do we have, sir?'

'A few days. With the seasonal storms becoming more frequent, and the delay caused by all this, things have become more urgent.' He tried to sound matter of fact. 'One thing, Richard. You are not to see her in Sydney.' He saw him start. 'And as a favour to me, I'd like you to remain aboard until you weigh, *except* on matters pertaining to duty and the ship's affairs.'

Bolitho stood up. 'I understand.'

'Good. I have too much respect for you to give you a lecture. But time passes, old pains are forgotten. You are going to need all your wits. Tuke is a vicious pirate and no hero, as some legends would have him. I believe he is here to *sell* his special services to someone, which is why he is arming and storing his vessels at our cost. Maybe he seeks respectability under a letter of marque, to become a mercenary instead of a hunted pirate. It is common enough.' He lowered his voice. 'And you will have Raymond watching and waiting for you to make a mistake.'

Bolitho said, 'The French and the Dons have long been interested in these waters, but without much success.'

He felt nothing. Could find no excitement at the prospect of a new mission, a chance of running Tuke to earth.

Sayer nodded. 'In the last despatches they speak of starvation and riots in France, even in Paris. So the King will be too busy to cast his eyes towards us. But Spain?' He shrugged. 'No matter what flag the devil flies, I want him taken and hanged before his fire spreads. One good thing though, the *Bounty* has vanished. Foundered, I shouldn't wonder. One less worry.'

'Sir?' Bolitho looked at him blankly.

Sayer crossed the cabin and gripped his arm. 'No matter, you were leagues away. But take heart. Think of Cornwall. Do your work. The rest will unfoul itself.'

Bolitho replied, 'Aye, sir.'

He had in fact been thinking of Cornwall. The big grey house in Falmouth. A few moments ago it had begun to come alive again in his thoughts. She would like it there, and they would all love her as they had his mother, and the other captains' ladies who had walked on the sea wall and watched for their husbands' ships, some in vain.

And now, because he had lowered his guard, he had betrayed the one person he really loved. Because of the resulting hatred and envy, Raymond was risking everything, and would do so even if it cost Viola's life.

'I'd like to return to my ship, sir.'

Sayer watched him. 'Yes. I'll send word if I hear anything. They're gathering some hands for the *Eurotas*, and you will have to supply an officer to take charge of her.' He added firmly, 'An officer, Richard. *You* must remain in your own ship. Once established in the Levu Islands, *Eurotas* will act as accommodation vessel. She can be safely left with someone junior until I can send more replacements. But you will act as you see fit when you have made the place secure.'

Bolitho held out his hand. 'Thank you, sir. For doing what you must hate doing. I know plenty who would have made it short and sharp.'

Sayer smiled. 'True. But mark what I said. I cannot save you if you cross Raymond. He is the sort of man who looks for scapegoats well in advance of anything he attempts. I do not wish to fit that role. Nor do I wish to see you as one.'

Bolitho went on deck and paid his respects to the quarter-deck and to *Hebrus*'s captain.

A gun boomed dully in the distance, and the other captain said, 'There go your two captured pirates. They don't waste time on trials out here for such carrion.'

With the execution gun still echoing over the harbour Bolitho climbed down to the gig where Allday stood to receive him, his face expectant.

'To the jetty, Captain?'

Bolitho looked past him towards the slow-moving crowd of people who had gone to see two men kicking out their lives on a gibbet.

She was there somewhere.

'No, Allday. To the ship.'

Allday barked, 'Shove off! Out oars!' Something had gone badly wrong. 'Give way all!'

He shaded his eyes to look across at the anchored transport, recalling the screams and frenzy of hand to hand fighting and killing.

What did these poxy dolts know of such things? He looked down at Bolitho's shoulders, the way he was gripping the hilt of that old, tarnished sword.

Once, Allday had been thankful to see Viola Raymond parted from Bolitho. He had known what might happen, as it was happening now. But as in a fight, once committed, Allday believed in seeing it through. He would think about it. Slip in a good word or two when he got the chance.

Bolitho watched the rise and fall of the oars, the carefully blank faces of the pigtailed seamen. They all knew. Some would be glad, others sympathetic. All would be interested in what was to happen next.

He heard the creak of the tiller as Allday steered the boat past the stern of a Dutch trading schooner.

Him most of all, he thought. He could almost feel Allday's mind working. All of his loyalty, courage and cheek could not help him this time.

He saw the side party mustered at *Tempest*'s entry port. The blue and white of the officers, the scarlet of Prideaux's marines. *Stand by to receive the captain.*

He straightened his shoulders and looked up at the ship. He was sailing as escort. It was not much of a bridge, but it was better than nothing. There was hope, and his determination, like Allday's, was stronger than ever.

7

The Narval

Lieutenant Thomas Herrick sipped at a mug of scalding, bitter coffee and watched Bolitho making notes beside his chart.

A week out of port, and Herrick for one was glad to be at sea, doing something he understood. Six days they had lain at anchor, and it had been painful to watch Bolitho's efforts to hide his anxiety, to contain his dismay as he looked at the anchored *Eurotas* and the town beyond.

Even now Herrick was not sure what Bolitho was really thinking. To anyone who did not know him as he did he seemed his usual alert, interested self. He was studying the chart with care, comparing his notes with those of Lakey, the sailing master.

Herrick did not know much about the Levu Islands, except that they were some two hundred miles to the north of where they had recaptured the *Eurotas*. Now they were plodding along, held back by the slower merchantman, while *Tempest* stayed watchfully to windward of her.

Bolitho looked up, his eyes bright. 'D'you remember old Mudge, Thomas?'

'Aye.' Herrick smiled. Mudge had been the sailing master in *Undine*. 'Must have been the oldest man in the King's service. The oldest afloat maybe. He admitted to sixty, and kept to that. A great lump of a man, but a fine master. Pity he didn't meet Mr Lakey. Maybe they'll have a yarn in heaven one day.'

Bolitho looked wistful. 'He knew a lot about these waters. How he rebuked me when I ordered every sail to be set. But how he grumbled when we crawled like this.'

Herrick looked up as Keen's feet moved across the deck. Borlase was in charge of the *Eurotas*. It was a pity in some ways, he thought. Borlase might say too much to Raymond. He was like that. On the other hand, he was glad to be here with Bolitho. If he had gone across to the merchantman instead he might have spoken too forcefully to that scum Raymond.

He asked, 'What d'you expect to find in the Levu Islands, sir?'

Bolitho walked to the stern windows and stared at the sloping horizon. There was mist about, and the glittering sea looked as if it was boiling from some great marine cauldron.

'A flag on a pole, Thomas. A few hard-working servants of the country. Much what we're used to.'

Noddall pattered into the cabin, the coffee jug in his paws. 'There's some more 'ere, sir.'

'Good.' Bolitho thrust out his mug. 'It makes me sweat, but it is good to taste something which is neither rotten nor rancid for a change.'

He held the mug to his lips, feeling it burning down to his stomach.

Another day. The same empty sea. He had taken to counting seconds whenever he went on deck to consult the compass and their estimated position. *Seconds* before he had to look towards *Eurotas*'s fat hull. She always seemed to remain in the exact position, held in the frigate's shrouds as if snared in a giant web. In fact, she was well down to leeward, too far to examine without a glass. Those occasions too had to be measured, rationed.

He heard some muffled shots and knew the marines were practising again, firing their muskets from the tops at makeshift targets which Sergeant Quare had hurled overboard. He wondered if one of the marksmen was the ex-gamekeeper, Blissett, and whether or not he was remembering the man he had silently killed on the beach.

Herrick said suddenly, 'It's no use, sir. I must speak my mind.'

'Good.' Bolitho turned towards him. 'I have been expecting something, so be done with it.'

Herrick put his mug very carefully on the table.

'It's all been said before. But I'm no less concerned. Me, I don't count. I'll never rise above wardroom rank, and I think

I'm glad for it, having seen what command can drag out of a man. But you have a family tradition, sir. When I saw your house in Falmouth, those portraits, all that history, I knew I was lucky to serve under you. I've been at sea since I was a lad, like most of us, and I know the measure of a captain. It's *not right* that you should be in jeopardy because of all this!'

Bolitho smiled gravely, despite his inner ache.

'By *all this*, I take it you mean my indiscretion? My discovery that I could fall in love like other men?' He shook his head. 'No, Thomas, I'll not let anyone abuse that lady just to hurt me. I'll see Raymond in hell before that!' He turned away. 'Now you've made me abandon my self-control.'

Herrick replied heavily, 'At the risk of offending you further, I still believe Commodore Sayer was right to,' he shrugged awkwardly, 'to keep you occupied aboard ship.'

'Perhaps.' Bolitho sat down again and rubbed his eyes with the palms of his hands. 'If only – '

He looked up sharply. 'What was that?'

'A hail from the masthead.'

Herrick was already on his feet as the call floated down again. 'Deck thar! Sail on the lee bow!'

They both hurried from the cabin and collided with Midshipman Romney who was on his way aft.

'Sir! Mr Keen's respects and – '

Herrick brushed past him. 'Aye. We know.'

Bolitho strode past the wheel, feeling the sun across his shoulders as if he were naked. A glance at the compass and to the trim of the sails told him all he needed. *Eurotas* was still on station, her big courses filling and deflating, depriving her of any beauty.

'Anything further?'

Keen looked at him. 'Not yet, sir.' He trained his telescope. 'Nothing.'

'Hmm.' Bolitho tugged out his watch. 'Send another lookout aloft, if you please.' He searched round for Midshipman Swift. 'Make a signal to *Eurotas*. Sail in sight to the nor'-east.' He looked at Herrick. 'Though in God's name they should have seen it themselves.'

Herrick held his peace. Merchantmen rarely maintained a

good lookout, especially when they had a naval escort. But there was no point in mentioning it now. He could tell Bolitho's anxieties were only just below the surface. One spark and . . .

Bolitho snapped, 'In heaven's name, what are our people *doing*?'

'Deck there!' It was the new lookout. 'She be a man-o-war, zur!'

Bolitho turned to Herrick again. 'What can she be about, Thomas?'

'One of ours maybe?'

'Bless you, Thomas!' He clapped him on the shoulder. 'We are the only *one of ours* in this whole ocean! Even the Governor of New South Wales is having to plead for ships!'

Herrick watched him, fascinated. The prospect of action was making Bolitho react, no matter what he was enduring privately.

Herrick said, 'And we've absolutely no idea what's happening in the world. We may be at war with Spain or France, anybody!'

Bolitho walked aft to the wheel again and examined the compass. East-north-east, and the wind still comfortably across the starboard quarter. The stranger was on a converging tack, but it would take hours to come up with her. What would he do if the newcomer turned and fled at the sight of them? He could not leave *Eurotas*.

But as the hour ran out and another began the lookouts' reports showed that the other vessel gave no sign of going about.

'Set the forecourse, Mr Herrick.' Bolitho crossed the quarter-deck and climbed into the mizzen shrouds. 'I shall feel happier if we lie closer to our charge.'

The hands hurried to their stations, and a few minutes later the frigate's big foresail filled to the wind and sent a tremor running through the shrouds and rigging like a message.

Bolitho steadied his glass, waiting for the long, undulating swell to lift the other ship long enough for him to examine her. Then he saw the ship with surprising clarity as with a freak of nature she and *Tempest* rose together.

For just a few moments he held her in the lens, then mist

and distance distorted the picture, and he lowered himself to the deck.

'Frigate. French by the cut of her.'

He peered up at the masthead pendant. 'Be up to her in two hours if this wind holds. Within range of a long shot before that.'

Lakey observed quietly, 'We're not at war with France, sir.'

'So I believe, Mr Lakey. But we'll take no chances all the same.'

He glanced along his command, picturing her wreathed in smoke and flying iron.

But not this time. The Frenchman was taking his time and making no effort to change tack enough to grapple for the wind-gage.

He added, 'Send the hands to quarters in good time, and make sure we have some experienced eyes at the masthead to see if the Frenchman does likewise.'

He took the glass again and trained it on the *Eurotas*. He saw the flash of a gown as she walked across the poop, one hand holding the big hat to prevent the wind taking it from her.

Oh God. He lowered the glass and she dropped into distance, leaving only the ship.

'Deck there! She's run up 'er colours!' A pause. 'Frenchie, right enough, zur!'

Even without a glass Bolitho could see the tiny patch of white breaking from the other ship's peak as she tacked heavily to hold the wind, her yards braced round until they were all but fore and aft.

It was a strange feeling. Like many of the men aboard, Bolitho had rarely met a French ship other than across the muzzles of a broadside. He thought of Le Chaumareys and was suddenly sad for him and the waste of his life. Captains were like kings in their own ships, no matter how small. But to the powers which manoeuvred and used them they were expendable pawns.

He made himself leave the deck and return to his cabin, almost blind from staring across the shining blue water.

Allday entered the cabin. 'I'll tell Noddall to fetch your coat and hat, Captain.' He grinned. 'Those breeches, patched or not, will do for a Frenchman!'

Bolitho nodded. If the French captain was new to these waters he would want to see every other captain he could. Would he come to *Tempest*, or would he go to him?

Noddall scuttled through from the sleeping cabin, carrying the coat over his arm, tutting to himself.

Bolitho had just finished transforming himself into some semblance of a King's officer when he heard the pipe, 'All hands! Hands to quarters and clear for action!'

The drums rolled, and he felt the hull quiver as her company rushed to obey.

By the time he had reached the quarterdeck it was done, even to the sanding of the planking around each gun. It would not be needed, he was quite certain, as he watched the other frigate's approach. But sand was plentiful, and every drill gained experience for some.

'Load and run out, sir?'

'No, Mr Herrick.' He was equally formal.

He looked along the black guns and bare-backed men. He found he was wishing it was the pirate Mathias Tuke lifting and plunging across the water towards him.

Midshipman Fitzmaurice came running aft to the quarter-deck ladder and called, 'Beg pardon, sir, but Mr Jury sends his respects and says that frigate is the *Narval*, thirty-six, and that he saw her in Bombay.'

Bolitho smiled. 'Give my thanks to the boatswain.'

He looked at Herrick. It was always the same in a ship. Always someone who had seen or served in another. No doubt the French captain was receiving similar news about the *Tempest*. Thirty-six guns. The same as his own. Ball for ball, if so ordered.

He watched the other ship shortening sail with professional interest. A lighter, sleeker hull than *Tempest*, well-weathered, as if she had been at sea for a long time. Her sail-handling was excellent, another mark of long usage.

Bolitho shaded his eyes and looked up at the peak. Out here *Tempest* sailed under the white ensign, and he wondered if the French captain was looking at it. Remembering.

'She's hove to!' Keen strode across the gundeck, ducking to peer over a twelve-pounder. 'And dropping a boat!'

Herrick grinned. 'Just a lieutenant, sir. Probably wants us to put him on the course for Paris!'

But when the young lieutenant eventually clambered aboard from the longboat he seemed anything but lost. He doffed his hat to the quarterdeck and then presented himself to Bolitho.

'I bring the respects of my *capitaine, m'sieu*, and the invitation to visit him.' His dark eyes moved swiftly around the manned guns, the swaying line of armed marines.

'Certainly.'

Bolitho walked to the entry port and glanced down at the French longboat. The seamen were neatly dressed in striped shirts and white trousers. But they had no life in them. They looked afraid.

'And who is your captain?'

The lieutenant seemed to draw himself up another inch or so.

'He is Jean Michel, Comte de Barras, *m'sieu*.'

Bolitho had never heard of him.

'Very well.'

He said to Herrick quietly, 'Retain the wind-gage, and make sure *Eurotas* keeps proper station until I return.'

Then with a nod to the rigid side party he followed the lieutenant into the boat.

The oarsmen pulled steadily across the water, taking and mounting each round-backed roller with practised ease. He felt the spray stinging his cheeks refreshing him. A vast ocean and the ships meeting by accident on one tiny pinpoint of it.

A French count and an English captain from Falmouth.

The officer snapped an order and the boat's oars rose dripping in two pale lines, while with a flourish the bowman hooked on to the *Narval*'s main chains. It was expertly done, but Bolitho had the feeling it was as much from fear as from experience.

He grasped his sword and pulled himself up towards the entry port, very aware of the eyes watching him from the deck above.

The *Narval*'s great cabin was in total contrast to Bolitho's own. Once aboard, he had been met by her captain with barely a word and had been hurried through the formality of the guard and side party with what had seemed like discourtesy. Now, sitting in an ornate gilded chair, his eyes half-blinded by the sunlight, Bolitho examined his host for the first time.

The Comte de Barras was of very slight build, and framed against the sloping stern windows appeared almost girlish. His dress coat was slightly flared and of superb cut, and Bolitho wished he had not allowed Allday to talk him into coming across in his seagoing breeches.

The only other occupant of the cabin was a youth, either Indian or Malay, who was busily arranging glasses and a beautifully carved wine cabinet on one of the two tables.

But the cabin was quite breathtaking. *Tempest*'s builders had used all their skills in carving and shaping her captain's quarters with the finest woods in their yard. *Narval*'s were only to be described as elegant and fanciful in contrast. Rich, beautiful curtains hid the usual screens and doors, and across the deck were several large rugs which must have cost a fortune.

He realized de Barras was watching him, awaiting his reactions.

Bolitho said, 'You live well, *Capitaine*.'

De Barras's smooth forehead wrinkled in a brief frown. Bolitho's failure to use his title perhaps, or his treating him as a fellow captain might have offended him.

But the frown vanished just as quickly, and he sat down very carefully in another gilded chair, the twin of Bolitho's.

'I live as best I can in these frugal circumstances.' He spoke perfect English with a slight lisp.

He snapped his fingers at his young servant. 'You must take some wine, er, *Captain*.' He watched the boy as if daring him to spill any on a carpet.

It gave Bolitho more time to study de Barras now that his eyes were growing used to the cabin. He could be any age between twenty-five and thirty-five. With delicately fashioned nose and small chin he looked more like a member of some exclusive court than a sea captain. He was, Bolitho had observed when coming aboard, wearing a wig. That too was unusual, and only added to the sense of unreality.

But the wine was good. More, it was excellent.

De Barras seemed pleased. 'My father owns many vineyards. This wine travels quite well.' Again the small, petulant frown.

Like Borlase, Bolitho thought.

'Which it needs to do. This vessel has been in unbroken service for three years now, and I have held command for two.

'I see.'

Bolitho watched him, wondering what this strange man really wanted. He noticed how the boy was hovering by de Barras's elbow. He was not merely attentive. He was terrified.

De Barras murmured, 'And you are bound for?'

There was nothing to be gained from secrecy. 'The Levu Islands.'

'You are expecting, er, trouble?' He waved one hand carelessly towards the sea, allowing a great show of lace shirt to froth from beneath his sleeve. '*Two* ships?'

'We have had trouble.'

Bolitho wondered if Raymond had a telescope trained on the *Narval*. He hoped so. Hoped too he was fuming at being excluded.

'Pirates?'

Bolitho smiled gently. 'I can see you are not surprised.'

De Barras was taken off guard. 'I am merely curious.' He prodded the boy's shoulder sharply. 'More wine!'

Bolitho asked, 'And you are bound for New South Wales?'

'Yes.' De Barras stood up and walked quickly to the bulkhead and adjusted one of the curtains. 'Clumsy fools. They live like swine themselves and have no thought for fine things!' He curbed his sudden irritation and sat down again. 'I intend to pay my respects to the governor and replenish my stores there.'

Bolitho kept his face stiff. The governor would really explode when he saw a French frigate in his bay.

De Barras added quietly, 'I am looking for one such pirate, and have been for many months. He is an Englishman, but a pirate nonetheless. We are both bound to his eventual destruction, eh, *m'sieu*?' It seemed to amuse him. 'He was plundering the waters of the Caribbean, from La Guaira to Martinique. I pursued him to Port of Spain and lost him when his men sacked and burned a village nearby.' His chest was moving with agitation.

Like a spoiled child, Bolitho thought. Frail he might appear, but he was as dangerous as a serpent underneath.

Bolitho said, 'It is a lot of concern for one man.' He watched for some hint, some sign of what lay behind de Barras's confidences.

'He is a man who attracts others.' De Barras sipped his wine delicately. 'One without loyalty himself, but one who can instil it in those he leads. I was going to explain these matters to the Governor of New South Wales, but it seems that he may be better informed than I realized.' He came to a decision. 'The pirate is called Tuke. He has with him a man who was awaiting deportation from Martinique to France. That was to be one of my missions.' He spat out the words. 'This *cochon* Tuke aided his escape, and now has him with his own foul company!'

'May I ask about this *other man*?'

'It is no matter.' De Barras shrugged. 'A traitor to France. An *agitateur*. But he must be taken and punished before he can cause more unrest.'

When Bolitho remained silent he added vehemently, 'It is in England's interest also. This traitor will use Tuke's strength to spread trouble, to rob and sack more and more ships and islands as his own power expands!' He dabbed a droplet of sweat from his chin. 'It is your *duty*!'

Something threw a shadow across the cabin, and when Bolitho turned towards the windows he imagined he was seeing a spectre from a nightmare. Dangling outside was a man, or what was left of him. Suspended by his wrists, with ropes attached to his ankles and which disappeared towards the rudder, he was naked, and his body was a mass of bloody lacerations and great gaping wounds. One eye had been torn from his head, but the other stared fixedly at the ship, while his mouth opened and closed like a black hole.

De Barras was almost beside himself with anger. '*Mon Dieu!*' He pushed the frightened boy towards the bulkhead door, pursuing him with angry words and threats.

Voices sounded overhead, and the dangling body dropped swiftly from view. Bolitho sat stock-still in his chair. He knew what was happening. Had heard about the savage and barbarous custom of keelhauling from old sailors. To punish a man in this manner was to condemn him to an horrific death. The victim was lowered over the bow and dragged along the keel, his progress controlled by lines attached to his hands and feet. After three years in commission, coppered or not, *Narval*'s keel and bilges would be covered with tiny, razor-sharp growths which would tear a man to fragments unless he was sensible and let himself drown. But man's instinct was to survive, even when the case was without hope.

Bolitho stood up and said, 'I will leave now, *M'sieu le Comte*. I have my *duty* to attend to. So if you would excuse me.' He turned towards the door, sickened and disgusted.

De Barras stared at him. 'That man was a trouble-maker! I will not tolerate such insolence! *Filthy, degraded beast!*'

Bolitho walked into the sunlight, remembering Le Chaumareys, the way his solid courage had inspired and welded his ship together. By comparison, de Barras was a monster. A vicious tyrant who had probably been appointed to *Narval* to keep him away from France.

By the entry port de Barras said sharply, 'Save your anger for your enemies!'

Then as Bolitho took his first step through the port he swung on his heel and stalked aft towards the poop.

The lieutenant who had escorted Bolitho aboard accompanied him back to *Tempest*. When they were almost alongside Bolitho asked, 'Is that how your ship is run, *m'sieu*? By terror?'

The young officer stared at him, his features pale under the tan.

Bolitho stood up in the boat, eager to be back in his own ship. Then he added, 'For if that be so, watch out that the terror does not consume *you*!'

Within minutes of returning to his ship Bolitho received a signal from Raymond. A summons to attend him aboard the *Eurotas* without delay.

Although still appalled by what he had seen aboard the French frigate, Bolitho could nevertheless find room for personal satisfaction. In his heart he had known that Raymond would insist on his going across to the transport, even at the risk of his meeting Viola. Raymond needed to display that he and not Bolitho held the reins of command, and his curiosity at what had passed between him and the Frenchman would do the rest. Also, Bolitho suspected, Raymond felt less in control when he was aboard a King's ship.

Herrick watched him anxiously as he prepared to make another crossing, this time in his own gig.

Bolitho was changing into some clean breeches, and had just finished his description of de Barras and the atmosphere of tyranny aboard the *Narval*. He guessed Herrick was probably comparing de Barras with the captain of the *Phalarope* where they had first met. Only seven years ago? It did not seem possible. They had seen and done so much together.

Herrick said eventually, 'I hate even the *sound* of his kind, and I for one'll be a sight more happy when his tops'ls dip below the horizon!'

'I'd wager you'll be disappointed, Thomas.'

Bolitho took a glass of wine from Noddall. It was as much to destroy the French captain's taste as to clear the salt from his throat.

Herrick looked at him with surprise. 'But I thought you said *Narval* is steering for New South Wales?'

Bolitho tugged his neckcloth into position and smiled grimly. 'She *was*. My guess is that de Barras has hot irons under him to recapture this mysterious Frenchman, and now sees us as a better chance. He may be right.' He snatched up his hat. '*Well?*'

Herrick sighed. 'Fine, sir.' There seemed no point in further protest. Bolitho's eyes were shining more brightly than they had for some time.

He followed Bolitho to the entry port and stood with him above the swaying gig. A quick glance aft told Herrick that Keen and Lakey, and even young Midshipman Swift, were all watching and smiling like involved conspirators. It only made him depressed. They did not understand that this was not just a man going away in the hopes of seeing his love, but one who could easily be casting his career into ashes.

Borlase was at the *Eurotas*'s side to greet Bolitho, but his childlike features were carefully set, giving nothing away.

Bolitho looked around the maindeck, and was thankful to see there appeared to be quite a number of competent-looking seamen amongst the replacements for those killed or maimed by the pirates. In every scattered seaport, even one as new as Sydney, there always seemed to be a few abandoned sailormen who were ready to chance one more strange ship. *Just once more.* All sailors said that.

'How are the prisoners, Mr Borlase?' It was strange that the term prisoner seemed to carry more dignity than convict.

'I've had them put to work in small parties as you suggested, sir.' A mere hint of disapproval here.

'Good.'

Maybe Borlase found them too much responsibility and worry. Or perhaps he thought they should be kept penned up as before. But once ashore in the Levu Islands they would need all their health and agility to stay alive. Deported convicts in the Americas, and now in New South Wales, had left plenty of bitter examples in their wake. They *must* survive, like those who guarded and directed them, upon their own resources.

They moved into the poop's shadow and made their way aft to the great cabin.

Raymond was waiting there, sitting at the desk, his body silhouetted against the reflected glare from the tall windows.

He said crisply, 'You will remain here, Mr Borlase.'

Bolitho waited impassively. Raymond was keeping the lieutenant as a defence or a witness. Or both.

'And now, Captain.' Raymond leaned back, his fingertips pressed together. 'Perhaps you will be so kind as to inform me of your discourse with the *Narval*'s captain.'

'I would have sent you a report.'

'Of that I am certain.' It sounded like sarcasm. 'But give me the bones of the matter for now.'

Borlase made as if to get a chair for his captain, but after a glance at Raymond seemed to change his mind.

Curiously, Bolitho felt better because of Raymond's attitude. No pretence, no change between them. Nor would there be.

He listened to his own voice as he explained briefly what had passed between him and the Frenchman. Calm, unemotional. Like evidence at a court martial, he thought.

Raymond dismissed the keelhauling as 'a matter for each country to decide'.

Bolitho said quietly, 'France decided long ago. But out here, de Barras is their country.'

'It is not my concern.' Raymond's fingertips drummed rapidly together in a silent tattoo. 'But the *Narval* most certainly is.'

'She will not dare to – ' Bolitho got no further.

Raymond snapped, '*Really*, you sea officers are as one! We are not at war with the King of France now. You must adjust to your new role, or exchange it for another.' His voice was louder and crisper. It was as if he had been rehearsing for just such a moment.

'With French aid we can explore all possibilities of trade and the mutual defence of it.' The fingers tapped in and out to mark each item. 'The crushing of piracy and plundering for instance. The covering of greater sea areas for our combined benefit. If one day we are forced to fight France again, and I think it unlikely, no matter what I have heard to the contrary, then we will be better placed because of this co-operation now. *Know your competitor*, every merchant will tell you so. A pity that those entrusted with our protection cannot bring themselves to do likewise.'

In the sudden quiet Bolitho could feel his own heart beating with anger and caution. He could tell from the manner in which Borlase's eyes were flickering back and forth between them that he was expecting him to lash out at Raymond's last remark. A calculated insult, doubly so as Bolitho's men had saved his life and restored his freedom with no little risk.

Raymond frowned. 'Have you no comment?'

'I know little of merchants, sir. But I do know an enemy from a friend.'

Borlase shifted his feet noisily.

Raymond said, 'Anyway, you sent the *Narval* on her way, no doubt with fresh fuel to burn at our expense.'

'I expect de Barras will be close to us for this passage, sir. He is determined to recapture his prisoner, and if we fall on the pirate Tuke his chances of doing so are good. From his point of view.'

'Quite. Tuke hanged and this renegade restored to his chains may in some way make up for what has happened already.' He paused, waiting to see if Bolitho would take up the bait. When he remained silent he snapped, 'When do you expect a landfall?'

'If this wind holds it will be under three weeks. If not, it could take two months.'

It was pointless to compare the sailing ability of the unmatched vessels, just as it was dangerous to be too optimistic. Raymond was waiting for a weakness. A flaw.

Raymond pulled out his watch and said, 'Tell my servant to bring some wine, Mr Borlase.' He looked at Bolitho coolly. 'I am sure my wife would wish to join us here also.' He glanced around the cabin. 'Yes, I am certain of it.'

Bolitho looked away. He should have expected it. Raymond's top card.

To Borlase it may have sounded a formal or expected invitation. Out of custom or courtesy. The senior official sharing his wine with the captain of a naval escort.

But the way his voice had lingered on the word *here*. Bolitho needed no other key to his reasoning. For *here* was the cabin where Bolitho had met with his wife. Had held her to drive away the terror and despair of the *Eurotas*'s capture. Had kissed the cruel burn on her shoulder. Where they had loved with all passion and simplicity.

The screen door opened and she stepped into the cabin. Despite her daily walks on deck she looked pale, and there were shadows under her eyes which filled Bolitho with pain.

'A visitor, my dear.' Raymond half rose and sat down again.

A red-coated captain of the militia sent as guards for the convicts had followed Borlase into the cabin too, and was beaming at Bolitho and the wine, totally ignorant of the real drama around him. *Another witness.*

Bolitho crossed the cabin and took her hand. As he put it to his lips he lifted his gaze to her face.

She said softly, 'It is *good* to see you again, Captain.' She

E

tossed her head. 'It has been too long.' She looked at her husband as she spoke. 'Under any circumstance!'

Borlase said, 'A toast to the King!' He sounded as if his neckcloth was strangling him. He at least guessed what was happening.

'Indeed.' Raymond sipped at his glass. 'Perhaps after I have completed my affairs out here the Palace of St James will be ready to offer me an appointment which will keep me suitably employed in London.'

Bolitho watched him. Again the hint was there for Borlase and the militia captain to note. That Raymond was a man of influence, with more advancement on the way. Not one to cross or deny obedience.

Surprisingly, he thought at that moment of his dead brother Hugh. Always hasty to react, always the leader. In this instance he would most likely have searched out some 'point of honour' on which to challenge Raymond to a duel. He would not have stopped to consider the consequences, the risk to all parties concerned. To him it would have been the simplest solution. Swords or pistols, he was more than a match with either.

He realized that Viola had crossed the cabin and had deliberately turned her back towards Raymond.

She asked, 'Do you know of these islands, Captain?' But her eyes were exploring his face, his expression. Consuming him with their need.

'A little. My sailing master is better versed.' He dropped his voice. 'Please take care, once ashore. It is a cruel climate, even for one as used to travel as yourself.'

'I am sorry, I did not hear that?' Raymond stood up and lurched against the desk as the ship wallowed steeply. Then he added, 'I think the wind may be rising, Captain.'

Bolitho looked at him, his eyes hard. 'Aye. Mr Borlase, would you signal for my gig.'

He hesitated by the door. Knowing he was beaten, and that the battle had not even been joined as yet.

Raymond nodded curtly. 'I hope the wind does stay fair.' He smiled. 'Why not see the gallant captain to his boat, m'dear?'

On deck the heat was oppressive, and the sea had risen slightly to a lively breeze. *Tempest* was standing to windward, her sails flapping in disorder as she lay hove to and awaited his return. The French ship was already well away, her courses and topsails hardening to the wind, and to all intents still set on her original destination.

Bolitho saw all and none of these things.

He stood by the bulwark, looking at her eyes, watching her hair breaking free and streaming into the wind like fluid bronze.

'I cannot stand it, Viola. I feel like a useless traitor. A buffoon.'

She reached out and laid a hand on his cuff. 'He is baiting you. But you are so much stronger.' She made to touch his face and then lowered her arm. 'My darling Richard. I cannot bear to see you so sad, so despairing. I am still full of happiness that we found each other again. Surely we could not be parted again. *Forever?*' She raised her chin. 'I would rather die.'

'Boat's alongside, sir!'

Raymond's feet scraped across the deck, and Bolitho saw him watching from below the poop.

Just to snatch her in his arms and be damned to Raymond and all else. Even as he thought it, Bolitho dismissed the dream. Raymond would use all he had to keep her out here. Like a beautiful prisoner. A possession.

Bolitho raised his hat, his hair ruffling across his forehead. 'Rest easy, my love. I do not intend to strike just yet!'

Then with a nod to Borlase he climbed down into the tossing boat.

8

Short Respite

Bolitho's estimate for a landfall at the largest island of the Levu Group was closer than he had imagined, the total passage from Sydney having taken only twenty-six days. The first few hours at anchor in the mushroom-shaped bay were busy for everyone aboard the *Tempest*, for quite apart from the importance of selecting a safe anchorage with room to swing and little chance of dragging in a sudden gale, the company were further hindered by a growing collection of native craft from this and surrounding islands.

They were different from other islanders which *Tempest* had encountered. Their skins were paler, their noses less flat, and their bodies for the most part devoid of violent tattoos and tribal scars. The girls who crowded the canoes, or swam happily around the frigate's stem as she glided to her anchorage, caused plenty of comment amongst the seamen, and were obviously well aware of the interest they were arousing.

As Scollay, the master-at-arms, remarked sourly, 'There'll be trouble with that lot, you see!' But he was quick to wave and grin with the best of them.

Herrick came aft as soon as the anchor was down and reported to Bolitho on the quarterdeck.

Bolitho moved his glass past the anchored *Eurotas* and trained it slowly along the shoreline and creamy-white beach. Low surf, lush green trees which held the shade to the water's edge, and bright blue water. Beyond, partly hidden by haze or low cloud, the island's tallest point shone like polished slate, towering above the other hills and forest like a perfect pyramid. It was like some part of paradise.

This, and probably nothing more, could have caused the

Bounty's company to mutiny. How different from the slums and seaports from which so many sailors were drawn. Warmth, friendly and hospitable natives, abundant food. It was a margin between hell and heaven.

He steadied the glass on the settlement. Here, the paradise was less evident.

Herrick was also looking at the stout wooden palisades and blockhouses, the larger building beyond the outer perimeter with the flag above it. There were places like this all over the Pacific, the East and West Indies, and as far north as China, some said.

'Well sited.' It was all Herrick could find to describe his feelings. He was probably thinking, like Bolitho, of Viola left with her maid and no friends in this remote outpost of trade and empire.

There was a small schooner moored to a frail-looking pier and several longboats tied up nearby. She would be used for visiting the other islands, no doubt. Against her, *Eurotas* and *Tempest* would appear like giants.

Keen strode aft, looking worried. He touched his hat. 'What do I do about the natives, sir? They want to come aboard. They'll overrun us!'

Herrick glanced at Bolitho for confirmation and said unfeelingly, 'Let 'em come in manageable groups, Mr Keen. Keep them from sneaking below, and watch out for local drink being smuggled inboard.' He grinned then at Keen's confusion. '*And* a weather-eye for some of our own Jacks, too. Remember, they've not seen girls like these for a long time!'

The first natives came eagerly, and within minutes the deck was strewn with gaily coloured garments, piles of fruit and coconuts, and to Keen's astonishment, a young, squealing pig.

It was like watching children, Bolitho thought, as some of his seamen struggled to break the language barrier, and the giggling girls with their long black hair and barely concealed bodies pointed at their knives or their tattoos, touching each other and shrieking with uninhibited laughter.

Lakey said glumly, 'How long before they ruin this place too, I wonder?' But nobody took any notice.

It was not so easy to get the visitors to leave and make way for the next group, and some of the seamen aided Keen in his efforts by picking up the girls and dropping them overboard, where they dived and surfaced like Neptune's handmaidens.

Bolitho said at length, 'I will have to go ashore, Thomas. Set a good anchor watch and put out a guard boat. It all looks peaceful. But . . .'

Herrick nodded. 'Aye, sir, *but* always seems to mar things.'

He followed him down the companion and aft to the cabin where Noddall and Allday were peering through the stern windows and waving to some hidden swimmers below the transom.

Bolitho added, 'Mr Bynoe will be going ashore to obtain fruit and other fresh supplies, I have no doubt.'

Herrick understood. 'I'll have the purser guarded too, don't you fret, sir.' Inwardly he was wondering how it was Bolitho never seemed to forget anything. Even when his heart was elsewhere.

'And Mr Toby. I'm fairly certain the carpenter will be off as soon as he can to seek useful timber for his store.'

Herrick said quietly, 'I'll *remember*, sir.' He waited for Bolitho to look at him. 'You go ashore and do what you must. I'll have a safe ship for your return.' He hesitated, hoping he had not used his friendship to go too far. 'And I mean that both ways, sir.'

Bolitho picked up his hat and replied simply, 'I never doubted it, Thomas.' Then more sharply, 'Allday, if you can drag yourself away from the contemplation and selection of your lust, I'd be obliged to be taken ashore!'

Allday sprang towards the screen door, his face under control. 'Never faster, Captain!'

Left alone with Herrick, Bolitho added quietly, 'The *Narval*.'

'Aye, sir.'

Herrick waited, knowing the Frenchman had been on Bolitho's mind. They had sighted her several times, just a tiny sliver below the horizon. Following. Waiting like the hunter.

Bolitho said, 'He'll not anchor here. But as soon as I am sure what we are required to do I would like to discover his whereabouts.'

Herrick shrugged. 'Some would say it was a sort of justice if this de Barras got his grappling irons into Tuke before we did, sir. I think we're too soft with bloody pirates of his kind.'

Bolitho looked at him gravely. Hanging would certainly be too soft in de Barras's book.

'Have you considered the reverse side of the coin, Thomas?' The grey eyes watched Herrick's uncertain frown. 'That Tuke may have the same plan in mind for the *Narval?*' He walked towards the square of bright sunlight below the companion, adding, 'He nearly took *Eurotas* into his brotherhood, and he certainly captured enough heavy guns to make him a power to reckon with.'

Herrick hurried after him, his mind hanging on to Bolitho's words. Mutiny in a King's ship was bad enough, but to contemplate that a mere pirate could attack and seize a man-of-war was impossible to accept.

He said grudgingly, 'Of course, *Narval is* a Frenchie.'

Bolitho smiled at him. 'And that makes a difference to your conscience?'

'Aye.' Herrick grinned awkwardly. 'Some.'

There was even more fruit on the gundeck now, and the shrouds and gangways were festooned with plaited mats, strange-looking garments and long, delicate streamers daubed in bright colours.

Herrick said, 'What would the admiral say to all this?'

Bolitho walked to the entry port, noticing the instant attention and interest his appearance was causing. Several girls crowded around him, trying to hang garlands over his neck, while others touched his gold-laced coat and beamed with pleasure.

One old man kept bobbing his head and repeating 'Cap-i-tain Cook' like a sailor's parrot.

It was probable that Cook had once visited the islands, or maybe the old man had carried the story of his ships and his sailors with their pigtails and oaths, rough humour and rum, from another part of this great ocean entirely.

Bolitho heard Allday call to his gig's crew, 'There'll be a few little maids here who'd suit me, lads, an' that's no error!'

Bolitho lowered himself into the boat, while the calls shrilled and brought more cheers and laughter from the onlookers.

It was like it all the way to the little pier, with girls and young men swimming on either beam, touching the oars, and turning Allday's stroke into confusion. Even his threats made no difference, and Bolitho was glad for his sake when they were safely ashore.

He paused with the sun beating down on him, tasting the different aromas, of thick undergrowth and palms, of wood-smoke and drying fish.

Allday said, 'It looks a bit rough, Captain.' He was looking at the wooden wall around the main settlement.

'Yes.'

Bolitho straightened his sword and started to walk along the pier towards a group of uniformed militia who were obviously waiting to escort him. Close to, their red uniforms with yellow facings were shabby and badly patched. The men were well browned by the sun and, he thought, as hard as nails. Like the Corps in New South Wales, they were adventurers. Of a sort. Unwilling to risk the discipline and regulated life in the army or aboard ship, but without the training or intelligence to stand completely on their own.

One, with shaggy hair protruding beneath his battered shako, brought up his sabre in a salute which would have made Sergeant Quare faint.

'Welcome, Captain.' He showed his teeth, which only made him appear more wild. 'I'm to take you to see the resident, Mr Hardacre. We've been watching your ships coming in all day. A fair sight they made too, I can tell you, sir.' He fell in step beside Bolitho, while the rest of his party slouched along behind.

On the short walk to the settlement Bolitho discovered that Hardacre had built the place with very little help from anyone, and had somehow managed to win the respect of most of the islanders for several miles around. It was unlikely he would take very kindly to Raymond, Bolitho thought.

The militia had been collected mostly in Sydney, and their numbers had dwindled over the past two years to a mere thirty men and two officers. The rest had either deserted, leaving the islands by native craft or the occasional trading schooner, or had gone to make their lives with one of the local tribes, enjoying an existence of women, plentiful food and no work at all. And a few had disappeared without any trace.

The talkative lieutenant, whose name was Finney, confided, 'I came to make my fortune.' He grinned. 'But no sign of it yet, I'm thinking.'

Below the gates of the settlement, protected by little block-houses above and on either side of them, Bolitho paused and looked back at his ship. Herrick had been right about it. It was well sited, and a handful of men with muskets, even these ruffians, could hold off twenty times their number. He frowned. Provided they were armed with nothing heavier.

Inside the gates Bolitho stopped and stared up at a crude gibbet. The halter was still attached but had been cleanly cut with a knife.

Finney sucked his teeth and said, 'T'was a mite awkward, Captain. We'd no idea that a real lady'd be coming to a place like this. We had no warning, y'see.' He sounded genuinely apologetic. 'We cut him down sharply, but she saw the poor devil all the same.'

Bolitho quickened his pace, filled with hatred against Raymond.

'What had he done?'

'Mr Hardacre said he'd been after the daughter of a chief on t'other side of the island. He forbids any of the men from going there, an' says the chief is the most important friend we have among the tribes.'

They reached the deep shade of the main door.

'And he had the man hanged for it?'

Finney sounded subdued. 'You don't understand, Captain. Mr Hardacre is like a king out here.'

Bolitho nodded. 'I see.' It was getting worse instead of better. 'Then I am looking forward to meeting him!'

John Hardacre made an impressive sight. Well above average height, he was built like a human fortress, broad and deep-chested, with a resonant voice to match. But if that was not enough to awe his visitors, his general appearance was of a self-made king, as his lieutenant had described. He had bushy hair and a great, spade-shaped beard, both once dark, but now the colour of wood ash. Somewhere in between, his eyes stared out beneath jet-black brows like two bright lamps.

He wore a white, loosely folded robe which left his powerful legs bare, and his large feet were covered only in sandals, and held well apart as if to sustain the weight and strength of the man above.

He nodded to Bolitho and studied him thoughtfully. 'Frigate captain, eh? Well, well. So His Majesty's Government appears to think we may need protection at last.' He chuckled, the sound rising like an underground stream. 'You will take refreshment with us here.' It was not a suggestion but an order.

Raymond, who was standing beside an open window and mopping his face with a sodden handkerchief, complained, 'It's hotter than I thought possible.'

Hardacre grinned, displaying, disappointingly, Bolitho thought, a set of broken and stained teeth.

'You get too soft in England! Out here it is a man's country. Ripe for the taking, like a good woman, eh?' He laughed at Raymond's prim stare. 'You'll see!'

Two native girls padded softly across the rush mats and arranged glasses and jugs on a stout table.

Bolitho watched Hardacre ladling colourless liquid into the glasses. It was probably like fire-water, he thought, although Hardacre seemed willing enough to drink it, too.

'Well, gentlemen, welcome to the Levu Islands.'

Bolitho gripped the arm of his chair and tried to stop his eyes from watering.

Hardacre's ladle swept over him and refilled his glass. 'Damn good, eh?'

Bolitho waited for his throat to respond. 'Strong.'

Raymond put down his glass. 'My instructions are to take overall control of these and other surrounding islands not yet under common claim by another nation.' He was speaking quickly as if afraid Hardacre might fly into a rage. 'I have full instructions for you also. From London.'

'From London.' Hardacre watched him, swilling the drink

around his glass. 'And what does *London* think you can do which I cannot, pray?'

Raymond hesitated. 'Various aspects are unsatisfactory, and, besides, you do not have the forces at your disposal to support the King's peace.'

'Rubbish!' Hardacre turned towards a window. 'I could raise an army if I so wanted. Every man a warrior. Each one ready to obey *me*.'

Bolitho watched him, seeing his anxiety which he was trying to hide, and his obvious pride in what he had achieved on his own.

Hardacre swung towards him violently. 'Bolitho! Of course, I recall it now. Your brother. During the war.' He sighed. 'That war made many a difference to a lot of folk, and that's true enough.'

Bolitho said nothing, watching Hardacre's eyes remembering, knowing that Raymond was listening, hoping for his discomfort.

The great bearded figure turned back to the window. 'Yes, I was a farmer then. Lost everything because I was a King's man when we had to take sides. So I pulled up my roots and set to work out here.' He added bitterly, 'Now it seems it is the King who wishes to rob me this time!'

'Nonsense.' Raymond swallowed his drink and gasped. 'It will not be like that. You may still be needed. I must first – '

Hardacre interrupted, 'You'll first listen to me.' He flung aside the plaited screen and pointed at the dark green trees. 'I need trained men to help me, or those I can instruct before I get too old. I don't want officials like those in Sydney or London, nor, with all respect, Captain, do I need uniforms and naval discipline.'

Bolitho said calmly, 'Your discipline appears somewhat harsher than ours.'

'Oh that.' Hardacre shrugged. 'Justice has to be matched against the surroundings. It is the way of things here.'

'*Your* way.' Bolitho kept his voice level.

Hardacre looked at him steadily and then smiled. 'Yes. If you'll have it so.'

He continued gruffly, 'You've seen what can happen in the

islands, Captain. The people are simple, untouched, laid open
for every pox and disease which a ship can drop amongst them.
If they are to prosper and survive they must protect themselves
and not rely on others.'

'Impossible.' Raymond was getting angry. 'The *Eurotas* was
captured, and retaken by the *Tempest*. Every day we're hearing
worse news about marauding pirates and murderers, and even
the French are disturbed enough to have sent a frigate.'

'The *Narval*.' Hardacre shrugged. 'Oh yes, Mister Raymond,
I have my ways of learning news, too.'

'Indeed. Well, you'll not seek out and destroy these pirates
with a trading schooner and a handful of painted savages!'
Raymond glared at him hotly. 'I intend to make it my first task.
After that, we will talk about trade. My men will begin landing
convicts tomorrow, and clear more land near the settlement
where huts can be built for them.' He sounded triumphant. 'So
perhaps you can begin with *that*, Mr Hardacre?'

Hardacre eyed him flatly. 'Very well. But your wife, I trust
you'll not detain her here longer than necessary?'

'Your concern moves me.'

Hardacre said quietly, 'Please do not use sarcasm on me.
And let me tell you that white women, especially those of gentle
birth, are no match for our islands.'

'Don't your people have wives?'

Hardacre looked away. 'Local girls.'

Raymond looked at the two who were standing near the
table. Very young, very demure. Bolitho could almost see his
mind working.

Hardacre said bluntly, 'Two girls of good family. Their
father is a chief. A fine man.'

'Hmm.' Raymond pulled out his watch, the sweat running
off his face like rain. 'Have someone show me my quarters. I
must have time to think.'

Later, when Bolitho was alone with him, Hardacre said,
'Your Mr Raymond is a fool. He knows nothing of this place.
Nor will he want to learn.'

Bolitho said, 'What of the French frigate? Where did you see
her?'

'So you had it in your mind to ask, eh? Like a teazel in the brain.' Hardacre smiled. 'Traders bring me information. Barter and mutual trust is our best protection. Oh yes, I have heard about *Narval* and her mad captain, just as I know about the pirate, Mathias Tuke. He is often lying off these islands with his cursed schooners. So far he has thought twice about trying to plunder the settlement, damn his eyes!' He looked at Bolitho. 'But your frigate will be outwitted, my friend. You need small craft and strong legs, and guides who can take you to this man's hiding places, and he has several.'

'Could you discover them for me?'

'I think not, Captain. We have survived this far without open war.'

Bolitho thought of the *Eurotas*, the superb planning which had gone into her capture. That and the ruthless cruelty to back it would be more than a match for Lieutenant Finney's militia.

Hardacre seemed to read his mind. 'I brought stability to the islands. Before I came the chiefs had fought each other for generations. Stolen women, taken heads, adopted barbarous customs which even now make me breathe a little faster to think of them. You are a sailor. You know these things. But I made them look to *me*, forced them to trust me, and from that small beginning I founded the first peace they had enjoyed. *Ever.* So if someone breaks it, he or they must be punished. Instantly. Finally. It is the only way. And if I began to use their trust to cause havoc amongst them, by allowing you or the Frenchman's cannon to smash down their primitive world, these islands would revert to blood and hate.'

Bolitho thought of the laughing, supple girls, the sense of freedom and simplicity. Like the shadow of a reef, it was hiding what lay just below the surface.

Hardacre remarked absently, 'You know of course that *Narval*'s captain is more concerned with recapturing a prisoner of France than he is in killing Tuke.' He nodded. 'I see from your face you had already thought as much. You should grow a beard, Captain, to hide your feelings!'

'What you were saying earlier about white women.'

Hardacre chuckled. 'That too you could not hide. The lady means something to you, eh?' He held up his hand. 'Say nothing. I have severed myself from such problems. But if you want her to continue in health, I suggest you send her back to England.' He smiled. 'Where she belongs.'

There was a commotion of voices and hurrying feet in the yard below the window, and moments later Herrick, with Lieutenant Finney panting in his wake, strode into the room.

Herrick said, 'The guard boat found a small outrigger canoe, sir.' He ignored Hardacre and his officer. 'There was a young native aboard. Bleeding badly. The surgeon says he is lucky to be alive.' He glanced at Hardacre for the first time. 'It would appear, sir, that North Island in this group was attacked by Tuke and two schooners, and is now in their hands. This young lad managed to escape because he knew of the canoe. Tuke burned all the other boats when he attacked.'

Hardacre clasped his big hands together as if in prayer. 'God, their boats are their living!' He turned to Herrick. 'And *you* are?'

Herrick regarded him coldly. 'First lieutenant, His Britannic Majesty's Ship *Tempest*.'

Bolitho said quietly, 'So it seems you do need us after all.'

'North Island is the hardest to defend, its chief the least willing to learn from past mistakes.' Hardacre was thinking aloud. 'But I know how to seek him out.' He looked at Finney. 'Muster the men, and take them to the schooner. I will leave immediately.'

Bolitho said gently, 'No, you will stay here. *I* will take the schooner in company with my command, and with your permission some of your men and a few reliable guides.' He added, 'You will serve your islanders the better if you stay here.' He saw his words sink in.

Hardacre nodded his massive head. 'Raymond, you mean.' He frowned. 'No matter. I understand, even if you cannot say it.'

Bolitho said to Herrick, 'Recall the shore parties, Thomas. News travels fast in the islands apparently. We must travel faster. The wind is still with us, so we shall clear the anchorage and reefs before dusk.'

Herrick nodded, absorbed in the only world he understood and respected. 'Aye, sir, Lady Luck permitting.'

He hurried away, and Bolitho heard him shouting for his boat's crew.

'A resourceful lieutenant, Captain.' Hardacre watched him grimly. 'I could use him here.'

'Use Thomas Herrick?' Bolitho picked up his sword. 'I've not seen any man, including his captain, do that as yet!'

He strode from the room, leaving the bearded giant and the two silent girls to their thoughts.

Then he stopped dead as he heard her voice. '*Richard!*'

He turned, holding her against him as she ran down the narrow wooden stairs. She felt hot and shaking through her gown, and her eyes were desperate as she asked, 'Are you leaving? When will you return?'

He held her tenderly, putting aside the mounting demands and questions which only he could answer.

'There has been an attack. Tuke.' He felt her shoulders go rigid. 'I may be able to run him to ground.' In the courtyard he heard Finney bawling orders, the clatter of boots and muskets. 'The sooner I can do it, the quicker you will be free of this place.'

She studied him, stroking his face with her hand as if trying to mould it in her memory.

'Just be careful, Richard. All the time. For me. For us.'

He guided her back into the shade and walked into the harsh glare again.

Raymond was already in the courtyard, he must have run from his room to find what was happening for himself.

He snapped, 'You *were* going to tell me, Captain?'

Bolitho looked at him gravely. 'Yes.'

He touched his hat, the movement needing all his self-control. 'Now, sir, if I may go to my ship?' He turned away, seeing the brief twist of her gown on a stairway above the yard as she watched him leave.

Allday already had the gig prepared, the crew ready.

Bolitho sat in the boat and tried to think clearly as the oars churned the water alive. Tuke, de Barras, Raymond, they all seemed to revolve and blend into one enemy. A last barrier between him and Viola.

Borlase met him at the entry port.

'I have reported back to duty, sir.'

'So I see.'

Bolitho looked past him at the mingled brown figures of the islanders, the familiar ones of his own seamen and marines.

'Clear the ship, Mr Borlase. Then let me know when the schooner is ready to make sail.' He saw the confusion in his eyes. 'Come along! Let us not be all day!'

Herrick came hurrying towards him. 'I am sorry I was not here to greet you, sir. You must have the wind under your gig!'

Bolitho nodded vaguely. 'I'll want you to take command of the schooner, Thomas. Use the native crew and Hardacre's militia. But take Prideaux and twenty marines.' He clapped him on the shoulder. '*Action*, Thomas. What a way to begin the New Year, eh?'

Herrick stared at him as if he had gone mad. Then he nodded. 'Of course, sir. Tomorrow is the first day of seventeen hundred and ninety. I have been checking the log on each and every day and had forgotten all about it.' He strode towards the quarter-deck ladder calling for the boatswain.

Aft by the taffrail Bolitho paused to collect his thoughts into some semblance of order. Another year. He had hoped it might be different. The beautiful surroundings and quiet shore made it harder still to accept that she was here also, and denied him. He sighed deeply. And tomorrow, because circumstances insisted, they might be fighting for their lives yet again.

He watched the boats pulling from different angles towards the ship. The carpenter's crew and the purser, the guard boat and the surgeon, who had probably been ashore to examine the local vegetation.

Some of his men had been thinking more of other distractions, and almost everyone had expected at least a few days and nights at anchor.

He shaded his eyes to look up at the masthead pendant. Still whipping out strongly enough.

He started to walk towards the companionway. As captain of a man-of-war you must earn respect. But to obtain and hold popularity was somewhat harder.

Bolitho paced deliberately up and down the weather side of the quarterdeck, his mind going over the sketchy plans while his eye wandered towards the nearest islands as they moved slowly abeam. Their hills and crags were painted like dull copper by a magnificent sunset.

Ahead, just off the lee bow, was Hardacre's little schooner, and beyond her a deeper curtain of shadow to mark the closeness of night.

On the opposite side of the deck his officers chatted quietly and watched the view as they discussed their ideas of what would happen.

It was strange not to see Herrick moving about the deck, or hear his familiar voice. In some ways his absence was a blessing, and allowed Bolitho to stay remote, more able to contain his thoughts.

He heard Lakey murmuring with his two mates, and guessed he was repeating his earlier doubts and anxieties for their benefit. Hereabouts, the straggling islands and humps of the Levu Group were less well charted, some barely at all. Depths and distances were vague and probably pure guesswork.

But the schooner's crew knew them well enough, and Herrick would be sure to impress upon them the need for absolute caution when comparing their own draught with that of the frigate. North Island was very small, high-crested, and with a deep inlet to the north-west like something carved by a great axe. The population lived in one village, and as Hardacre had said, drew a regular harvest from the sea. Maybe Tuke had gone there to set up a new base, or to gather stores and water for his ships. So he did have at least two schooners. Viola had been right about that also.

He found himself thinking about Raymond again, wondering what his hopes really were. He would probably stay in the islands until more help arrived. The usual caravan of secretariat and overseers which always followed. Most of his original staff had either been murdered by Tuke's men or had stayed in Sydney to recover fom wounds, and to put affairs in order for friends and relatives who had also been killed or captured.

Raymond had been lucky, or was it that Tuke was cleverer than everyone gave him credit for? To single out Raymond as a hostage, to know he was aboard even before the attack, showed a far superior mind to the usual kind of pirate.

Borlase crossed the deck. 'Permission to shorten sail, sir? It is close on time to change the watch.' He waited, uncertain of Bolitho's mood. 'You did order it, sir.'

'Yes.' Bolitho nodded. 'Call the hands.'

There was no sense in driving the ship through the islands in pitch darkness. He thought he heard Lakey breathe out with relief as the boatswain's mates piped the watch on deck to reduce sail.

The attack would have to be quick and efficiently executed. He moved aft to avoid the hurrying marines and seamen. *Tempest* would cross and if need be enter the inlet while the schooner's party landed and attacked the village from the rear. Tuke must feel safe enough. He would not expect one youth to have escaped, to have had the courage to take a canoe all on his own and carry the news to the main island.

High above the deck he heard the seamen calling to one another as they hung over the yards and fisted the canvas into submission.

Two of their number had not returned to the ship with the other shore parties. Bolitho had ordered Borlase not to mark them in the log as 'Run', for desertion carried only one penalty. He had heard that Hardacre's village were planning to hold a *heiva* to welcome the ships and their companies amongst them, with feasting and dancing, and doubtless some of that drink which had cut his breath like fire.

Out of a whole company, two desertions were not so bad under the tempting circumstances. If the men returned freely, he would think again. If not, they would most likely end up as unwilling 'volunteers' in Hardacre's militia when the frigate had departed for good.

He thought about Hardacre, and could find nothing but a grudging admiration. His motives were obscured behind his power, but his feelings for the natives and the islands were sincere enough. But he would lose against Raymond. Idealists always did with men like him.

He moved to the wheel and examined the compass. North by west. He nodded to the helmsman.

'Steady as you go.'

'Aye, zur.' The man's eyes glowed dully in the last of the sunset.

Bolitho heard Borlase rapping out orders in his shrill voice. As acting first lieutenant he would let nothing slip past him. After his last experience and the subsequent court martial, he dare not.

He would take a few hours' sleep if he could. Another glance at his command, feeling the gentle thrust of wind and rudder, listening to the familiar sounds of rigging and canvas. They were so much a part of his everyday life that he *had* to listen to hear them.

Allday was in the cabin, watching Noddall filling a jug with fresh drinking water and placing it beside two biscuits.

Bolitho thanked him and allowed his coxswain to take away his coat and hat, the trappings of command. He looked at the offering on the table. Water and biscuits. Much what the prisoners eat in the Fleet Prison, he thought.

Allday asked, 'Shall I get the cot ready, Captain?'

'No. I'll rest here.'

Bolitho laid down on the stern bench and thrust his hands behind his head. Through the thick glass he could see the first stars, distorted in the stout windows, so that they looked like tiny spears.

He thought of Viola, pictured her lying in her strange bed, listening to the growls and squeaks from the forest. Her maid would be with her, protecting her new mistress in her quiet, stricken manner.

His head lolled and he was instantly asleep.

Allday pulled off his shoes and removed the deckhead lantern.

'Sleep well, Captain.' He shook his head sadly. 'You worry enough for the lot of us!'

9

Decoy

'God's teeth, Mr Pyper, what is taking you so long?'

Herrick mopped his face with his sleeve and peered up at the brightening sky. Below him, some waist-deep in boiling surf, were the remainder of his landing party, while others, notably Finney's militiamen, were already higher up the steep rocky slope which they had confronted when the schooner's two boats had carried them here.

Herrick watched Midshipman Pyper staggering in the water while several brown-skinned islanders tried to keep a boat from smashing itself on the rocks. He hated it when things went wrong because of careless planning or, as in this case, no planning at all.

Finney and his other lieutenant, a dull-eyed man called Hogg, had been certain of the right place to land the party. Herrick glared at the pitching schooner which had anchored nearly a cable offshore. That showed just how much *they* knew of anding places!

The result had been several long trips back and forth with the two small boats, and by now it was well past the time when they should have been moving inland.

Pyper scrambled up the slope, water trickling from his shirt and breeches, his face beset with worry. Like Swift, he was seventeen, and looked forward to promotion if and when a chance came. He did not want to irritate his first lieutenant.

'All ready, sir.'

Captain Prideaux called from the top of the slope, 'I should damn well think so!' Despite the discomfort he, of all present, looked impeccable as usual.

Herrick bit back an oath. 'Send the marine skirmishers ahead, if you please.'

'Done.' Prideaux's foxy face gave a sly smile. 'I've got those bloody guides to hurry their carcasses, too!' He drew out his slim hanger and lopped the head off a plant. '*So?*'

Herrick gritted his teeth. 'So be it.'

He waved his hand over his head, and with some further delay his mixed party started to move inland.

Finney observed cheerfully, 'The village is right at the top of the inlet. Most of the huts are on stilts, their backs in the hill-side. If Tuke's men are in there, they'll be like rats in a cask when your ship blocks the seaward end!' The prospect of a fight seemed to please him.

Down the straggling line of guides and marine skirmishers came the message. There was smoke in the air. Strong stench of burning.

Prideaux said, 'They must be destroying the village.' He did not sound as if he cared.

Herrick slapped a stinging insect from his neck and tried to fathom it out. Tuke had attacked the island, and was creating his usual terror and murder. But why? If he needed supplies, which seemed unlikely after his rich haul from the *Eurotas*, why waste time in sacking the place? Likewise, if he was setting up a new hiding place, why burn it down first? Nothing made sense. He thought of discussing it with Prideaux but checked himself. The marine always seemed to be sneering at everyone he considered beneath his station in life. Too bloody clever by half.

He glanced at the two militia lieutenants as they strode easily amongst their ragged retainers. They would know nothing. It seemed likely they left all their thinking to Hardacre.

Herrick thought about Bolitho and pictured him here. *Now*. What would he do? He grinned in spite of his apprehension. He was not here. He had sent his first lieutenant.

He looked up, sniffing the air. There was the smoke right enough. It was shimmering over a low hill, staining the sky.

Prideaux said harshly, 'By God, this is hard going!'

Midshipman Pyper turned to Herrick and said, 'I think I should go ahead with a guide, sir.' He was rather a serious youth, but likeable.

Herrick paused, hiding his surprise. *That* was what Bolitho would have done.

'I was thinking along that tack, Mr Pyper. But I'll go myself.' He waved to Finney. 'Halt the men and put out your pickets. I want the best guide, double-quick!' It was amazing how easily it was coming to him now. 'Right, Mr Pyper, you can come too.' He slapped his shoulder.

Pyper stared at him, unaware what he had done to excite his lieutenant.

'Aye, sir.'

Prideaux said wearily, 'Attack from the rear. Five or six volleys and a charge of canister would do just as well. Less work, too. They'd run like rabbits. Right under *Tempest*'s guns.'

Herrick looked at him, trying to mask his anger. Prideaux always swept other people's plans away with a few simple remarks. The trouble was, he always sounded so confident.

'We shall see,' Herrick replied stiffly. 'And in the meantime . . .'

He turned and hurried towards the waiting guide, a squat native, quite naked, and whose ears were split and transfixed by sharp bones.

Pyper grimaced. 'He stinks a bit, sir.'

The guide showed his teeth. They were filed like marlin spikes.

'*God.*' Herrick examined his pistol and loosened his sword. 'Come along then.'

The island was tiny, but after blundering and crawling over scrub and stone, and thrusting between tightly interwoven fronds, Herrick imagined it must be twice the size of Kent.

The guide bobbed round some rotting trunks and jabbed his hand towards the thickening smoke. He was excited.

Herrick said tightly, 'We'll have a look.'

He dropped on his knees once again and followed the guide's scarred and dusty rump through a clump of prickly scrub.

Pyper exclaimed, 'Masts and yards, sir! They're anchored right below the village, where the smoke is coming from!'

Herrick shook his head. 'Insolent buggers. They are *that* sure of their safety while they do their work.' He rubbed his hands. '*Tempest* will be able to take her time and blow them apart as she pleases.' He turned round with difficulty. 'We'll tell the others.' He looked at the midshipman. 'Well?'

Pyper flushed. 'I thought – well, I was once told – '

'Spit it out or we'll be here all day!'

Pyper said firmly, 'Hadn't we better look at those vessels first, sir? One might be better armed than the other. Perhaps we could get our sharpshooters to pick off her seamen if she seems likely to weigh first.' He added lamely, 'I am sorry, sir.'

Herrick sighed. 'You are quite right.' It must be the heat. 'I should have thought of it.'

Leaving the perplexed guide amongst the scrub, Herrick and the midshipman wriggled further towards a dip in the hill. Then they saw the inlet, a line of huts blazing and crackling along the far bank like torches, and smoke hiding the water beneath them.

To the left was a jutting wedge of land, while closer to the hill and partly hidden from Herrick were the other huts. But he could only stare at the jutting piece of land and the beach below it.

'There are the *ships*, Mr Pyper.'

He could still not really accept it. The masts and yards looked real enough, but they were rigged to stand on the short beach, held upright by long stays and plaited creepers. There was even a masthead pendant on one of them, and Herrick realized that the loosely brailed-up sails were in fact crude matting.

The truth thrust into his dazed thoughts like ice water. If they seemed genuine to him this close, to *Tempest*'s masthead lookouts as she forged towards the headland they would appear perfect. Two vessels at anchor, their crews intent on pillage and murder ashore.

Pyper stared at him, his face filled with confusion.

'What will we *do*, sir?'

Herrick felt his throat go dry. Just above the out-thrust wedge of land he had seen something move. *Tempest* was here already. He could picture her exactly as if she were not hidden. Guns manned. Officers at their stations. Bolitho and Lakey on the quarterdeck.

He felt something akin to panic. *What was waiting for her?*

Where were the pirates? He could hear occasional musket and
pistol shots, and there was much more smoke now.

Something glinted beyond the burning huts, and Pyper said
thickly, 'A battery. Some big guns, sir.'

So that was it. It was all frighteningly clear to Herrick. Like
walking to the edge of a grave and seeing yourself there.

The message, the dummy masts, the burning village had
been a combined plan. To lure *Tempest* to the inlet.

Herrick stood up, regardless of the danger. Due to the
wretched schooner, to everything which had happened since
their arrival in the islands, Bolitho was unwarned and unready.

He heard himself say, 'Run back! Tell Captain Prideaux I
want a full-scale attack here and now!' He saw the shocked
understanding on Pyper's face. 'I know. We'll not be able to
get away. But we'll save the ship. Remember that.'

Then, as Pyper stumbled away and the naked guide watched
him with fixed fascination, Herrick cocked his pistol and drew
his sword.

'By th' mark seven!'

Bolitho looked at Lakey's intent face as the leadsman's voice
drifted aft from the chains. He restrained himself from using a
telescope again and stood with his hands on his hips, trying to
visualize his ship and the narrowing strip of water, the undulating barrier of land as a single panorama. After coming on deck
before dawn, and going over the charts and calculations with
Lakey and his two lieutenants, Bolitho was as prepared as any
captain could be when approaching a little-known island.
Island? It was not much more than the ridge of a drowned
mountain, he thought.

He watched the surge of current around the nearest clump
of rocks, the drag of it as it receded in a bright welter of spray.
But the wind, hesitant though it was so near to land, was still
holding, and steady. He glanced up at the long masthead
pendant as it licked away towards the starboard bow. *Wind and
depth.* The ability to stop the ship and anchor. The procession
of thoughts and precautions trooped through his mind like
persistent beetles.

'Deep eight!'

Lakey said sharply, 'More like it.'

Bolitho walked to the quarterdeck rail and looked down at the guns. Here and there a man moved nervously or took another pull on a gun tackle. Bare feet scraped on the sanded decks, and high in the maintop some marines were swinging a swivel gun back and forth in a silent bombardment. He saw Lieutenant Keen standing between the lines of twelve-pounders, bending at the waist to peer through one of the open ports, but keeping his arms folded as if to show how calm he was.

Two midshipmen were assisting him at the divisions of guns, the pug-faced Fitzmaurice and the slight figure of young Romney. Swift stood with his signal party on the quarterdeck, while Borlase, puffing and emptying his cheeks like a fretful baby, moved restlessly by the starboard gangway.

All there. Ready and waiting for something to happen.

Bolitho glanced at the half-hour glass beside the compass. He wanted to take out his watch to be sure, but knew it would be seen as agitation, uncertainty. He had been aware of the men nearby, watching him. Looking away quickly as his gaze had passed over them.

But it was taking far too long. If they had to change tack now it would be an age before they could work back towards the inlet. He studied the out-thrust wedge of land, the only thing recognizable from the bald description on his chart. It was pale, probably some sort of rock, and strangely at odds with the lush green background. Beyond it, glittering now above the starboard carronade, was the first hint of an opening. He bit his lip. If Herrick stayed silent he would have to drive past the inlet, and lose precious time in so doing. If there were ships still there, they might even slip past before he could come about and spread more canvas. He looked up, slitting his eyes against the glare. The sunlight angled down between the shrouds as if through windows in a cathedral, he thought vaguely.

Topsails and jib, with the forecourse so tightly reefed it was barely filling. But it was dangerous to make more speed.

He saw Allday watching him from the companionway, his heavy cutlass across one shoulder. Allday was waiting his moment. He knew his captain's moods so well that to speak now would only bring a swift rebuke.

The realization, even amidst all his uncertainty, moved Bolitho. He said quietly, 'I can almost *feel* the island.'

Allday walked to his side. 'The smoke is thinning a bit, Captain.'

'No. I think it's being fanned further inland.'

'Mebbee. It's my thought that the first lieutenant has found nothing. The pirates have gone, and knowing Mr Herrick, I'll wager he's looking after the dead an' wounded left behind.'

'Deck there!' The urgency of the cry made everyone look up. 'Ships at anchor around the point! Two on 'em!' A pause. 'Tops'l schooners!'

Bolitho turned to Allday, his eyes gleaming. 'Well?'

Allday seemed troubled. 'I was wrong then.'

'Yes.' Bolitho strode to the rail. 'Shake out the fores'l, Mr Borlase! There's no sense in losing that pair.' He smiled at the lieutenant's anxious expression. 'We might even catch them as prizes if they've the wit to strike to us!'

He turned away, trying to contain his anxiety for Herrick and his men. They must have lost their way, or perhaps the schooner had grounded?

The big forecourse boomed and filled importantly from the foreyard. In response, the land seemed to move abeam more quickly, while spray spattered over the bow and across the crouching seamen there.

Keen was shouting, 'Starboard battery will fire by division! On the order, gun captains, and not before, d'you hear?'

Bolitho looked at him at the opposite end of the ship, or almost. How far he had come to gain such confidence and authority. Without becoming a tyrant on the journey, which was even more important.

It did not occur to Bolitho that Keen's captain might have had something to do with it.

He said, 'Stand by to alter course, Mr Borlase. Pipe the hands to the braces. We will steer nor'-east.'

How many times had they altered tack and course during the long night? But it had been usual enough for these men. This was different. They had made their landfall. They would do what they were ordered.

He listened to the bark of commands, the clatter of halliards and blocks as belaying pins were removed and the hands prepared to trim the yards.

The pale wedge of land was almost past now, and he could see fires burning, and hissing clouds of steam from the opposite side of the inlet.

'By th' mark five!'

Lakey said, '*Ready*, sir.'

Bolitho looked at him gravely. It was all on the sailing master's lean face. Responsibility. Anxiety. Determination. The ship, and it was always *his* ship to a master, had to have room to come about should the water become too shallow or the wind die. At worse they must anchor, but still hope they could fight clear of the shoals and the angry-looking spray below the foreshore.

'Very well.' As the seamen hauled at the braces, and the big double wheel was put steadily over by Lakey's best helmsmen, Bolitho cupped his hands and yelled, 'Masthead! What of the ships?' The seaman must have been so enthralled by his place as spectator that he had not added to his first report.

'Still at anchor, sir!' The man was probably peering down at the deck, but the blinding sunlight hid him.

Bolitho consulted the compass and then the set of the sails, feeling the ship leaning less steeply as she came into the land's shelter.

Borlase was yelling, 'Belay there! Take that man's name, Mr Jury!'

Bolitho had no idea who *that man* was, nor did he care. He was staring at the reflected fires on the water, leaping and glowing dull red despite the sun's power, making the inlet ahead of the bowsprit glitter like one great flaming arrowhead.

'Take in the forecourse, Mr Borlase!'

As the sail was brailed up to its yard again, Bolitho studied the blazing village and charred boats with mounting anger. Where was the point of it? What prestige could a pirate like Tuke hope to gain by destroying and murdering these simple people?

'Deep six!' The leadsman sounded completely absorbed.

Ninety feet above the deck Marine Blissett, ex-gamekeeper and now one of *Tempest*'s best musket shots, stood with his companions beside the little swivel gun and watched the stick-like masts above the barrier of land.

Once round it and the starboard battery would begin to fire. Slow and deadly. The first shots were always under control. He peered over the barricade at the intent figures between the black guns, the lieutenants and warrant officers pacing and worrying, or snatching a look aft at the captain.

He saw Bolitho almost below him. He was carrying his hat, and his black hair was moving in the hot breeze.

Blissett remembered the other island. The girl he had found stripped and murdered.

Blissett was always amazed at his fellow men. They were often forced to live and work in unbearable hardship, and no matter how the captain kept an eye on such matters, there was always some bully ready to make things worse when he got the chance.

Yet these same men who could face a broadside with outward calm, or watch a flogging of one of their mates with barely any emotion, could rise to madness if an outsider kicked a dog, or as in that case, killed an unknown girl who was probably a slut anyway.

Blissett was not like that. He thought things out. What you needed to stay out of trouble. But also what you had to do to get noticed. He wanted to be a sergeant like Quare. He might as well, now that he was one of them.

He wondered why he had not been one of the party sent ashore with that pig Prideaux.

The captain of the maintop, legs braced, his back against the massive blocks of the topmast shrouds, asked, 'Wot you dreamin' about, Blissett?'

The captain of the top, a giant petty officer called Wayth, was very aware of his responsibility, the maze of cordage and spars, the great areas of canvas which he might be ordered to repair or reset at any moment of the day. And he disliked marines intensely without knowing why.

Blissett shrugged. 'We'll have no chance of taking these

buggers. They'll fight to the finish and take their bloody ships to the bottom with 'em. No prize money. No nothin'!'

The mast trembled, and Wayth forgot the marines as he peered up at his topmen.

Blissett said to his friend, 'We'll be up to 'em shortly, Dick.'

'Aye.' The marine at the swivel swung it towards the land. 'We'd never even reach the ships with this poor cow!' He grinned. 'Now, if we was shootin' on the larboard beam we might 'it a couple of fat 'ogs for our supper, eh?'

Rising to his friend's joke, Blissett turned away from the rocky shoreline and the two sets of masts and playfully pointed his musket towards the opposite side.

'One for the pot, Dick!' He froze. '*Jesus!* There's a bloody cannon over there!'

Wayth snarled, 'I've 'ad about all . . .'

The rest of his anger was blasted away by the crash of a heavy gun and the immediate shriek of iron as it smashed between *Tempest*'s masts.

Blissett fell to his knees, ears ringing, the breath pounded from his lungs by the closeness of a massive ball. Dazedly he stared at the length of severed rigging, and then, as he retched helplessly over the barricade, at the pulped remains of the maintop's captain. The ball had cut him completely in half, leaving his stomach against the mast like a pancake.

Somehow Blissett managed to shout, 'Deck! Battery on th' larboard bow!'

It was then he realized that apart from the corpse he was alone. His friend and the other marine must have been hurled bodily to the deck below.

Blissett leaned his musket against the barricade and trained the swivel towards the shore.

The first shot from the shore was followed instantly by another, bringing cries of alarm from the *Tempest*'s gundeck as it passed between the masts and ploughed into the beach on the opposite beam.

Bolitho yelled, 'Engage with both batteries, Mr Keen!'

He turned away as blood and flesh fell across the nets which had been spread above the guns. Someone had been killed on the maintop, and two marines had gone over the side after hitting the same nets then bouncing into the water, dead or alive, he did not know.

Some of the men at the starboard battery were shouting and cheering, the sound strangely wild. They were probably trying to drown their sudden surprise at the bombardment, the unexpected deaths right amongst them. But soon they would hit back themselves. *Even the score.*

The shouting faltered and broke up into more confusion as the hidden guns fired again, putting down a heavy ball almost alongside.

Bolitho watched the spray falling across the hammock nettings, a seaman peering up at it as if expecting to see a boarder. He felt chilled, unable to move his thoughts in time with the swift change of events.

Bang! That was surely a third gun, perhaps halfway up a slope and above the blazing huts. The ball went wide, and he turned to see it raise a tall waterspout near the rocks.

Keen had his sword above his head. 'Ready, lads! *Ready!*'

Bolitho saw the sword drop to Keen's side and for an instant feared he had been hit by some hidden marksman.

Then Keen came running aft, heads turning from each gun to watch his passing.

'What the *hell*, Mr Keen?' Borlase's voice was shriller than ever.

But Keen ran halfway up the larboard ladder and shouted to Bolitho, 'Sir! The masts are false! *There are no ships!*'

To add menace to his words a shot crashed through a gunport and upended a twelve-pounder over two of its crew; the air rent with screams and sobs as the ball shattered in fragments on a gun across the deck. Men fell kicking and plucking at their bodies with hands like claws, their dying progress across the planking marked by trails of dark blood.

'Engage to larboard!' Bolitho walked quickly to the compass. 'Broadside, and then reload with grape!'

Through his reeling thoughts came a spark of hope. That they might hit some of the carefully sited guns and give themselves time to beat clear of the inlet.

'*Fire!*'

The ship bucked and vibrated as if she had struck a sandbar, the smoke rolling away downwind in a dense pall from the uneven broadside. Shouting like madmen the gun captains urged their men to reload with heavy grape, while around them the ship's boys darted with more powder, dodging the gaping corpses and crawling wounded, their faces like tight masks.

'Ready!'

Hand by hand each gun captain looked at Keen, his trigger line pulled almost taut.

'On the uproll! *Fire!*'

This time it was better timed, and Bolitho thought he saw the trees and burning huts shiver as the packed grape sliced through them.

But the reply came just as swiftly, almost two together. One hit the forecastle, and Bolitho heard the crash and whine of splinters, saw men flung down as if by a terrible wind. He felt the air throb over his head, and winced as a ball cut through rigging and clawed down another seaman who was pulling himself aloft to repair some of the damage.

The man fell with a sickening thud across one of the quarterdeck guns, and for a few moments he moved like some obscene, bloody creature before he died and was hauled away by the stone-faced crew.

'We will come about, Mr Lakey!'

Bolitho staggered as the deck jumped to another long-drawn-out broadside. Thank God the smoke was going towards the hidden guns. It was their only protection.

Lakey nodded, his head jerky. 'At once, sir.' He cupped his hands. 'Man the braces if you please, Mr Borlase!'

Borlase peered aft, his eyes bulging from his head. Another shot whined low over the nettings, and it seemed to bring the lieutenant's limbs back into motion.

'Man the braces! Clear the starboard battery if you must but *lively* there!'

Bolitho watched coldly. No room to wear and take full advantage of the wind. They would have to pass right through its eye, pivoting round with those four mocking masts their only adversary. He could feel the anguish blinding and choking him.

It was his fault. He should have seen the flaw, felt his enemy's cunning. No, *skill*.

'Ready ho!'

Several men let go a brace as a ball splintered through a portion of the gangway and ground three men into a writhing shambles.

Bolitho saw it all. Felt it. One second a scene of pain and survival as two men dragged a wounded companion towards a hatchway and safety. Now they kicked and screamed in one hideous gruel.

'Put the helm down!'

Bolitho ran to the lee side to try and see any sign of the enemy. But apart from several scattered fires on a hillside, caused no doubt by Keen's grapeshot, it was as before.

He watched the men hauling at the braces, their features grim and shining with sweat. Here and there a warrant officer, even some of the wounded, added their weight to drag the great yards round, while above the proud figurehead the jib with broken rigging drifting amongst it like weed flapped in abandoned confusion.

'Helm a'lee!'

The quartermaster had to repeat it as the guns hurled themselves inboard on their tackles, one of them making red tracks through the remains of a fallen seaman.

'Off tacks and sheets!' Borlase's voice was like a scream through the speaking trumpet.

'Let go and haul!'

Bolitho watched, hardly daring to breathe, as the land began to move very slowly to larboard as his ship responded to rudder and canvas.

A grating crash brought more startled shouts, and he saw a ball upend another gun, slewing it right round amidst its severed tackles and gasping men as if to turn upon its own ship in revenge.

Rigging fell from the maintopmast in black, glittering coils, and heavy blocks bounced and trailed over the nets like live things.

Through it all, urging and threatening, sliding in blood or colliding with men employed at trimming the yards, Keen and his subordinates sent more hands across to the still unfired starboard battery.

All these things were recorded in Bolitho's brain like writing on parchment. Keen was keeping his head, knew that once around they might have a faint chance of finding and hitting their attackers before they reached open water again.

Crash! Lakey yelled, 'Main t'gallant, sir! *Watch out on deck!*'

Like a giant, murderous tree, the whole topgallant mast and yard, all its canvas, blocks and shrouds swept down and through the flimsy protection with the sound of an avalanche. It fell across the larboard side, breaking down nettings, whipping men from their feet and flinging them aside like dolls.

Bolitho felt the ship stagger under the onslaught, sensed the change in motion as the tangle dragged at the hull like a great sea-anchor.

Jury was booming, 'Axes there! Clear it away! Get those wounded below!'

His great voice seemed to rally the dazed gun crews along the side where the topgallant mast had fallen. More trailing halliards and ratlines, followed by the masthead pendant, splashed over the side, surging around some corpses and a few frantic swimmers as if to suck them under.

Somewhere through the din and smoke Bolitho heard the foretopsail filling to the change of tack, and saw the land loom dangerously close while *Tempest* continued to turn.

The planks bucked beneath him, throwing up splinters like jagged darts as a ball smashed through the poop and explored the semi-darkness between decks in a trail of destruction and terror.

In disbelief Bolitho saw the sun glinting on clear water, a distant island very green in the untroubled light. In the opposite direction the trailing smoke from his ship mingled with that of the inlet and glowed above the burning village.

One more ball struck the hull right aft, a great hammer-blow, as if to mark the final seal of defeat.

Bolitho listened to voices resuming command and order, the cries of the wounded becoming fainter as men died or were carried below to the orlop for Gwyther and his mates to tend as best they could.

F

The broken mast and spars were drifting clear of the stern, and he saw one man sitting astride the crosstrees, staring after his ship, too stunned to know what was happening.

Borlase lurched towards him. 'We are out of range, sir.' It seemed as if he had to speak, although his voice was thick and unsteady.

Midshipman Swift was on his knees beside one of his men.

'Hold on, Fisher!'

He peered round desperately for aid, his powder-grimed face streaked with sweat, or perhaps they were tears, Bolitho thought.

The wounded seaman was one of the older hands, and had been put in the signals party because of his inability to swarm aloft as he had once done. Two bad falls had rendered him almost a cripple, and by rights he should have been ashore with his family, if he had one.

Now he lay staring up at the trailing rigging, his face ashen as he gripped Swift's hand between his as if in prayer.

He asked in a strong voice, 'Be Oi goin', zur?'

Swift stared blindly at Bolitho. Then he seemed to draw on an inner reserve and pulled a flag up and over the man's waist. A ball, split in half by striking an upended gun, had almost severed one of his legs, and had laid open his groin like a cleaver.

Swift said haltingly, 'You'll be all right, Fisher, you see.'

Fisher tried to grin. 'Oi don't feel all right, zur.' Then he died.

Swift stood up violently and vomited on the deck.

Bolitho glanced at Allday. 'See to him. He was worth six men today!'

'Aye.' Allday sheathed his cutlass and walked to the midshipman's side.

Swift did not look at him. 'All these men. We never stood a chance.'

'Look at Fisher, Mr Swift.' Allday's voice was calm but firm. 'He could have been any of us.' He waited for the youth to face him. 'Or all of us. He did his best. Now there are other poor fellows who need help.' He turned as the midshipman hurried to the quarterdeck rail. Then he said, 'He'll do, Captain. Just give him something to bite on.'

He watched Bolitho's face, seeing the strain clouding over it like pain. He'd not heard a word of it.

Lakey asked. 'What orders, sir?'

Bolitho looked past Allday towards the island and its pall of smoke.

He said, 'We could enter and re-enter that place with little change in result. Until – ' he thrust his hands behind him, gripping his fingers until the pain steadied him, ' – until our damage became fatal. Then, we would lie aground or sinking until we agreed to terms, or until we were all killed.'

He forced himself to look up at the men who were already climbing up the shrouds towards the gap left by the lost top-gallant mast. They were moving slowly. The confidence and the will gone out of them.

Almost to himself he said, 'They have the upper hand.'

In his brain a voice insisted. *They beat you . . . you . . . you.* Until he thought his mind would burst.

'We will rejoin the schooner and anchor, Mr Lakey.' He turned to Borlase. 'I want a list of dead and wounded. Soon as possible.'

They were all looking at him. Accusing, sympathizing, hating? He could not tell any more.

Lakey murmured, 'Very well, sir.' Then in a louder voice, 'Watch your helm, damn your eyes!'

Bolitho crossed to the weather gangway and took several deep breaths. In a moment more he would step inside his role again. Plan a suitable approach, lay his scarred ship on her rightful tack to rejoin Herrick with least delay. Bury the dead, attend the wounded. See to the repairs, discover the reason for failure no matter how painful it was to swallow.

But first . . . He let his gaze move over the quiet shore. The huts were hidden as were the dummy masts. It was a savage lesson. What he had seen as his last moments on earth might now be viewed as a last chance to redeem a terrible mistake. He made himself turn away from the land and examine his ship, as if to punish himself even further.

Borlase asked, 'Secure guns, sir?'

He nodded. 'Then have the galley fire lit and see that the people are fed directly.' He looked at the dangling rigging, the long smears of blood on the decks, already brown in the sunlight. 'There is a lot to be done.'

Allday said awkwardly, 'I'll fetch something to drink, Captain.'

Bolitho looked at him sharply, something in Allday's tone dragging him from his own despair.

The big coxswain added, 'That last ball, Captain. It did for poor Noddall.' He looked away, unable to watch Bolitho's eyes. 'I'll fetch it for you.'

Bolitho took a few paces, hesitantly and then with sudden urgency. Poor, defenceless Noddall. Loyal and uncomplaining, who despite his terror of the din of battle had always been ready to serve, to watch over him.

It seemed impossible he was not below now. Hands like paws. Shaking his head and fussing.

Lakey watched him grimly, while from nearby Jury, the boatswain, paused in his work with the scrambling, grimy seamen to study Bolitho. He had heard Allday's words, and marvelled that with all this hell the captain could find time to mourn just one man.

Bolitho's eyes lifted suddenly and settled on him. 'Your men are doing well, Mr Jury. But not yet well enough to idle, I think.'

Jury sighed. It was a relief to see Bolitho returning from inner hurt, no matter how bad the consequences might be.

10

Too Much Courage

'Fix your bayonets!'

Herrick gritted his teeth to contain his impatience as Prid-eaux brought the marines into a single line, while further along the uneven slope Finney's militia were following their example, faces tight with concentration.

The air shook to the sudden boom of cannon, and Herrick knew the hidden battery had opened fire. The gunners would be able to see *Tempest* beyond the point, even though it still hid all but her topmasts from Herrick.

Prideaux snapped, '*Advance!*' His slim hanger shone in the sunlight, moving from side to side like a steel tongue as he strode through the scrub and sun-dried stones.

More shots, and before he followed the main part of his men towards the burning huts Herrick turned and watched the waterspouts rising like spectres on the frigate's shadow as she continued to force the inlet.

His mind repeated warnings and dreads, so that for precious seconds he could only stand and punish himself with what he saw. The inlet was too narrow. The ship would strike. She might be pounded into submission without even sighting her executioners.

He swore savagely. He was here, not on the quarterdeck where he belonged.

He shouted, 'Fast as you can!'

Then with the others he was running and stumbling down the slope, the marines starting to cheer like madmen as they charged into the drifting smoke and sparks.

If they could overwhelm just one of those guns they could train it towards the others. The shock of an attack from behind might cause enough confusion and give Bolitho the diversion he desperately needed.

A seaman fell kicking and clasping his head, blood soaking his hair and shoulders. Herrick stared at him as seamen and marines faltered or blundered against each other in the choking smoke.

Then, as if to a signal, the air was filled with flying rocks and sharper pieces of stone. Herrick heard them hitting flesh and bone, men cursing and staggering while they tried to see their attackers.

Prideaux shouted, 'Look! Across that clearing!' He raised a pistol and fired. 'Natives from the village!'

More stones hurtled through the smoke, and two men fell, knocked senseless.

Midshipman Pyper crouched beside Herrick, his teeth bared. 'What are they attacking *us* for? We're here to help!' He sounded more angry than frightened.

Herrick raised his pistol and fired, feeling nothing as a dark figure cartwheeled down the slope and through the charred wall of the hut.

'They think we're all the same!'

He swore obscenely as a stone hit his shoulder, numbing the whole of his arm so that he lost his grip on the pistol.

'Come on, Prideaux!'

The marine captain was peering through the swirling smoke, his eyes smarting as he watched the naked figures becoming real and menacing as they started to pound up the hillside.

'Ready!' His hanger did not falter as a marine fell sobbing beside him, his jaw broken by a rock. 'Aim!'

Herrick dashed sweat from his eyes, gripping his sword with his left hand. He could hear them now. Like baying hounds, rising to a crescendo of hate and despair. It would be better to die than to linger on at their hands, he thought.

'*Fire!*'

The muskets cracked together, the stabbing flames making the smoke lift above the grim-faced marines.

'Reload! Keep your timing!'

Slightly above them, Finney's men began to fire, with neither timing nor preparation. Herrick could hear the balls cracking into trees and rocks, the sharp screams which told their own story.

But they were still coming.

Herrick cleared his throat. It felt raw.

'Up, lads!' A spear passed over his head. He saw it, but through his racing mind it meant nothing. He balanced himself carefully on the treacherous stones. 'Keep together!'

His eye took in the fact that the marines were moving with practised, jerky motions, like red puppets, arms rising and falling as one while the ramrods tamped home another volley.

'*Take aim!*'

A marine shrieked and dropped down the slope, his bloodied hands trying to drag a spear from his stomach.

'*Fire!*'

Again the musket balls swept across the crouching men in a lethal tide. Controlled, but with less authority as two more men fell under the ceaseless bombardment of rocks and spears.

A great chorus of shouts from the militia made Prideaux lose his outward calm. He looked at Herrick. 'Finney is being attacked from the other side.' His hanger fell to his side, and he added with bitter disbelief, 'God, the buggers are running for it!'

Herrick snatched up a musket from a fallen marine and cocked it, ignoring the agony in his shoulder as he made sure it would fire.

Through his teeth he said, 'Send someone to the top again. See if the ship is safe. Quick as you can.'

Prideaux nodded. 'Mr Pyper. You go.' He ducked as a spear hissed between them. '*Tempest* will be dismasted, I shouldn't wonder.' He took a reloaded pistol from his orderly. 'Here they come again.' He smiled tightly. 'Put a ball in me rather than leave me, eh?' He walked back to his men. 'I'll do the same for you.'

Herrick watched him. For those few seconds he almost liked the man.

Then they were firing again, reloading and fumbling, firing and crouching together like the last men on earth. Herrick heard ragged shooting from some way off, and guessed that

Finney's men were retreating back to the schooner, all thought of defiance gone out of them.

He pulled the trigger. *A misfire*. He stood with his legs astride and used the musket like a club, feeling the pain run up his wrists as he smashed down a screaming savage and struck out at two more. All round him the sounds were of people now, the muskets used only for their bayonets, or as crutches for the wounded.

Herrick hurled the musket into a man's face, noting briefly that his eyes were almost red with fury and the lust to kill. Then he drew his sword again, parrying aside a spear and hacking open a brown shoulder with the same movement.

Above and through it all he heard Pyper calling his name, then, 'The ship's gone about! She's clearing the entrance!' Then he fell silent, terrified, even dead, Herrick did not know.

He yelled, *'Fall back! Carry the wounded!'*

He slashed at a figure which had somehow got past the gasping, thrusting marines. Herrick slipped and almost fell, searching wildly for his sword, knowing that his loss had halted the man, that he was turning towards him, his voice lifted in one terrifying shriek.

Another figure ran through the smoke, holding a pistol outstretched in both hands, as if it was taking all his strength to use it.

The heavy ball took away the native's forehead and hurled him across Herrick in a welter of blood and convulsing limbs. He had been carrying a long, wavy knife, which fell across Herrick's shoe and slit it open, merely with its own weight.

Herrick picked it up and recovered his sword. 'Thanks, Mr Pyper.'

He waved his arms in the air, realizing that the attackers had melted into the smoke, leaving dead and wounded entwined amongst their discarded weapons.

Prideaux said tersely, 'They'll try to cut us off, damn them!' He watched his marines reloading their muskets and those of their dead or wounded comrades.

Herrick nodded. 'It gives us a little time.'

Prideaux regarded him coolly. 'For what? Praying?' He swung round angrily. 'Be careful, you dolt! You nearly dropped it!' His orderly had been reloading a pistol, and was shaking so badly he seemed barely able to stand. 'Go and help the wounded, man. You're more menace than aid in your state!'

Herrick wiped his face and blinked at the sky. So clear above the smoke. Mocking all of them for their antlike confusion.

A seaman said, 'Four wounded or stunned by them rocks, sir. Five killed. I dunno 'ow many of the militia's still with us, but I can see several corpses on th' 'illside.'

Prideaux said angrily, 'To *hell* with them, I say. If I meet *Mr* Finney again I'll give him cause to regret he survived!'

Herrick said, 'Ready to move.'

He had seen it before. The wildness of a battle going with the suddenness of a squall, leaving men like fallen trees. Useless. Broken.

'Yes.' Prideaux waved his hanger. 'Two scouts up ahead!' He glanced at Pyper. 'You take charge of the wounded.' His head darted forward. *'Is that clear?'*

Pyper nodded, his eyes glassy. He was probably remembering how he had nearly been cut off. How he had held the heavy pistol, feeling it gaining weight with each second as he had tried to clear his vision of sweat and fear as the naked, yelling savage had lunged towards the first lieutenant.

'Aye, sir.'

'That is a relief.'

Prideaux strode off again, his heels striking up dust as he hurried after his marines.

Herrick watched the clearing. It was wrong to leave the dead marines, but what could he do? He must lead and rally the survivors. The pirates might be after them as well, although it was unlikely they would wish to cross swords in wild country with natives whose village they had just burned.

He waited for Pyper and his stumbling group of wounded to pass and then walked towards the same rounded hill he had seen just hours ago. And he had acted on his own initiative. The thought troubled him as he walked, and he searched his mind for satisfaction or justification.

Tempest had got away, although she must have suffered under those powerful pieces. His action to attack and divert the gun-

ners may have made little difference, although the pirates must
have heard the din they were making.

But Bolitho would *not* know. That they had tried to help, to
prevent the ship's destruction with the only means they had.
Their lives.

A marine turned and looked back at a companion who had
been hit in the leg by a spear. He was leaning on Pyper's
shoulder, his eyes bright and feverish as he stared after the rest
of the men.

The marine called, 'Come on, Billy, not long now! You'll
get a double tot o' rum for this, I shouldn't wonder!'

Herrick swallowed hard. They were *not* done for yet. Not
with men like these.

When eventually Prideaux's scouts signalled that the landing
place was in sight, Herrick knew even his moment of frail hope
was extinguished.

As they crawled into whatever shelter they could find and
shaded their eyes against the fierce glare from the sea, Herrick
saw Finney's men surrounded by even more natives than had
originally attacked them near the village. It was made worse by
the silence, the pathetic attitudes of the militiamen as they
stared out at the hostile faces.

Finney had thrown down his sword, probably because he
had been here before, or had met some of these same natives
during his service with Hardacre. The other lieutenant, Hogg,
was standing well back with his men, his terror evident even
at this distance.

And beyond the little scene of fierce tension the schooner
idled clear of the rocks, her mainsail already set and drawing as
she moved further from the shore. Her small native crew
would imagine the raid had been a complete failure, and why
not? They would try to save themselves. Get home.

A seaman muttered, 'There's one o' the boats still here, sir.'

Herrick did not answer. He had already seen it, known that
it had been stove in. By the rocks or the natives no longer
made any difference.

It was then the silent figures exploded into the militiamen
in a solid naked wall. The light glinted on stabbing and plunging weapons, on limbs waving above the swaying crowd like

scarlet roots, while through the heated air Herrick and his men listened to the rising roar of jubilant voices.

There was nothing they could do. It was still too far, and they would probably refuse to move even if he ordered it. They would wish to stay together at the end. It was not because they were frightened, they were beyond that. Nor was it caused by any sort of revenge for being left abandoned by those same men who were being mercilessly hacked to death.

It was the way of sailors, and on land or sea it was the only one they knew.

The crowd began to break away from the trampled sand and scrub. It was like some great obscene flower. Scarlet in the heart, with trailing ends, and parts which still moved until pounced on and clubbed or cut to death.

Only Finney was left, and he was being stripped naked and bound, trussed to a pole. Being saved for something even more horrific.

A marine said hoarsely, 'I might hit him with a long shot, sir.'

'No.'

Herrick turned away. All these men to save one. He would not expect it even of himself. But it was hard to form the word.

He said, 'Time enough when they discover what's happened to the rest of us.'

Herrick rolled on to his back and stared at the sky. He remembered with stark clarity when he had been a small boy and had been playing with his friend on the bank of the Medway. He had thrown a stone through the rushes. Meant as a joke, like those they always played on each other, it had hit his friend in the eye, nearly blinding him.

Herrick had screwed up his face, willing that it was a dream. That when he looked again it would all be clean and as before.

But then, as now, it was real. If he looked, the litter of corpses and torn limbs would still be there. And the schooner would be gone.

Prideaux was saying to his corporal, 'Put all the muskets together and then inspect the powder and shot. The wounded can do the loading, right?'

'Sir.' Attentive, even now.

Pyper said quietly, 'Will it be soon, sir?'

Herrick did not look at him, but watched a bird with scimitar-shaped wings circling far, far up against the washed-out blue sky.

'I expect so.' He added, 'But no quarter. Nor do we surrender.'

'I see.'

Then Herrick did turn his head to look at the midshipman. *Do you see?* The boy who had started to become a man. Did he not ask why he was to die, here of all places?

Someone said, 'The buggers are searchin' about on t'other side of th' hill, sir.'

Prideaux sounded irritable. 'Yes. Well, it won't take a foxhound to pick up our trail, will it?'

Herrick raised himself carefully amongst the prickly gorse and looked at the sea. The schooner was stern-on now, standing well out from the landing place.

We could light a fire, make an explosion, but it would only bring down the savages that bit sooner. Anyway, the schooner would not dare to come inshore.

He looked again at the schooner, his mind suddenly clear. The wind. It had shifted. Quite a lot. He stared at the hillside bushes and scrub and tried to fathom its direction.

Prideaux asked, 'What is it?'

He was trying to sound disinterested as he always did, and the fact he was not succeeding gave Herrick sudden desperate hope.

He replied quietly, 'The captain will come to look for us. The wind. It could make a world of difference. Give him a day's start.' He looked at Pyper's strained features. 'A whole day. If we can just hang on here.'

The marine who had been speared in the leg said huskily, 'That would be fine, sir.'

His friend grinned. 'Wot did I tell 'ee, Billy-boy?'

Prideaux scowled. 'Don't raise their hopes. The wind, what is that? Time, how do we know anything?'

Herrick looked at him. 'He'll come. Mark me, Captain Prideaux.' He looked away. 'He must.'

Bolitho sat in the cabin going over his written log while a lantern swung back and forth above his head.

All yesterday, and through the long night, they had sailed with as much canvas as they could carry. No one had spoken of risk or caution this time, and he had seen men look away when his gaze had passed over them.

He glanced at the stern windows, realizing with surprise they were already paling with the dawn. He felt suddenly empty and dispirited. Noddall would have reminded him. Hovered around the desk.

He thought of all the faceless bundles sewn in hammocks which he had watched dropped overboard. It could have been ten times worse, but it did not help at all to remind himself.

Wayth, captain of the maintop. Sloper of the carpenter's crew, and who had done more than anyone to make the newly built jolly boat a success. Marine Kisbee, maintop. Old Fisher, able seaman. William Goalen, second quartermaster, Noddall, cabin servant, and too many others beside. In all fifteen had been killed, and as many more wounded. And for what?

Death for some, discharge for others, and advancement for the lucky ones who filled their shoes.

He rubbed his eyes again, trying to quell the ache in his mind.

There was a tap at the door and Midshipman Swift stepped into the cabin.

'Mr Keen's respects, sir, and we have just sighted a light to the north'rd.'

'A ship?' He cursed himself for passing back the information as a question. He stood up and placed the thick book inside his desk. 'I'll come up.'

He had been wrong about Herrick too, it seemed. The light must be the schooner. Although even with the shift of wind it seemed strange she had reached this far. He thought about the wind and how they had cursed it so often in the past. When Lakey had told him of the sudden change he had found it hard to conceal his emotion from him.

On the quarterdeck the air was almost chill after the heat of the days and the stuffy restriction below. A quick glance at the compass bowl and another at the flapping mainsail and driver told him the wind was holding as before, and the ship was steering to the north with the island hidden somewhere on the larboard beam. But for the wind, they would have taken perhaps two days, even more, to beat back and forth, to fight round the southern end of the island before returning to search for the schooner's landing place.

He took a glass from Swift, knowing there were more than the duty watch on deck, watching and waiting.

He saw the vessel straight away, and even in the few moments since Swift had reported it to him the light had strengthened, so that he could make out a darker smudge which would be the schooner's big driver.

'How roundly the dawn comes up.' That was Mackay, the first quartermaster. He sounded calm enough. Glad perhaps that his mate, Goalen, and not himself had gone several hundred fathoms down in a hammock, with a round-shot at his feet to speed the journey.

'Aye.' Lakey's coat rustled against the compass as he moved about in the gloom like a restless dog. ' 'Nother ten minutes it'll be blinding your eyeballs out!'

True to the sailing master's prediction the daylight swept across the islands like the opening of a vivid curtain.

Bolitho watched the schooner, sensed the uncertainty as she tacked, hesitated, as if to turn away.

From the masthead, where Keen had sent him, Midshipman Swift shouted, 'No sign of red coats aboard, sir!'

'Blazes!' Borlase had appeared now. 'They must have left them there. Or . . .' He did not finish.

'Signal her to heave to.' Bolitho's voice cut through the speculation like a rapier. 'Stand by the quarter boat, Mr Borlase.'

Bolitho watched the wave troughs changing from black to deep blue. From dark menace to friendly deception.

He felt his anxiety giving way to unreasoning impatience. 'And pass the word for Mr Brass. Tell him to prepare a bow-chaser directly. If the schooner does not respond, I want a ball as near to her bilge as makes no difference!'

By the companionway, his thick arms folded, Allday listened and watched Bolitho's words having effect. He saw Jack Brass, the *Tempest*'s gunner, bustling forward with his mates, and knew he too was well aware of Bolitho's mood.

'She's heavin' to, sir.'

'Very well.' Bolitho let his thoughts carry him along. 'We will fall down on her to within hail. It will save time.' He looked at Allday. 'We will probably need the launch. Select the best hands you can.'

He slitted his eyes to watch the rolling schooner as the frigate ran down on her. Empty, or all but. Perhaps there *was* no more time. That would make the defeat even more complete, an acceptance of it impossible. He looked at the quarterdeck rail, remembering Herrick.

He said harshly, 'See that the people are well armed. Tell Sergeant Quare to lower two swivels into the launch, and provide some good marksmen for the quarter boat as well.'

Like extensions they were moving from him, acting on his wishes. His ideas.

The schooner was much nearer now. He lowered his telescope and said, 'Give them a hail, Mr Keen.' He had seen the schooner's master, a great hulk of a man, probably born of mixed blood right here in the islands.

Keen's voice re-echoed across the water, distorted by his speaking trumpet.

Bolitho listened to the hesitant replies, some barely understandable. But the main message was clear enough. The schooner had left without Herrick's party. They might be dead, as were all the militia. Butchered.

Bolitho glanced at the men around him. With the company already depleted by death and wounds, by Herrick's landing party and marines, *Tempest* was getting more and more shorthanded.

He made up his mind. It could not be helped.

He said, 'Tell the schooner to stand by to receive a boarding party.' He looked at Borlase. 'You will take command here until our return.' He snapped, 'Well, *come along*, let us be about it!'

Midshipman Pyper said huskily, 'I think we may be safe, sir.'

The sun was beating down on the saucer-shaped depression where Herrick had gathered his party of seamen and marines.

He felt as dry as the sand and rock which burned through his clothing like hot metal, and he had to force himself almost physically not to think of water. There was precious little left, and what there was was needed by the wounded. Especially Watt, one of the marines. He had been hit in the shoulder, either by a dart or spear, nobody was sure, or could remember.

He was lying with his head on the marine corporal's knees, gasping, and drawing his legs up in deep convulsions of pain.

Herrick said, 'Too soon to know yet.'

He listened to the marine's groans. He was in agony. Maybe his wound had been deliberately poisoned, he had heard of such things. Darts which left men or animals to die in dreadful suffering. Once, the corporal had tried to adjust the crude bandage, and Herrick had been forced to look away from the wound, in spite of all he had seen during his years at sea. Like a ripening, obscene fruit.

Prideaux sat with his boots out-thrust, dragging a stalk of sun-bleached grass through his teeth. His eyes were distant as he said, 'We've got to keep Watt quiet. Those devils are not far off. I know it in my bones. Watt'll raise an attack if we're not careful.'

Herrick looked away. Prideaux was doing it again. Passing an idea, like a hint. Leaving it for him to decide.

He said, 'Corporal Morrison, give the man some water.'

The corporal shook his head. 'Not much in the flasks, sir.' He shrugged and held one to the man's lips. 'Still, I suppose . . .'

A seaman on lookout called sharply, 'Some of 'em comin' now, sir!'

The dull acceptance and lethargy vanished as they struggled to their allotted places, seizing weapons, screwing up their faces.

Herrick watched as a file of natives came down a narrow gully on the opposite side of the hill and padded swiftly towards the sea. They did not hesitate even to glance at the carnage which lay rotting in the sun, but hurried on into the shallows by the rocks where Herrick and his men had come ashore.

Pyper said, 'They're looking at the longboat.'

Herrick nodded. Pyper was right. He remembered then seeing the village boats all ablaze. Their only way to reach other
islands. To trade. To seek revenge. *Or to escape.*

'They must have been back to their village. That means the
pirates have gone. Probably had a boat standing offshore all the
while.'

Herrick could not disguise his bitterness. While *Tempest* had
tacked round the point and into a trap, and he and his men had
fought for their lives, the pirates had carried on with their well-
laid plan. They might have failed to sink the frigate, but they
had shown what they could do with a mere handful of men.

He saw the longboat lifting sluggishly in the surf, the water
sliding across her bottom boards as the natives hauled and
guided it into the shallows.

Herrick tried not to listen to another man being given water.
He watched the natives, knowing he would have to do something and soon. The night had been friendly enough, apart
from the insects. After the horror of the day, the systematic
massacre of Finney's men, and their own desperate plight, all
they had wanted to do was fall into exhausted sleep.

But like the memory of his boyhood friend on the bank of
the Medway, the menace and danger were still waiting with the
dawn. There were no more rations, and certainly not enough
water for another day. If they left the depression to search for
a pool they would be seen or heard.

Prideaux had remarked during the night, '*Tempest*'ll not
come. The captain'll think we're dead. We will be, too.'

Herrick had turned on him with such force he had said very
little since. But when their eyes had met in the first light, after
they had searched an empty sea, Herrick had seen the same rebuke, the same contempt.

He heard the corporal say, 'It's all gone, mate. See? Empty!'

'Mother of God! The pain! *Help me!*'

Herrick pushed them from his mind, watching the busy
figures in and around the beached longboat. He thought he
saw water through the starboard side between the planks. That
was not too bad. Not like being stove in from the bottom.

He rolled over and propped himself on one elbow, ignoring
the rawness of his throat, the cracks in his lips. He had started

up from that beach yesterday morning with twenty-nine others, excluding Finney's men. Five had been killed, and four were badly wounded. Hardly anyone had survived without a cut or bruise to remind him of their struggle.

He took each man in turn. Some were almost finished, barely able to hold a musket. Others lay hollow-eyed and desperate. Watching the sky over the rim of their heated prison. Pyper looked weary. But he was young, as strong as a lion. Prideaux; he of all of them seemed unchanged.

Herrick sighed, and shifted his attention to the boat. It was half a cable over open land. If they waited until night it was likely the boat would be gone, especially if the natives wanted it to raise an alarm in other islands.

He pictured them running down the slope, the satisfaction of being the ones with the upper hand, as they shot and cut their way to the boat. Then he thought of the others. Too sick or wounded to move on their own.

Prideaux said very quietly, 'We could rush the boat and make certain that none of those savages is left alive. How many are there? Ten at most.' He did not drop his eyes as Herrick faced him. 'The rest of the village would think we'd run for it. Once in safety we could send help for the wounded.'

Herrick studied him. Loathing him for reading his mind, for his casual dismissal of those who were dying behind him. For being able to think clearly and without sentiment.

He replied hotly, 'Or we could kill them ourselves, eh? Make it easier all round!'

Prideaux said, 'Oh, for God's sake!'

Herrick felt suddenly light-headed. Wild. He turned towards the others and said, 'Now, lads, this is what I intend.' When he began he found he could not stop. 'We'll wait a mite longer until they've done some repairs on *our* boat.' He felt a lump in his throat as the marine with the spear wound tried to grin at his feeble joke. 'Then we'll go. *Together.*' This last word seemed to hang above all of them.

Herrick continued, 'Half of us will fight, the others will help the injured.'

He tried not to picture that long, naked slope. Half a cable. One hundred desperate yards.

'What then, sir?' It was the corporal.

'We'll head for the nearest island where we can take stock. Get some – ' he tried not to lick his parched lips, ' – water.'

Pyper said, 'They're moving the boat again, sir.'

They peered over the rim, and Herrick saw the boat was riding up and down in the surf, while three of the natives worked inside and the rest steadied it as best they could while the search for leaks went on.

They must need the boat more urgently than I thought.

Now that he had made some sort of decision, Herrick felt better. He had no idea how many of them would be able to get away, but anything could be faced if the only alternative was being rounded up and slaughtered like beasts.

'*Damn!*' Prideaux scrambled up beside one of his men who was pointing inland. Another party was coming from the direction of the village, and there were many more this time.

Prideaux looked at Herrick. He said nothing, but it was as clear in his eyes as if he had. *This is our only chance.*

Herrick stood up. 'Collect your weapons. *Easy*, lads.' He examined his own pistols and loosened his sword. Thinking of Bolitho. Of all those other times. 'Corporal, select the best marksmen.' He looked at Pyper. 'Stay with Corporal Morrison and make sure he leaves some fit men to carry the wounded.' He gripped his wrist. 'We've not much time.'

Herrick's mind was cringing from the swiftness of events. He tried to concentrate on the boat. The distance from it. If they held off the newcomers, the wounded and their helpers would be killed by the men on the beach. If they charged down and attacked them now, the wounded would be left behind.

He looked at Prideaux's thin features. 'Well? You're the marine. What should I do?'

Prideaux eyed him with surprise. 'Attack now. Leave two sharpshooters with the wounded. When we've taken the boat, the rest of us can cover their retreat. The others from the village will make perfect targets as they come down the slope.' His lips twisted in a brief smile. 'That is how a *marine* would do it.'

Herrick rubbed his chin. 'Makes sense.'

He looked at Pyper. All of them.

'Ready, lads.'

He glanced at the glittering bayonets, the crossbelts of powder and shot. The extra muskets, loaded and slung on anyone with a shoulder to spare.

He drew his sword and saw there was a dried bloodstain on it.

'Follow me.'

It was at that moment, as two of the men hoisted the marine, Watt, that he gave a terrible scream of agony. It seemed to strike everyone motionless, even the natives in and around the boat stood stock-still, their eyes white as they stared up the hillside.

A man called, 'God, the wound is broken, sir!'

Watt screamed again, his legs kicking as the pain tore through him.

There was a crack, and Herrick saw Watt's head jerk back from the corporal's fist.

Morrison gasped, 'Sorry, matey, but we've work to do!'

Prideaux shouted, '*Charge!*' And the handful of marines ran down the slope, yelling enough for a full platoon. Herrick, Pyper and two seamen went with them, eyes blind to everything but the boat and the startled, scattering figures.

Spears were seized and hurled blindly, and one of the seamen fell gasping on the sand, a broken shaft sticking from his chest.

Then they were up to them, and the frantic anger of their attack almost carried them straight into the surf. Pistols banged and bayonets lunged through the powder smoke in a confusion of killing and fury. Three of the natives ran along the beach, but one fell to a marine's musket. The rest lay either dead or wounded around the boat.

Herrick yelled, 'Here they come, lads!'

He waved his sword towards the lurching group of wounded and the two marines who had fallen back to give them some cover. He watched as Prideaux's men began to fire over their heads towards the rushing tide of figures at the top of the slope. Again, the torrent of stones and spears, the air rent with voices.

Then he and Pyper and the remaining seaman clambered around the boat's stem and thrust at it with all their strength, feeling it fighting back, thrusting at them with each lift of breakers around the rocks.

'It's no use.' Pyper was almost sobbing. 'Can't do it. Too heavy.'

Herrick snarled, 'Push! *Harder*, damn your eyes!' He shouted at Prideaux, 'Two more men!'

As he twisted round, the water swirling and clinging to his clothing, he saw the little procession staggering past the body of the speared seaman. They were too slow, and the nearest natives were less than fifty yards behind them.

Prideaux called, 'Man the boat! It's our only chance! We'll all die if we wait here!'

Herrick waded ashore, his sword above his head. He felt half mad with anger and disappointment, but he would not leave those men behind.

'Go to the devil!'

He ran towards the corporal who was carrying Watt bodily over his shoulders like a sack. The others, including the one with the wounded leg, hobbled and hopped after them. Herrick saw that two men had fallen together further away, and before they could get up again were pounced upon and brutally hacked to pieces, despite the sporadic musket-fire from the the beach.

Herrick ran through the reeling men, not knowing what he hoped to do.

The two marines at the rear saw him and yelled, 'No good! Done for!'

One of then threw away his empty pouches and raised his bayoneted musket.

'Come on then, yew bastards! Let's be 'avin yew!'

The other fell choking on blood as a spear hissed out of the sun.

Herrick saw it and heard it, even watched their faces as they came towards him.

He could not see the boat now, not that it mattered. Nobody would escape.

He moved his sword slowly, seeing the crouching figures fanning out on either side. He could sense the power of them, smell them.

The sun was almost in his eyes, so that there was no shadow for him or the solitary marine. It was as if they were already dead.

To one side of the slowly advancing crowd he saw a spear
raise itself carefully and deliberately. *Now*.

The bang, when it came, was almost deafening in the terrible
silence.

Herrick heard startled shouts from behind, and then as if
torn from a man's heart, a strangled cheer.

Herrick said harshly, 'Stand still, man! *Don't look round!*'

The marine, blinded by sweat, his musket and bayonet as
rigid as before, said from one corner of his mouth, 'I'm with
yew, sir!'

Slowly, uncertainly at first, the front rank of natives began
to move back. When another bang shook the air they retreated,
bounding up the slope, seemingly without effort.

Then, and only then, did Herrick turn.

Just inside the rocks was *Tempest*'s launch, a smoking swivel
mounted in the bows. Where the canister has struck, Herrick
neither knew or cared. It must have gone into the sky, for had
it been aimed at the slope it would have killed more of his men
than their attackers. Perhaps the sound, and the sight of the
long launch, with the frigate's quarter boat coming up astern,
had been enough.

Herrick crossed to the marine and clapped him on the
shoulder.

'That was bravely done.'

Together they walked towards the surf, where men were
leaping from the boats to help and support the others through
the shallows.

Bolitho stood quite still on the sand, his hands at his sides,
as he waited for his friend to reach him. But in his mind he
could still see Herrick as moments earlier the launch had thrust
through the rocks after being towed at full speed by the schooner. Herrick, sword in hand, his back to the sea, as he stood
with one marine to face a mob, and certain death.

It was something he would never forget. Nor would he wish
to.

He clasped Herrick's arms and said simply, 'You have too
much courage, Thomas.'

Herrick tried to grin, but the strain prevented it. 'You came,
sir. Said you would.' His head dropped. '*Told them.*'

Bolitho watched, unable to help, shocked to see Herrick's shoulders shaking. *I did this to him.* He looked round at the beach, now empty but for the dead. *For nothing.*

Pyper came up the beach and hesitated. 'All inboard, sir.'

Bolitho said to Herrick, 'Come, Thomas. There is nothing we can do now.'

They passed the abandoned longboat, and it was then that Herrick seemed to come out of his shock. The boat had begun to sink again, the primitive repairs already leaking to the surf's rough motion.

He said, 'Damn thing would have sunk anyway.' He looked at Bolitho steadily. 'It would have served bloody Prideaux right.'

Bolitho was the last to climb into the launch. He paused, the sea surging around his waist, slapping the old sword against his thigh. One day he would meet with Tuke. No ruse, no trick would save him then.

He allowed Allday to haul him over the gunwale.

But this time it had been a defeat.

11

'Make the Best of It'

James Raymond ignored the seamen who were spreading awnings above the quarterdeck, while others swayed out boats for lowering alongside. He had come out to *Tempest* within minutes of her dropping anchor in the mushroom-shaped bay, and was almost beside himself with anger.

Bolitho watched him grimly, seeing his efforts to build a picture for himself of what had happened. Not that it was difficult, especially for one who travelled so far and so often as Raymond.

'I just will not accept it! I cannot believe that a King's ship, a thirty-six-gun frigate to boot, could be thwarted and almost sunk by a damned pirate!'

There was no point in arguing, Bolitho thought wearily. There was enough to do without trying to change Raymond's opinion. One he had been holding and preparing for some while. Probably since his lookout had first sighted the returning vessels. The little schooner had hurried on ahead to prepare him. Then *Tempest*'s silhouette, her missing topgallant mast and yard which had left such an obvious gap to mar her beauty, would have added more fuel to the fire.

He saw Isaac Toby, the carpenter, his owl-like face almost as red as his familiar waistcoat, rolling amongst his depleted crew, pointing at damage, marking a splintered timber with his knife, or indicating something which needed immediate restoration. He would be missing his mate, Sloper, Bolitho thought.

Some of the more badly wounded had already been ferried ashore. The rest had to work all the harder. *Especially now.* He looked across the shining water, knowing Raymond had stopped his ranting to study his reactions. Poised above her reflection like one of a matched pair, the French frigate *Narval* swung easily at her cable. Her awnings were spread, and there were boats in the water, while a solitary cutter pulled around her on guard duty.

Raymond snapped, 'You may well look yonder, Captain. You turn up your nose at a Frenchman because his ideas are different from your own. How d'you think I feel, eh? A representative of King George and a country which supposedly supports the world's finest navy is made to ask for the service of a *foreign* man-of-war! God damn it, Bolitho, if the Emperor of China offered me a ship I'd take her, and double-quick, believe me!' He moved about the deck, his shoes catching on splinters. 'Always the same. I am expected to perform miracles. Opposed by hidebound fools and pig-headed soldiers!' He glared at him, oblivious to the heat. 'Sailors too, it seems!'

Herrick came aft and touched his hat. 'All the wounded listed by the surgeon have gone ashore, sir. I've ordered the boatswain to begin work on the topgallant – '

Raymond interrupted sharply, 'Quite right, too. Make her nice and pretty again, so that Mathias Tuke can have another game with her!'

Bolitho jerked his head and Herrick withdrew. He said, 'Mr Herrick does not warrant that, sir. He is a brave man and an excellent officer. Some good men died, one just this morning.' It had been the wretched marine, Watt. Gwyther had said he was surprised he had survived that far with such a wound. 'I command this ship, and I am responsible.' He looked at Raymond squarely. 'Tuke is cleverer than I thought. Perhaps I only saw what I wanted to see. But either way, it was my decision.' He dropped his voice as Keen hurried past. 'It will only make things worse if we allow personal feelings to become involved.'

Raymond replied, 'I had not forgotten who commands the *Tempest*. And I shall make sure you get a full report when I send my despatches to London. And you do not have to tell me how to behave. I have made my feelings towards you quite clear, I think. So it is quite useless to start asking favours now that your stars are less agreeable, eh?'

'Is that all, sir?'

Bolitho clenched his fists behind him, realizing how neatly he had been goaded into the trap. Maybe he was just too tired, or, like Le Chaumareys, was losing his grip on reality.

'For the present.' Raymond mopped his face. 'I will be calling a conference shortly to plan a campaign against Tuke and any of his associates. If in the process we can recapture the French prisoner for de Barras, then all well and good. Under the circumstances it is the very least we can do.' He sounded less sure as he added, 'De Barras has the authority of his country, and the means to execute his orders. We are not at war, and he at least seems to know what he is about.'

Bolitho thought of the cabin, the rich carpets and the frightened boy with the wine. Above all, de Barras's indifference to brutal and sadistic treatment of his own men.

He made himself ask, 'How did Hardacre take the news?'

Raymond shrugged. 'I am not certain which he grieves over the most. His precious natives who killed his men as well as some of yours, or the fact that he no longer has his own army to crow over! I'll be satisfied only when I get some proper soldiers here. I cannot abide amateurs in any walk of life!'

Raymond moved to the gangway and paused, looking down into his boat.

'There will be a brig from England shortly. She will call here on passage to New South Wales. She can take the guards back to Sydney where they came from. Then there will be no excuse for not sending me some troops.'

Despite his hatred for the man, his hurt over what had happened, Bolitho sensed an inner warning.

The burning village and what Herrick had told him about the natives of North Island made a mockery of Hardacre's hopes. Revenge for what Tuke had done to them had killed Finney's militiamen and had nearly done for Herrick. The old hatreds could soon come alive again and turn island against island, tribe against tribe.

One of the most noticeable things he had seen when *Tempest* had re-entered the bay had been the absence of canoes and swimming villagers. The same girls and young men had been there well enough. On the beaches and below the thick green fronds. But they had kept their distance, as if fearful that by coming too close they would gain some infection and lose their simplicity and safety which they must have come to take for granted.

'And until they arrive, sir?' He already knew the answer.

'The responsibility will be yours, Captain. Hardacre has enough men still to take care of the settlement. The protection of its progress I am giving to you, and will be saying as much in my report. It is a heavy responsibility.' He looked round, his eyes almost hidden in shadow. 'I will be interested to watch your, er, success.' Then with a curt nod to the side party he lowered himself into his boat.

Herrick walked across the deck and said bluntly, 'I could live very well without *that* one!'

Bolitho shaded his eyes to peer at the settlement with its palisades and rough blockhouses. She might be watching the ship, knowing of her husband's eagerness to get out to *Tempest*, if only to add weight to the captain's burden.

Apart from the lack of laughing islanders, things seemed much as before. The little schooner was already being loaded with bales and baskets, and he guessed she would soon be sailing to other islands nearby. To keep trade moving. To regain confidence. Hardacre was taking a great chance, but then he had done that for a long time now.

He said, 'I want this ship ready for sea as quickly as possible. Work the hands while there's daylight, and make sure you put a picket ashore if you're sending anyone for fruit or water.'

Herrick nodded. 'I couldn't help but hear the last thing he said, sir. I think it's damned unfair to hand you the extra role of guarding over the convicts.'

Bolitho smiled gravely. 'The convicts will be no trouble. I doubt if they'll want to stray far from the settlement.' He turned away to watch new cordage being hauled aloft. 'However, we do what we are paid to do.' He walked towards the companionway. 'Tell Noddall . . .' He stopped short.

Herrick looked at him. 'Sir?'

'Nothing. I'd forgotten.' He vanished below.

Herrick walked slowly to the nettings and looked at the inviting beaches. Inviting? He thought of the great bloody stain on the sand, the human fragments rotting in the sun, and shivered. Just to see St Anthony's light in the English Channel once more. To walk beside the Medway, to smell the fruit trees, and the farms. He would not want to stay ashore too long. But to know he would be able to see it again.

Borlase joined him. 'Now, sir, about the promotion to quartermaster. I've a good man in my division.'

Herrick moved his shoulders inside his coat. Like getting back into things. Men had to be moved, a shortage of hands in one watch must be remedied from the other. The whole watch-bill would have to be rearranged, with the unfit men put to work where they would find it less of a burden but still do a good job.

Someone would have to be found to replace poor Noddall.

He turned as the gangway sentry called, 'Jolly boat returnin'!'

Borlase said harshly, 'The pickets are bringing off the two who deserted! They should be flogged senseless after what we've been through!'

'I think not.' Herrick watched the approaching boat, the two figures sitting dejectedly between some marines. 'We need every fit man, and by God are those two going to work!'

He saw Jury coming towards him with one of his petty officers and the carpenter's red waistcoat looming from the opposite direction. Questions, things wanted, things destroyed. He smiled. All in a day's work for any first lieutenant.

It was a mixed gathering. Raymond, very composed and unsmiling, sitting at a large, locally carved table. John Hardacre, his bushy hair and beard, his strange, loosely folded robe very much at odds with Raymond's neat elegance.

Seated at the far end of the room, one leg negligently crossed over the other, *Narval*'s captain, the Comte de Barras, with his senior lieutenant whose name was Vicariot, made bright figures of blue and white, while de Barras's curled wig added another touch of unreality. Both the Frenchmen were so smartly attired that Bolitho felt crumpled by comparison, and when he glanced at Herrick he guessed he was thinking much the same.

A scar-faced overseer from the settlement, a half-caste called Kimura, who looked more like an executioner than anything else, completed the gathering.

Bolitho tried to sit easily in the cane chair, wondering how this place would have changed in a year or so. A big, well-built house and a thriving community of traders and administrators. Clerks and managers, experts on this and that from England. Or would it be like others he had seen in the Great South Sea, overgrown again by the jungle, deserted even by the natives who had once come to depend upon such outposts?

Through a long window, well-screened with plaited mats, he could see the end of the bay, a dark green point of land, with the sea rising beyond it like water penned in a dyke.

Tempest had been at anchor for five days. Days of ceaseless work and short tempers. Three men had been flogged over incidents which at any other time would have been trivial enough to be overcome. Bolitho detested unnecessary punishment, just as he despised those who preferred it to righting the wrongs.

It had been made worse by the nearness of the French ship, the faces lining her gangways to watch the bitter ritual of punishment under the lash.

Bolitho had been ashore several times to report progress to Raymond, to consult with the Corps guards, who had come with the convicts from Sydney, on the matter of security. Also, he had had plenty of opportunity to meet the deported prisoners for himself. Even after all the long months awaiting trial and making the voyage to the opposite end of the earth, they seemed dazed. But they looked well enough, and were not so cowed as when Bolitho had seen some of them aboard the *Eurotas*.

He wondered about the *Eurotas*. Why she could be spared merely to lie idle in the bay. Accommodation ship she was not, and apart from her depleted company, she appeared to provide nothing but a possible way of escape if things went wrong. Bolitho knew that Herrick had been across to her on two occasions to try and obtain men for *Tempest*. He had, by means which Bolitho could only guess at, procured six new hands, all seamen. No matter what it had cost him in patience and humour, they were worth their weight in gold.

No doubt like all the other hints and promises in Sydney somebody would eventually arrive with a new warrant to work the *Eurotas* in the government's service, and she would sail away.

He tried to concentrate on the men around him, to fit them into the puzzle. But it was too easy to think instead of Viola Raymond. He had seen her once only since his return while her husband had been aboard the French frigate enjoying de Barras's hospitality. Just for an hour he had stayed with her. But not alone. To save her as best he could from further gossip, Bolitho had accompanied her to the new clearing where some of the convicts were building a line of huts for their own occupation.

Her silent maid, the only female deportee to be allowed in the Levu Islands, had followed them, looking neither right nor left as they had passed amongst the amateur builders.

He had said, 'There is a brig coming from England soon.' He had looked at her, the way she held her head, the rich hair shining beneath her large straw hat. If anything she was lovelier than ever. 'If you insist on going in her to Sydney, her master cannot refuse. And neither can your husband. You obeyed his wishes. The gesture was made. Nothing can be gained by your staying, and I'll not let him stand by and watch you endanger your health.'

It was then that she had stopped and had taken his hands, pulling him round to face her.

'You don't understand at all, do you, Richard?' She had smiled up at him, her eyes shining. 'What if I did as you suggest? Take the next available ship to England, pack my belongings and go to your house in Falmouth?' She had shaken her head before he could protest. 'I love you dearly, and because of that I *want* to stay. I need to be here! To be hundreds and hundreds of miles away, wondering, fearing for you and waiting for your ship to anchor would only add to my torment. Here, at least, I can see you. Touch you. Be near to you. I know that if I allow us to be parted again, it will be forever. If you are ordered to New South Wales, to India, to the ends of the globe, then I will go to your Falmouth, and gladly.' She had shaken her head again. 'But leave you at James's hands, *never*!'

Bolitho thought about it as he watched Raymond's fingers leafing through his official papers.

She had been right. He had not understood. All he had considered had been her safety, her freedom from Raymond. But love pushed caution aside and made a fool of prudence.

'And now, gentlemen.' Raymond looked up. 'This is what I believe to be our next objective. For myself, the expansion and protection of this settlement and its trade routes is important.' He smiled at de Barras's finely chiselled features. 'And you, *M'sieu le Comte*, will wish to recover your renegade and return to your homeland as originally intended.'

De Barras nodded slightly, his lips pursed, cautious, unwilling to show his hand too soon.

Raymond looked at Hardacre. 'I know how *you* feel about what has happened, but I imagine it has been coming for months. Those who live in the midst of a problem are often the last to be aware it exists.' A gentle smile. 'However, we are here, and whether they like it or not a few natives are going to have to put up with us. This is not one of John Company's concessions now, nor a private enterprise. These islands are claimed by the Crown and are entitled to its protection.'

Bolitho watched de Barras. That last part had made him glance quickly at his lieutenant. Raymond was making his own position very clear, just supposing that the French might also have their eyes on the Levu Islands.

Then he looked at Herrick. Arms folded, blue eyes on the opposite wall. He was feeling out of place, uncomfortable. He was probably thinking of the ship. Repairs done, and all that still awaited his attention.

For a moment he saw Herrick again on that terrible beach. Sword in hand, his face towards a pack of angry, blood-maddened natives. A minute – no, seconds longer, and that chair would now be empty.

Raymond went on smoothly, 'With the assistance of the *Narval* and her excellent crew, I trust that all our objectives can be gained. It is in our interest that the pirate Mathias Tuke and his men be excised and punished without further loss to us.'

Bolitho knew de Barras was looking across at him, to remind him no doubt of their other meeting. They were almost his exact words.

Raymond said, 'In return we will do all we can to recapture the Comte's prisoner.' He looked directly at the French captain. 'I am certain that when I send my despatches to London to announce our success they will be equally well received in Paris, eh, *M'sieu le Comte?*'

De Barras stretched his legs and smiled. 'I understand.'

And so do I. Bolitho would not have believed it, had he not been present. De Barras must have entertained Raymond very well, there was even a goodly supply of wine being carried into the settlement by some of his seamen as Bolitho had arrived. And yet, like all tyrants, de Barras was still open for compliments, ready to accept Raymond's hint of a word in high places which could eventually benefit him in France. If, as Bolitho suspected, de Barras had been given his lonely command to keep him out of his own country until some trouble had been forgotten, then Raymond's casual offer would mean even more.

The door opened slightly and one of Hardacre's servant girls peered inside, obviously overwhelmed by the presence of so much authority.

Raymond snapped, 'See what she wants.'

The half-caste, Kimura, muttered something and then said, 'The chief is here.' He gestured to the window. 'He waits in the yard.'

'Let him wait.' Raymond seemed ruffled by the interruption.

Hardacre said, 'Tinah is a great chief, Mr Raymond. A good friend. It would be wrong to treat him in this fashion.'

'Oh, very well. You go to him if you must.' Raymond eyed him coldly. 'But none of your promises, d'you hear?'

Hardacre strode out, his big sandals flapping on the rush mats. 'I *hear*.'

'Ah well.' Raymond realized the overseer was still present. 'You can leave, too.' He smiled. 'It is hard for them to appreciate progress.' The smile disappeared. 'The youth who came from North Island with the news of the attack has not been found.'

Bolitho said, 'He probably thought he would be seen as a

traitor, sir. But it does prove that even on North Island there are some who trust Hardacre enough to come to him for aid.'

'Maybe. But the damage is done now. Tuke attacked your ship, but that was the deed of a felon and a murderer. Those *friendly* natives tried to kill your people and butchered most of Hardacre's militia. That, in view of what you were *trying* to do at the time, is unforgivable!'

'They did not understand any difference between Tuke's men and my own, and why should they?' Bolitho knew it was useless.

'Well, they will now, damn them!' Raymond swung round in his chair as Hardacre came in again. 'What *is* it?'

Hardacre replied, 'The chief says that his people are ashamed of what happened to my men.' He looked at Bolitho. 'And yours. But the chief of North Island was killed at the first attack. Less stable heads are in charge there now. It has never been the most friendly of islands, and now because their boats are burned they will be in hard times. Our people here are afraid to visit them.'

Raymond sniffed. 'I'm not surprised. And what did you promise them? A ship full of fat pigs and new boats?'

De Barras chuckled.

'I promised that you would give them help, sir, leave them unpunished –'

'*You did what?*'

Hardacre went on stubbornly, 'In return they will bring news of Tuke. Do all they can to help in his capture. They have no cause to like him, and every reason to fear your reprisals.'

Raymond dabbed his mouth. 'Help in his capture, you say?' He looked at de Barras. 'Well now.'

He made up his mind. 'Captain Bolitho. Go and speak with this, er, chief. Tell him you were a personal friend of Captain Cook, anything you like. But get him to talk with you.'

Hardacre followed Bolitho out of the room and stood outside the door breathing heavily, the planks creaking beneath his weight.

'He is a great chief! Not an idiot child!' He turned to

G

Bolitho. 'I could kill that man with less emotion than crushing a beetle.'

Bolitho went down the wooden stairway and towards the glaring sunlight. In the middle of the compound yard, on a small, ornate stool, the chief was sitting very erect and still, his dark eyes fixed on the empty gibbet. He was younger than Bolitho had expected, with thick, bushy hair and a small beard. His garment was of green cloth embroidered with coloured beads, and around his neck he wore a simple loop of gold wire.

His eyes shifted to Bolitho as Hardacre said, 'Tinah, this is the English captain. From the ship.' He hesitated before adding, 'A good man.'

Tinah's eyes had not flickered or moved from Bolitho's face during the introduction, but now he smiled, suddenly and disarmingly.

Bolitho asked, 'What you have told Mr Hardacre about the pirates. Is it possible you can find them for us?'

'Everything is possible.' His voice was deep, his accent halting, but Bolitho doubted if anyone could have looked more like a chief. 'We have peace now. We wish to keep it, Captain. Your men were attacked. But what would your heart say if you saw your women being used and then killed, your home burned before your eyes? Would you stop to say, these men are good, those are bad?' He raised a thick, intricately carved rod and drove it hard into the ground. 'No. You say, *kill*!'

Herrick came out of the building and looked at the seated chief and his small group of retainers who were waiting by the gates of the compound.

He said, 'Pardon the interruption, sir, but Mr Hardacre is wanted upstairs.' He smiled. 'I almost said, *on deck*, sir. It seems the gallant French captain wishes to enquire about water and provisions on the surrounding islands.'

Hardacre nodded grimly. 'I'll go. It is vital that his ship enters each anchorage in a peaceful manner. I don't want these people to see him as an enemy.' He added, 'No matter what *I* think.'

Herrick looked hard at the chief. 'There was a man taken prisoner. His name was Finney.'

'I knew Finney.' Tinah glanced at the building. 'I did not tell my friend how he died. Just that he did die.'

Herrick asked harshly, 'Can you tell me?'

'If your captain wishes.' The chief sighed. 'North Island is not like this one. Finney was tied to a stake and covered with clay taken from the stream. His breath was kept for him by a reed through the clay.' His eyes were fixed on Herrick's. 'Then his body was held over a very slow fire.'

Herrick turned away, revolted. 'Baked alive, for God's sake!'

Tinah shrugged. 'My father told me of such things. But in North Island . . .'

Herrick nodded. 'I know. They are different from your people.'

The chief watched Herrick as he returned to the building. 'That must be the strong one. The man who stood alone.' He nodded. 'Yes, I have heard of him.'

Hardacre came back and said, 'It is done.' He looked at Bolitho. 'If that's all, Captain?'

Bolitho touched his hat. 'Yes.'

Hardacre and the chief obviously had things to discuss. A rift to heal before it could destroy both of them.

In Raymond's room again he found the others taking wine.

The other door opened, and a servant stood aside to allow Viola Raymond to enter.

Raymond introduced her to de Barras, who bowed from the waist and kissed her hand, saying, 'My dear lady, I was so grieved that you did not come to my humble quarters with your husband, the Resident.'

She replied, 'Thank you, *M'sieu le Comte*, perhaps another time.'

The French lieutenant bowed stiffly and mumbled something in very broken English.

Viola looked at Herrick and held out her hand. 'Why, Lieutenant, it is so nice to see you again.'

Herrick's tan hid what must have been a blush. 'Er, thank you, ma'am. It's good to see you, too. Indeed it is.'

She crossed to Bolitho and offered her hand. 'Captain?'

Bolitho touched her fingers with his lips. 'Mrs Raymond.'

Their eyes met, and he felt the gentle pressure of her fingers on his.

As she moved away to speak with the servant, de Barras walked to Bolitho's side and said softly, 'Ah, now I think I know why she did not come to my ship, *oui*?'

He returned to his lieutenant, laughing quietly to himself.

Herrick whispered, 'Did you hear that, sir? Impudent dog!' He turned his back to the others. 'But you see how it goes, sir? You must take care!'

Bolitho looked past him, watching her hair lying across her shoulders. *Take care*. Herrick did not know what it was like to stand meekly by and watch the one you loved so dearly held at arm's length.

The only bright piece of news had been that brought by the young chief, Tinah. If they could run the pirates to earth, and destroy their power once and for all, there was the very real possibility that *Tempest* would be ordered home, to England. And then?

Herrick watched his captain sadly. It was hopeless. It was like telling a bull not to charge, a cat not to chase mice.

He saw a table being prepared in the adjoining room and counted the chairs.

Well, we might as well make the best of it while it lasts, he decided.

12

The Worst Enemy

The French frigate weighed and put to sea two days after the conference in Raymond's spartan headquarters.

Her departure seemed to restore some of the readily offered hospitality from the islanders, and it was rare not to find some of them on *Tempest*'s deck or alongside in their swift-moving canoes. Bartering, bringing gifts, or merely watching the hands at work on the dwindling list of repairs, it all helped to ease the tension.

The islanders had no cause to fear or dislike the French sailors, and in fact they had had no opportunity of meeting many of them. Only small parties had gone ashore to gather fuel or supplies, each escorted by heavily armed men.

Bolitho had decided that despite or because of their simple standards and judgements the islanders had sensed the oppression aboard the *Narval* as he had done, and not understanding it had rejected it.

Life aboard *Tempest* was hard enough, especially at anchor in a sheltered bay, with the sun seeming to grow hotter each hour to add to the discomfort. But in the dog watches it was rare not to hear the scrape of a shantyman's fiddle or the slap of bare feet as off-watch seamen took part in one of their ritual hornpipes.

From the Frenchman they had heard nothing. Just the chime of a watch-bell, the occasional order being piped between decks. Cowed, humiliated, the ability to seize even the smallest enjoyment had been crushed out of them.

With *Narval* gone from the bay, Bolitho soon discovered that Raymond intended to keep his word on the matter of responsibility. When not being employed aboard, *Tempest*'s specialists, like the carpenter and the cooper, the sailmaker and the boatswain, would be required on the island, using their skills to help with the modest but much needed building programme, both of huts and the blockhouses to defend them.

The surgeon too was more on land than in his sickbay, tending to the wounded and the rarer illnesses amongst the villagers. It was an arrangement which suited Gwyther very well, Bolitho knew, and when he returned to the ship he rarely appeared without some tropical find, a violently coloured plant or some strange-looking fruit.

Captain Prideaux attended to the siting of the new blockhouses, despite the obvious resentment of the two Corps officers.

When they had protested to him he had snapped, 'You keep telling me that this or that is not your job. That you should not have been sent here by the Governor of New South Wales anyway, and I am heartily sick of it! In a King's ship you have to be ready to attempt anything, no matter how you may feel about it.'

One of them had replied hotly, 'You insult us, sir!'

Prideaux had looked almost happy. 'Then I will give satisfaction, to both of you if need be!'

To his disappointment they had retired with some haste.

As he had walked through the village or down along the glistening beach Bolitho had wondered what *Narval* was doing. De Barras had promised to make a long patrol around North Island and on to the next group. To see, and be seen. If he was lucky enough to flush out one or more of Tuke's vessels, he would certainly exploit the victory and press on with his search.

Bolitho had enough to keep him occupied for most hours of every day. In mounting heat, he went about his duties with impassive determination, knowing Raymond was waiting to complain, to criticize, if he lowered his guard.

It was common enough for sea officers to do what he was doing. Even the commander of a modest sloop-of-war or brig was expected to show his King's authority when need be. As Prideaux had hotly remarked, *no matter how you may feel about it*!

But he felt vulnerable, knowing she was never far from him

and yet rarely able to meet her without Raymond being present. Was Raymond trying to pretend that everything was as before as far as she was concerned? Or was he merely enjoying Bolitho's dismay and want whenever they met?

And although he tried to tell himself he was being too protective, he was worried for her health. She spent some of her time accompanying the surgeon on his rounds, and did not spare herself or share the attitude of the islanders – *when it bears heavy on you, stop work.*

Lieutenant Keen was employed in charge of the shore parties, and Bolitho had seen him more than once with a native girl of slender beauty who seemed to regard him as one of the gods. In his turn, Keen watched her with an expression of one completely lost. Bolitho had found himself feeling depressed and envious of their blissful understanding.

By the end of the month Herrick took him on a tour of inspection of the ship, and Bolitho shared some of his well-justified satisfaction. Under the hands of his craftsmen, the cunning uses of wood and tar, paint and hemp, *Tempest* showed little sign of the terrible moment when she had been snared and mauled in Tuke's well-laid trap.

Later he reported as much to Raymond, who for once had little complaint to make, nor did he offer his usual comparison with the efficient de Barras.

Instead he said, 'I am uneasy about the brig from England.'

'It is common enough to be delayed, sir. It is a demanding passage around the Horn.'

Raymond did not seem to hear him. 'I feel deaf and blind here. I get no messages from Sydney, and nobody brings me the support I need if I am to make anything of this place.'

Bolitho watched him guardedly. So that was it. Raymond was feeling left out, abandoned, as he himself had done more than once over the past years.

He was saying, 'I do not want another *Eurotas* incident. Nor do I want another *anything* until I am ready here. It is as I suspected. I am always learning how misguided I have been to trust others. That damned chief, Hardacre's *friend*, for instance. Where is the intelligence he promised, eh? Tuke's head in exchange for my leniency? My *weakness*, he thinks, no doubt!

And Hardacre, mooning about his affairs like the mad monk himself!' He sank into a chair and stared at a half-empty wine bottle.

Bolitho said, 'I understand that the expected brig is the *Pigeon*, sir?'

'Yes.' He looked at him suspiciously. 'What of it?'

'I know her master, or did the last time I heard of her whereabouts. William Tremayne. He comes from my home town. Used to be in one of the Falmouth packets. He'd never allow himself to be hoodwinked by Tuke. When you've been master of a packet, had to sail alone through every sort of sea to the ends of the globe, you must learn to fight off everything to stay alive.'

Raymond shifted uneasily. 'I hope you are correct about him.'

'I would like to take my ship and patrol to the sou'-east of the group, sir.'

'No.' Raymond glared at him. 'I need your presence here. When I have heard from de Barras, or the brig, I will know what to do. Until then, I will trouble you to continue with your work.'

He said it so vehemently that Bolitho wondered what else was worrying him.

'Suppose, for instance, the King of Spain has *not* withdrawn his claims to possessions and trading facilities, eh? For all we know there might be six Spanish sail-of-the-line sweeping right through these waters!' He shook his head. '*No*. You'll remain at anchor.'

Bolitho left the room. If only there was some way of getting word to Commodore Sayer in Sydney, not that he could do much. It was strange when you thought about it. Three ships, the *Hebrus*, Sayer's elderly sixty-four, *Tempest*, and now the overdue brig *Pigeon*. As unmatched as any vessels could be, and yet each of their senior officers was a Cornishman, and each was known to the other.

As he reached the pier he saw Hardacre striding from his schooner.

'Good. You'd better come, too.' He sounded troubled. Angry. 'Tinah has news. Of the pirates and that other bloody madman, de Barras.'

Once more in Raymond's room Hardacre exploded. 'Did you know that de Barras has been amongst the islands in the north, acting like Caesar! Canoes have been fired on, and the whole area is smouldering like a tinder-barrel! In God's name, what were you thinking of to leave him the field, to do as he pleases?'

'Control yourself!' Raymond sounded startled nevertheless. 'How did you hear of all this?'

'At least I am still trusted by some of them!' His massive chest heaved painfully. 'The chief sent word. Tuke's anchorage is at Rutara.' He jerked his head towards the ceiling. 'The sacred island.' He looked at Bolitho. 'Do you know it?'

'Only from sparse detail.'

'Aye.' Hardacre strode this way and that, his hands clasped as if in prayer. 'It is a harsh place, without much water apart from rain pools. Just the sort of hole that a man like Tuke would use for a short while.' He sounded worried. 'No native would dare land there.'

Raymond licked his lips. 'Well, that is good news, surely, if we can trust on it.'

'*Trust?*' Hardacre looked at him with unmasked contempt. 'It has cost Tinah several of his men to get it, and will probably turn some of the other islands against him for helping *you*.'

Raymond looked down at the table, his fingers drumming on it, loud in the sudden silence.

'De Barras will anchor off North Island after he has carried out his search. You can send your schooner to him forthwith. I will write a despatch for his immediate attention.'

'She is the only vessel I have here at my disposal!'

'That is not my affair. This is.' Raymond eyed him coldly. 'I can commandeer the schooner, you know?'

Hardacre turned to the door. Beaten. 'I will see the master. Now.' He slammed the door.

Raymond breathed out very slowly. 'Well, well, Captain. Moments ago we were in the dark. Now, if it is to be believed, the news sounds promising. Very.' He gave a thin smile. 'Perhaps it is as well that the role of Tuke's executioner falls to the French. If there are repercussions in high places, we are in a stronger position.'

'I would like to go too, sir. If not instead of, then with de Barras.'

'You think he will be unable to deal with Tuke? Because of your own rough handling, is that it?' His smile broadened. 'Really, you disappoint me to show your pique so openly!'

'It is none of those things, sir.' He looked away, seeing the man dangling from *Narval*'s stern, dying as he had watched. 'Two ships would be better than one. I respect Tuke's cunning, just as I mistrust de Barras's ability to contain his own brutality. These islands could become a battleground because of him!'

'You had your chance, Captain Bolitho. The objectives are clearer cut now, and I think de Barras will be eager to fulfil my requirements when he reads the despatch I will send to him.'

'More promises?'

Raymond ignored it. 'See that you are in readiness to weigh anchor when I need you. The trap is closing around the pirate, but we still have our work to do here. If only that damned brig would come!'

As Bolitho turned to leave Raymond added casually, 'The *Eurotas*. What is your, er, report on her?'

Bolitho paused. 'She is guarded by her own people, and my boats pull round her after dark.'

'I would have been displeased to hear the contrary.' Raymond tapped the table again. 'No, I was referring to her readiness for sea.'

'As ordered.' Bolitho watched him, trying to see through his prim severity. 'As ready as my own command.'

'Good. That helps me to plan.'

Bolitho returned to the pier and watched his gig pulling towards him. Raymond's attitude over the transport was a mystery. *Eurotas* had no master, and a depleted company. If Raymond imagined she could be used beyond an extreme emergency he was going to be disappointed. *Unless* . . . He rubbed his chin thoughtfully. Unless he intended to transfer his papers and plans on board her and leave the settlement to Hardacre. Could it be he was inwardly afraid of the unseen events? *I feel deaf and blind here.* Sailors were used to relying on their own meagre resources, but perhaps men like Raymond, trained and educated to ways of Parliament and government, could not survive without news and guidance.

Bolitho awoke violently from a heavy sleep, fighting aside his sheet as he tried to discover what had disturbed him. Then he saw a pair of eyes glowing in the gloom like pale lamps, and he remembered that Orlando, the giant Negro, had been given the chance of acting as his servant. It had apparently been Allday's idea soon after Noddall's death, and as he was still going about his new duties, Bolitho assumed his coxswain was satisfied. Although with the amount of cursing and blaspheming he had heard, he might have expected otherwise.

'What is it, man?'

He struggled to sit up, his practised mind taking in that the cot was steady and unmoving, and only the normal sounds of a vessel at anchor penetrated the cabin. It was stuffy, almost airless, and the effort of moving made the sweat trickle across his bare skin.

Orlando bobbed his head and dragged Bolitho's sheet from the cot, bowing to feel for his shoes.

Allday loomed through the darkness. 'Boat alongside, Captain.' He peered at the Negro. 'Mr Raymond wants you ashore. The master of the *Pigeon* is with him, it seems.'

Bolitho lowered his legs to the deck, grappling with the news. Yesterday, his hilltop lookout had reported the sight of a sail to the south-east. Within hours it was recognized as the overdue brig *Pigeon*, and once more Bolitho had felt the excitement run through his ship like a fresh breeze. News from home. Keeping a memory alive. All things to all men.

Some of the interest had transmitted itself to the settlement and fires had been lit to bring the heavy scent of wood-smoke and cooked meat to the secluded bay.

And then the wind had dropped, and when darkness had swept over the islands the brig had anchored, to await the safety of the dawn and a secure passage through the reefs.

He heard feet on deck, the rattle of blocks as a boat was hoisted outboard. That would be Herrick's doing. Making sure his captain had his proper gig and not one of Hardacre's scarred longboats.

He asked, 'What is the time?'

Allday said, 'Morning watch has just been called, Captain.' He rubbed his chin. 'The *Pigeon*'s master must have been brought in by boat.'

Bolitho stared at him. How easily Allday got to the bones of it. It had to be something very urgent to bring a brig's captain ashore after such a long and wearying voyage from England. Was it war with Spain? Would *Tempest* be ordered home? He thought of it carefully, matching his need against that of his training. She would be safe in Cornwall, while he . . . He swore as Orlando jabbed his stomach accidentally with a massive elbow.

Allday lit one of the lanterns and grinned. 'That's the best of being mute, Captain. You never have to apologize!'

Bolitho peered at his reflection in a mirror. Naked and tousled, his hair black across his forehead, he looked more like a vagrant than a captain.

But Orlando bustled about him, fetching lukewarm water from the galley, and while Allday got busy with soap and razor, laid out Bolitho's clothing as instructed. He did it far better than he should after so brief a training, and Bolitho suspected the Negro had once served in some great estate, or had been in a position to watch others attending their masters. Perhaps, like his ability to speak, his memory had been cut short with some terrible experience.

Herrick came aft and tapped the door. 'Gig's ready, sir.' He watched the little scene in the cabin. 'I see that I need not have worried.'

Bolitho slipped into his clean shirt and allowed Allday to fasten the neckcloth. 'No more new information?'

'No.' Herrick looked tired. 'But the *Pigeon* has brought some bad news, I think. The good always seems to drag its feet.'

Bolitho snatched up his hat. 'We will see.' He hesitated, allowing Allday to hurry on ahead to his gig. 'Be ready, Thomas. We may have to weigh at dawn.'

'Aye.' He had obviously thought of little else. 'There are only the shore parties unaccounted for. Young Valentine Keen will have to manage.'

Bolitho ran lightly up the companion ladder and felt the

cooler air on his cheek. Just past four in the morning, and the decks moist under his shoes. He peered up at the crossed yards and thought the stars were already fading between the shrouds and neatly furled sails.

Men stood aside, and others doffed their hats as he lowered himself into the boat. Through open gunports he saw blurred faces, the watch below trying to guess what was happening. Where he was going in such haste.

As the gig rushed across the smooth water he sat in silence watching the trailing phosphorescence around the dipping blades, the surge of foam from the stem. He saw the *Eurotas* loom above the fast-moving boat and heard the harsh challenge, '*Boat ahoy!*' and Allday's prompt reply, '*Passing!*'

With so many rumours of unrest and trouble amongst the islands, the ship's sentries were more alert than usual. Failure to acknowledge a challenge might bring a blast of canister into the boat.

Bolitho saw the lights beyond the pier and knew the whole settlement must be awake.

'*Oars!*'

Bolitho watched the pier rising above him and heard the clink of metal as the bowman caught a ringbolt with his boat-hook.

Then he was up and striding along the pier, marvelling that the place had become so familiar to him after so short a stay.

He passed one of Prideaux's pickets, the marine's crossbelts gleaming white in the darkness. Through the wide gates and past the gibbet where he saw the overseer, Kimura, waiting for him.

'Well?' He could smell the man. Sweat and the pale drink which tasted like rum and which would kill if taken in quantity.

Kimura said in his strange voice, 'They wait upstairs, sir. They not tell me nawthin'.'

After the gig and the rough track from the pier Raymond's room seemed blinding with light.

Raymond was standing in an ankle-length satin coat, his hair ruffled as he glared at the open door. Hardacre was sitting in a chair, his fingers interlaced across his belly, face very grim.

And beside a screened window the *Pigeon*'s master made a shaggy contrast, bringing the ocean right into the room.

William Tremayne had changed little, Bolitho decided, as he

strode towards him and gripped his hand. Broad and short, with spiky grey hair, and eyes so dark they glittered in the lanterns like black coals.

Tremayne grinned. 'Dick Bolitho!' He wrung his hand, his palm as rough as timber. 'How are ye, me 'andsome? Still a captain, eh?' He chuckled, the sound coming out of the depths to bring Bolitho instant memories. 'I'd thought you master o' the King's Navy at least be now!'

Raymond said sharply, 'Yes, yes! Please sit down, the pair of you. The fond greetings can wait.'

Tremayne peered round under his chair, his dark eyes innocent.

'*Now* what is it?' Raymond seemed to be verging on an explosion.

Tremayne looked at him sadly. 'I am sorry, sir. I thought you were talking to a dog an' was looking for him, like!'

Raymond cleared his throat, and Bolitho saw that his hands were shaking badly.

He said, 'The news is serious, Bolitho.'

Tremayne interrupted cheerfully, 'Aye, 'tis that, Dick. The whole of Europe is quaking fit to bust open!'

Bolitho watched Raymond's hands. 'Spain?'

'Worse.' Raymond seemed to have difficulty in forming his words. 'There has been a bloody revolution in France. The mobs have taken the country, thrown the King and his Queen into prison, and they may already be dead, even as we sit here. According to these despatches, thousands are being hunted down and beheaded in the streets. Anyone of noble birth, or touching on the smallest authority, is being taken and butchered. Our channel ports are crammed with refugees.'

Bolitho felt his mouth go dry. Revolution in France. It did not seem possible. There had been food riots and disorders, but so had there been in England after the war. He could well imagine the effect of the news at home. Amongst the foolish and unthinking there would be short-lived enjoyment at seeing an old enemy brought down in confusion. And then would come the cold logic and understanding. The might of France separated only by the English Channel, and with the rule of Terror at its head.

While he had been worrying about *Tempest*'s role, or had taken the news from Timor to Sydney about the *Bounty* mutiny, the real world had been put to the torch.

Raymond said, 'It will mean war.' He looked at the wall as if expecting to see an enemy. 'But nothing like the last one. By comparison that will be remembered as a skirmish!'

Tremayne eyed him curiously and then said to Bolitho, 'It all started last July. May have turned into something worse b'now. But still, I reckon it'll seem like good news to the Frenchie, Genin, or however you pronounces it.'

Bolitho looked at Raymond. *'Genin?'*

'Yes. Yves Genin. One of the minds behind the revolution. Yesterday he had a price on his head as far as we were concerned. Now . . .'

Bolitho stared at him. 'Is that the man de Barras wants to capture?' He saw the uncertainty change to guilt. 'You *knew*! All this while and you knew Genin was no felon, but a man wanted for political reasons!'

'De Barras entrusted me with the news, certainly.' Raymond tried to recover his composure. 'I do not have to tell my subordinates everything. Anyway, what is it to you? If de Barras succeeds in taking Genin alive it is his affair. He will be serving new masters himself when he returns to France.'

Tremayne said gruffly, 'He'd be a fool to go. They'd have his head in a basket before he could say "knife". If half the things I've heard are true, it must be like Hades in Paris.'

Hardacre spoke for the first time, his voice very slow and level. 'You do not understand a word, do you, *Mr* Raymond?' He stood up and walked to the nearest window and threw aside the blind. 'Captain Bolitho can see it, even I, a landsman, can understand, but *you*?' His voice rose slightly. 'You are so full of your own greed and importance you see *nothing*. There has been a revolution in France. It may even spread to England, and God knows there are some who will never get justice without it. But *out here*, in the islands which you only see as stepping-stones to your damned future, what does it really mean?' He strode across to the table and thrust his beard at Raymond. 'Well, tell me, *damn your eyes*!'

Bolitho said quietly, *'Easy*, Mr Hardacre.' He turned to the table. 'Had you told me that Genin was the man who had found sanctuary with Tuke, I might have foreseen some of this. Now it may be too late. If Tuke knows about the revolution, he will see Genin not merely as a useful hostage but as a means to an end. Genin is no longer a fugitive, he represents his country, as much as you or I do ours.'

Raymond looked up at him, his eyes glazed. 'The *Narval*? Is that it?'

Bolitho looked away, sickened. 'When *Narval*'s people are told of the uprising in France they'll tear de Barras and his lieutenants to pieces.'

Tremayne said bluntly, 'I reckon he'll know b'now. I heard of two French packets which rounded the Horn within days o' me. The news will be across the whole ocean, if I'm any judge.'

Bolitho tried to think without emotion. All the sea fights, the names of captains, French and English alike, which had become a part of history. History which he had helped to fashion. As had Le Chaumareys.

This great sea was alive with countless craft of every kind. From lordly Indiamen to brigs and schooners, and down further still to the tiny native vessels which abounded here. Like insects in a forest, or minute sea creatures. Yes, the news would spread quickly enough.

In the seven months since the revolution had begun the whole world might have changed yet again.

Only one thing was clear and stark, like a wreck on a reef.

Tuke would capture the *Narval*. It was so simple it made him want to walk out into the darkness. De Barras's men would rise to their new banner willingly. After the barbarous way they had been made to live and serve de Barras, it would be like a flood bursting.

And then Tuke would emerge in his new role, not merely a troublesome pirate, but a real force to be reckoned with. Raymond was correct in one thing. It would mean war. England would never stand by and watch a new France expanding at her expense. Every ship would be needed desperately. They had been unready for a clash with Spain over trade concessions. What would they do when confronted with a freshly blooded France?

Tuke, with his small but unchallenged flotilla of vessels, would do as he pleased, take what he wanted. Found an empire if he so wished. He looked at Raymond again. And he had known about Genin all the time.

Tremayne said, 'I will put to sea tomorrow.' He grinned. '*Today*, that is.'

Raymond said tonelessly, '*Pigeon* is carrying despatches for the Governor of New South Wales.'

Tremayne winked. 'And for Commodore Sayer. He'll be writing fresh orders for *you*, Dick, double-quick!'

Hardacre leaned over the sill and sniffed the air. 'Light soon now.' Without turning he said, 'And my schooner is out looking for de Barras. If Tuke already knows about these things, he'll come out of hiding. He'll not risk attack from a frigate. The *Narval* would pound his little vessels to boxwood before they got in range.'

Bolitho remembered the powerful guns, *Tempest*'s topgallant mast plunging down to the deck, killing and maiming as it went.

Almost to himself he said, 'All Tuke has to do is wait. If de Barras learns the news, he'll be even more desperate to recapture his prisoner. His ship is all he has now. Without her, he is as good as dead.'

Tremayne stood up, his sea-boots creaking. 'I'll be off directly, Dick. If you have any despatches, I'd be obliged to get 'em afore noon.' He tried to grin. 'But you're all safe and snug here. Your fifth-rate and th' big transport in the bay. You could hold off an army, eh?'

Raymond spoke up sharply. 'De Barras is no longer our concern. This settlement is. I will be getting more men and supplies soon. Once they arrive, Tuke and his followers will sheer off and go to another hunting-ground.'

Tremayne regarded him calmly. 'If you think that . . .' He turned away. 'I'll have a boat alongside *Tempest* till an hour afore I up-anchors. Send your despatches into her.' He gripped Bolitho's hand. 'I'll tell 'em about you, Dick, when I drops the anchor in Carrick Road again. I often sees your sister. I'll pass it kindly to her.'

'Thank you, William. But I may be there before you.'

As the other captain left the room Bolitho felt suddenly heavy. It was like an evil dream, when nobody would listen or understand what you were trying to say.

With Tuke on the rampage, and the forces of authority unable or unwilling to contest his power, the islands would fall on one another's throats as in days past. The spear and the war club would lay the islands open for traders and pirates to plunder as they thought fit.

He saw Hardacre watching him. *He knew.* A betrayal. There was no other word for it.

But would the French sailors rise against their officers? No matter what Tuke or Yves Genin told them, could they bring themselves to mutiny and smash down all they had been disciplined to obey without question?

When a nation rose against its King and turned murder loose on the streets it could face up to almost anything, Bolitho decided grimly.

He said, 'I am requesting permission to put to sea, sir. I'll find de Barras and tell him what we know. It would be far better to send him and his ship away than to bring superior forces down on our heads by remaining silent.'

'No.' One word, and yet it rebounded around the room like an iron shot.

Hardacre said, 'Then I'll be down to the village and speak with Tinah. There are things to prepare.' He glanced at Bolitho. 'I've no doubt you wish to discuss matters, too!'

As the door closed behind him Raymond said, 'I have my own responsibilities, and you are here to support me to the best of your ability.'

'I know my orders, sir.' Was it possible to sound so calm, when all he wanted to do was pull Raymond by the lapels of his beautiful coat and shake him until his face was blue.

'Good. In my opinion de Barras will either defeat Tuke or return to France if he learns what has happened. Either way it is no longer our affair. War will come, if it has not already begun, and we must prepare the Levu Islands as instructed.' His mouth hardened. 'And I imagine that you will be able to drive Tuke's schooners away, should they come too close, eh?'

'D'you know what I think, sir?' Bolitho leaned out of a

window and gripped the sill to prevent his hands from shaking. 'I believe that there will be no bases here, not now, nor any time in our lives. The war we knew was a sounding-brass, the one to come will be fought with giants. There will be neither need nor time for islands and governors to control them.' He drew in a breath very slowly, tasting the sea, feeling it pull at him. 'No supplies or soldiers will come either.'

Raymond exclaimed, 'You're mad! What do you think I was sent for?'

Bolitho did not face him. 'Think about it. I was kept out here because of you. Because I challenged your authority five years ago and stood between you and a man you wronged and allowed to go into oblivion. Because of other, more personal matters also, you used your skills to maroon me here. De Barras is another. But he was driven out of France too late. By then his sort had created anger and hatred, which in turn will try to destroy our world, too. And you? Do you not think it strange that you have joined our little world?'

When he received no reply he turned and saw Raymond staring at the table, his open despatches spread between his out-thrust arms.

Then he said hoarsely, 'You are wrong. Of course I will get support. I have worked all my life for proper recognition. I will not stand by and see it all . . .' He lurched to his feet, his eyes blazing. '*I am the governor here!* You will do as I say!'

They stayed quite still, facing each other like strangers.

Then, as Bolitho made to leave, he heard voices in the compound and feet on the stairs outside.

It was neither Hardacre nor his overseer, but Lieutenant Keen. He was dressed only in shirt and breeches, and he looked beside himself with anxiety.

'I am sorry to disturb you, sir.'

He looked so wretched that Bolitho took his arm and guided him out on to the stairway beside another window.

'Tell me.'

'I have a friend, sir. She, she . . .'

'Yes, I have seen her.' He still could not even guess. 'Continue.'

'I was with her. I had attended to my duties with the working party and seen them in their huts, and then . . .' Sweat ran down his face as he blurted out, 'In the name of God, sir, I believe there is fever amongst us!' He turned away, his shoulders shaking. 'She just lies there. She cannot speak. I didn't know what to do.' He broke down completely.

Bolitho stared past him at the trees and the glow of water beyond. Another dawn? It was more like the day of reckoning. *I must think.*

'I'll come with you.' He strode back into the room and searched amongst the litter of papers until he found something to write on. 'I must send a message to the pier. For Allday.'

Raymond asked dully, 'What are you muttering about?'

Bolitho said, 'I would suggest you close the settlement gates, sir. There may be fever on the island.'

Raymond's jaw dropped. 'Impossible! You are just trying to parry aside my orders!' He saw Bolitho's expression and added, 'Your lieutenant is mistaken! *He must be!*'

Bolitho walked from the room. Revolution on the other side of the world, and the islands waiting to watch their new masters fighting amongst themselves. And now, like a trident from hell, had come the worst blow of all. The one enemy which came from within, and from which there might be no quarter.

13

Volunteers

Bolitho knelt on a rush mat and looked at the young girl. In the hut, which had been erected a few days earlier by some of *Tempest*'s working parties, there was almost complete silence, and Bolitho was conscious of it. As if the surrounding trees, even the island, were listening. Above his head he heard the quiet buzz of insects hitting Keen's lanterns, and the young lieutenant's irregular breathing as he looked over his shoulder.

He had the girl's wrist in his hand, but there was barely any movement in it. Her smooth skin felt wet, and the beat of her heart was fast and urgent.

Hardacre came into the hut, brushing between a marine picket and two natives as he strode under the lantern light. He ran his big hands across the girl's body and then looked up at Keen's anxious face.

'She has the fever. How much do you care for her?'

Keen answered brokenly, 'With everything I have. She must live. She *must*!'

Hardacre stood up. 'Cover her well. No matter if she tries to throw it off, keep her warm.'

He looked at Bolitho and walked with him out of the hut. The sky was much paler and some birds had started to sing.

'It has come to the islands before. Last year. Early. Many died. They have little resistance.' He glanced at the hut door. 'I am afraid your lieutenant will lose his friend.' His grim features softened. 'They hardly know a word of each other's language. I have watched them together. She is Malua, Tinah's sister. She will be much missed.' He studied Bolitho gravely. 'I will go to the village. They have certain roots, herbs also.

There might be a chance.' He shrugged. 'But who knows what may follow?'

Bolitho heard feet on sand and saw Allday hurrying towards him.

'You were supposed to take my message to Mr Herrick!'

Allday looked at him calmly. 'Aye, Captain. I sent my second coxswain with the gig. He's a fair hand.' He squared his shoulders. 'I know about the fever. And I've seen what it can do, an' that's no error. My place is here. With you.'

Bolitho looked away, deeply moved by Allday's staunch loyalty, despairing because of what it really meant. For both of them.

Keen came out of the hut, his eyes very bright. 'She seems easier, sir.'

Bolitho nodded. *How we delude ourselves when the worst is about to happen.*

'Hardacre has gone for aid. He is the best hope.'

Keen sounded dazed. 'But I thought the surgeon would come, sir?'

Bolitho turned towards the dawn sky. 'You must know, Mr Keen, what might well happen. To all of us. The fever may be local and easily held. Again, many diseases are new to these islands, their cure unknown as they were brought by outsiders. Like ourselves. *But –*' he watched the dismay clouding Keen's face, 'we have to think of the ship and what we are ordered to do. To bring Mr Gwyther ashore would deprive the ship of help should she need it. For once he comes I cannot allow him to return until we know the worst.' He forced a smile. 'Or the best.'

Keen nodded jerkily. 'Yes, sir. Yes, I think I understand. Now.'

Bolitho watched his emotions, his anguish. How well he knew him. To think it should come to this.

Almost harshly he said, 'So we must be about it. You are my second-in-command. I believe you have Mr Pyper ashore with you, so from today he will be acting-lieutenant. See to it. I have already passed word to Mr Herrick to appoint both Mr Swift, and Mr Starling, master's mate, to the same positions. We will need all our skills, and it were better that we have as

many with the proper authority as we can. Although from what
I have learned from my people these past months, I would
promote every man-Jack if I were free to do so!'

Allday said, 'Here comes another, Captain.' He added
hurriedly, 'Be easy with him. He thinks he is doing the best he
can.'

Orlando's tall figure came out of the grey light, shining and
running with water as he squelched over the sand towards the
huts.

Bolitho looked towards the bay but the ships were still
hidden in shadows. Orlando had taken it on himself to swim
ashore. He must have heard Herrick giving his new orders, or
someone spreading word of the fever. Either way, he had
come. Unable to speak or ask, he was just standing there,
watching Bolitho as if he expected a blow in the face.

Bolitho said quietly, 'I am afraid there will be no cabin for
you to fuss over, and precious little of anything else for a
while.' He reached out impetuously, as Allday had seen him do
many times, and touched Orlando's arm. 'So I am placing you
in charge of our food supplies.'

The Negro lowered himself noiselessly on to his knees and
nodded very slowly.

As Bolitho turned away Allday touched the Negro with his
shoe. 'Stand up, you ignorant bugger!' He grinned to hide his
sadness. 'Can't you see what you're doing to him, man?'

By the time the first sunlight had touched the hills and
filtered through the trees towards the bay Bolitho had discovered the extent of his resources. Apart from Keen and
Pyper, he had Sergeant Quare and Jack Miller, boatswain's
mate, to support his authority. Two marines and six seamen
only remained of the working party.

Most of the wounded had recovered sufficiently to be returned to the ship, leaving only the marine with the spear-thrust
in his leg and two seamen. If things got worse, even they would
have to be put to work.

Keen came back, his eyes on the hut. 'I've mustered the hands
together, sir. They seem to know what's expected from them.'

Fortunately, most of the shore parties had been chosen for
their skills and reliability. Men like Miller, who had proved a

first-class hand, even if he changed into a wild-eyed killer in battle. Penneck, ship's caulker, who had been putting finishing touches to one of the huts. Big Tom Fraser of the cooper's crew, trustworthy except where drink was concerned. Jenner, the dreamy American, and another wanderer, Lenoir, who was of French birth, and the ex-gamekeeper, Blissett. The latter would most likely see this new isolation as yet another chance to obtain his corporal's stripes.

'Thank you.' He smiled. 'Go to your Malua. I'll not need you for a while.' He beckoned to Allday. 'We will walk to the settlement and speak with Mr Raymond. I shall want the convicts kept separate from the village and from ourselves. That way the Corps guards can watch over them and also attend to the defence of the compound and anchorage.'

He found himself marvelling at the easy way his ideas translated themselves into actions. It was sheer madness. What could he and a handful of men do here? If the natives started to drop with fever the situation would get ugly and quickly. It would not be a siege for long. It would be a massacre.

He passed the long hut which Gwyther had used as his hospital and saw the wounded marine and his two companions sitting by the entrance. He could feel the uncertainty, the new fear.

Bolitho said, 'Don't worry. You're not forgotten.'

The marine known as Billy-boy asked, 'We'm in for troubles, sir?'

'Can you still hold a musket?'

He bobbed. 'Can that, sir. I'm gettin' better all the while. Just me leg.'

Bolitho smiled. 'Good. You'll be armed directly. I'm mounting you as picket on the weapons.'

He strode on with Allday beside him. Weapons. The compound had its swivels and a few six-pounders. Not exactly artillery, but they could sweep any attackers from the pier like gravel from a road.

He paused on a slope and looked towards the sea. *Tempest* lay as before, serene above her image, distance hiding the confusion which his message must have created. Poor Thomas. He would be here too but for his sense of duty.

Bolitho glanced at the *Eurotas*. It would be best to transfer

the convicts into her rather than keep them ashore and add to
any risk of infection. He tried to scrape his mind further, to
discover some weakness or flaw in his hastily assembled plan.
Just hours ago, that was when it had all started. Like a line in
a ship's log, a hint of some new disturbance on the sea's face.
Your life could change with the speed of light, the merest
whim of an idea.

The pier was deserted, and below it Hardacre's longboats
swung gently to their lines, their gunwales so blistered they
showed no trace of paint or colour.

They reached the big gates, and Bolitho saw two Corps
soldiers watching him from one of the little blockhouses.

Allday shouted, 'Open the gates! It's Captain Bolitho!'

An officer appeared on the rampart, his coat like blood in the
sunlight.

'I am sorry, Captain! But the governor has ordered me to
keep them closed! For the safety of my men and all those on
duty within, and for the security of the settlement, it is considered the best arrangement.'

Bolitho looked at him steadily, his mind like ice, despite the
enormity of Raymond's betrayal.

He called, 'We have to stand together. The ships are one way
of life, the islands another. If we are to meet any threat from
attack or from sickness we must –' He stopped, sickened. His
words had sounded like pleading.

Allday said thickly, 'Let me get up at the bastard, Captain!
I'll gut him like a herring!'

'No.'

Bolitho turned away. Raymond could do as he pleased.
There was an underground stream within the compound, endless drinking water. Hardacre had chosen the site wisely. They
would have plenty of food, far more than they needed with the
militia scattered and less mouths to feed. If every man outside
the palisades died and the islanders were decimated, Raymond's
stand, his decision to save what he could, might be seen as
brilliant planning. Especially across a fine desk on the other
side of the world.

With Europe moving towards another conflict, even the
smallest deed might be welcome.

'We will go back to the huts.'

He glanced quickly at Allday as they walked down the slope towards the trees. When did you begin to see signs of fever in a man? It was the dread of every sailor. He could understand the feelings of the Corps soldiers on the palisades. But it was a fool's protection. Tropical fever could soon scale a wall.

He found Pyper making a list of supplies and said, 'Put a man by the pier. To keep watch on the ship.' He said it briskly. Matter of fact. There was no point in putting thoughts in Pyper's mind if they were not already there. The mention of the ship. Security. Amongst one's own. While here . . .

Pyper nodded. 'Aye, sir.'

Despite being made an acting-lieutenant he looked very young. Vulnerable. As Keen had once done when he had first joined Bolitho's previous command.

It felt cool inside the hut, and Bolitho looked down at the girl, shocked to see that she had changed in so short a time. Her face was drawn, her mouth twitching, as if she were in a trance.

Hardacre was wiping her forehead with a cloth. He stood up and said, 'I heard about Raymond. Might have guessed he'd be useless. Government spy. Lackey!'

Bolitho said, 'Can you spare a few minutes?'

Outside again, Hardacre took a flask from his robe and offered it.

'Safer than water. Makes it easier to stay calm, too.'

Bolitho let it trickle across his tongue. It was fiery, and yet took away his thirst.

He said, 'I remembered what you said about Rutara Island. About its being a good hiding place for Tuke.'

Hardacre smiled. 'How can you still think of such things? They are beyond us now.'

'You described it as the Sacred Island.'

'True. It is a rough, rocky place. Not suitable for habitation. Superstition and fear grew out of it. The people will not land there. To do so is desecration. A sign of war. Tuke would know this.'

'And de Barras?'

'I think not.'

Bolitho remembered the false masts, the pain and the shock of the bombardment. He had known that Tuke would have a plan. Maybe all the rest had been a rehearsal just for this. De Barras would drive into the anchorage, guns firing, whether he knew about Genin and the revolution or not.

The wildness of battle would soon restore order in his ship, and Tuke's destruction would keep de Barras's security for a little longer.

But the islanders would see and care about none of these things. To them Tuke, de Barras and the English sailors were as one. Hostile, alien, feared. But as soon as they knew of their trespass on to their Sacred Island the last control would snap.

Tuke would stand off and await his chance as he had done before. *Eurotas* captured, villages burned and pillaged, people killed without mercy. And after challenging a King's ship with no more than a simple ruse, de Barras would stand no chance at all.

He looked at the palm fronds moving gently in a soft breeze. Hardacre's schooner was lively enough, but *Tempest* carried a tremendous spread of canvas. He made up his mind.

'Allday. Get a boat's crew together. One of Mr Hardacre's cutters. I am going out to the ship.' He saw Allday's disbelief and added, 'Well, *almost.*'

Later, as the boat rose and dipped in a slight swell, Bolitho knew what it was like to be parted from his command.

The boat kept station on *Tempest's* stern, and he was aware of the many figures on the poop and in the mizzen shrouds silently watching as the oars held it in position.

In the cabin windows Herrick and Borlase were staring down at him, and it was all he could do to remain outwardly calm, even formal.

'Tell Mr Lakey to lay a course for Rutara Island. I want you to weigh immediately and go there with every stitch you can carry.'

He could see his clerk, Cheadle, deeper within the cabin. He would be writing it all down. Bolitho never transferred his authority without setting it in writing. And even though his signature would not appear this time, it would be enough to safeguard Herrick if things went wrong. And two-thirds of the ship's company were listening. The best witnesses of all.

He added, 'It is sacred to the other islanders. I need you to anchor in the lagoon there, but do not put a single man ashore! Do you understand?'

Herrick nodded firmly. 'Aye, sir.'

'If Tuke's schooners are there, destroy them, do what you can to drive them away. Your actions will be seen. It will be known that we are not here to smear their beliefs and bring a war amongst them.'

'And if I meet with *Narval*, sir?'

Bolitho looked up at him, trying to feel his way. 'You read my instructions. If de Barras is still in command you must tell him about his country. If *Narval* is under new colours, you must stand off.'

'Not fight, sir?'

'Like it or not, Mr Herrick, we are not known to be at war with France.'

'Is there anything more I can do, sir?' He sounded wretched.

'Send a short report in *Pigeon*'s boat. In your own words. Someone should know what we are about.'

There was no point in mentioning that Raymond had shut them out of the settlement compound. Even Herrick might refuse to obey if he knew that.

'And, Mr Herrick.' He paused, holding his gaze. 'Thomas. You will stay at anchor off Rutara until you get contrary orders. We will be safe here. The defences, and the *Eurotas*'s remaining guns, still command the entrance.'

Quietly he said, 'Put her about, Allday. This is easy for no one.'

By the time the boat had reached the pier again there were men already swarming up *Tempest*'s rigging and out along her yards. That was good, Bolitho thought. It would keep Herrick too busy to think about those he was leaving astern.

He saw Keen at the inner end of the pier, his shirt open to his waist, his arms hanging at his sides.

He waited for Bolitho to reach him and then said huskily, 'She's gone, sir.' He looked at the sun. 'Just this moment.'

Allday said, 'I'll deal with it, sir.'

'*No!*' Keen swung on him. 'I will.' In a gentler tone he added, 'But thank you.'

Bolitho watched him go. It had of course been a dream, hopeless from the beginning. In these beautiful surroundings. He let his gaze move over the beach and nodding fronds, the deep blue water. But they had stood no real chance. The young sea officer. The native girl from a barely known island.

He quickened his pace. But it had been *their* dream. No one had had the right to break it.

'*Richard!*'

He swung on his heel, seeing her running down from the makeshift hospital towards him.

He seized her and held her against him. 'Oh, Viola, why did you leave the compound?'

But she was clinging to him, laughing and weeping all at once.

'I don't care! Don't you see, my darling Richard? No matter what happens, for the very first time *we are together*!'

Acting-Lieutenant Francis Pyper watched as they walked into the long hut. He had been feeling afraid, especially after seeing the activity aboard *Tempest*. Even now she was shortening-in her cable, and within the hour might have disappeared around the headland.

But he was no longer afraid.

Sergeant Quare crunched towards him. 'Sir? Message for the captain. Two natives sick in the village. He should be told at once.'

Pyper nodded, his mouth dry. 'I will tell him.'

Quare removed his hat and wiped the inside with his hand. Poor little bastard, he thought. Won't be long now. They'll start to drop like flies. He had seen it in the Caribbean. In India. All over the bloody place.

He saw Blissett walking towards the pier and bellowed, 'Do your tunic up! Where the hell d'you think you are, man?'

That made him feel slightly better.

'*Halt!* Who goes there?'

Bolitho stepped into a white patch of moonlight and showed himself.

'Sorry, sir.' Sergeant Quare grounded his musket. 'Wasn't expectin' you again.'

'All quiet?' He leaned against a tree and listened to the hissing roar of surf along the outer reef. Timeless. Confident.

'Yessir.' The marine sighed. 'They've been burnin' some more poor devils in the village. Heard 'em chantin' and wailin'.'

'Yes.'

Bolitho checked himself from sitting down. He was tired out. Sick and weary from the constant work. It had been eight days since *Tempest* had set sail, and there was still no word from anybody. Not that he expected much help from the village. There had been several deaths, and Hardacre had told him that some more natives had been found dying in a canoe on the other side of the island. They had been strangers, and had probably brought the disease with them. Itak was the name given to the fever. It wasted its victims away in no time at all. Threw them into a desperate struggle for breath while they burned up from within.

Each day Bolitho inspected his men, searching for any sign of it. But apart from weariness and strain, they were behaving well. Which was more than could be said for the men inside the compound. Bolitho had sent Keen to request that food and drink be lowered over the palisade. In fact it had been thrown down, and Keen had heard sounds of drunken laughter, as if the place was turning into a madhouse.

So next day Bolitho had gone himself. After waiting in the sun for a long time, watched, and he suspected covered, by two guards in a blockhouse, Raymond had appeared above him.

Bolitho had said, 'We need help, sir. If the people in the village are left to themselves they may become too weak to burn their dead –'

He had got no further.

'So you have come to beg, have you? You thought you could override me by sending your ship away! Well, you've got your *new command* now! A native hut, and a handful of ruffians to do your bidding! My precious wife will soon come running back when she sees what she has thrown away!' He had sounded wild, even jubilant.

Bolitho had made another try. 'If I take the watch off the

Eurotas I will have enough hands to manage until the fever is gone.'

'You keep your men away from my ship!' His voice had risen almost to a scream. 'My men have orders to open fire if a single boat puts off to her! You've lost your ship, Captain, and I'll not have you touch mine!'

He had found Keen and the others waiting for him with the news of another death. It was pitiful the way the natives were accepting it. *The gods were angry.* Tinah knew about Tuke and the sacred island. If the whole of his people discovered the truth too they would see their suffering as the direct result of intrusion.

He looked at the stars and shivered. If he had acted sooner he might have been able to seize the *Eurotas* under cover of night. But that was too late. Raymond's threats, and their own fear of the Itak, would make sure of a hot welcome from the loaded swivels.

If he could not get word to Herrick, and the schooner failed to return soon, he would know *Narval* had been taken. In the name of the Revolution or through an open mutiny made no difference now. Tuke would demand payment for his help to Genin's cause, and the Frenchman could hardly refuse. But how would he do it? A legalized position with the new regime, a ship, a letter of marque, or the promise of gold when Genin eventually reached Paris?

To make the wound more bitter, Bolitho realized that as soon as *Narval* had gone and Tuke had obtained the reward he was seeking, news would quite likely arrive to say that England and France had been at war for months.

It would be the end of Bolitho's career. In Raymond he had a deadly enemy. And in London they would be looking for a scapegoat to cover their anger at losing both the French frigate and a pirate who would still need to be hunted by men-of-war desperately required in the line of battle.

He thought of Raymond's words when he had shouted down at him. That was his only comfort. Viola had worked ceaselessly at his side, carried encouragement from her makeshift hospital to the village where she had helped to nurse the sick and take care of the children left behind.

She was lying in the hut where he had just left her. He had knelt over her, listening to her regular breathing, afraid to touch her and break her sleep.

The sergeant asked, 'I hope you'll pardon me, sir, but what are we goin' to do?'

'*Do?*' He ran his fingers up through his hair. 'Wait. When the schooner comes I'll get a message to her master. At least we will know if *Narval* is still hereabout.'

'Er, this island, sir. The one you told us of. 'Ow far away is it?'

'Rutara is well north of here. Some five hundred miles.'

Bolitho thought of it even as he said the words. The winds had been light but favourable. Herrick should have taken up his station even if he had been unable to destroy Tuke's schooners. He would certainly not run into the trap which had caught them before.

He watched the stars growing smaller and fainter. It would soon be time to begin again. Issue rations, make sure his men were clean, and try to keep up their spirits. At least the Itak was not the pox which he had known to kill two-thirds of a ship's company in a matter of weeks. On land they could build fires, boil water and pursue some sort of routine.

He said, 'Walk with me to the pier. It will be light very soon.'

How quiet it was in the village. It was hard to believe the beach and shallows had been full of laughing girls and youths. Like Keen's beautiful Malua.

'Sir!' Quare's voice jerked him from his thoughts. 'I think I saw a sail!'

Bolitho jumped on to a slab of rock, straining his eyes into the gloom. But all he saw between sky and sea were breakers, a necklace of surf cut short where it met the headland.

But it was brightening fast, and he could already see *Eurotas*'s portly outline, an anchor light still flickering.

Bolitho looked towards the settlement, but there was no sign of life.

Quare said stubbornly, 'There, sir.'

This time he did see it, like a pale fin rising above the distant surf, shivering through the spray, but moving inshore even while he watched.

A schooner. Small and well handled.

He said, 'Go and rouse Mr Keen. Tell him I want a message sent to Hardacre to say his schooner is returning.'

The vessel's master would take more notice of him than of Raymond, that was certain. He heard Quare's boots crunching back up the slope, and somewhere a child crying, the sound strangely sad.

Then from behind him she said, 'I woke up. You'd gone.'

She came to his side and he put his arm around her shoulders, feeling her warmth.

'It's the schooner.' He tried to sound calm. 'I wonder what news she'll bring.'

The sails were end-on now, tilting steeply to the wind. It must be much stronger outside the bay's protection, he thought. Being ashore was like being crippled. You had to wait for others. He could even imagine how Raymond felt about it.

He squeezed her shoulders. 'Please God let it be good news!'

Hazy light played across the horizon, like smoky liquid spilling over the edge of the earth. It touched the twin masts, Hardacre's rag of a pendant, as the vessel drove close to the reef and tacked expertly in a welter of spray and spindrift.

Keen came along the path, tucking his shirt into his breeches. He saw Viola Raymond and said, 'Oh, good morning, ma'am.'

'Hello, Val.' She smiled, seeing the dark shadows under his eyes, sharing his pain.

Bolitho said, 'Hardacre will be here soon, I expect.'

He glanced at the palisades. He would wait until the schooner was warped alongside the pier and then walk down to her deck. Nobody from the settlement would be able to prevent him, and they were too frightened to leave the compound's protection.

The bay was opening up on either hand, and they stood in silence watching the colours emerge from the darkness, the still and threatening shadows come alive with movement and simple beauty.

Keen would be thinking of her, running down the beach into the sea with him. Laughing.

'She's back then.' Hardacre stood on the hard sand, hands on hips, watching his schooner take on personality. 'And about time, too.'

H

Bolitho shaded his eyes and watched for some sort of signal from the *Eurotas* or from the palisades. If Raymond ordered her to anchor and await his pleasure he would have to think of something else.

Hardacre remarked suddenly, 'That's very unusual.'

Bolitho looked at him. 'What?'

'The master knows this bay like his own soul. He usually begins to wear ship at that point, when the wind stands as it does today.'

Bolitho turned back to the little schooner, a sudden chill of warning pricking his brain.

'Mr Keen, go to the gates and rouse the sentry! Tell the fools to challenge the schooner!'

He watched the small vessel, and then heard Keen shouting up at the blockhouse by the gates. He stiffened, she was altering course yet again, towards the *Eurotas*.

Hardacre said, 'In God's name, what is the madman doing?'

Bolitho snapped, 'Get me a musket!' He saw Quare on the slope. 'Quick! Fire yours!'

Damp, or over-eagerness, made the musket misfire, and Bolitho heard Quare growling like an angry dog as he prepared another shot.

From the palisade came a thick, unsteady voice, full of sleep and protest, and Keen returned, saying angrily, 'That man should be . . .' He saw Bolitho's expression and turned to watch the ships.

Even the crack of the musket did not break their fixed attention, although the chorus of awakened birds was enough to alarm the whole island.

Slowly, faintly at first, and next with terrible resolve, a column of smoke erupted from the schooner's deck. Then a flame, licking out from a hatch like an orange tongue, consuming the jib sail in ashes.

Keen said with a gasp, '*Fireship!*'

'Rouse the men!'

Bolitho saw the schooner stagger as part of her maindeck collapsed in a great gust of flame and sparks. Like things released from hell the fires exploded across sails and tarred rigging, changing the little ship into one massive torch. Bolitho could even see the blaze reflected in *Eurotas*'s furled canvas and shrouds as the wind carried it unwaveringly towards the anchored ship's side.

'A boat's cast off, sir!' Quare was reloading frantically. 'The buggers will get away!'

He stopped loading as the schooner shuddered against the *Eurotas*'s hull and hurled a fresh column of smoke and swirling sparks high over her mastheads.

Bolitho could hear the fires taking hold, could picture the tinder-dry wood, the tarred cordage all joining together in one terrible pyre. He thought he saw some men jump into the sea, and imagined the terror below decks as the off-duty watch awoke to their own awful execution.

He felt her quivering, sobbing quietly against his shoulder.

He said, 'There is nothing we can do, Viola. Some will reach the beach, but I fear that most will die.'

So *Eurotas* had been cut out right under Raymond's guns. His ship, his life-line if all else failed, was blazing and crackling, the smoke rolling downwind in a great choking bank. Masts and spars were consumed and fell into the sparks, internal explosions hurled fragments high into the air to pock-mark the surrounding water with feathers of spray. One great bang rocked the gutted hulk and rolled an echo around the bay like thunder. As it finally died away, *Eurotas* started to settle down, the steam spouting and hissing to cover her last agony before she went to the bottom, leaving her charred poop still visible above the surface.

Keen asked quietly, 'Why, sir?'

'It was our message, Mr Keen.' Bolitho turned away from the water, his eyes smarting from smoke, or was it the added bitterness of his discovery? 'Tuke has chosen his reward.' He looked at Hardacre and added, 'It is this place. Without *Eurotas*'s protection we cannot hold it now. Once installed, it would take a regiment of marines to flush him out again.'

Keen said in a small voice, 'And we have no way of getting help, sir.'

As if to emphasize his words the schooner's bows broke surface and floated away from the great frothing whirlpool of flotsam and charred remains.

Bolitho said abruptly, 'Follow me.'

He found Pyper and the rest of the men grouped near the hospital hut, the wounded beside them.

Bolitho looked at them as individuals and then said, 'It is my belief that Mathias Tuke has seized the means to attack this island and those others which depend on it. Otherwise he would not waste a schooner by using her as a fireship, she is too valuable for his flotilla.' He saw his words hitting home. 'He will kill any natives who oppose him, and you have already seen his methods, both aboard *Eurotas* and ashore.'

He knew she was watching him, remembering her own torment when the transport had been captured. She even touched her shoulder at the place where her gown hid the livid brand he had set on her.

He continued, 'Not one of us has caught the fever, although many have died all around us. So perhaps we are safe. Maybe we are too evil to go just yet!'

Bolitho saw Miller and Quare grin, as he knew they would. On the other side of the clearing Allday was watching him calmly. He had heard this sort of thing before.

Bolitho said, 'Only one ship can offer battle to Tuke, and no matter what forces he now has, I think *Tempest* is more than a match for them.'

Blissett nodded, and he noticed that Lenoir, the French seaman, was crossing himself. Orlando stood apart from the rest, arms folded, one foot on the last case of biscuit. He looked powerful, and somehow regal.

He added slowly, 'There are *five hundred miles* between us and *Tempest*, lads.'

He could see their doubt. What did the distance mean? Five hundred. It might as well be five thousand miles.

Bolitho looked along their intent faces, wishing he could spare them.

'I intend to take a cutter and as many volunteers who are willing and find our *Tempest*.'

There was a long drawn-out, stunned silence. Then as Pyper stepped forward with a makeshift watch-bill, Allday said, 'Wouldn't it be better to take both cutters, Captain?' He smiled lazily. 'More of a chance, I reckon.'

Pyper called, 'All volunteers hold up your hands.'

The boatswain's mate, Miller, replied, 'No need. We'll all go.' He showed his strong teeth like a wild animal. '*Two* cutters, eh, lads?'

They all crowded forward, slapping each other and grinning as if they had just been offered something precious.

Bolitho glanced at his hands, expecting to see them shaking. He heard her say, 'You cannot leave me, Richard.'

He looked at her, his protest dying as she took his hands. Then he nodded. 'Better together, my love.'

Allday cleared his throat. 'Beg pardon, ma'am, an open boat full of sailors is no place for a *lady*!' He sounded shocked. 'I mean, Captain, it would not be right!'

She looked him up and down. 'I have seen it all. And I believe you need me to sustain your impudence, Allday!' She smiled. 'When do we start?'

Bolitho took out the watch, seeing her eyes on it as he opened the guard.

'Dusk. If we attempt to leave earlier the guards may panic and open fire to stop us.'

He led her away from the others and their strange, released excitement.

'I don't know, Viola. I'm not sure I can do it. Five hundred miles. And even then . . .'

She took his elbow and turned him gently towards the huts.

'Look at the marine, Richard. The one called Billy-boy. He has been badly wounded, but now he is on his feet. And the other two are much better. With men like these, of *course* you can do it!' She made to leave him and then said quietly, 'And do not ask Hardacre to look after me until you return. We go together.' She watched him steadily. 'It is our promise.'

He nodded. 'If you are determined.'

She tossed her head and he saw her as he had first done, five years back. All her strength and as he had thought then, her arrogance. Despite her torn gown and scarred shoes, that lady was still very much there.

'Never more so, my darling Richard. About *anything*!'

14

When, *Not* If

Bolitho eased the tiller bar slightly and said, 'We will drift for a while, Mr Pyper. Hail the other boat.'

Gratefully they hauled the long oars across the gunwales of the cutter and drooped over them like men at prayer. Getting the boats away from the pier without being seen or challenged had been child's play compared with making a safe passage through the reefs. The undertow had been very strong, and as if to taunt their puny efforts the wind had attacked them around the headland with unexpected vigour, and it had taken every man's strength to reach open water.

Now, with the sun already high in an empty sky, it was difficult to imagine it.

Bolitho looked along the boat, watching each man's reaction, his adjustment.

Close astern the other cutter was pulling towards them, and he saw Keen at the tiller, pointing to one of the oarsmen, or advising somebody on how to get better results from his stroke.

In his own boat Bolitho could readily understand Keen's problems. The two crews were as evenly matched as possible, with the few seamen spread between the rest, the marines and the injured.

He looked down at Viola's hand on the gunwale. She had hardly said a word during their violent, tossing progress through the broken water, but when he had reached out for her she had looked up at him and had smiled. Just that. And yet it had offered him more confidence, more peace at that moment than he could remember.

He made himself think about his task. Five hundred miles.

At the very best, with all in their favour and no one falling sick, it would take over a week. The boats had no sails, but Miller had discovered some scraps of canvas and had promised to try and rig something which might help steady the boat and spare the oarsmen some of the back-breaking strain.

What a mixed bunch, he thought, as he looked at each weary, stubbly face. Miller, and the marine, Blissett. Jenner and Orlando, and two of the injured, the marine called Billy-boy and Evans, the ship's painter.

He met Allday's gaze from the stroke oar and nodded. If Allday showed resentment at crewing a boat instead of coxswaining it, he did not show it.

'At any other time it would make a fair sight, Captain.'

Bolitho looked abeam. The islands all seemed the same, blue and hazy in the morning sunlight.

He wondered if Hardacre was even now shouting his message to Raymond from the gates, telling him what these men were trying to do to save him and his cowardly guards.

He thought too of the moment when the cutter had surged past the still-smouldering wreck of the *Eurotas*. Only her blackened poop and taffrail remained above the surface, but it had been enough to make Viola seize his hand and press it against her in the darkness. The sight of that stark outline, surrounded with breaking spray and trailing fragments of cordage, must have brought it all back in an instant. It had been in the poop where she had faced Tuke. Where he had taunted and humiliated her.

'Boat your oars!' Keen leaned over the gunwale of his boat as it nudged alongside the other one. He said, 'Wind's dropped, sir.' He smiled at Viola. 'I hope you were able to sleep, ma'am.'

But the smile only made him look sadder, Bolitho thought.

'I hope it remains so.' Bolitho kept his voice level and relaxed.

Unlike a ship, there was nowhere he could hide from those who depended on him. Like this moment. The beginning. Five hundred miles with neither chart nor sextant. All he had was a small boat's compass, and the barest amount of food and water. Hardacre had managed to smuggle some wine and a flask of rum to him, and this he would keep for anyone whose

health wilted under the torment of heat and exposure. They had
six muskets between the two boats, and apart from the officers'
pistols there were some cutlasses and a boarding axe which
Miller always carried in his belt. It was not much, but if they
could keep up a regular daily total they had a chance. Any
tropical storm, or sudden fever amongst the boats, and they
had no chance at all.

To remind everyone of the need for care and vigilance, a
shark had joined them at dawn, and even now was cruising
lazily a cable or so astern.

Bolitho fixed the islands in his mind like an unmarked chart.
The Levu Group, and then north like the point of the compass
to the Navigator Islands, directly adjacent to which lay Rutara,
and with luck, the *Tempest*.

He said, 'We will keep our water ration the same in each
boat, Mr Keen. But tomorrow I intend to beach in the best-
looking bay or cove and supplement our stores with coconuts.
We might even find some shellfish in the rocks.'

He wanted to add that a hot meal, no matter how frugal or
coarse, was better than anything to keep the men in good
health and spirits. As soon as they got ashore on one of the
islands he would tell Keen. To shout it now over the lolling
heads of his men would sound like an early acceptance of failure.

Miller looked up from his efforts with needle and palm.
'I've got some canvas left over, sir.' He held a ragged piece
about the size of a hammock across his knees. 'It'd make a fine
shelter for you, ma'am.'

She smiled. 'I'll not refuse such kindness.' She ran one
finger around the neck of her gown. 'It is strange that it should
be hotter on water than on land!'

Miller chuckled. 'Lord love you, ma'am, we'll make a
seaman of you yet!'

Some of the men in the other boat nodded and grinned like
unshaven galley slaves. Bolitho watched them, and then
touched her shoulder.

He said quietly, 'You are worth a lot more than muscle.
You make them smile, when they must be thinking of nothing
but escape and sleep.'

Bolitho looked at the sun. 'Take the tiller, Mr Pyper. I will have a turn on the oars.' To the marine he said, 'Go aft and attend to the injured.' He waited for the man to look at him. 'Then examine the weapons, and make sure our powder is protected.'

The two boats drifted apart, suddenly very small and frail on the great expanse of blue water.

Across Allday's broad shoulder he saw her watching him, her eyes shaded by her straw hat, speaking to him as if with her voice.

Pyper cleared his throat, nervous, even with so much before him, at the prospect of giving orders to his captain.

'Out oars!' He looked down at the little compass. 'Give way *all*!'

With his shoulders propped against the side, the wounded marine squinted up at Viola Raymond. Like everyone else, he thought of her as 'the Captain's Lady', it had a good ring to it. She was good to him. Had watched over his wounded leg better than any surgeon, and was as gentle as an angel. He could not distinguish her face because of the sun's glare around the brim of her hat, but he could see the grime on her gown and shoes which she had gathered from the pier. A fresh pain lanced through his leg and he moved uneasily.

She asked, 'How is it, Billy-boy?'

The marine grimaced. 'Fair, ma'am. Just cramp.'

The other injured man, Evans the painter, said nothing. He was watching the woman's ankle below her gown and imagined the smoothness of her leg beyond. Then he thought of his wife in Cardiff, and wondered how she was managing without him. She was a good girl, and had given him four fine daughters. He closed his eyes and let himself drift into sleep.

By Pyper's feet, Blissett made sure the powder and shot were well stowed, and then looked up at the sleeping Evans. It was suddenly clear to him. As if a voice had shouted it in his ear. Evans had started to die. The realization frightened him, and he did not know why. Blissett had seen many men go. In battle, in brawls, or merely because they were taken by one bout of illness or another. But seeing Evans' face, and knowing what he did, was like falling on another man's secret, and it disturbed him deeply.

Behind Bolitho, the American called Jenner pulled and thrust easily with his oar, his mind lifting away on one of his many imaginary journeys. When he was paid off he would buy a farm in New England. Miles from anywhere. And settle down with a girl. He tried to picture her, and then started to create his perfect mate in his imagination.

Next was Orlando, using his oar with clumsy precision, taking his stroke from the others. He ducked as Miller stepped over his oar to take his place in the bow, his sailmaking put aside until the next rest. For with only five oars in use it needed all their strength. Miller laid back on his loom and grinned at the sky. It was like a fight. And to Jack Miller that was meat and drink in one.

And so it went on, under a pitiless glare, or partly masked in low haze, the two boats crawled like ungainly beetles. Men changed round at the oars, rations of biscuit and a cube of salt meat were issued and washed down with a pannikin of water from the barrico.

Release from heat and torment came with the night, but their efforts to make steady progress continued as before.

His back aching from the unfamiliar oar, his palms blistered, Bolitho sat at the tiller, Viola's head cushioned across his knees. Once she gripped him with her fingers and moaned softly in her sleep as Bolitho brushed the hair from her mouth.

Pyper had taken one of the oars, and Miller was bailing water from the bottom of the boat. They sounded worn out, half beaten already. He tightened his jaw. And this was the first full day.

After the cutter's pitching motion the firm sand at the top of the beach felt as if it too was moving.

Bolitho watched Keen and Miller making sure both boats were properly secured, and heard Sergeant Quare ordering lookouts to either side of the small cove. Again, it looked and felt idyllic. Lush greenery with the regular swish and gurgle of breakers along the pale sand. But he knew how deceptive it could be, just as he knew of the vital need for watchfulness.

Pyper came to him, his face seared by the sun. 'Shall we unload the boats, sir?'

'Not yet.' Bolitho trained his small telescope on the far side of the cove, suddenly tense. But what he had thought to be a plume of smoke proved to be nothing more dangerous than a swaying cloud of insects. 'We will wait a while and see if we are discovered here.'

He wanted to unload the boats, if only to lighten them and stop their unnecessary pounding in the surf. But he felt uneasy. Apprehensive. He tried to tell himself he was being over-cautious, that the need for rest before the challenge of the final haul to Rutara was more important.

He saw Evans and a seaman called Colter lying beneath some shady palms. The other injured man, the marine, was propped against a tree, helping Viola to unpack some dressings. The rest of the small party moved about restlessly, feeling their way, recovering their wits after the hard work at the oars. He watched her smiling at Evans, wiping his forehead and trying to make him comfortable. Looking back over their day and two nights in an open boat, he was deeply moved. She had not once complained, nor had she asked for the slightest privilege. Before a boat half full of strained and anxious men she had performed her own needs with only Miller's crude screen to offer a pretence of privacy. Now she was on the beach with the wounded men. If she knew Evans was dying she was hiding her dismay very well.

Quare strode across the sand. 'All clear, sir.' He gestured along the curving wall of trees. 'I'll put the hands to work getting nuts.' He forced a wry smile. 'I could manage a gallon of Devon ale right now, sir.'

Keen joined them. 'Shall we start a fire, sir?' He rubbed his hands and gave a great yawn. 'Maybe we could kill a bird or two. Frazer had the fine sense to bring a cooking pot with him from the village.'

Bolitho nodded. 'Directly. Shellfish, and some cubes of salt pork, any sort of fowl, too. It would not go down well at an admiral's table, but something hot, no matter how doubtful, will do our people a power of good.'

He sat down and rested his head in his hands, grappling

with the problems of his journey, the mounting strain it would make on all of them. He looked at her again. Especially on a woman. Yet in some ways she had more inner reserves and courage than any of them.

He heard a man laugh, and another respond with a stream of obscenity as a coconut was dropped on to his head. The luckless man on the ground swung round and gasped, 'I begs yer pardon, ma'am!'

She laughed at his confusion. 'My father was a soldier. I've heard worse from him!'

Her words struck another note for Bolitho. How little he really knew about her. She had gained more knowledge of *him* by reading the *Gazette* and speaking with his superiors, and yet in five years of separation his love had gained rather than faded.

Allday trudged towards the boats carrying a net of coconuts. He paused, drew out his cutlass and then selected a nut with great care.

'Here, Captain.' The blade flashed in the sunlight, lopping off the top of the nut like a scalp. 'A local brew!' It seemed to amuse him.

Bolitho raised it to his lips and let the milk run over his tongue.

'Thank you. It is like . . .' He put the nut on the sand between his legs, his mind racing. 'Allday.' Bolitho's tone made him stiffen. 'Do not turn. On the other side of the cove. Right by the water. I saw a face.'

Allday nodded and called to Frazer, 'Big Tom! Put these in the boat.' He turned and walked back up the beach, pausing only by Viola Raymond to pass a brief message.

Bolitho stood up slowly and stretched his arms. There it was again. A quick movement amongst the thick fronds, the sun's glitter on something bright.

It was taking too long. Men were walking back towards the water, stiff-legged, like bad players in a travelling band of mummers.

Quare hurried towards Bolitho, his musket over his shoulder. 'Where, sir?'

As if to a signal, several figures began to emerge from

amongst the thick foliage, fierce-looking natives, totally unlike those Bolitho had seen around the settlement. From North Island or elsewhere hardly mattered now. They had probably hidden themselves much earlier, even before the boats had been hauled ashore. He counted them. More than twenty, and all armed with spears and short, wide-bladed knives. One, obviously a leader of some kind, was adorned with several strings of glass beads. In the reflected sunlight they had betrayed his hiding place.

Bolitho measured the distance. From the top of the beach to the boats. From the silent, watching natives to his own men.

He said quietly, 'Stand still, lads. They are trying to discover what we are about. If they think we are from a ship nearby they may go. If not, we could have a fight on our hands.'

Pyper said desperately, 'There are some more yonder, sir. By the red flowers.'

No wonder Quare's lookouts had not seen them. They must have crept along the water's edge and through the surf itself to bypass the tired sentries.

The one with the beads raised his hand and called something in a thin voice. Then he pointed at Bolitho, recognizing him too as a leader, and then very slowly turned his arm towards Viola Raymond. He bobbed his head and grimaced, then poked his bushy black hair, while those around him did likewise and grinned. He was fascinated by the colour of her hair, and yet his simple mime was more menacing than any open attack.

Bolitho held up his hand. '*Friend!*'

A few of the natives wandered vaguely by the hissing surf, and Bolitho saw the pattern changing even as he said, 'Fall back to the boats, but do it slowly!' He had seen that the apparently aimless movement was an attempt to get between the sailors and the boats, or separate them from the little group beneath the trees.

He thought suddenly of Herrick. This time there was no last-minute help or swivel guns to strike fear into the silent figures on the beach.

He said, 'Mr Keen, we will use my boat only. Take charge of it now and get it launched. Sergeant Quare, have some men aid the injured.' He saw Allday and Miller watching him. 'We will stand here. Make no further move.'

Bolitho heard the cutter's keel grating on sand, the heavy gasps from those who were manhandling it into deeper water. To try and escape with both boats would be madness. It was probable the natives had canoes nearby and would soon overhaul the slow pulling boats and attack them individually. You could not pull an oar and fight at the same time when you were so shorthanded.

The natives were starting to move nearer, and he heard them murmuring between themselves, the sound strangely inhuman, like the twittering of birds.

Allday said, 'Something to the left, Captain. More of the buggers. This lot must have been waiting for reinforcements. Just to be on the safe side.'

Bolitho called sharply, 'Lively, lads!'

Then he turned as several figures separated from the main group and streaked across the sand towards Viola and the helpless Evans. The wounded marine swung up his musket like a crutch and fired, the ball hitting the first native in the stomach and hurling him down to spatter the pale sand with blood.

The sudden move and the crack of the musket acted like a clarion call, and with a great whoop of frenzy and hatred the natives hurled themselves towards the boats, the air instantly alive with spears and jagged pieces of stone.

Sergeant Quare dropped to one knee and fired, followed immediately by the other muskets. The effect was immediate, and still yelling and whooping the attackers fell back into the green foliage, leaving three of their number dead or dying.

Bolitho drew his pistol and shouted to Pyper, 'Get those men down here!'

A spear flitted across his vision and stuck quivering in the wet sand.

The second wave would come at any moment. He saw Blissett and another marine reloading beside Quare, and their wounded comrade hopping down the slope towards the boats, his face twisted with pain and exertion. Orlando was carrying Evans, who was moaning and struggling weakly in his arms, while the other injured seaman was being bustled into the cutter by Frazer and Lenoir.

'Here they come again!'

This time it was more determined, the rocks and stones raining down on the reeling, dazed seamen and marines, and then spears from two angles at once.

But the muskets replied briskly, and Bolitho fired his pistol at a screaming native who had weaved around the crouching marines and was charging straight at the boat. He was knocked sideways, his limbs flailing as he fell into the surf, turning it bright pink.

Bolitho thrust the pistol away and drew his sword.

'*Hurry!*'

He turned, sickened, as the marine with Blissett gave a terrible shriek and fell on his side, a spear driven hard into his chest.

'This way, sir!'

Keen was standing in the cutter's bows, firing his own pistol and waving for the others to clamber aboard. Bolitho saw Viola's hair blowing above the gunwale and realized that he and the marines were the only ones still on the beach.

Blissett was trying to drag his companion towards the surf, but Quare punched his shoulder and yelled, 'Leave him! He's done for! Get his musket and move yourself, my lad!' He fired as he spoke and sent another dark figure sprawling.

The next few minutes were a confusion of desperate purpose mixed with revulsion as their attackers turned on the dead marine and started to slash and hack him into an unrecognizable bundle.

Then the oars were out and the cutter was moving swiftly into deep water, the speed of the stroke laying bare their horror and their fear.

'No canoes in sight, sir.'

Bolitho nodded, unable to answer as he sucked in air. By his feet he saw a net full of coconuts, but by having to abandon the other boat they had lost half their supply of food and water.

Sergeant Quare said roughly, 'Marine Corneck was a good hand, sir. Came from the next village to me.'

Blissett lay across an oar, his eyes smarting. He had never

liked the dead marine much. But to see him cut apart like a carcass made him burn with anger and disgust.

Bolitho watched their varying reactions and matched them against his own. Some small warning had prevented all of them ending up like Corneck. A few more minutes and he might have ordered the boats to be unloaded, fires to be lit. He met her gaze along the boat as she tied a bandage around Jenner's head. He had been badly cut by a piece of rock. She looked very calm, but her eyes were misty with suppressed emotion. But for the wounded marine's swift action they might have seized her and dragged her away before anyone could intervene. Even the thought of it made him feel sick.

The only compensation was that there were more men to work the oars and so allow small snatches of respite for the others. Against that . . . he looked at Evans, who was now barely conscious, and at Penneck, the ship's caulker, who had received a bad gash on the neck from a spear. He took out the flask of rum, feeling their eyes on it, seeing Big Tom Frazer look away to hide his own want.

'A tot each to Evans and Penneck.' He looked at her across their heads. 'And, I think, for the lady.'

Keen said hoarsely, 'Aye, sir. She most of all.'

But she shook her head. 'No. Rum is something I have not been able to admire.'

Several of the men laughed, haltingly at first, and then in a tide of uncontrolled noise which none seemed able to stop.

Bolitho touched Keen's shoulder. 'Let them get it out of their souls. They have enough to face.' He saw Pyper joining with the rest, his laughter changing to helpless tears which ran unheeded down his face like rain.

After a while they pulled themselves together, some surprised, others ashamed, but not one making any comment on their behaviour. The oars began to move up and down again, and within another hour the small cove was lost in a blur of haze which covered the islands astern like fine netting.

Then they rested, issued rations, drank their water, looked around at the sea and each other with dulled acceptance.

Ahead and on either bow the islands were breaking up and growing smaller. They would have to land again and find water, gather supplies. And all the time the sun pursued them, seared down on them, burning away their determination, their will to survive.

And when night eventually found them it was without comfort. For after the shock and fear of their experience on the island, and the heat of the long day, the air seemed like ice, so that those not employed on the oars clung together in shivering cold.

The next day, despite all their caution, the same danger showed itself. Behind the lush vegetation of one island watching eyes followed their weary approach. When they prepared to beach the boat they were attacked as before, beaten and almost knocked senseless by rocks and flying stones, until they were forced to pull into deeper water to find refuge.

Bolitho watched Keen and Pyper issuing the rations, and looked for resentment or mistrust in the faces of the others. The rations had to be exact. One sign of greed or favouritism and these same loyal and disciplined men might fall on each other like crazed wolves.

If only they had been able to get more food before leaving. But if Raymond had found out what they were intending, either from his guards or from the village, they would not even have reached the pier.

Blissett picked up his musket. 'Permission to fire, sir!' He was watching a circling sea-bird, his eyes alive with sudden excitement.

Bolitho nodded. 'Wait until it is closer. Otherwise our friend will have it.' He glanced astern at the tell-tale dorsal fin. He could accept it now without fear or curiosity. It was just part of the whole. One more hazard.

The bird fell neatly to the first ball. It was a booby, about the size of a duck.

They all stood or crouched staring at it until Bolitho said quietly, 'We will divide it. But the blood must be given to the weakest.'

Revolted at first, the men took their little portions and then devoured them with sudden desperation. The blood, carried carefully through the swaying boat, was given to Evans, the wounded seaman called Colter and finally Penneck.

Just before sunset, and another bitter night, they sighted some fast-moving canoes to the north-east. Like harrying dogs, Bolitho thought. Running them down into weakness so they could be killed at leisure. Maybe they thought them to be some of Tuke's men and were trying to wreak a terrible vengeance. Or they might even be acting for Tuke under threat or promise of reward.

Miller had constructed a sea-anchor with the last scrap of canvas, and Bolitho decided to give everyone a chance to have a brief rest, unbroken by the groan and clatter of oars.

As the boat lifted and rolled across a succession of troughs, Bolitho sat in the sternsheets, his coat around Viola's shoulders, one arm encircling her and protecting her from the motion.

Once she said, 'I am not asleep. I was looking at the stars.'

He held her firmly, needing her, fearing for her.

Then she said, 'Stop discovering blame, Richard. I *wanted* to be here with you. Nothing is changed.'

When he made to answer he found she was asleep again.

As the dawn opened up the sky once more they saw even fewer islands, and the ocean seemed far greater and more invincible. They found too that Evans had died in the night.

Bolitho trained his small glass on the nearest land. It was very green, but without any sign of a beach. But it might be their last chance. He looked at Evans' body, lying on the bottom boards as if asleep. They could bury him there. It would prevent the shark from snatching him away, and so save his men from seeing it happen to one of their own.

When they got ashore they were not attacked, and although Quare's lookouts did find some old fire places, it looked as if they had lain unused for years. It was so difficult to get a boat inshore without pounding it against the rocks that perhaps native canoes stayed away, too frail to take the risk.

They found a tiny pool with some fresh water. It was from a rainfall, and barely enough to fill Frazer's cooking pot. But with some of their dwindling supply of salt pork, a collection of small oysters which Pyper discovered amongst the rocks, and a few ship's biscuits to give it body, Allday and Miller set about preparing their first hot meal. There was dried wood in plenty, and with Allday's tinder-box and a small magnifying glass which they removed from Evans' body they used the sun to get a good blaze going.

The little Welshman was buried on a slope under some trees, and the shallow grave covered with flat stones. It was a strange resting place for the *Tempest*'s painter, Bolitho thought. As he sat with his back against a palm and wrote carefully in a small notebook which was now becoming his log, he wondered how he would describe the place. Not that anyone would ever read about it.

Viola was lying in the shade beside him, the hat across her face.

'Call it Evans' Isle, Richard.'

He smiled. 'Yes. After all, he's the only one who will be staying here.'

Keen's voice came from the rocks where the boat was being watched and guarded. 'Just sighted some more canoes, sir!'

Bolitho thrust the little book inside his shirt. 'Very well. Douse the fire and collect the men. We're safer in the boat than up here.'

In grim silence they pulled away from the only place which had made them welcome. Sustained for a while by their meal and a brief rest, they turned the stem towards the north once more, leaving Evans alone with his last and only possession.

Like a dying water-beetle the cutter, her oars partly withdrawn and unmoving, rolled across an unbroken swell which stretched as far as an eye could reach.

Bolitho sat with his arm on the tiller bar, breathing very slowly and trying not to look at the sky. The heat was so fierce that the sea had no colour, and merged into the sky like blinding silver.

He thought of writing something in his little book, and knew it was getting harder every time to concentrate on the useless, empty words.

The oarsmen lay across the looms, faces pressed on their arms, the others either crouched against the side of the hull to try and find some shade or slept where they sat, like dead men.

Viola Raymond was beside and a little below him. She was

wearing his uniform coat, having removed her torn and stained gown to wash it in salt water. As he looked down at her, seeing the autumn-coloured hair tied back across the collar, he thought she could have been a captain.

She seemed to feel him looking at her and reached out to touch his hand. But she did not look up. Like her companions, she found the glare too painful, too demanding on whatever energy she still had.

'How much rest will you give them?' Her voice was low, but it no longer mattered. No eyes watched them together, and when they touched or held hands it was accepted. Part of their total strength, as it was part of his.

He slitted his eyes, measuring the sun's angle. 'Not much longer, Viola. We are making less headway every day.'

He wiped his forehead with his sleeve, the movement making the sweat pour down his chest and thighs. It had been four agonizing days since they had left the little island where they had buried Evans. Days and nights of unrelenting, sapping work. Pulling and bailing. Trying to snatch a few moments for sleep and then starting all over again. He considered their present circumstances. They had left the pier eight days ago. It was incredible even to think of the slow, wretched miles which marked their progress. The water was down to a gallon, if that. The salt pork was merely a fistful of rock-hard fragments. He had issued most of the wine in small cupfuls, and they had been lucky enough to hit and kill a noddy two days back. The bird had been divided as before and the blood given to the worst-off. The latter now included a seaman called Robinson who was suffering severely from both sun and thirst, and Penneck, whose spear wound showed signs of poisoning. The ship's caulker was the only one who was rarely silent. Day or night he moaned and sobbed, feeling his dressing around his throat and occasionally falling into semi-consciousness, still groaning.

Bolitho tightened the grip on her fingers, his eyes smarting as he thought of her husband and his callous indifference, his refusal to think of anything but himself.

'How do you feel?' He waited, knowing she was preparing her reply, then added, 'The truth now.'

She returned the pressure on his hand. 'Well enough, *Captain*.' She looked up at him, shading her eyes. 'Do not fret so. We *will* get there. You'll see.'

Allday stirred and shook himself like a dog. 'Ready, lads?'

Penneck started to groan again, and Blissett said savagely, 'Stow it, matey, in the name of pity!'

Quare removed his red coat and folded it carefully before taking over an oar. 'Easy now, Blissett! The poor devil can't help himself!'

'Out oars!'

Bolitho watched them, seeing their despair as they struggled with the long oars. Even thrusting them out through the rowlocks seemed as much as they could manage now.

'Give way all!'

Bolitho peered down at the compass. *North.* Maybe they would all die, and Tuke would fall upon the settlement just as he had always intended. Bolitho had once found a drifting boat full of dead sailors. He often wondered who was the last to die, what it must have been like to drift helplessly with men you had known, and having seen them go one by one, wait for your own summons.

He tried to shake himself out of his depression and concentrated on Miller's makeshift sail. It did little to add to their speed, but by helping to steady the hull it made the oarsmen's work a bit easier.

Bolitho took out his glass and trained it across the starboard beam. Just over the sea's edge he saw a hint of purple. A long, flat island. He felt his heart quicken. They were not lost. He remembered it from the description on his chart.

She stirred against him. 'What is it?'

He kept his voice level. 'Another island. Many miles away, and too far to use what strength we have to visit it. But it means we are making progress. Once or twice I thought . . .' He looked down at her and smiled. 'I should have trusted *your* judgement.'

He turned his attention to his men again. Pyper was doing his best not to show it, but he was in a bad way. Blistered by the sun, his shoulder like raw meat through a rent in his shirt, he looked near to collapse. None of them had any moisture in their bodies. Perhaps Evans was the lucky one after all.

Quietly he said, 'We must have water. I can't ask these men to go on until they drop.'

She nodded slowly. 'I will pray.'

He watched her bowed head, the hot breeze ruffling her hair across the blue coat, and almost broke down. He had brought all of them to this. She especially would suffer because of her love. The remainder would die because he had decreed it.

'There.' She looked up at him. 'It is done. Now I will see to the dressings.' She touched her gown as it lay drying on the thwart. 'I will use some of this after today. Poor Penneck has used almost the last of the bandages.' She stood up, swaying with the boat until Keen put up his hand to steady her.

She smiled at him. 'Thank you, Val.'

It was her special name for him, and Bolitho saw her receive the same grateful look. Next to himself, Keen had better cause than anyone to remember her kindness.

Sergeant Quare had to clear his parched throat twice before he could speak. 'Will I start to divide the rations, sir?' Even he looked dejected. Almost beaten.

Bolitho felt suddenly desperate. 'Yes. One cup per man. Half water, half wine.' He nodded heavily. 'I *know*, Sergeant. It is the last of it.'

As Viola reached the sick and injured men Penneck seized her borrowed coat and babbled wildly, 'Don't let me die! Please don't let me die!' He was pleading, his voice rising to a thin shriek.

Colter, the wounded seaman, snarled, 'I wish to God 'e *would* die! 'E'll drive us all mad, that 'e will!'

'That will do!' Bolitho stood up, his mind aching and throbbing. 'Orlando, hold that man's arms while his dressing is changed!'

He watched her above the slow-moving oars. In her captain's coat, her legs as bare as any sailor's, she looked even more beautiful. She paused with her work while Orlando pushed Penneck against the gunwale, and thrust some loose hair from her face. Again their eyes met, and she smiled at him.

Blissett pulled his oar across the boat and snatched up a

musket. ' 'Nother bird, sir!' He fired, but the bird continued as before.

Quare flung another musket to him, and with barely a pause Blissett fired again. The sea-bird dropped close abeam, and within ten minutes had been divided and eaten.

As they sipped their watered wine and tried not to swallow it in one gulp, Pyper said brokenly, 'When I get back to the ship I'll never complain again!'

Bolitho watched him, seeing how close he was to breaking.

Almost gently he said, 'You will all right, Mr Pyper. You said *when*, not *if*. Hold on to it with all your strength, and that applies to the rest of us. Thank you, Mr Pyper. I feel somewhat better now.'

Allday looked up from his oar and smiled sadly. Inwardly he felt he could weep. For the lady in his captain's coat, for young Pyper, for Billy-boy who was trying so desperately not to show his distress from his wounded leg. But most of all for the captain. He had watched him, day after rotten day, using every trick, everything he had learned and experienced since first going to sea at the age of twelve, just to hold them all together.

In the line of battle it was terrible, but the suffering and hardship made some sort of sense to the survivors. But this was a side of the Navy which landsmen never knew of and cared about even less. And yet the rules were the same, and the burden to each commander just as definite.

Bolitho looked at him, perhaps feeling his thoughts.

'Ready for another pull, Allday?'

Allday smiled, sharing the game.

'Aye, Captain, if you'd care to join us poor sailormen.'

Jenner managed to give a croaking laugh, and Miller said, 'Anyway, sir, *you* don't wear a captain's coat no longer, eh?'

Bolitho seated himself on the thwart beside Allday, while Pyper took over the tiller.

He had to ask. 'What d'you think, Allday?'

The broad shoulders gave a slight shrug. 'They say the devil looks after his own. I reckon we stand a chance, and that's no error.'

Bolitho laid back on the oar, shutting his eyes to the pitiless sun. No more water, and just a few coconuts and some biscuits. And yet they still trusted him. It did not make any sense.

He thought of Pyper's pathetic courage and made himself say, *when*, not *if*.

His oar blade collided with another, and he realized he had almost fallen asleep or into a daze. The realization helped to sharpen his thoughts again, and he heaved on the oar with unexpected vigour.

When next he glanced outboard he saw there was quite a sharp wash coming back from the stem to mark their efforts. He closed his eyes tightly and thrust down on his loom.

When, not *if*.

15

A Power of Strength

Two nights after Bolitho had issued the last of the wine and water a storm broke over them with such ferocity he thought that everything was finished. It hit the cutter shortly after nightfall and transformed the sea into a crazy torment of bursting waves with crests large enough to swamp almost anything.

Hour after hour, stumbling and falling in swirling water, they fought to keep the boat from broaching to. Miller's sail, complete with its spar, was torn away into the spray-filled darkness within minutes, while loose gear, clothing and one of the oars followed soon after.

It was a frantic, unyielding struggle for survival. No orders were given, and none expected. The weary, battered men bailed or stood to their oars, blinded by spray, almost deafened by the thunder of bursting crests and the jubilant wail of the wind.

And then, as Bolitho sensed a slight easing in the wind's force, the rain came. Slowly at first, the heavy drops striking their heads and bodies like pellets, and then with a hissing roar, the very weight of which seemed to beat the waves into submission.

He yelled hoarsely, 'Quick, lads! *The rain!*'

It was pitiful to watch as they floundered in the waterlogged boat, groping for canvas, pannikins, anything which would catch the precious rain. The sick and injured, and the handful of men on the oars, kept their faces turned into the downpour, eyes tightly shut, mouths wide to receive what must seem like a miracle.

Bolitho dashed water from his face and hair and said, 'Viola! Your prayer was answered!'

They reached out blindly, their hands meeting and slipping in an onslaught of rain and sea.

If only it had come sooner and had spared them the last agonizing day. They had drained the last of the coconuts and then broken the shells to try and suck moisture from the fruit itself.

In the afternoon, while the boat had drifted beam-on to the sea, their torpor had been broken by an insane yell from Penneck.

He had cried, *'Water! In the name of Jesus!'*

And before anyone could move he had dragged himself up and over the gunwale, floundering wildly, yelling and weeping, while the boat had drifted away from him.

Where he had gathered the strength, Bolitho had been unable to imagine, but as he had swung the tiller and the blistered oarsmen had come back to life, Orlando had risen in the bows and had dived cleanly overboard.

Penneck had been hauled roughly over the stemhead with little pity for his injury. His thirst-maddened action had cost far more than a loss of strength and progress, for even as Orlando had paddled towards the boat, supporting the raving Penneck, the shark had struck with the speed of a battering-ram.

Helpless, the rest of them had watched the water frothing bright red, and had seen Orlando's upturned features contorted in agony, his poor mouth open in a silent scream. Then mercifully he had been dragged down even as Blissett had fired a ball at the tell-tale dorsal fin.

Allday called, 'Th' wind's dropping, Captain!' Like the rest, he was wringing wet, hair plastered across his forehead, his shirt moulded to him like another skin.

'Yes.'

Bolitho came out of his thoughts slowly. Penneck now lay in the bottom of the boat, his arms tied, but his legs jerking in irregular convulsions as he gaped at the clouds and giggled while he let the rain sluice over him.

Orlando was gone. Rather as he had first come amongst

them. From the sea and back to it. Nobody knew any more about him than when he had been rescued, only that he was grateful to remain with them.

As his friend Jenner had said brokenly, 'At least the poor devil was happy while he was with us, sir. When he was given the job of being your servant he was fair bustin' with pride, bless him!'

Unconsciously, Bolitho spoke aloud, 'Aye, bless him.'

Allday stared at him. 'Captain?'

'I was thinking. Adding another name to my list.'

When dawn came up with its breathtaking haste it was as if little had changed during the night. The clouds were gone, and the sea's face was as before in regular, undulating swells. As the sun rose and felt its way into the boat the woodwork and the dazed occupants steamed as if about to burst into flames. They peered around at their tiny world, examining each other, looking for signs of hope or the opposite.

They had collected over ten gallons of water, and there was still a little rum for those who needed it most. The food was gone, and unless Blissett was able to shoot another bird things would quickly deteriorate.

The only noticeable change from yesterday was that the shark no longer followed them. That too was strange, and to some, chilling. It was as if it had been waiting. To collect Orlando for the ocean he had cheated for just a short while.

Keen joined him during one of the short rests. He looked fitter than most of them, although his arms were burned by the sun and blotchy from salt sores.

He said, 'We saved the compass, sir.'

Bolitho kept his voice down. 'Have you noticed the driftwood?'

He watched Keen as he shaded his eyes towards the glittering horizon. Little pieces of flotsam floated towards the boat, black in the harsh light. There were birds too, but too far off for even a lucky shot.

Keen looked at him, his face incredulous. 'Land, sir?'

Bolitho wanted to contain it, in case he was wrong. But he looked along the boat and knew they could not last another day. With good news they might be able to hang on.

He nodded. 'Close. Yes, I believe so.'

Viola stood up and laid her hand on his shoulder, the other on Keen. She did not speak, but looked steadily towards the horizon, her hair lifting and falling over the coat.

Bolitho watched her, loving her, fascinated by her inner strength. Despite the sun, and what she must have endured, she looked pale compared with Keen and the others. He had only seen her break down once since leaving the islands, and that had been when Orlando had been killed.

She had said, 'He could not speak. He could not even cry out. And yet I seem to remember his voice.'

She said nothing more until the storm had burst over them.

They were all looking at him now, and even Penneck had fallen silent. He saw that the marine called Billy-boy was sharing an oar with Pyper, his injured leg propped on a musket. The other wounded seaman, Colter, had drawn enough strength from his ration of water to help look after Penneck and the one named Robinson who was in a very low state. But they were not so ill they could not sense something was happening.

Bolitho said, 'I believe we are near land. Whether we are close to Rutara Island, I am uncertain, for with storm and drift, and denied even a sextant, it is like groping in the dark. But whatever island we sight, we will land and secure food. After what we have seen and suffered together, I think it will take more than hostility to prevent us.'

Big Tom Frazer, his eyes red with strain, stood up and bellowed, 'A cheer for the cap'n, lads! *Huzza!*'

Bolitho could only stare at them. It was terrible to witness. These gaunt, blistered, unshaven men trying to stand at their oars and cheer.

He raised his voice. 'Enough! Save your strength!' He had to turn away. 'But I thank you.'

Keen cleared his throat and said, 'Out oars!' He met Viola's gaze and smiled like a conspirator. 'Give way all!'

By late afternoon Blissett and then Sergeant Quare were luckier with their marksmanship. One noddy and then a booby fell to their muskets, and although it took longer this time to reach them, they were retrieved and eaten with a full ration of water.

Then, as the sun touched the horizon, Miller shouted, '*Land*, sir! Fine on th' starboard bow!'

All thought of order and discipline broke down as they stood in the swaying boat, as if by so doing they might see it more clearly.

Bolitho held her arm and watched with the others. Land it was.

'We will reach it tomorrow.' He nodded firmly. 'Then we shall see.'

She answered simply, 'I never doubted you could do it.'

While Keen restored the stroke to the oars and the cutter started to move ahead again, Bolitho sat beside her in the sternsheets, as they had done every day since their journey had begun.

She leaned against him, Bolitho's coat tightly drawn around her. Her own clothing, like most of the articles in the boat, had gone outboard in the storm.

'Hold me. I feel cold, Richard.'

He put his arm round her. It would get even colder during the night, and protest or not, he would force her to take some rum. But when he cradled her against him he could feel the heat from her body like fire.

He said, 'Soon now. We'll build a fire. Then we will find the ship.'

'I know.' She moved closer and rested her head on his chest. 'A *big* fire.'

The boat settled down for another night. Quare and Blissett examined the muskets and powder. Keen made certain Penneck was still secured, in case he should throw himself overboard again.

But there was a different air in the boat. Not the fear and dread of another dawn, but a strange confidence in what it would bring for them.

Lieutenant Thomas Herrick moved restlessly about *Tempest*'s quarterdeck. At anchor, and despite the spread awnings and windsails, the ship was like a furnace, and only deep below on the orlop deck or in the holds could you find relief.

He had been in charge of the frigate for fifteen days, and should have been satisfied with the way he had handled her, and the fact that nothing untoward had occurred. But being Herrick, he felt like half a man, and even now, whenever he heard a footfall on the companionway, he almost expected to see Bolitho emerge on deck, his grey eyes moving automatically from one end of his ship to the other.

He walked to the nettings and looked at the island with something like hatred. To most people it would appear much as any other small point of land in the Great South Sea. To him it was a mocking challenge. A millstone which held him helpless.

He saw *Tempest*'s launch pulling lethargically between ship and shore, the sunlight glinting on weapons. For although they had found no sign of the French frigate or Tuke's schooners, they had company just the same. Large war canoes, crammed with dark figures, had moved as near as they dared. Watching or waiting for *Tempest*'s men to break the sanctity of their island by stepping ashore.

His mind returned frequently to the settlement and he wondered what was happening. No sign of the fever had appeared on board, so it seemed likely it was of a local nature and could bring down only those closely exposed to it and who lacked the toughness of the average sailor.

He had discussed it with the surgeon several times, but he had been unhelpful. He had explained to an impatient Herrick that a 'sniff of a cold' which would do no harm to a country parson in England could kill every man, woman and child on one of the islands if the conditions were right for it. On the other hand, no European could withstand the terrible torture of some initiation ceremonies which were performed and accepted without a murmur. Gwyther had said, 'It is all a question of *balance*, you see.'

Herrick mopped his face. Question of balance indeed.

Borlase appeared on deck and watched him guardedly. 'Have you made a decision, Mr Herrick?'

'Not yet.'

Herrick tried to turn it aside in his mind. It was fifteen days since he had left the Levu Islands and had watched Bolitho being pulled ashore. He ought to have heard something by now. He wondered what Bolitho would say when he discovered about the letter. In his own round handwriting Herrick had written a private report for Commodore Sayer at Sydney and had sent it across to the brig *Pigeon* before she had weighed anchor.

Herrick knew about courts martial and boards of enquiry. He understood that something in writing, put down at the time of the events under examination, carried far more weight than a carefully worded document written much later when the man concerned knew which way the cat would jump. Although what notice anyone would take of the view of a lowly lieutenant was harder to understand. But the thought of that pig Raymond using his influence and guile to destroy Bolitho was something he would not stand by and watch.

He looked at Borlase, waiting with his childlike smile.

'I have carried out the captain's orders. But there has been not even a smell of *Narval* or the pirates. If there had been a sea fight, we'd have discovered something surely? Driftwood, corpses, *something.*'

Herrick forced himself to think back. He had found Hardacre's small schooner off North Island, but her master had nothing to report. He had been very glad to see Herrick, happier still to be ordered to the settlement. There were too many war canoes in the vicinity for his liking. It was more than probable Bolitho would send the schooner back again, here to Rutara, with fresh instructions. He shook his head angrily. No, he was doing it again. Shutting his eyes. Turning from responsibility.

He considered it more calmly. It could happen at any time in a man-of-war. By accident, in battle, or from disease, a captain might die. Then his subordinate took charge, and so on. There was no other way. And here, thousands of miles from anywhere, it was his own burden now.

He said abruptly, 'I will weigh tomorrow.' He saw Borlase's eyes sharpen. 'That schooner should have brought us news.'

Borlase let his lashes hide his eyes. 'It is a heavy decision for you.'

'God damn it, d'you think I don't know that, you fool!'

Borlase flushed. 'I am sorry you take that attitude, sir!'

'*Good!*'

Herrick saw Acting-Lieutenant Swift walking wearily along the larboard gangway. He was on watch. It was like having a wardroom full of children and old men, Herrick thought angrily.

'*Mr Swift!*' He saw the youth jump. 'Recall the boat and change crews. It is your job to remember these things!'

Ross, the big master's mate who was also appointed acting-lieutenant by Bolitho's order, strolled across to him.

Herrick glowered. 'And don't *you* start asking what I am going to do!'

Ross kept his face stiff. 'Och, sir, I had no such intention.'

There was a scuffle of feet by the entry port and then Swift ran aft, his sun-reddened face alive with excitement.

'Sir! The sentry saw two men on the island! As I hailed the guard boat they seemed to appear out of nowhere!'

Herrick snatched the glass and trained it on the shore. For a moment he could not find anything because of a dancing haze which made the low hills quiver like jelly. Then he saw them, two staggering, bewildered figures, lurching against one another, sometimes falling, only to rise up and continue towards the sea. Like two drunken scarecrows, he thought.

Ross said sharply, 'Those canoes have sighted 'em, sir!'

Herrick swung his telescope round like a swivel gun, masts, rigging and then open water sweeping through the powerful lens and then settling on the nearest canoes. A mile distant, but there was no doubting their purpose. They must have seen the men on the island, too. The closest canoe was a grand affair, with a great castle-like structure in its stern, decorated with man-o'-war birds' feathers, and richly carved. Must be all of forty feet long, he thought, with professional interest.

He barked, 'Rouse the hands, but don't send them to quarters. Tell Mr Brass to clear away whatever twelve-pounder he thinks fit to bear on those fellows. I'll have no nonsense from them!'

Calls trilled below his feet, and seamen and marines appeared from all directions.

Borlase remarked, 'They're both white men anyway.'

The guard boat, still unaware of the two men ashore, pulled gratefully into *Tempest*'s shadow. Herrick ran to the gangway, and as he leaned out under an awning felt the sun on his neck like a branding iron. Schultz, the German boatswain's mate, was peering up at him.

Herrick yelled, 'Go back and lie offshore. Tell those two men to swim out to you. Put one of yours overboard if need be, but keep the boat away from the beach!'

The heads in the launch swivelled from the island to the canoes and back again.

Herrick added, 'And, Schultz, let somebody else do the hailing.'

'*Ja*, zur, I understand!' He grinned.

'God.' Herrick went into the shade again. 'This damned heat!'

He looked up at the loosely brailed sails. Ready to release and set in minutes. *Tempest* was desperately shorthanded, but as prepared to give fight as any ship could be.

A gunport opened, and one of the twelve-pounders trundled squeakily into the sunlight. Mr Brass, the gunner, stood hands on hips, watching the selected crew loading and ramming home a black, shining ball. Beside the gunner, Midshipman Romney, small and delicate against the muscular seamen, was trying not to get in anybody's way.

'Ready, sir!'

Herrick nodded. The canoes were much closer, the paddles rising and dipping in perfect unison. He shivered despite the heat. He remembered other times when he had watched them, without the stout timbers of a ship to protect him.

'May I speak, sir?' It was a young seaman called Gwynne, one of the volunteers Herrick had signed on from the *Eurotas*. He had settled in well and seemed quite happy with his somewhat harsher surroundings.

'Yes, Gwynne.'

The seaman shifted awkwardly on his bare feet as the officers clustered around him. Even Prideaux was here now, his foxy face set in disapproval.

I

'Them two fellows, sir. I knows 'em. They'm off *Eurotas*, same as me.'

Herrick stared at him. 'Take the glass, man. Have another look!'

Prideaux said softly, 'If it is true, they must have changed sides when Tuke captured the ship in the first place.'

'I know that!' Herrick controlled his frayed temper. 'Bring them aft when they get on board.'

Gwynne nodded firmly. 'Aye, sir. 'Tis them right 'nough. Tall one's Latimer, 'e was a foretopman, a simple sort. T'other is Mossel, able-bodied seaman.' He grimaced. 'A proper gallows-bird, that one.'

Borlase puffed out his cheeks. 'And that is *precisely* where he will end.'

Herrick nodded to Gwynne. 'Thank you. That is most helpful.'

He looked at the two figures who were wading and suddenly swimming towards the boat. The bottom shelved steeply and swiftly, as Herrick had discovered when he had anchored. But Schultz had reached the two struggling swimmers.

'Canoes sheering off, sir!'

Herrick peered towards the sleek canoes and their busy paddles. Maybe they had been waiting to capture these two scarecrows for themselves. Herrick thought of what Tinah had said about the militia lieutenant. *Baked alive in clay*. It was too horrible even to consider.

He called, 'Secure the gun. No sense in wasting a good ball.'

Brass touched his forehead. He looked disappointed, Herrick thought.

He saw the surgeon and one of his loblolly boys waiting at the gangway.

'Bring them to me when you're satisfied.'

Gwyther stared at him. 'They may be very ill, sir. You said there was no water on the island surely?'

'I said *satisfied*, Mr Gwyther.' Herrick was not prepared for another 'question of balance'. 'I did not mean when they have had a month's rest!'

In the cabin he sat at Bolitho's desk, while Cheadle, the

clerk, knelt by a small chest sorting through papers like a ghoul over a coffin.

Captain Prideaux rapped on the door. 'Ready, Mr Herrick!'

The two men came into the cabin, blinking dully, and being half supported by Pearse, the ship's corporal, and Scollay, the master-at-arms.

Gwyther hovered in the rear like an anxious bird. He said, 'I suggest they be allowed to sit down, sir.'

Herrick regarded the two men coldly. 'When I am ready.'

They were in a bad way. Gaunt and wild-eyed, their mouths and much of their skin were covered with sores, their lips cracked by thirst.

He remembered what Gwynne had said of Mossel, and could well believe it. Squat and beetle-browed, it could not have taken much to change him into a pirate.

Herrick said, 'You are from the *Eurotas*.' He saw the dazed exchange of glances. 'So you can spare me the story you were going to tell about being shipwrecked mariners and how you were the only survivors. It has been tried before by cleverer and more believable rascals!'

The tall, gangling seaman called Latimer tried to step towards the desk, but Scollay snarled, 'Stand still, you bugger!'

Latimer said in a husky, terrified voice, 'It wasn't my fault, sir!'

Prideaux was watching him fixedly, his fingers stroking the hilt of his sword. 'It never is.'

The man continued wretchedly, 'They took over the ship afore we could do anythin', I was plannin' to 'elp rescue the cap'n, but . . .'

The one called Mossel grated, 'Hold yer tongue, you fool!'

Herrick regarded him thoughtfully. They must have been hiding on the island for days. Fearful of the watchful canoes, and hoping against hope that a ship would pass close enough to rescue them. But not a King's ship. Only thirst, and the grim realization they would not stay alive much longer, had forced them to reveal themselves.

He said quietly, 'Send for the boatswain.' He saw Midshipman Fitzmaurice in the doorway. 'My compliments to Mr Jury.

Tell him I wish to have a halter run out to the mainyard immediately.'

The effect was immediate. Latimer fell on his knees, sobbing, 'It's not right, sir! Please don't 'ang me! T'others forced me into it! We 'ad no choice!'

Herrick said, 'There are plenty of men who did not join the pirates, and are alive to say so.'

Fitzmaurice asked politely, 'Shall I tell the boatswain, sir?'

'Let me consider.' Herrick watched Latimer being hauled to his feet.

Mossel said, 'We'll 'ang anyways, so what the 'ell.' He winced as the ship's corporal drove his fist into his side.

Herrick stood up, sickened at Latimer's grovelling, and his own part in bringing it about. But time was running out. There was more at stake than the neck of a bloody mutineer.

He snapped, 'Take him outside.' To Latimer he added, 'And *you*, sit on that chest. I'll not have your filth on the captain's furniture.'

As the door closed behind the other man, Latimer asked timidly, 'You are not the cap'n then, sir?'

'No. So you see, what my captain knows nothing of will not disturb him. I can hang you here and now, and no one will care a jot. I can take you back to land and say that you, er, aided my enquiries, and they will believe it. The captain is bound by certain rules. I am not.' He watched the lie exploring the man's mind, then he shouted, 'So tell me, damn you, or you will dance on air before eight bells!'

The story which Latimer blurted out was as fantastic as it was frightening.

In his cracked, husky voice the man who had been a foretopman under the murdered Captain Lloyd told of his service aboard one of the pirate schooners, the one which was commanded by Mathias Tuke. Feared, and with good reason, Tuke nevertheless built a sort of respect amongst his men. Latimer told of his attack on an island, how he had landed guns, and set fire to a village. He described acts of murder and bestial cruelty, which by his example had spread to his crew, so that death became almost too commonplace to mention.

He explained that the Frenchman, Yves Genin, had also been

aboard, but had taken no part in the killing and plunder. He seemed to have some sort of understanding with his brutal companion.

Latimer heard them having an argument one night, after a whole day of drinking. Tuke had raved that he did not need Genin at all, that just the rumour of his being aboard was enough to entice that madman de Barras into a trap.

Genin had replied just as hotly that his own men aboard the *Narval* would not act without his word.

Herrick listened, spellbound. So that was it, almost as Bolitho had described it would be. Genin was bait, but he had some of his followers already hiding amongst the French frigate's company. They probably signed on when de Barras was chasing after his escaped prisoner.

Latimer left the worst part until the end.

He said in his failing voice, 'Just afore Tuke put us ashore 'e fell on the schooner from the settlement. 'E tortured 'er master and threw 'im to the sharks. But not afore 'e'd discovered all about your ship and where you was. 'E laughed like a madman, and all the while 'e was burnin' the schooner's master with a red 'ot blade.'

Herrick stared at him. So the schooner had never even reached the settlement. *Tempest* was up here, and known to be here.

He asked, 'Anything more?'

Latimer looked at his tarry hands. 'We took a small trader, Dutch, I think she was. She 'ad letters aboard. News about the trouble in France.'

'God Almighty.' The fat was in the fire now. 'And then?'

'Me and Mossel was caught stealin' from the booty, sir. Cap'n Tuke marooned us 'ere. Knowin' there was no water an' that them black devils would kill us if we tried to leave.'

Herrick nodded. 'Your Captain Tuke is a clever man. He knew that we would come. That we would think those canoes were watching for us, and remain at anchor.' He looked at Prideaux. 'So when he passes the word to Genin's people aboard *Narval* there will be a mutiny, and in many ways I can understand that. But a pirate he will remain.'

Prideaux shook his head. 'I think not. If he can make use of

Narval, effect one great capture with her assistance, he might well seek respectability and recognition, and Genin could give it to him.'

Herrick bit his lip. 'Mebbe, but we're not in Henry Morgan's times now.'

Latimer was looking at them anxiously. 'I did 'ear tell of some supply ships, sir. The Dutch trader told Tuke. They're comin' round the 'Orn on passage for New South Wales.'

Herrick turned to Prideaux again. 'So there you have it. He'll find a new base for himself. Mount his captured guns and prepare to make the biggest capture of his life.' He glanced at the stern windows, seeing the purple shadows feeling out from the land. He made up his mind. 'Damn it, Captain Prideaux, we'll weigh tomorrow and return to the settlement. I daren't up-anchor now and work through these reefs in the dark. It was bad enough getting into the place.'

'An' *us*, sir?'

Herrick studied Latimer for several seconds. 'Your companion will hang, though not at my hands. I'll see what I can do for you. You may have saved many lives. It could help.'

He turned away as the man was bustled weeping from the cabin.

Prideaux said bitterly, 'Save lives, by God! We're incapable of being anywhere in time now! I think we should return to Sydney. Let the commodore take the responsibility.'

Herrick felt better now he had made a decision. Without the schooner Bolitho could not get word to him. It was up to *Tempest* to rejoin her proper commander, no matter at what risk from fever.

He said, 'Pass the word for Mr Lakey. I wish to discuss tomorrow's sailing plans. After that we will hold a conference in here.'

Alone in the cabin Herrick walked to the windows and stared out at the restless water. A light wind, but there had been quite a storm the previous night, a long way off, but the sea had been choppy even here. You could never be certain of weather.

Lakey stepped into the cabin.

Herrick said, 'We're going for the captain, Mr Lakey.'

The sailing master regarded him and answered dryly, 'About time.'

Blissett half-stood and half-crouched right in the cutter's bows, gripping the stemhead with his hands to retain his balance. He was desperately tired, and his stomach ached so much from hunger he felt sick and lightheaded. At his back the oars rose and fell, very slowly, the stroke ragged and uncertain.

He gritted his teeth against the bitter cold. In a matter of an hour or so it would be sun-up, and after that . . . he tried not to think of it, to concentrate on anything to stop his head from lolling. He heard the occasional squeak of the tiller and pictured Lieutenant Keen sitting there, using the stars to hold the boat roughly on course. The violent storm had swept away the lamp for the compass, and it took every ounce of skill to keep the boat from veering away, the oarsmen too fatigued to notice.

Which was why Blissett was posted in the bows. Apart from being one of the strongest men in the boat, his past life as a gamekeeper, used to peering over long distances of his master's estate, had blessed him with excellent eyesight. He had no idea if the island they had sighted before nightfall was the one they wanted, nor did he much care. But it was more than possible, worn out as they were, that they might pull right past it in the darkness. He yawned and tried to stop his shivering.

He could feel Penneck watching him from the bottom of the boat. Wild, crazy eyes. *You start your raving again and I'll drive my musket into your mouth.* He stiffened as something white moved in the darkness. But it was not a bird. Just a dart of spindrift whipped from the crest of a wave.

The sea already seemed brighter, he thought anxiously. The sun would come soon. The suffering.

Someone climbed over the thwart behind him and asked huskily, 'Nothing?' It was the sergeant. Getting ready to do his stint on an oar.

Blissett shook his head. 'Dawn coming up.'

'Aye.' Quare sounded very low,

'Never mind, Sergeant.' Blissett suddenly needed Quare to be the same as he always was. Confident. Hard. 'We'll manage.'

Quare smiled wearily, grimacing at the pain in his sore lips. 'If you say so.'

Blissett turned from him. *If Quare really thought* . . . He froze, blinking rapidly as something upset the sea's regular pattern.

In a small voice he said, 'Sergeant, up ahead! It's land!' He gripped Quare's arm. 'Please God, tell me I'm right!'

Quare swallowed hard and nodded. 'You're right, lad. I see it.' He swivelled round towards the stern. '*Land ho!*'

Oars went momentarily out of control as men struggled to their feet or fumbled blindly across the thwarts.

Bolitho could not move, as he had been drowsing, one arm around Viola's shoulders.

He said, 'Mr Keen! What d'you see?'

But it was Allday who replied, 'It's the one, Captain! I'm sure!' He looked around the boat. 'All those bloody islands, but we found it!'

Several of them tried to cheer, others wanted to weep, but were too parched even for that.

Bolitho said quietly, 'Wake, Viola. You were right. It must be Rutara, although it has to be some form of magic!'

Allday heard him and gave a great sigh, rubbing his sore palms on his trousers. He wanted to say something special at this moment. To hold them all together long after the boat and the misery of their endurance would be faded in memory.

He stared at Bolitho and then at Viola Raymond. He had been holding her against him, as he had for most of the night. But now as he tried to rouse her, her arm slipped from his grasp and hung down to sway with the boat's unsteady motion.

Then Allday was on his feet, his voice harsh as he called, 'Mr Keen! See to the captain!' He scrambled aft, knocking men aside, ignoring all of them as he added, 'Just do as I ask, sir!' Then he was by the tiller, his arms around both of them as he exclaimed, 'Here, Captain! *It's no use!* Let me take her, *please!*' And as Bolitho started to struggle he called, 'Hold him!' He turned his head, his voice breaking, '*For God's sake*, Mr Keen!'

Only then did Keen understand. He gripped Bolitho around

the shoulders while Jenner seized him from the opposite side. All he could say was, 'I must do it, sir. I must. I can't let you go.'

Allday gathered her up in his arms, feeling her hair blowing across his face as he carried her to the middle of the boat. Her body was still warm, but against his neck her face felt like ice.

He murmured to Miller, 'The anchor, Jack.'

Miller nodded, as if like the rest he was struck dumb by what was happening. Their suffering, the discovery of land, it all meant nothing.

Bolitho shouted, '*No!*' And Allday heard his shoes slipping on the wet boards as the others held him there.

Gently, Allday slipped Bolitho's coat from her body and held her above the gunwale, while Miller passed a bowline around her and attached it to the cutter's anchor. No shark or scavenger would disturb her now.

She was so light she barely made a ripple as he slipped her into the water, and even as he watched he saw her pale shape fading into the depths, until it was gone altogether.

Then Allday went aft and stood in front of Bolitho, powerful against the paling sky.

He said wretchedly, 'Use me as you will, Captain. But it was for the best.' He laid the coat beside him. 'She'll rest easy now.'

Bolitho reached out and gripped his hand. 'I know.' He could barely see. 'I know.'

Keen said heavily, 'Man your oars.'

The boat began to move again, and as the frail daylight felt its way across the water Bolitho looked astern and said, 'But for me she would not have been here.'

Keen replied quietly, 'But for her, sir, none of us would have survived.'

Half an hour later the light laid bare the island, and close inshore, her awnings and sails very clear against the land, they sighted the *Tempest*.

But this time there was no cheering, and as they moved nearer, hearing the sudden excitement on board, the trill of calls and the sounds of a boat being lowered, they were cruelly aware of loss rather than survival.

A boat from *Tempest* reached them in minutes and took them in tow, her crew suddenly aware of the silence.

As Bolitho pulled himself up and through the entry port he was only dimly conscious of the pressing figures around and above him.

Only one face stood out, and as he gripped Herrick's hand he was unable to speak, or to let go.

Herrick watched him anxiously. 'You came all that way, sir? What . . .'

He turned as Keen said, 'The lady has just died, sir. Within sight of this damned island!' Then he hurried away.

Herrick said, 'We will speak later, sir.'

He beckoned urgently to the boatswain, but the shocked and bewildered men were already being helped or hoisted inboard.

Bolitho nodded to each man in turn as they were aided or shuffled past. Acting-Lieutenant Pyper, being carried by two seamen, Billy-boy hopping with an arm around someone's neck. Jenner and Miller, Sergeant Quare and the unbreakable Blissett. The Frenchman Lenoir, and Big Tom Frazer.

Allday touched his forehead. 'All hoisted inboard, Captain.' He watched him, searching for some sign. Then he said, 'You can be proud of what you did, Captain, an' that's no error.' Then he too walked slowly towards the companion.

Herrick followed Bolitho aft, past the silent, watching faces. He noticed the way he was carrying his coat, as if it was the most precious thing he possessed.

He asked hesitantly, 'Do you have any orders, sir?' He fell back as Bolitho looked at him. 'It can wait of course, but . . .'

'It cannot, Mr Herrick.' Again the impetuous grip on his arm. '*Thomas*. We have work to do. Get the ship under way, if you please. We are returning to the Levu Islands.'

As Bolitho lowered himself through the companion, Lakey said in a fierce whisper, 'Five hundred miles, Mr Herrick. In that boat, and with nothing much to sustain them either.' He shook his head. 'They must have found a power of strength from somewhere.'

Herrick nodded sadly. 'Aye, they did. And now she's dead.

I could shoot myself for some of the thoughts I've had, some of the things I've said.'

He saw the boatswain watching him from the gangway.

'Mr Jury, be so good as to sink that cutter before we weigh.'

'But, sir, a boat, any boat, is valuable out here.' He sounded shocked.

'In this case I think it best to destroy it.' Herrick glanced at the cabin skylight. 'I would to God I could destroy its memory also!'

16

No Retreat

On the morning of the first full day at sea the wind backed considerably, and with the sudden change came a heavy downpour of rain.

Bolitho leaned over the stern bench and stared emptily through the thick windows, his vision twisting and swirling as the rain swept across the water and pounded over the deck above. He heard feet hurrying to various parts of his ship, men watching over sun-dried cordage to ensure it did not swell enough to foul the blocks. Others would be collecting the rain-water to supplement their stocks.

He sat down wearily, letting the vessel move his body without resistance. In his screened sleeping compartment he could hear Hugoe, the wardroom servant, completing his tidying, collecting clothing to be washed.

Herrick had suggested several men who would be willing or suitable to replace Orlando. But Bolitho could not bear the thought of beginning again. Not yet. Hugoe was always in demand in the wardroom, and was grateful to be freed from the cabin, and its brooding captain, he suspected.

Rain gurgled down the scuppers or pattered happily across the sealed skylight. *Water*. You were less than nothing without it. He pictured the thirst-crazed man leaping overboard to fill his stomach from the sea. Orlando's terrible agony as the shark had crushed him into a bloody pulp.

He forced himself to take out his watch, and hesitated further before he could open the guard. Even the engraving seemed to stand out sharper.

Hugoe stood in the screen door. 'I've done, sir. 'Less there's owt in 'ere?'

'No. You can carry on.' He saw the curiosity in his eyes. 'Thank you.'

The marine sentry at the outer door shouted, 'Midshipman o' th' watch, sir!'

'Enter.'

It was young Romney, very nervous as he presented a list of the day's work from his first lieutenant. The visitors would soon be arriving. Questions. Needs.

He scanned through Herrick's round handwriting. 'Very well.'

Romney hesitated, one foot scraping over the other. 'May I speak, sir?'

'Yes.' Bolitho turned his back as if to watch the water streaming down the tall windows.

'I – I, that is, we, sir, want you to know how sorry . . .'

Bolitho gripped his hands tightly to his sides until he could face him again.

'Thank you, Mr Romney.' He barely recognized his own voice. 'It was most thoughtful.'

Romney watched him, his eyes full of warmth. Like a dog's, Bolitho thought despairingly.

The surgeon peered through the door, and Bolitho snapped, 'Come in.'

He would immerse himself in his duties and what he must plan ahead. But the small touches of kindness which came without warning shattered his guard like a cutlass on a badly cast rapier.

Bolitho listened to Gwyther's sick report.

'The marine is doing well, sir.' Gwyther's Welsh accent was very pronounced. It always was when he intended to act out of character. 'But you seem not to have slept, sir? There's bad, it is, if I may presume to say so.'

'You may not!' He hurried through the list of names. 'And Penneck?'

The surgeon sighed. 'I fear his mind has broken, sir. And Mr Pyper is very sick from his exposure and burns. But – ' another sigh, ' – he is young.'

Herrick was the next visitor, his conversation full of technicalities and requirements for keeping a ship of war in proper order. Although he did not mention anything about Viola, his blue eyes were incapable of concealing his anxiety.

Bolitho stood up and walked to the quarter windows. Birds dipped and wheeled beneath the ship's counter, waiting for scraps, watching for incautious fish. He thought of Blissett. His perfect aim, despite his own suffering.

He asked, 'Did you tell Prideaux that I expect him to promote Blissett directly?'

'Aye, sir.' Herrick shifted as Bolitho turned to look at him. 'In case he was about to argue the toss, I told him it was neither a suggestion nor a request. But that it was a bloody order, sir! I hope that was all right.'

'Yes.' He looked up as more feet pounded overhead.

Herrick explained, 'I told Mr Lakey that you want as much sail as we can spread. The hands are turning to in both watches.' He tried to smile, to break through Bolitho's ache. 'Being the master of course, he wasn't too pleased to drive her in this rain.'

He waited, wondering how to continue. 'I can manage well enough, sir. No need to bother you until we sight the islands.'

Bolitho sat down on the bench and stared at the canvas-covered deck.

'We can exercise the twelve-pounders as soon as the sails are trimmed. As we are so shorthanded it will be necessary to shift the crews around again.' He pounded his hands together. 'I want this ship ready to fight, d'you understand?'

'Look, sir.' Herrick stood his ground. 'I've little love for the Frogs, as you well know. But they've been in their King's service too long to throw in their lot with a pirate, surely?'

Bolitho eyed him gravely. 'Suppose I were to go on deck, right now, Thomas, and have all the hands lay aft. And if I told them that we were already at war with France, that England was depending on their courage and tenacity, do you honestly believe there is one single man aboard, including yourself, who would dare to question it?' He shook his head. 'Do not bother to deny it. It is on your face.'

Herrick watched him and marvelled. How could he keep on worrying and altering the pattern of things uppermost in his thoughts?

He said, 'If the Frenchman, Genin, can rouse the company against that tyrant of a captain, there's nothing to prevent him telling them the same about us?' He pouted his lower lip. 'But I still don't see why.'

'It will be his bargain with Tuke. The ship's authority and Genin's safe passage set against Tuke's own reward. Supply ships, gold, patronage, it matters little. What does and will count is his need of a safe and powerful base.'

Herrick nodded glumly. 'And there is nothing to prevent it. 'Cept us.'

'Aye, Thomas. One frigate against a flotilla. Our depleted company against seasoned, maltreated veterans.'

There was a cry from overhead, and feet shuffled impatiently. Herrick was needed, but he was unable to break the spell of Bolitho's icy determination as he added, 'But we *will* prevent it. We will use what we have to destroy the pirate and everyone who stands with him. In months, if not already, we may be at war with France again, and I have no intention of allowing *Narval* the pleasure of fighting us in the future.' He looked away. 'I should have seen it before. Much earlier. But I was like Le Chaumareys, too sure of my own capacity.' He smiled, but the warmth avoided his eyes. 'Go to your men, Thomas. I will be up when you begin the drills.'

Herrick replied simply, 'I have not spoken before, sir, but I owe it to you now, and to the lady more than ever. I was wrong to criticize, and had no place to act as I did. Your need of each other is made so plain to me now, for I see what her loss has meant. I am sorry, not just as a loyal subordinate, but still, I hope, as a firm friend.'

Bolitho nodded, the lock of hair dropping over his eyes. 'My wrong was the greater. I should have taken your advice those five years back, and again just months ago. Because of my want, I put her life in danger. Because she trusted me, she is now dead.' He turned his back. 'Please leave me.'

Herrick opened his mouth and closed it again. He had never seen him like this before. Pale, despite his tanned skin, his eyes ringed with shadows like a man possessed.

On deck he could not even find reassurance in the way that the company was arranged to allow for the shortages.

He saw Blissett standing with the marines at the hammock nettings, his musket at his side. Apart fom looking thinner, he showed little sign of his ordeal.

He remarked, 'I am glad to see you well, *Corporal* Blissett.'

Blissett beamed. 'Sir!' For him, life had suddenly expanded. Another step.

Herrick walked to the quarterdeck rail, the last heavy drops of rain tapping down on men and sails alike. It would soon be as hot as hell. He glanced at the upturned faces on the gundeck, the bare-backed topmen who waited on either gangway ready to swarm aloft and loose the topgallants when ordered. A good company, he thought. As mixed as a crowd at a prize-fight, but none the worse for it. They had somehow come together. Learned to accept, if not agree with, the manner in which they served. He felt he should say something. Tell them just how much they would have to give and withstand if Bolitho was right.

There was a step on the deck behind him and Bolitho said, 'There seems to be a delay, Mr Herrick?'

Herrick looked at his eyes, grey and steady, but something else as well. Challenging, or was it pleading?

He touched his hat. 'I thought you'd be staying below for a while, sir.'

Bolitho looked slowly across the silent men and the ship herself as she laid over on the larboard tack.

'My place is here.'

He rested his hands on the rail, feeling the ship trembling through it, passing the unending messages to anyone who would listen. He recalled Viola's expression when he had explained how a ship performed and responded. At first he had been almost shy, a boy again, as he had described what to him was his everyday life. And she had not been bored, nor had she been politely interested. In time they could have shared it. Planted something as firm and as lasting as the old house in Falmouth. But now . . .

He said abruptly, 'Carry on, Mr Herrick. Hands aloft and loose t'gallants, if you please.'

The shrouds and ratlines became alive with scurrying figures, and the urgent shouts of petty officers shattered the calm and sent the sea-birds screaming across *Tempest*'s bubbling wake.

Bolitho began to pace up and down the weather side, a vital presence, and to all but those who knew him intimately, as outwardly calm as ever.

But each step was painful, and although his men bustled around him, or slithered down backstays to attend further tasks, and while canvas boomed and hardened to the wind, Captain Richard Bolitho walked entirely alone.

Tempest made a fast run south to the Levu Islands, and although they sighted no craft larger than an occasional canoe, Bolitho had the feeling that every mile of their progress had been watched.

He knew that most of the ship's company were trying to keep their distance and avoid his eye. In many ways the isolation amongst his closely packed world suited him, and yet he was equally conscious of his responsibility to them. Especially with what might be lying ahead. Tomorrow. Next week.

To be feared by the men whose lives he held in his hands was totally repugnant to him. He saw the glances, searching for his daily reaction to their needs. Sail and gun drill. Working aloft or about the decks, he knew they watched after he had passed them by. Concerned, or merely curious. Envious, despite his grief, for all his privileges compared with their spartan existence.

On the last day, as *Tempest* worked slowly towards the mushroom-shaped bay, her courses brailed up and two leadsmen in the chains, he watched the island taking shape in the early light, very aware of his own mixed feelings.

The masthead had reported smoke soon after dawn, and as the light strengthened over the humped hills and brought reflections back to the water, he saw a drifting pall above the bay like a low cloud, deep-bellied with rain.

Herrick said, 'From the settlement by the look of it, sir.'

Bolitho said, 'It would seem so.'

He examined his feelings again. Did he want to find Raymond already dead? Or was he merely seeing the smoke as proof that he was right? About Tuke and the *Narval*, above all about his own part yet to come.

He said abruptly, 'Give me a glass.' He took it from Midshipman Romney and trained it on the land.

As the telescope's eye passed over the bay he saw the remains of *Eurotas* glistening above the surface like decayed teeth. He had almost forgotten about it, and the sight cut into him like a dirk. It brought back too many memories. Of that night they had left the bay, more afraid of being fired on by Raymond's orders than the ordeal which they were only just beginning.

He moved the glass until he found the settlement. The smoke was from some outbuildings, probably the ones which had been built for the convicts. There were several holes in the palisades too, the work of heavy guns.

But the flag was still there. He closed the glass, angry with his acceptance. *Never again.*

'Send the hands to quarters, Mr Herrick. We will anchor two cables from the pier. I need to be able to leave with haste.'

He shut his ears to the squeal of calls, the immediate rush of feet along gangways and decks. On the forecastle, peering over the bows, was Borlase with the anchor party. He turned, startled by the sudden commotion, and Bolitho wondered briefly if he thought his captain was going mad, or had suffered so much in the open boat that he was beyond a proper decision.

Herrick hurried across the quarterdeck and touched his hat. 'Hands at quarters, sir.' He asked, 'Shall we clear for action?'

'Not yet.'

Bolitho lifted the glass again and saw several bare-backed figures ducking through the bushes above the nearest beach. So Tinah's village was not entirely destroyed. He found he was giving thanks, grateful they had been spared.

He lowered the glass and saw Keen on the gundeck, shading his eyes to stare ashore. Thinking of his beautiful Malua. Remembering the dream.

Lakey cleared his throat noisily. 'We're losing the wind, sir.'

Bolitho turned and saw the land sliding out to shield them, and heard the topsails banging restlessly overhead.

'Very well. We will anchor now.'

A long pull for the boats' crews. Equally, it gave *Tempest*'s guns command of the whole bay.

'Man th' lee braces! Hands wear ship!'

Bolitho took a few paces aft and watched his men, even more shorthanded with the bulk of the company standing at quarters in case the guns were needed.

They had learned a great deal together in two years. Heavy she might be for a frigate, but she had been good to them.

Seamen worked feverishly at sheets and clewlines, while others pulled on the braces to bring the yards round together.

'Helm a'lee!'

Bolitho crossed the deck so that he could keep a continued watch on the shore and the pier below the settlement.

'Let go!'

He barely heard the anchor fall as he said, 'I shall need my gig. Also the launch and full landing party of marines. Prideaux will take charge of them personally.' He beckoned to Allday. 'Make sure the gig's crew are properly turned out.' He saw the surprise, or was it hurt, in his face and added, 'I *know*. You'd already so ordered. But this has to look right.'

He saw the marines tramping from their stations on the poop and in the tops, Sergeant Quare shouting commands, his face so blistered from the open boat that it almost matched his coat.

Herrick watched the boats being swayed over the nettings, Jury, the boatswain, urging the lowering party with a voice like an angry bullock.

'It looks as if there has been an attack on the settlement, sir.'

'Yes.' Bolitho lifted his arms as Allday buckled on his sword. 'It proves we were right. Tuke is after this place for himself. He must have used the captured cannon to give Raymond a warning.'

Herrick licked his lips. 'He seems to have an edge on us every time, sir.'

Bolitho walked to the gangway and looked down at the boats.

'But for one thing. He seized Hardacre's schooner and knows all about your message.'

'I am deeply sorry, sir, I thought . . .'

Bolitho took his arm. 'No, Thomas, it is our only *strength*.

Tuke will think of you still anchored off Rutara Island, afraid
to disobey orders, even fearful that the Itak may have overrun
the settlement. Also, he will know that without the schooner
there is no sensible way of carrying messages between ship and
settlement.'

Herrick stared at him. 'I'd have thought the same, in his
shoes.' He shook his head. 'An open boat, with barely enough
water and food to last a few days, and through dangerous
islands at that, well, I can see his point of view.'

'It changes nothing.' Bolitho watched the launch, packed
with marines, as it pulled clear of the ship and waited for the
gig to move alongside. 'It does give us time. But for this, I fear
the island would already have fallen.'

Borlase called, 'All ready, sir.'

'What are *my* instructions, sir?' Herrick walked with him to
the entry port.

'The usual. A good lookout, and with maybe six guns
permanently manned. If all is safe ashore, I shall want a lookout
posted on the hill.'

He lowered himself into the boat while the trill of calls still
hung on the humid air.

Borlase asked irritably, 'Why all the show of strength?
The marines, the gig's oarsmen in their best chequered
shirts? It is more like a courtesy visit than a preparation for
evacuation.'

Herrick studied him calmly. 'Evacuation? Never. This is
the captain's way of showing that no matter what others may
think or dread, *Tempest* is as before. A ship of war, Mr Borlase,
not a hull full of frightened old women!'

Keen joined them by the entry port and asked, 'Who has
gone with the captain?'

Herrick replied shortly, 'Mr Swift. Good experience for him
when he does pass for the rank he has borrowed.'

He turned aside, remembering Bolitho's words in the cabin
before dawn.

'Not Mr Keen, Thomas. It is too soon. He'll see his Malua
by every tree, hear her voice. No. He needs time. I'll take young
Swift.'

Herrick sighed. How typical, he thought. He watched the

boats pulling into line and turning towards the pier. And how much worse it will be for *him*.

Bolitho stood beside one of the long windows in Raymond's room and listened to the insane screech of birds in the dense undergrowth.

He was surprised at his own calm, his inability to feel either disgust or hatred as he watched Raymond sitting at his carved table.

Below the window he heard some marines tramping across the compound, their voices and boots unnaturally loud. In the time while he had been away, as he and his boatload of men had fought out each painful day, the settlement itself had gathered a kind of decay.

Stores had been broached, and empty bottles and casks lay everywhere. Even Raymond had changed, hollow-eyed and dishevelled, his appearance made worse by his soiled shirt. Of all people he had altered the most.

Bolitho had almost expected the gates to be held shut in his face. Had that happened, he knew he would have been unable to restrain his feelings, or those of his men.

Raymond had been sitting at the table, as he was now, staring at the door. Perhaps he had never moved since the two boats had left under the cover of night.

He had said, 'So you survived after all? What are you going to do now?'

Hardacre had met the *Tempest*'s boats at the pier, and as they had walked together towards the palisades he had described in grim detail what had happened. Over a third of the islanders had died from the fever, and while the guards had cowered behind their defences, and had gone through one drunken escapade after another, Hardacre had done his best to give the others the will to survive.

Raymond had even driven the convicts from the settlement, and had ordered them to remain in their huts and manage as best they could on their own. Hardacre had helped them also, and had been rewarded by their willingness to ignore Raymond's unjust order and to assist him in the villages.

And then, just two dawns ago, the island had awakened to the violent crash of artillery, the splintering destruction of trees as the balls had smashed across the bay from the headland. A schooner had been anchored offshore, and during the night some of Tuke's men had ferried two big guns on to the island, ready to open fire as soon as they could determine the range.

It seemed that Raymond had failed to see that sentries were posted, and as neither of his Corps officers had been sober enough to have taken much part in matters, the attack had been swift and completely unexpected.

Hardacre said bitterly, 'It went on for two hours. Some of Tinah's people were hurt and two killed. The settlement was also hit, but more as a threat than to do damage. Then they withdrew. It may be that they got warning that *Tempest* was returning. But they did leave a message for Raymond.'

The 'message' had been pinned to the mutilated corpse of a French officer, the one named Vicariot, who had been de Barras's senior lieutenant. It had stated that if Raymond and his defenders were to withdraw from the settlement they would be given safe conduct to another island to await rescue. If they did not, they would suffer Vicariot's fate, as would all those who resisted them.

Bolitho stood silently by the window, thinking and remembering. If Tuke had known about *Tempest*'s return he would have attacked earlier without waiting for dramatic gestures. It seemed to be as much a part of the man as his cunning. The ability to use savage cruelty to break down resistance before it had begun.

One thing was no longer in doubt. *Narval* was taken, and the flag she would wear was immaterial. Her thirty-six guns, backed up by whatever other forces Tuke could offer, would more than swamp the defences.

He asked quietly, 'Did you know about the village? The numbers who died?' It was incredible and unnerving, but not once had Raymond asked about Viola. Something seemed to snap and he said, 'And your *wife*. She died at sea.' Just to say it aloud was like a betrayal. To share her memory with this selfish, vindictive man was more than he could bear. He added harshly, '*She* had great courage.'

Raymond turned slowly on his chair, his eyes in shadow as he answered, 'I guessed as much. She would rather have died with you than live with me.'

He stood up violently, and an empty bottle rolled unheeded from beneath his pile of documents.

'You've heard about Vicariot? Of the attack?' Raymond spoke quickly, as if afraid of interruption. 'They'll come again. I saw the Frenchman. They had mutilated everything but his face. So I would know. Be in no doubt.' He swung round, his features working wildly. 'I have written orders for Hardacre. He will take over the settlement until . . .' He scattered the documents, searching for the one which would give back Hardacre all that he had lost. Except that it would be for a very short time now. 'My guards will take the convicts aboard your ship today. *Now.* In Sydney there may be fresh instructions.'

Hardacre had remained silent until that point. 'You'd leave? Quit the settlement and lay us open to massacre? No militia, not even a schooner, thanks to you!'

Bolitho looked at him, his mind suddenly clear, like brittle ice.

'We are not leaving. I too have a *document.*' He turned to Raymond again. 'Remember, sir? My orders from you as to my duties here?' He walked to the window again and watched the fronds moving in the breeze. 'We are not running. I do not care what forces come against us. I have listened for too long about the stupidity of sea officers, the ignorance of common sailors. But when things get bad, *they* are the ones who seem so important all of a sudden. I have heard you talking of war as if it were a game. Of a *just* war, or a wasted one. It seems to me that a *just* war is when you in particular are in jeopardy, Mr Raymond, and I am heartily sick of it!'

Raymond stared at him, his eyes watering. 'You're mad! I knew it!' He waved an arm towards the wall. 'You'd throw away your life, your ship, everything, for this dunghill of a place?'

Bolitho smiled briefly. 'A moment ago you were its governor. Things were different then.' He hardened his voice. 'Well, not to me!'

The door banged open and Captain Prideaux marched into

the room, his boots clashing across the rush mats like several
men at once.

'I have examined the perimeter, sir.' He ignored Raymond.
'My men are setting the convicts to work. The breach in the
northern palisade was the worst. Sergeant Quare is dealing
with it.'

Hardacre said, 'I will speak with Tinah. He may be able to
help.'

'No.' Bolitho faced him, suddenly glad of Hardacre's presence, his strength. 'If we fail, as well we might, I want his
people spared. If it is known they were aiding us, they would
have less chance than they do now.'

Hardacre watched him gravely. 'That was bravely said,
Captain.'

'I told you, *you are mad*!' Raymond was shaking his fists in
the air, and spittle ran down his chin as he yelled, 'When this
is over, I will . . .'

Hardacre interrupted hotly, 'You saw that French officer,
you damned fool! There'll be nothing left to hate or destroy if
Captain Bolitho cannot defend us!' He strode to the door. 'I
will see what I can do to assist the marines.'

Swift coughed by the open door. 'Beg pardon, sir, but I'd
like some advice on the best siting of the swivels.'

'At once, Mr Swift.'

Bolitho turned on his heel, wondering if both Prideaux and
Swift had lingered nearby by arrangement, fearing that he
might fall upon Raymond and kill him. He found his hatred for
the man had gone. Raymond seemed already to have lost sub-
stance and reality.

At the darkest bend in the stairway he saw a quick movement
and felt a girl's hands gripping his arm. As Prideaux pushed
between them, cursing with surprise, the hands slipped, but
still clung to Bolitho's legs, then his shoes.

He said, 'Let her alone.' Then he stooped and aided the girl
to her feet. The poor, demented creature was staring at him,
her eyes brimming with tears.

Bolitho said gently, 'I loved her, too.' It took all his strength
to keep his voice level. 'As you did.'

But she shook her head and pressed her face against his hand.

Allday was at the foot of the stairs. 'She can't believe it, Captain.' He gestured to a marine. 'Take her to safety, but don't touch her.'

'I cannot believe it either.'

Bolitho stood in the blazing sun, his eyes smarting in the glare. He realized dully that Allday carried a bared cutlass. He must have drawn it as the girl had hurled herself from the shadows. To defend him.

He added simply, 'Who will take care of *her*, Allday?'

'I dunno, Captain.' He fell in step beside him. 'There should be a place for everybody.' He looked away, his voice suddenly husky. 'The bloody world is big enough surely!' He sheathed his cutlass angrily. 'I'm fair sorry about that, Captain. I forgot myself.'

Bolitho said nothing. *I would have it no other way.*

Then he took the watch from his pocket, and found he could do so without hesitation. Her strength was still with him.

He said, 'Come. We'll go round the defences and see for ourselves.'

Allday grinned, relieved and strangely moved. 'Aye, Captain.'

As they walked towards the gates and a marine sentry stamped his boots together, Prideaux remarked, 'God's teeth, Mr Swift, you would think they were on Plymouth Hoe!'

The youth nodded, aware he was seeing something fine, and yet unable to put a name to it.

Prideaux stared at him and exclaimed, 'Not you, too! Be about your duties, sir, or acting-lieutenant or not, I'll set my sword to your rump, damme if I don't!'

For the remainder of the day, and all through the following one, boats plied busily between *Tempest* and the shore. Bolitho seemed to be everywhere, listening to ideas, which slow to come at first, grew and became more adventurous at the slightest encouragement.

Allday stayed with him the whole time, guarding and worrying, seeing the strain and determination laying firm hold in his captain. He did not care that even the shamefaced members of the Corps had returned to their duties at the settlement and had taken Prideaux's orders without a murmur. Nor did he find comfort in the fact that even the laziest and most unreliable seaman was working through each watch without a rest, and with little more than a grumble. He knew better than most that without Bolitho none of the plans would be worth more than a wet fuse.

As Bolitho stood on the hillside watching the seamen gathering bales of dried grass and palm leaves, or shoring up the battered palisade, Allday waited. He saw the way he seemed to grow more content with each new challenge. As if he was trying to please someone nobody else could see. And he knew well enough who that was.

Just before the darkness threw shadows over the bay the lookouts reported a sail to the east.

Bolitho returned to his ship, strangely calm and without any sort of tiredness.

The sand had run out, and he was glad. One way or the other, they would end it here.

17

A Stubborn Man

Herrick hesitated by the screen door and watched Bolitho for several seconds. He must have fallen asleep at the desk, and as he lay with his face pillowed on his arms the lantern which swung from the deckhead threw his shadow from side to side, as if he and not the ship were moving.

'It's time, sir.'

Herrick laid his hand on Bolitho's shoulder. Through the shirt his skin felt hot. Burning. He hated disturbing him, but even Herrick would not risk his displeasure on this morning.

Bolitho looked up slowly and then massaged his eyes. 'Thank you.' He stared around the dark cabin and then at the windows. They too were black and held only the cabin's reflections.

'It will be dawn in half an hour, sir. I've sent the hands to breakfast, like you said. A hot meal, and a tot to wash it down. The cook will douse the galley fires when I pass the word.'

He paused, annoyed at the interruption as Allday entered the cabin with a jug of steaming coffee.

Bolitho stretched and waited for the coffee to burn through his stomach. Strong and bitter. He imagined his men eating their extra ration of salt pork or beef, jesting with each other about the unexpected issue of rum. Yet he had slept like the dead, and had heard nothing when his ship had awakened to a new day. For some, if not all of them, it might well be the last.

'Will I fetch Hugoe, Captain?'

Allday poured some more coffee. He had been out of his hammock and down to the galley for Bolitho's shaving water much earlier, but showed little sign of fatigue.

'No.' Bolitho rubbed his hands vigorously up and down his arms. He felt cold, and yet his mind was crystal-clear, as if he had enjoyed a full night's sleep in his bed at Falmouth. 'He'll be sorely needed in the wardroom.'

Allday showed his teeth, knowing that was not the reason at all. 'Very well then. I'll get some breakfast for you.'

Bolitho stood up and walked to the windows. 'I couldn't eat. Not today.'

'You must, sir.' Herrick gestured to Allday and he left the cabin. 'It may be a while before we get another chance.'

'True.'

Bolitho peered down at the water below the counter. But there was only the merest glint to show the pull of the current. It still surprised him at the speed with which the dawn broke. Many throughout the ship would be wishing it might never come.

He said quietly, 'If we fail today, Thomas.' He stopped, uncertain how to continue. He did not wish Herrick to accept a possibility of defeat, but he needed him to know how much his friendship meant, how it sustained him.

Herrick protested, 'Bless you, sir, you mustn't talk like that!'

Bolitho turned and faced him. 'There is a letter in the strongbox. For you.' He held up his hand. 'If I fall, I want you to know that I have arranged some benefits for you.'

Herrick strode to him and exclaimed, 'I'll hear no more, sir! I – I'll not *have* it!'

Bolitho smiled. 'So be it.' He walked up and down the cabin. 'I would it were as cold as this for a whole day. A sea-fight is blistering enough without the sun's distractions!'

Herrick dropped his gaze. Bolitho was shivering badly. Lack of sleep, total exhaustion from the open boat, it was all starting to show.

He said, 'I'll be off, sir.'

'Yes. We will go to quarters as soon as they have eaten.'

He saw Herrick's apparent satisfaction and waited for him to leave. Then he sat down and started to go over his plans again, searching for flaws, or improvements.

He poured another mug of coffee, picturing his ship as she lay in darkness. Two guard boats pulled around her at all times, while on shore Prideaux had mounted pickets to patrol the beach and headland. They would have to be withdrawn when it was light. *Tempest* was so shorthanded, whereas the enemy . . . he shivered and drained the last of the coffee. *Enemy.* How easily the word came. He recalled the French seamen he had seen when he had visited *Narval.* With such cruel treatment they would probably have mutinied anyway, revolted against de Barras and his sadism. The uprising in France gave them even wider scope for vengeance. A battle would seem a small price to pay for their release.

Bolitho tried to form an image of Tuke, but the memory of the livid brand on Viola's shoulder made him close his mind to him. Instead he thought of her, hanging on to each detail, afraid something might be lost in his memory.

Allday brought his breakfast, but said nothing as Bolitho pushed it aside. In silence he shaved him, and brought a clean shirt from the chest as he had seen Noddall do so many times.

The ship felt very quiet, with just the sluggish motion and the creak of timbers to break the stillness.

Light filtered through the windows and across the chequered canvas of the deck.

Bolitho slipped into his coat and grimaced at himself in the bulkhead mirror. In the weak light he looked pale, so that his coat and breeches and the gold lace stood out in sharp contrast.

Allday said quietly, 'We've stood like this a few times, Captain.' He glanced up at the skylight as feet moved restlessly overhead. 'I never get used to it.'

Bolitho felt his coat, glad of it for once to hold the chill at bay until the sun rose above the islands once again.

'Nor I.'

The door opened slightly and Midshipman Fitzmaurice poked his pug-face around it.

'The first lieutenant's respects, sir, and he wishes to clear for action if it is convenient?'

Bolitho nodded, conscious of the youth's formality. 'My compliments to Mr Herrick. Tell him I am ready.'

Moments later the stillness was broken by the twitter of calls, the stamp of running feet and all the preparation for battle which to a landsman would appear no better than chaos.

The staccato beat of the two drums on the quarterdeck echoed around the bay, reaching the settlement and further still to the village. To the tired sentries on the headland, and to the wounded marine called Billy-boy who had been given his own special task ashore.

And also to a wild-eyed girl who lay alone in her hut, her mind destroyed, but her memory hanging on to the one person who had helped and protected her.

As the sun found the *Tempest*'s main topgallant masthead, and made the whipping pendant change from white to copper, Herrick touched his hat and reported, 'Cleared for action, sir.' He said it proudly, for despite his shortages, the operation had been completed in less than fifteen minutes.

Bolitho walked to the quarterdeck rail and looked down at the silent figures. He recalled Allday's remark. *We've stood like this a few times.* And his own response.

The shadowy figures below him, and crouched around the quarterdeck, would they understand when the call came? He wondered if de Barras was still alive, how it must have been for him when the latent hatred had exploded into mutiny.

'Deck there! Ship to the east'rd! At anchor, sir!'

Bolitho walked to the nettings, his hands behind his back. Still just the one. Bait perhaps to draw him into another trap. A watchdog, while others prepared a different form of attack. It was too early even to guess.

He saw Fitzmaurice speaking to the signals party, and considered the change which had affected all of them. Swift now walked the gundeck with Borlase, and Keen stood aft, watching over the quarterdeck six-pounders. He saw Pyper too, doubled up with pain from his burns and salt sores, standing with the carronade crews on the forecastle.

He heard the American, Jenner, say something to another seaman, and half expected to see Orlando with him. He shivered. Boys into men. Men into oblivion.

The masthead again. ''Tis a schooner, sir!' He would have a perfect view. The strengthening glow directly behind the other vessel, while *Tempest* still lay in deep shadow.

Bolitho said, 'We will know soon what to expect.'

'Aye, sir.' Herrick was on the opposite side of the deck, and raised his voice so that it would carry more easily. 'Not really worth our while, is she, sir?'

It brought a few laughs, as both of them knew it would.

Bolitho turned and saw Ross watching him closely. 'Get aloft with a glass, Mr Ross. I want you to take your time. Examine the schooner as you have never done before.'

He watched him thrust through the boarding nets and climb nimbly up the main shrouds, the telescope bobbing on his shoulder like a poacher's gun.

Then he looked at the masthead pendant. The wind had backed during the night, but was steady enough from the north-west. It was well sheltered in the bay, but the schooner would not venture inside the reef and risk being grounded, for she would be anchored right in the wind's path.

Everything must happen here. Hardacre had added his knowledge to Lakey's, and it was quite impossible for an attack to be launched overland from the other side of the island. There was no safe landing place, and the threat of attack from hostile natives, no matter what Tinah had promised, would need treble the force which Tuke and his men possessed.

Sunlight slipped gently across the upper yards and sails, and the hill above the settlement stood out from shadow as if detached from all else.

Ross, one-time master's mate, now acting-lieutenant, called sharply from his high perch, 'They're lowering a boat, sir.'

More dragging minutes and then, 'The boat's standing in towards the reef!' His Scottish voice was indignant as he added, 'A flag o' truce, b'God!'

Bolitho looked at Herrick. The first move was about to begin.

The boat hoisted a small scrap of sail as soon as it was clear of the schooner's side, and as it gathered way Bolitho recognized their intention to pass through the reef and enter the bay.

'Gig, Allday!' Bolitho looked at Herrick as the gig's crew scampered from their various stations. 'I don't want them to see how thin we are on the ground. Signal the shore party. They must act quicker than I had planned.'

He knew Herrick was forming a protest, but brushed him aside and almost tumbled into the gig in his haste to get away.

'Quick as you can!' He gripped the gunwale as the oars dug

into the water and sent the boat over a trough like an excited dolphin.

Allday said, 'God, look at them!' He chuckled. 'They've just seen *Tempest*!'

The boat had certainly slowed its approach, but after a momentary pause started to move again towards the surging water between the reefs.

As it drew closer Bolitho saw it was crewed by a motley collection of men, mostly bearded and as dirty as their boat. But they were well armed, and the tattered white flag which flew from the mast made the contrast more evident.

Bolitho snapped, 'Tell them to heave to. They're near enough.'

Allday's hail, and the fact the gig's crew were resting on their oars, made the other boat rock dangerously in the steep swell as she idled beam on to the nearest spur of reef.

A powerful, bearded figure with two crossbelts of pistols and pouches stood and cupped his hands. He sounded English, but was certainly not Tuke.

Bolitho wished he had brought a telescope, but knew it was doubtful if he would have been able to use it. The violent pitching of the gig and the rising nausea in his stomach would have seen to that.

The voice shouted harshly, 'So you got here, Cap'n?'

Almost what Raymond had said. Bolitho raised one hand, his eyes watering in the pale sunlight.

The man continued, 'The message stands as before. You carry your people away, an' be damned to ye! We are taking the island, an' you too, if you stay an' fight!'

His words brought growls of anger from the gig's crew.

Bolitho stood up carefully, his hand gripping Allday's shoulder.

Then he shouted, 'Under what flag? Will you hoist your own cowardly rag, or shall you hide under French colours?'

Despite the boom of surf on the reef he heard the confusion of voices from the other boat.

Then the man called, 'We have the *Narval*! You'll live to regret your bloody arrogance, Cap'n!' He waved his fist and another figure was hauled upright from the bottom of the boat.

For an instant Bolitho thought it might be de Barras, and then saw it was a young lieutenant, his arms pinioned, his face almost black with bruises.

Another visual proof of victory. Bolitho glanced at his oarsmen, seeing their mixed expressions of disbelief and horror.

Bolitho shouted, 'Release him! None of this is his doing, and you know it!'

The man laughed, the sound distorted on the offshore wind. 'D'you not know of the *Revolution*, Cap'n?' He waved his hand over the boat. 'These lads do, an' with bloody good cause, eh?'

So Tuke had put some of the French sailors in each of his vessels. It would be safer that way. With the French officers killed or in irons, Tuke would have had to take command of *Narval* himself. Not that he would need much encouragement, and his experience as master of a privateer would have provided him with as many skills as any sea-officer in the King's service.

Allday said quietly, 'They're going to kill him, Captain.'

As he spoke one of the men in the other boat seized the lieutenant's hair and pulled his head backwards, so that they could see his eyes glittering in the light, his face distorted with pain and terror. A knife rose and flitted across the Frenchman's throat with such speed that there was neither a cry nor a struggle. Then the corpse was flung overboard, leaving a scarlet smear on the boat's planking.

Bolitho snapped, 'A *pistol*! That's no damned truce flag!'

But the shot went wide, and by the time he had reloaded the schooner's boat was already moving swiftly away from the reef.

From seaward came a sudden bang, and seconds later a tall waterspout lifted between reef and headland, the spray from the heavy ball spreading out in a great white circle.

'Return to the ship.'

Bolitho seized the gunwale and tried to control his sick hatred. That might be their intention. To lure him from the bay before he knew the enemy's exact strength.

While the gig pulled swiftly towards the *Tempest*, Bolitho looked across at the settlement, picturing the defences which now seemed so puny when set against what he had just witnessed.

K

Fires had been lit to give an impression that the settlement was occupied by far more men than the small force there actually was. Some red tunics had been placed on the palisades, and from a distance would be seen as vigilant sentries at their posts.

A deception, and that was *all* it was.

He winced as another ball whimpered overhead and cracked into some rocks below the headland.

When he reached the *Tempest*'s quarterdeck he found Herrick, armed with a telescope, watching the other vessel. Out of range of *Tempest*'s twelve-pounders, yet she was slamming shots into the land without effort. When the shadows eventually departed from the beach and settlement they would start to shoot in earnest.

Herrick observed, 'Twenty-four pounder, sir. At *least*. Must have got it off the *Eurotas*, I reckon.' He looked at Bolitho worriedly. 'I was bothered by those devils in the boat. They might have opened fire on *you*!'

Crash. Bolitho heard the ball ploughing through the trees on the far side of the bay, and saw enraged birds spreading out above them like splinters.

Herrick persisted, 'We will have to up-anchor. If they shift their aim to us they could dismast the ship and leave us crippled, no more'n a floating battery!'

Bolitho removed his hat and wiped his forehead. It was what the enemy intended. Draw him out, leave the bay undefended. The schooner might not be able to outsail *Tempest*, but she could lose her amongst the litter of islets and reefs without difficulty.

He looked up at the masthead pendant. Steady as before from the north-west. He took a telescope and walked to the nettings, his mind grappling with the danger, with what he was asking of his men.

He said over his shoulder, 'Send word ashore. When we make the signal, they must start the fire.' He heard Herrick sigh. 'I *know*. It was for a last hope. We just have to reverse things.'

Bolitho steadied his glass against the hammock nettings and trained it on the anchored schooner. He was in time to see a puff of smoke from her forecastle as she loosed off another ball.

The schooner was in direct line with the headland. And the wind.

He heard a boat pulling towards the shore and then a violent splintering noise as another ball landed on the little pier and brought down the outer end in a welter of broken woodwork and lashings. It was luck, for no gun captain could see through shadows. But it told very clearly of what would happen soon if they did nothing to stop it.

He said, 'Boarding party, Mr Herrick. Launch and cutter. If the wind holds we will fire the headland as planned. The smoke will drift down on the schooner. That is when the attack must begin.'

Bolitho thought of the long pull, and pictured the wounded marine on the hillside with his collected heaps of dried grass and underbrush, liberally dosed with coconut husks and grease. With luck the enemy gunner would think that one of his shots has started a fire ashore. If it failed, both boats' crews would be slaughtered before they could lay a finger on the schooner's hull.

A moment later Fitzmaurice called, 'Quarter boat's reached the shore, sir!'

Bolitho nodded. 'Man your boats, Mr Herrick. Keep them on the concealed side until the fire begins.'

He made himself take a few paces back and forth, his feet stepping over gun tackles and rammers without conscious effort. It would take ten minutes for the word to be passed to the makeshift beacon.

He heard men clattering into the boats, the clink of weapons.

'Bend on the signal, Mr Fitzmaurice.'

Bolitho wiped his face. He was sweating badly, but without warmth.

'Quarter boat's shoved off again, sir.'

The message had been passed.

Bolitho snapped, 'Hoist the signal now.'

The flag broke from the mainyard, its appearance timed by coincidence with the next bang from the schooner's heavy cannon.

Bolitho trained a glass on the headland and the hillside beyond. Faintly at first, rising from some lingering shadows like dirty stains against the sky, the smoke began to roll downwind. The filthy concoction of grease, oakum and waste which they had mixed with the tinder-dry grass and rushes held the smoke down towards the water in a thickening, evil-looking pall.

The marine called Billy-boy was exceeding even the bravest hope, and a short explosion echoed from the hillside to add to the deception. They would hear it in the schooner, and might think it was a magazine exploding.

Herrick asked quietly, 'Permission to leave, sir?'

Bolitho looked past him at the two boats alongside, their crews peering up at the ship like strangers. Hand-picked every one, and some of the best men in the ship. If the worst happened it would strip *Tempest* of hands so sorely that her defences would be halved.

He held Herrick's gaze. *And he was the best of all.* But he could not let anyone else command the attack. Now they needed every ounce of confidence, every bit of experience, and to the ship's company Herrick had all of it and more to spare.

Was this the time which he had dreaded for so long? It must come one day. But surely not here, in this godforsaken corner of the world where so much pain had already been suffered.

Even as he thought about it he knew it could happen anywhere.

He said, 'Take care, Thomas. Have the swivels ready to shoot. Retire if you are sighted before you can grapple.'

Herrick took off his coat and hat and handed them to a marine. In the boats there was no mark of rank or station either. They had planned it this way in the short reprieve they had been given by Bolitho's five hundred mile passage in the boat.

Herrick turned to watch the spreading fog of smoke. It had already reached the reef, and the schooner's outline faded suddenly in the man-made haze.

Maybe he was thinking the same. What they had done in so short a time. Like the fire. Oakum and tar from the ship, pig's fat and grease from the village, coconut husks and fibres, even molasses which the purser had been hoarding for an emergency. Plus all the other combustible material, it was making an impressive screen.

It should have been for later. If and when *Narval* tried to force the entrance to the bay, the smoke was to have confused her gun crews so that *Tempest* could draw her to close action while she was near the reef. But that was before this had happened. Anyway, the wind might have changed and reversed the advantage.

Herrick said, 'Lady Luck is with us, sir.'

Then with a wave to the quarterdeck he lowered himself into the big launch. The two boats began to pull away immediately, the oars' speed indicating the measure of time and survival.

In the cutter, Jack Miller, boatswain's mate, crouched intently by the tiller, a boarding axe protruding from his belt.

Allday said softly, 'God help those buggers if *he* gets amongst 'em!'

It would take over half an hour for the boats to get anywhere near the anchored vessel. The smoke had to stay as thick as ever until then. Also, the schooner's crew must not suspect that anything untoward was happening.

Bolitho said, 'Mr Borlase, we will commence firing with the starboard battery. Load and run out, if you please.'

Borlase stared at him anxiously, a nerve jumping in his neck. 'At what target, sir?'

'To the right of the schooner. I want them to see our shots dropping short. It will make them believe in their safety, also that we are not attempting to weigh anchor and use the smoke ourselves.'

Minutes later the starboard twelve-pounders crashed out one by one in a slow broadside, the smoke rolling downwind to join the rest. The schooner had all but vanished beyond it now, and when Bolitho looked for the two boats he saw only the wake of the rearmost one, the hulls, like the headland, completely hidden.

He pulled out his watch. The sun was well up, and no longer could they rely on shadows to protect the settlement. He wondered briefly what Raymond was doing. If he was thinking of Viola.

'Signal from the hilltop lookout, sir!' Fitzmaurice had his telescope to his eye.

Bolitho walked beneath the mizzen shrouds and shaded his

face against the growing glare. The stench from the burning
hillside was bad enough here, what it was like in the boats was
hard to imagine. He felt sick and suddenly dizzy, and wished
he had taken Allday's offer of breakfast.

He felt angry with himself. Well, it was too late now.

He saw the flash of light from near the hilltop, the reflected
sun caught in a mirror, as he had seen the foot soldiers do it in
America. It was limited but very quick, provided you had in-
vented enough simple signals well in advance.

Fitzmaurice said in his haughty voice, 'Sail to the north, sir.'

Bolitho nodded. It was like the start of a great drama in
which no one was certain of his role. The sail must be the
Narval, sweeping down from some hiding place in the north,
probably expecting to find the schooner in sole possession of
the bay or its approaches.

He tried to remember the time on his watch. Where the two
boats would be. How long before the other ship hove in sight
around the headland.

He moved to the rail above the gundeck and watched the
twelve-pounders being hauled up to their ports again.

Swift was looking aft towards him. 'Again, sir?'

Bolitho heard Lakey say, 'Can't see nothing of the schooner
or the reef now. God, what a fog!'

Allday was standing by the companion, his arms folded as
he watched the idle crews around the quarterdeck guns. He
turned to watch the captain and saw him stagger and almost
fall. Everyone else was watching the smoke or the men at the
twelve-pounders.

He reached Bolitho's side in three strides. 'I'm here, Captain.
Easy now.' He looked at Bolitho's face. It was shining with
sweat, and his eyes were half-closed as if in terrible pain.

Bolitho gasped, 'Don't let them see me like this!' He swallowed hard, his arms and legs shivering violently in gusts of
icy cold. As if he were on the deck of a North Atlantic patrol.

Allday murmured desperately, 'The fever. It must be. I'll
fetch the surgeon.' He saw one of the seamen staring and barked, 'Watch your front, damn you!'

Bolitho gripped his arm and steadied himself. 'No. Must
hold on. This is the worst time. You must see that!'

'But, *Captain*!' Allday was pleading. 'It'll kill you! I'll not stand by and let it happen!'

Bolitho took a breath and thrust himself away from Allday's support. Between his teeth he said deliberately, 'You . . will . . do . . as . . I . . tell . . you!'

He made himself walk slowly to the nettings, and curled his fingers into them as he tried to control his shaking body.

He said, 'Tell them to continue firing.' The din might help, if only to keep their minds off him.

The crash of the broadside thundered across the water, the balls going downwind into the smoke.

He heard himself say, 'Please God let Thomas succeed. We cannot move with so few hands.' The words spilled out of him and he could not prevent it. 'No way to die.' He let go of the hammock nettings and walked carefully to the compass. 'We'll have to lie here and fight!'

A blurred shape hurried past, carrying a shot-cradle. It paused and then turned towards him. It was Jenner, the American.

'Couldn't help but hear what you said, Cap'n.'

He seemed to swim in Bolitho's vision as if under water.

'I heard tell of somethin' durin' th' war. Of an English captain who was so short-handed his sloop was almost run ashore and taken by the Frenchies. I also heard tell that the captain was *you*, sir.' He ignored Allday's threatening look and added, 'You used wounded soldiers instead, right, sir?'

Bolitho tried to see him properly. 'I remember. In the *Sparrow*.' He was going mad. It had to be that. Speaking like this about the past.

'Well, I got to thinkin', why not use them convicts?'

'*What?*' Bolitho stepped forward and would have fallen but for Allday.

'I just thought . . .'

Bolitho seized his wrist. '*Fetch Mr Keen!*'

Keen's voice came from his side. 'I'm here, sir.' He sounded worried.

'Send the other boats ashore immediately and go with them. You worked at the settlement, they know you better than the rest of us.' He leaned closer and added fervently, '*I must have men*, Val.' He saw Keen's expression and knew he had used Viola's name for him without realizing it. 'Do what you can.'

Keen said despairingly, 'You're ill, sir!' He glanced at Allday's grim features. 'You must have caught . . .'

'You're *delaying*!' He pushed him away. 'Get them here. Tell them I'll try and obtain their passage back to England. But don't lie to them.'

The guns crashed out again, the trucks hurling themselves inboard on their tackles.

'Enough.' Bolitho tugged at his neckcloth. 'Cease firing. Sponge out and reload.'

He saw the surgeon standing directly in his path, his face grave as he snapped, 'You will go below, sir. As the surgeon it is my duty . . .'

'Your duty is on the orlop!' He dropped his voice. 'Just fetch some drops, anything to keep my mind alive. A few more hours.'

'It will certainly kill you.' Gwyther shrugged. 'You are a stubborn man.'

Bolitho walked unaided to the weather side and stared at the nearest land.

'I'm so cold, Allday. Some brandy. Then I will be myself again.'

'Aye, Captain.' Allday watched him helplessly. 'At once.'

Lakey had been near the wheel with his quartermaster and had seen Keen's anxiety and the hasty arrival of the surgeon. As Allday hurried to the companion he opened his mouth to ask what was happening. Allday always knew. Instead, he turned away, unable to believe what he had seen.

Mackay, his quartermaster, spoke his own thoughts aloud. 'In God's name, Mr Lakey, there were tears in his eyes!'

'Avast, Mr Herrick! I can hear the buggers!'

Herrick lifted his arm and the muffled oars rose dripping on either side of the launch. He hoped that Miller, following closely astern, would have his eyes open and not collide with them.

He heard the distant murmur of voices, then the clang of

metal. He swallowed hard and made a circular motion above his head with his sword. They must be almost up to the schooner, but because of the smoke could see nothing. Earlier they had seen her masts poking through the drifting fog, and Herrick had been thankful that nobody had had the sense to send up a lookout.

The men in the boat shifted uneasily, watching his face. Their eyes were red-rimmed from the smoke, and their bodies stank from its filth and greasy persistence.

Herrick looked at those nearest him. Grant, a senior gunner's mate, who came from Canterbury, not that far from his own home. Nielsen, a fair-haired Dane, who shared an oar with Gwynne, the young recruit he had got from the *Eurotas*. He knew them all, as he did those in the other boat.

Something tall and dark loomed above them, and as they drifted beneath the schooner's long jib boom they almost became entangled in her anchor cable.

Not a second left for hesitation. Herrick snapped, 'Grapnel! *Boarders away!*'

Then, pushed and jostled by his men, Herrick fought his way up and over the bulwark, seeing faces above him, and hearing the muffled voices change just as quickly into violent yells and oaths. Pistols banged, and a seaman fell back into the launch, knocking another down with him.

Herrick sat astride the bulwark, seeing it all through the drifting smoke. The massive gun, the additional tackle it had needed to restrain it on the narrow deck. A man ran at him with a cutlass, but Herrick twisted it with his hilt and flicked it clattering into the scuppers. Now he had both feet inboard, and slashed the man across the face and neck before he could pull out of his charge.

They were outnumbered, but with trained determination the *Tempest*'s men made a tight little wedge, backs to the bulwark, their feet already slipping in blood as they clashed together with their enemy.

The clang of steel, the fierce, wild cries of the men, were matched by the screams of the wounded and dying.

But from right aft came the thud of another grapnel, and Miller's men swarmed over the taffrail yelling and cursing like

fiends. Steel on steel, the pent-up fear and hatred bursting in a
tide of unrestrained killing. Men rolled upon one another,
fighting with dirks, cutlasses, axes, or anything which would
beat a man into submission.

Herrick parried a sword aside and realized it was the bearded
man who had met Bolitho under a flag of truce. He was even
bigger near to, but Herrick had endured enough.

He had never had much time for the fancy swordsmanship
of men like Prideaux, or from what he had heard, Bolitho's
dead brother, Hugh. He was a fighter, and relied on his
strength and staying-power to carry him through.

He took the man's heavy sword just six inches above his
hilt, forcing him round, but keeping both blades crossed.

The bearded giant shouted, 'You bloody bastard! This time
you die!'

Herrick's eye flickered to a patch of blood on the deck, and
thrust his hilt away from him with all his strength. He saw the
cruel grin of triumph on the man's face as he was allowed to
draw back the full length of his blade. Then it altered to sudden alarm as his heel slipped on the fresh blood, and for a mere
second he was off balance.

Herrick thought suddenly of the tiny scene he had watched
through his telescope. The terrified French officer, his throat
cut in the twinkling of an eye. Like a slaughtered pig.

'*No, you die!*'

His short fighting-sword seared diagonally across the man's
stomach, just above the belt, and as he dropped his weapon and
clutched the torn wound with both hands, Herrick hacked him
once and hard on the neck.

There was a wild cheer, and Miller, his axe red in his filthy
fist, yelled, '*She's ours*, lads!' It was done.

The cheers altered to cries of alarm as the deck gave a violent
shiver and threw several men kicking amongst the dead and
wounded.

Herrick yelled, 'The reef! They cut the cable!'

There was another great lurch, and part of the mainmast
thundered across the deck and crushed Gwynne dead, his
mouth still open from calling.

Herrick waved his sword. 'Fall back! Man the boats!'

He heard the water swilling through a nearby hold, the sounds of loose cargo and stores being hurled against the bulkhead. The reef would make short work of her, and anyone stupid enough to remain aboard.

Carrying the wounded, and kicking the pirates' weapons into the water, the seamen retreated to their boats.

Half-mad at the swift change of events, some of the pirates, and several whom Herrick guessed to be Frenchmen from the *Narval*, turned on each other, while with each violent lurch the schooner lifted and ground still further on to the reef.

Miller's cutter discharged its swivel gun for good measure as they pulled away.

Herrick shouted, 'To the ship! Give way all!'

He held his breath as a great shoulder of shell-encrusted reef rose out of the sea almost under the bows. He waited for the crash, the inrush of water, and then as the boat pulled clear he turned his thoughts to his men. Poor Gwynne. A volunteer for so short a time. He looked at Nielsen, the young Dane, rocking from side to side, his face ashen with agony. He had dropped his cutlass, and one of the pirates had lunged at him with a sword. Nielsen had seized the swinging blade with both hands, and had hung on even as his attacker had pulled the razor-edged weapon through his palms and fingers.

Grant, the old gunner's mate, showed his tobacco-stained teeth in a tired grin. 'We done it, sir. One down.' He turned as the schooner rolled over in a welter of spray. ''Nother to go.'

'Aye.' Herrick looked along the boat, sharing their pain and their pride. 'Well done.' He thought of Bolitho and what he would say.

It was only a beginning, but they had shown what they could achieve.

18

On This Day

Bolitho made himself stand very still as Herrick hurried aft towards him. The nausea came and went, and several times he thought he was going to fall to the deck. And yet he was acutely aware of what was happening around him, as if he could see without being seen. As if he were already dead.

Even his voice seemed to come from far away. 'Thank God you are safe, Thomas!' He looked towards the gangway where the boatswain's party were helping some of the scarred and battered seamen up from the boats.

Herrick said, 'They did well. When that smoke clears you'll see naught but a few spars across the reef. I lost three good hands though . . .' He stopped short and saw Lakey trying to signal him.

Then, as the exhaustion and fury of the fight left him, he looked closer at Bolitho.

He said, 'I – I'm sorry, sir. I was thinking of myself.' He did not know how to continue. 'You must go below. *At once.*' He studied the firm line of Bolitho's jaw. Like that of a man preparing for the first touch of a surgeon's blade. 'How could this have happened?'

Voices called from forward, and he turned, off guard and confused, as he saw the remainder of the ship's boats moving slowly from the shore. They were packed beyond capacity, bodies lumped over the oars and gunwales like sacks of grain, with only inches of freeboard above the water.

Borlase said hoarsely, 'Convicts. *He* sent for them.'

'Yes.' Bolitho walked slowly to the side to watch the first boat hook on.

The drops which the surgeon had allowed him had given

him a small relief, and Allday's brandy lingered on his throat like fire. He had to blink to clear his vision as the convicts scrambled awkwardly on to the gangway and through the boarding nets. Against his own men he could see little difference. He felt a sudden sense of urgency. He must talk with them. Tell them. He saw Keen coming towards him and waited for him to speak first. He felt he had to save every breath. Each small effort brought the sweat across his body in a flood.

Keen said, 'The marine sentries think that the schooner may have landed spies in the night, sir.' He glanced helplessly at Herrick. 'They're not certain, but it's possible.'

Bolitho waited for the next spasm of giddiness to pass. 'I feared as much. They could lie hidden for hours, days.' The bitterness crowded into his tone. 'They will soon see through our pathetic disguises.' He walked to the rail and looked at the gundeck, at the jostling figures below him.

Herrick said quickly, 'Let me, sir. I'll tell them what they must do.'

'*No.*' He did not see the despair on Herrick's face. 'I am asking too much of them already, without . . .' He swayed and added, 'Thomas, old friend, if the enemy knows of our weakness, we are done for. They will pound us to pieces while we lie at anchor. We *must* meet them in open water. To do that we need men. *Any* men.'

He looked at the sky, the streaming pendant high above the deck.

'There is little time. When I have spoken to these people you will withdraw our remaining pickets from the island.' He spoke slowly and with great care. 'Whichever of these people wishes to go ashore, have them taken there before we weigh. With this wind, the *Narval* will be around the headland before noon. By then I intend to be in the best position I can find.'

He swung away and raised his voice. 'Listen to me, all of you! A French frigate is coming to engage this ship, and she will most likely have another vessel to support her. I am short-handed, more so now because of losses against that pirate schooner. You have no cause to love the authority which brought you to this place, nor have you a firm promise that I can get you passage home to England, if that is what you want.'

He turned slightly towards the sun so that they would think he
was shutting his eyes against the glare and not to control a bout
of nausea. 'But you have seen what Tuke and his men have
done, and *will* do if they overwhelm this ship. Your support
may do no more than delay a defeat. But without that aid we
are already dead men.'

There was a pause, and he could almost feel their torn
emotions.

Then a voice called, 'All I done was steal a pig, sir! They
sent me to Botany Bay for that. Me family was starvin', what
else could a man do?'

Another said hotly, 'My woman was slaughtered by that
bastard Tuke after 'im an' 'is devils 'ad done with 'er as they
wanted!' His voice shook. 'I got nothin' to go back to England
for, Cap'n. But by the livin' Jesus I'll fight for you if you tells
me what to do!'

Uproar broke out on the gundeck, and while the seamen and
marines watched spellbound the jostling convicts faced each
other in argument and anger.

Bolitho said heavily, 'It did not work, Thomas. I cannot find
it in my heart to blame them.'

Herrick snapped, 'Have the boats ready, Mr Keen. Mr Fitzmaurice, make a last signal to the settlement.'

They turned as a man called, 'We know what you done for
us, Cap'n, an' what you *tried* to do. When you've been used to
little better'n kicks and curses you soon gets to know what you
values. Aye, Cap'n, I'll fight for you too, an' be damned to
tomorrow!'

A few voices still yelled out in protest, but they were drowned by a great wave of cheering, which even Jury's resonant
voice could do nothing to quell.

As it slowly died down Bolitho said quietly, 'Put them on
the gun tackles and braces. Their strength and our skills are
all we have. We must use them well.' He turned away, retching
violently. 'Move yourself, Thomas!'

Herrick tore his eyes away. 'Man the boats!' He watched as
several of the convicts clambered down into them, pursued by
ironic cheers from their companions. 'Mr Keen! This will be
the last time, so be as quick as you can.'

He saw the small red figures by the smashed pier, one hopping on a crutch. Sick and wounded, convicts, everyone who could draw breath was needed today. But all he could see in his mind was Bolitho, fighting his own war, hanging on as his life swayed between reality and total collapse.

Bolitho did not move or speak again until the last boat came alongside and off-loaded some marines. He had expected to see Raymond come aboard, although he could find no reason for it. So he intended to remain behind his frail defences to the end. To take credit for the victory, or as was more likely, barter for his life yet again with the attackers.

He saw Herrick waiting by the quarterdeck rail, his face full of anxiety.

'Drop a buoy here and moor all but the quarter boat, if you please.'

Herrick understood. 'Aye, sir.' This was one day when they would need no boats, and if all failed, they might help Hardacre and some of the others to escape.

'Very well.' Bolitho looked around the crowded quarterdeck. 'We will weigh directly. Have the capstan manned.' He nodded to Lakey. 'Lay a course to weather the headland and the reef as close as you can manage.'

He turned and saw Midshipman Romney waiting to assist Fitzmaurice.

'Run up the colours, and tell Sergeant Quare to have his fifers play us out.'

As *Tempest* weighed anchor once more and tilted reluctantly to the wind, figures moved slowly from the trees along the beach and ran to the water's edge to watch. They saw the sails breaking out from the great yards, the minute figures scrambling above the deck like monkeys, the mounting foam beneath the gilded figurehead, and though most of them did not understand why it was so, many were deeply moved by what they saw.

Their young chief, Tinah, stood beside Hardacre's massive figure and raised one hand to his ear, as faintly at first, then more strongly, he heard the strains of music.

He looked enquiringly at the big man by his side.

Hardacre said quietly, '*Portsmouth Lass*. I never thought to hear it in these islands.'

Hardacre, who hated the signs of authority and spreading power from a land he had almost forgotten, who had sought only security and peace amongst the people who had grown to trust him, was unable to control his voice as he added, 'God bless them. We'll not see their like again.'

Once free of the land's protection the north-westerly wind laid into *Tempest*'s canvas and held her hard over on the larboard tack.

'East nor'-east, sir! Full and bye!'

Bolitho nodded and walked up the tilting deck to the wea-ther side. The rising din of shrouds and canvas, the clatter of blocks and the hiss of the sea were joined in his mind as one great tumult. He felt the deck quivering to the wind, and when he peered along the larboard twelve-pounders he saw them hanging on taut tackles as the ship heeled further and further to the thrust.

Spray spurted over the nettings and stung his cheeks, but he barely flinched. He saw faces he did not know being hustled to various parts of the ship, some gazing at him as they hurried past. He no longer thought of them as convicts, but found himself wondering what they had once been. Again, much like his own men. Driven from the land by necessity, or lured to the sea by impossible dreams. But for their circumstances they might have ended in a King's ship anyway. The impartial cal-lousness of a press-gang, a need to escape like Jenner or Starling, it might be fate after all which set the stage for man.

'More brandy, Captain?'

He turned, holding firmly to the hammock nettings, and saw Allday watching him.

'Later.' He forced a smile. 'You'll have me three sheets to the wind!'

Allday did not smile. 'Help me, Captain. I don't know what to do. I can't stop you, an' I can't aid you either.'

Bolitho reached out and gripped his arm. 'You *are* helping me. As you have always done.' He saw Allday's face fade mo-mentarily as if a mist had formed over it, and added tightly, 'Just by being here.'

'Deck there! Sail on th' larboard quarter!'

Herrick swore, 'Damn! They will hold the weather-gage.'

Bolitho beckoned to Romney and seized the telescope from him. His heart was going like a smith's hammer, and it took time and effort to steady the glass. He saw the blurred outline of the headland falling rapidly away on the quarter, its silhouette made more confused by the spray which was bursting across the reef in wild abandon.

There she was, just as he remembered, thrusting towards him with all but her royals set to the following wind. Her beak-head vanished repeatedly in great swooping plunges, and he could imagine the sea sluicing over her guns as she was driven to her capacity.

He heard Lakey say, 'Pity the wind don't shift and dismast the bastard!'

Bolitho forgot the voices around him as he concentrated on a sliver of sail which had appeared almost astern of the other frigate. The second schooner. He lowered the glass, biting his lip to control his reeling thoughts. Viola had told him about the other schooner. When she had been Tuke's captive. There would probably be another heavy cannon aboard her, too. Some may have been transferred to *Narval* also.

He pulled himself along the spray-soaked planking until he had reached the rail above the nearest twelve-pounders.

He saw Borlase and Swift pause in their walking between the guns and called to them, 'I want you to double-shot the guns.' He held up his hand to silence Borlase's protest. 'After the first broadside there'll be no time. It'll be gun for gun.' He felt the grin prising his lips apart. 'What say, lads! Give him a headache from the start!'

Somebody gave a cheer, and he saw Blissett, his corporal's chevron very bright against his scarlet tunic, waving his hat in the air.

Sprawled in the maintop, the marine called Billy-boy examined his long musket and eased the stiffness in his leg.

Behind him the captain of the maintop asked uneasily, 'What d'you reckon?'

The marine shrugged. 'Two to one. I seen worse. Anyroad, I'd rather be here than on some poxy island.'

The other man looked at the mast, trembling to the great weight of spars and rigging. He was thinking of the man he had replaced. Blasted to bloody pulp by one of those iron balls.

Bolitho said, 'Prepare to shorten sail, Mr Herrick. We'll have the t'gallants off her directly.'

He pictured the other ship in his mind, flying downwind towards their quarter. Tuke would be expecting a fight, and would need to get to grips while he held the wind. Against that, *Tempest*'s heavier build would slow her when she came about on the opposite tack. It would be a temporary advantage, but it was all they had. They would never match the French ship for agility. He knew Herrick was thinking the same.

Herrick raised his speaking trumpet. 'Hands aloft! Take in the t'gans'ls!'

Romney peered up at the tightly braced yards. It would be no easy work up there today, with the wind buffeting the bulging canvas and trying to dislodge the topmen one by one.

Bolitho felt the deck trying to level off as the sails were fisted and hauled into submission and lashed to the yards.

He made himself look towards the *Narval* again, and saw she was much closer. No more than a league away. He saw a brief puff of smoke, and flinched as a ball moaned overhead to raise a feather of spray on the opposite beam.

Keen said, 'They must have one of *Eurotas*'s twenty-four-pounders as a bow chaser.'

No one answered him.

Bolitho concentrated on the other ship, expecting her to follow his example and shorten sail. There was some activity on her upper yards, but not enough to hold her headlong attack. If Tuke tried to make a violent alteration of course in either direction, to follow *Tempest* or to track her round on a new tack altogether, he would, as Lakey remarked, tear the masts out of the ship.

'Stand by to come about!' Bolitho had to cup his hands because of the boom of canvas. 'Mr Borlase! Are you ready to engage with the starboard battery?' He saw him nod, confused no doubt by the fact that the enemy was on the opposite side. Bolitho added, 'Well, tell me in future! I am not a magician!'

He walked back to the nettings, fighting for breath, angry with himself for wasting energy, with Borlase for being so stupid.

Herrick looked up the slanting deck, his eyes very clear in the light. 'Ready, sir!' He glanced up with a start as a ball whipped between the main and mizzen without hitting even a halliard. He had not even heard the gun fire.

Bolitho glanced quickly aft to the helm and the leaning group of men around it. Lakey, dependable and as steady as a rock. Keen with his gun crews, and the marines spread along the nettings behind him, their muskets already cradled over the tightly packed hammocks.

He turned to look forward, seeing the new men at the braces, grim-faced, some no doubt wondering if their momentary heroics were worth all this.

The older men were waiting to let go the headsail sheets so that *Tempest* would swing unhindered across the wind's eye, and near them he saw Pyper and the crews of the two carronades waiting for a chance to pour their murderous charges into the enemy's stern if a chance offered itself.

'Ready! Put the helm down!'

Slowly and noisily, *Tempest* started to swing to windward, the air shaking to the onslaught of shrouds and vibrating rigging. He saw men hauling at the braces, one falling in a confused heap as he lost his footing, only to be chased and pushed back to his position by Schultz, the boatswain's mate.

Round and further still, the tossing panorama of breaking crests and glass-sided troughs swinging across and under the jib boom while every stitch of canvas protested noisily.

And there, like an hitherto unseen vessel, was the *Narval*, rising above the starboard bow instead of the opposite quarter, her pyramid of sails creamy white in the sun's glare.

Bolitho saw the deep shadows on her forecourse and topsail and knew she was trying to alter course. The sails hardened again, and he guessed Tuke knew it was impossible to match his opponent's manoeuvre.

Bolitho ignored the confusion on deck, the whine of blocks and the overwhelming groan of spars as the yards were hauled still further round to lay *Tempest* on the opposite tack. He watched intently, seeing the other ship forging towards his jib boom, making an arrowhead between them. It was the best part of a mile away, although it looked from aft as if both bowsprits would lock like tusks.

'As you bear, Mr Borlase!' He felt unsteady and sick.

Borlase sliced the air with his hanger. '*Fire!*'

Double-shotted, the starboard guns crashed out in one tremendous broadside, the trucks hurling themselves inboard while dense smoke funnelled through the open ports in a choking cloud.

Above the receding echo of the broadside Bolitho heard a terrible scream and saw blood splashed across the deck close to where Borlase was standing. One of the convicts had changed his position at the moment of recoil and had been smashed in the chest by one of the guns as it came hurtling inboard.

Borlase tore his eyes from the droplets of blood which had spattered across his legs and yelled, 'Stop your vents! Sponge out! *Load!*' His voice as shrill as a distraught woman's as he peered through the swirling smoke.

Bolitho saw the smoke swirl and quiver as the French frigate fired back. Iron hammered into the lower hull, and he heard the whine of more balls passing overhead. *Tempest*'s sudden change of tack had confused their aim.

The smoke thinned and billowed away downwind, and Bolitho caught his breath as he stared at the enemy. Sails punctured in several places, and at least two gun ports empty of muzzles.

Herrick yelled, 'Well done, lads!'

Prideaux said, 'We'll not surprise that one a second time.'

Bolitho strode to the compass, ignoring the stained faces of the men who watched him pass. At the compass he consulted the set of the sails, the position of the other ship as she carried on downwind, her topmen already reducing her show of canvas.

He tried to hold the sickness aside, but it was dragging at him. Pulling him down with relentless strength.

It was all suddenly quite clear. He was going to die. This day, on this deck. It was merely a matter of time.

He dashed the sweat from his eyes and peered at the compass.

South-west, and there were two islands overlapping across the bows, misty and beckoning as in a dream.

'Let her fall off two points, Mr Lakey. We will follow *Narval* round.'

'Steady she goes, sir! Sou' sou'-west!'

There was a rumble of cannonfire, and men ducked in confusion as *Narval*'s next broadside swept over the water. A different sound this time. Chain and bar shot, in an effort to cripple *Tempest*'s rigging.

The nets above the gundeck bucked and rebounded under an onslaught of severed cordage, blocks and a man who had lost both legs yet was still trying to drag himself to safety.

'*Fire!*'

Tempest shook violently, the guns spitting out their long orange tongues, deadly and vivid in the choking smoke.

The frigates were a bare half-mile apart now, with *Tempest*'s bowsprit level with the other's mainmast. Again and again the guns thundered across the water, the passage of their shots marked on the sea by burning wads and by the force of their wind above the waves.

Tempest's forecourse and main were punctured in several places, and above the sweating gun crews the torn rigging trailed in the wind with few men spare to repair it.

A violent flash exploded from *Tempest*'s poop, as if a magazine had ignited deep in the hull. Bolitho slipped and fell to the deck as splintered planks, upended cannon, men and pieces of men were flung about him. Voices called and screamed, and as he struggled to his feet he saw that half of the helm had been smashed to fragments, the quartermaster and his mates strewn around it like bloody rags.

Lakey was unmarked and unharmed, although he had been standing just inches away. As others ran to assist him he croaked, 'That schooner! The bugger's put a shot through our counter!'

Herrick pointed to the smoke which billowed up through the shattered skylight and companion. 'Must have been double-shotted with a load of grape for good measure!'

He hurried aft as Jury, his legs and shoes splashed with blood, yelled, 'Steerin's carried away!'

True enough. With power gone from her rudder, *Tempest*
was already falling away downwind, exposing her stern towards
the other frigate.

More shots tore into the hull, and others raised fountains of
spray against the side.

Bolitho shouted, 'Must get steering-way!'

He turned, sickened, as a ball crashed through a port and
took the head from a crouching gun captain, leaving the torso
standing for just a few terrible seconds.

Herrick shouted, 'What'll we do, sir?'

Bolitho squinted through the smoke, watching the *Narval*'s
yards swinging round as she halted her charge and began to
turn in pursuit. He saw the schooner closing from the opposite
quarter, her captured gun firing again, the ball shrieking
through the rigging, breaking the maintopsail yard like a carrot.
The great spar, and all the weight of rigging and sail, plunged
through the smoke and across the gundeck, ripping the main-
course into flapping streamers as it fell. Men cried out in terror
as they were pinned or trapped by the wreckage, others searched
for friends, or struggled to free their guns and train them on the
enemy.

Swift, his mind and body reeling with horror as he stared at
Borlase crushed and mangled beneath the broken yard, one arm
still moving frantically, fought to stop himself from running
below to hide.

Then he saw something pale across the larboard quarter
and shouted desperately, 'The schooner! *Stand-to!*' He raised
his arm and saw with astonishment that he had lost two fingers,
but had felt nothing. '*Fire!*'

The ragged, badly aimed broadside spouted from *Tempest*'s
side, although less than half of the twelve-pounders would
bear, or were still able to shoot.

The schooner's foremast quivered, the sails all in torment,
and slid down into the smoke, slewing the vessel round and
rendering her helpless.

Bolitho saw it and more beside, although faces and events
were all somehow merged in his cringing mind. The schooner
was out of the fight. But for her he would have been able to
take on the enemy ship to ship. But now . . . He stared at the

havoc, the struggling, filthy figures who were trying to clear the wreckage from the decks. Dead and dying were everywhere, and there was blood running down the foremast, while high above the torn body of a topman dangled and swayed with the wind, snared in some of the broken rigging.

'It's *no use*, sir!' Lakey's lean face swam before him. 'We'll never get the helm rigged afore that bugger's up to us!'

Bolitho looked at Herrick. 'You know what you always said about this ship?' He drew his sword and tied the lanyard around his wrist.

'Aye.' Herrick watched him, fascinated and aghast. 'She's stout enough to take the heaviest battering. She's not taken a drop of water in the well, in spite of all . . .' He ducked as more iron smashed through the nettings, hurling men and hammocks aside in scarlet profusion.

Bolitho nodded, gritting his teeth. The sight of the men nearest him, of Midshipman Fitzmaurice lying on his side staring wide-eyed at the blood which was soaking out and around his slight body, had decided him.

'Tell the hands to reload and then stand down!' He shook Herrick's arm. 'It's our only chance. *Narval* can get on our stern and pound us to pieces. Without steerageway I can do nothing to stop it. Arm the people. *Be ready!*'

Herrick stared at him, seeing the torment and the feverish wildness in his grey eyes. But there was nothing he could do to stop him now.

He turned to Allday. 'Keep with him.'

Then a silence seemed to engulf the drifting ship as the tattered sails whipped and curled without effect, while from astern the merciless bombardment ceased. It was replaced by a mingled roar of voices, rising above the cries of the wounded and dying until it was like one great, savage bellow of triumph.

Unaware of their own strength or numbers, *Tempest*'s company crouched or lay beneath the fallen debris, or hid under gangways beside the guns which were still hot from their firing. Pikes and cutlasses, axes and belaying pins. The men, deafened by cannonfire, almost out of their senses by the sights and horrors all around them, stared at the stout timbers which had protected them and waited for the nightmare to end.

A few muskets hammered across the water, and Bolitho could hear Billy-boy yelling abuse as he shot again and again at the enemy. He could tell from his voice that he was badly wounded, dying even as he kept up his firing.

Slowly, and then with frightening suddenness, the *Narval*'s sails and yards lifted over the starboard quarter.

Bolitho stood by the rail, his sword dangling from his wrist. So the horror was not yet done. He watched the other ship's jib boom rise high above the nettings, the broken yard, and the untidy cluster of corpses. Dangling from the bowsprit, bobbing to the motion as if still alive, was the severed head of de Barras.

Bolitho felt the brittle strength coursing through him. He yelled, 'Fire as you bear!'

Like rats and moles, his blackened seamen scrambled from hiding, and down the *Tempest*'s battered side every gun which could find a target exploded in an ear-shattering crescendo, the noise made twinfold by the double-shotted charges and the closeness of the other ship.

He felt the deck lurch as *Narval*'s jib boom drove through the foremast shrouds, the grinding crash of the two hulls dulled by the terrible screams of those who had been caught in the murderous broadside.

'*Boarders away!*'

Yelling and cheering like madmen, what was left of *Tempest*'s company hacked their way across to the other ship, some falling before they could find a handhold, others held and crushed between the two swaying hulls.

Bolitho found himself on *Narval*'s gangway with steel clanging on every side. He slipped on blood left by that last onslaught, and knew Allday had saved him from pitching over the side.

Marines ran past, with Prideaux leading the attack.

Sergeant Quare waved his musket. 'At 'em, marines!' Then he took a full charge of canister in the chest and stomach, ripping him to fragments.

Blissett saw the marines hesitate, their faces like stone as they stared at Quare's corpse. He yelled, '*Charge!*' He was mad, exhilarated, and sad for Quare all in one brief second. Then he was amongst the defenders on the forecastle, his bayonet lunging and stabbing, while his companions closed around him in a tight, merciless group.

Bolitho reached the frigate's quarterdeck, his mind clear again as he saw his own ship through the drifting smoke.

All around him men were reeling and staggering, crossing cutlasses or fighting with fists and anything they could find. He saw Miller slashing a path towards the poop with his axe, watched him suddenly fall, pinioned by a pike, and covered by his killer as a British seaman hacked him down.

And then, beside the abandoned wheel, his legs astride two dying seamen, he saw Mathias Tuke. He was amazed to find that he felt no sense of surprise. Tuke was exactly as he had imagined. As she had described him.

Now, with his chest heaving, his fist bright red from the blood which ran from his sword, Tuke was staring at him, his eyes blazing with hatred.

He said harshly, 'Well, well, Captain! We meet at last! Did she tell you of the mark I put on her soft body, eh?' His mouth opened in his thick beard like an obscene hole and he laughed, throwing back his head, but keeping his eyes fixed on Bolitho.

From the opposite side of the deck Herrick saw it clearly, even as he cut down a screaming pirate and waited for his party of seamen to establish their hold of the gangway above the gundeck.

From two crews they had broken into separate parties. Then into groups. Now into individual fragments of defence and attack.

He saw Bolitho step towards Tuke, watched the two blades circling each other warily, could feel the tension.

He barked, 'Haul down their flag! Follow me!' With his fighting sword swinging before him, Herrick charged to the attack.

Bolitho saw none of them. Only Tuke. And even he seemed to be growing in size and stature, his body surrounded by enclosing darkness.

Tuke took a deep breath, startled by Bolitho's failure to respond.

Then he bellowed, '*Now!*' And with a wild yell he lunged forward.

Bolitho saw the blade slicing towards his stomach and knew he could do nothing. The strength was gone from his arm, and he felt the deck jar his legs as he stumbled on to his knees. Men were cheering from the other end of the ship, and he knew the flag which was being waved and then thrown over the side was that of the enemy. But he could feel and do nothing.

His vision was obstructed by a white-clad leg, and he heard Allday's voice break in a sob as he shouted, '*Back!*' There was a clang of steel. 'And *back*, I say!' More clangs, and Bolitho was able to see Allday driving Tuke towards the side. He was holding the cutlass with both hands like a broadsword, something he had not seen before. He wanted to call to him, to stop his fury before he was cut down.

Allday was almost incoherent with anger and grief, oblivious to a cut on his shoulder and to everything but the towering man before him.

Between blows he gasped, 'You bloody, cowardly, murdering bastard!' He saw the man show fear for the first time and brought the heavy cutlass against Tuke's hilt with all his strength, hurling him to the deck. Then as he made a shadow fall across Tuke's head and neck he sobbed, 'I wish to God this was not so quick for you!' The cutlass swung down once, then twice.

As Herrick and the others rushed to drag him away, Allday hurled his cutlass over the nettings and ran to Bolitho's side.

Bolitho gripped his arm, wanting more than anything to reassure him. But he was shaking violently and could barely whisper.

Allday said, 'You'll be *all right*, Captain.' He looked wretchedly at Herrick. 'Won't he, sir?'

Herrick replied, 'Help him up. We must get him aboard *Tempest*.' He saw Keen running towards him. 'Take command here.'

With Herrick and Allday guiding and half-carrying him, Bolitho returned to his own ship.

There were no more cheers, and his men parted to let him pass, their strained faces looking and searching for something.

Bolitho saw the shattered companion and knew he had some-how reached the *Tempest*. But the companion, and the place where he could hide his final shame from his men, still seemed a mile away.

He heard himself murmur, 'See to the people, Thomas. After that we'll . . .'

Herrick looked at him despairingly as the surgeon hurried to meet them, his butcher's apron covered with the stains of his trade.

'After *that*, sir, we'll be going home.'

Gwyther watched Allday lower the captain on to a cot. 'He does not hear you, Mr Herrick.' He knelt down and loosened Bolitho's neckcloth.

Allday looked at Herrick. 'You go, sir. He'd want it. It's your responsibility now. I'll tell you when the captain's feeling better.'

He said it so fervently that Herrick could only reply, 'I'm depending on it.'

Above, the cheering was beginning at last, as the two drift-ing ships were secured, and those who had expected to die were made to accept that they had won a victory.

But to Herrick, as he paused in the square of sunlight below the companion, there was no such feeling, and only a sense of stricken disbelief.

Gwyther said, 'There is little I can do.'

He was needed in a dozen places at once, and had already operated on more men than he could have believed possible in so short a time. Yet he could not move, and was held here by Allday's simple belief.

He added quietly, 'We can only wait. And hope. No man in his condition should have done what he has today.'

Allday looked at him and replied firmly, 'But he's not just any man.' He nodded. 'I'll watch over him.'

He heard the muffled cheering and said to Bolitho brokenly, 'See, Captain? We did it. Just like we said.'

Silently, Gwyther turned and made for the orlop again. The surgeon had served with Bolitho for several years but had never really got to know him. After this, live or die, he knew he could never forget him.

Epilogue

On a bright summer's day in 1791, almost eighteen months since he had been carried more dead than alive to his ship from the captured *Narval*, Captain Richard Bolitho knew he had won the greatest fight of all.

Only those who had been with him, who had watched over his daily struggle against the fever, knew the whole story. To Bolitho it had been like one long nightmare, with brief moments of clarity and others of overwhelming suffering.

He remembered little of the voyage to New South Wales and his stay in the governor's house. Or of his farewells to Herrick and the others who had visited him before *Tempest* had sailed for England. At a slower and less demanding pace Bolitho, with Allday ever at his side, had taken passage in an Indiaman.

Again the pictures in his mind were blurred and painful. Of his married sister, Nancy, organizing his reception in the old grey house below Pendennis Castle, being very brave and hiding her dismay at his gaunt appearance and inability to speak more than a few words to her. Of Mrs Ferguson, his housekeeper, red-eyed and fussing over him between bouts of weeping. Of Ferguson, his one-armed steward, helping Allday to settle him in the great bed. The one where if you sat up you could see the blue line of the horizon and a corner of the castle on the headland.

Except that nobody had really thought he would be able to leave his bed again. Nobody but Allday, that is.

But as the months dragged past, days and weeks of emptiness and nausea, he realized he was gaining new strength. He was able to ask about people, of what was happening in the world outside his bedroom.

At the first hint of better weather he took a few short walks, using Allday like a prop for most of the time.

And he had a visitor. Captain William Tremayne of the brig *Pigeon* came to the house within an hour of dropping anchor in Carrick Roads. It was like rolling back the months. Bolitho sat in a high-backed chair by the window, while Tremayne sat nearby, a goblet of wine in his big fist.

Pigeon had come home with despatches. Tremayne had brought it all back. The islands, the swaying palms and laughing girls. It seemed that Hardacre had been given permanent control of the Levu Islands as government agent. There had not been much choice in the matter, for Raymond had been found dead, apparently by his own hand.

The most unexpected news had been about Yves Genin, seized with the rest when *Tempest* had won her bloody battle against the *Narval*. Although the frigate had been handed over to a prize court, Genin had been allowed to return to France. More because he was an embarrassment than as a mark of goodwill towards the Revolutionary Government. Genin, who had done so much to pave the way for rebellion, was rewarded by a quick end on the guillotine. The new government took the view that a man who could plan a major uprising might well do it a second time.

And on this particular day Bolitho was standing by the open window, watching the various hues of green, the rippling fields which ran down the hillside towards the sea.

He thought a lot about *Tempest* and wondered where she was. He had heard she had been at Plymouth completing a refit and preparing to commission with a new company. His one wish was that he could have been with her before she had paid off. A few of the old hands were still aboard, and her captain should be grateful to have them. Lakey, the taciturn sailing master, Toby, the carpenter, Jury, the boatswain, and a few more beside.

The rest had scattered to the needs of a growing fleet, to ships which would be desperately needed again when the clouds of war eventually broke across the Channel. Even little Romney had found another ship, and Bolitho hoped he would be luckier this time. Keen, Swift, so many he had grown to know, were beginning all over again.

He sighed. And Thomas Herrick? He had not heard where he was, other than at sea.

He heard the clock chime above the Falmouth church of Charles the Martyr, and took his watch from his pocket and examined it slowly in the warm sunlight.

Behind him Allday opened the door, a bottle of wine balanced on a tray.

He stood very still, seeing it all. Bolitho's silhouette against the sunlight, and the watch, *her* watch, in his hand. It needed no words to describe what Bolitho was thinking. Remembering.

Bolitho turned and saw him. He smiled and thrust the watch into his pocket.

'I thought we might take a *longer* walk today. There's a frigate coming into the Roads. We can carry a telescope along with us, eh?'

Allday replied doubtfully, 'We'll see, Captain. It's a fair way to the old battery on the headland. No sense in tiring yourself.'

Bolitho eyed him fondly. 'Thank you for that. And so much more.'

'My pleasure, Captain.' Allday looked towards the sea. 'It will need time. But we'll walk a deck again, and that's no error!' He grinned and added, 'Come then, I'll fetch your coat and a telescope.'

Bolitho walked slowly to the door and let his gaze linger on the room. *She would have been happy here.*

Then he said, 'Lively now, and we'll take some ale on the way back.'

The battle was won.